Birds in the Graves

MARK BASFORD

Published by Mark Basford, 2015

ISBN: 978-0-9934345-0-1

CHAPTER 1

'Lot one seven five is a painting by George Bakewell of his house in Norfolk. This may surprise those of you who thought he always lived in Shawton. In fact he had two houses, which ordinarily would be seen as something to be envied; however, he also had two wives, which was rather frowned upon at the time.' Jonathan, the auctioneer, waited for the amused murmurs to die down.

His next words were directed at the huddle of dealers standing in their usual position at the far corner of the elegant auction room, hired from the Shawton Country Estate to provide that special ambience which adds credibility to an auction house and boosts bids from amateurs. 'I have several commissions.' He conducted a personal dialogue while nodding in turn at his left and right hands, rapidly reciting in increments of ten the five numbers from one sixty to two hundred.

Raising his head, he scanned the room in anticipation. 'Do I see two twenty?' A leather-jacketed dealer in the back corner of the room jerked his shorn head. 'I have 220, 250 with me.' The dealer turned away. A young man sitting on the back row gave an exuberant flick of his number card and began to wave it. '280; thank you sir, I have your bid.' He nodded at his left hand. '300.' The young man competed with the book bids as the auctioneer changed up effortlessly to top gear. '320, 350, 380, 400, 420, 450, 480, 500, 520, 550, 580, 600, 620, and I'm out. The bid is with you, sir. Do I see 650 anywhere?'

A middle-aged woman stared nervously at the auctioneer from her seat on the front row as she raised her upside down number card a few inches. '650 I have; do I see 680?' The young man remained motionless. 'The bid is against you sir. I can take 660 if you wish.' Jonathan acknowledged another flick of the young man's card. 'I have 660. Do I see 670?' The auctioneer turned to the spotter, who indicated there were no other bidders. '660, going, going, gone.' In tandem with the last word, the auctioneer struck a disc-shaped mahogany sounding-block with his yellowy-white ivory gavel. 'Sold to the gentleman seated at the back. Please raise your number again, sir. Thank you.' He scribbled the bidder number and the amount of the winning bid on a paper docket and passed it to the fourteen-year-old boy to his left; the lad rushed to the entrance hall and passed it to his mother who was sitting at a table facing a computer screen.

Before continuing to the next lot, Jonathan glanced around the room: all eyes were fixed on him with an intensity that added to his sense of anticipation. He raised his eyes heavenward and to his right, then followed to the back of the hall the line of fine plasterwork that bordered the ceiling in pink and gold, noticing in passing a few patches that needed regilding.

Moving his focus to a heraldic shield centred halfway up the far wall, he began his brief eulogy. 'We now have lot one seven six: *Robin*, Britain's favourite feathered friend, and a fitting finale for Milo Piscaro's Birds series. Sadly, Milo died recently at his home here in Shawton; I am sure you will all wish to join with me in offering sincere condolences to those who knew and loved him. He was our brightest son, the leading light of the art movement known as English Geometricism. Those of us who had the honour of knowing him personally will feel an intense sense of loss that perhaps only his legacy of artworks can begin to assuage.' He performed a show of respect, bowing his head and half-closing his eyes.

After several seconds he looked up and presented his portrayal of a sympathetic vicar, his smile tinged with sadness and his eyes seeing through the ornate ceiling to a paradise beyond. After a few seconds more, he overpainted his compassionate visage with the more businesslike countenance to be expected of an auctioneer. 'There has been an upward re-evaluation of his work since the catalogue was printed; I have to start the bidding at twenty thousand pounds. Do I see twenty thousand anywhere?' The dealers in the corner turned their backs and began to talk amongst themselves. Graham, a regular assistant who had helped set up the display stands, raised his arm to indicate a telephone bid had been received. Jonathan translated. 'I have twenty thousand pounds on the telephone.' The seventeen-year-old youth seated at his right pressed a few keys to update the computer; seeing an immediate response, he drew Jonathan's attention to the bright green panel that was indicating a bid had been received at the invited level. Jonathan scrutinised other information on the screen before announcing, 'Twenty-two thousand on the internet.' He looked to his left at Graham, who gave a deep nod of the head. 'Twenty-four thousand I have on the telephone.' The computer screen panel changed to red and then quickly back to green. 'Twenty-six on the net.'

Graham was taken by surprise when his bidder missed out a step. He tried to speak normally, but his delivery of "Thirty" faltered, the tail of the word catching in his throat; he gave a slight cough to clear it. Jonathan transposed to a deeper, more confident-sounding voice that masked his personal unfamiliarity with this level of bidding. 'Thirty thousand on the telephone, Thirty-two on the net.' He interpreted Graham's nod. 'Thirty-five on the telephone.' Another glance at the screen confirmed the online bidder was still active. 'Thirty-eight on the internet.'

Graham overcompensated for his earlier stumble on the word "Thirty" by making a loud call of "Forty."

Jonathan stood erect as he announced, 'I have forty thousand pounds on the telephone.' Seeing the screen panel remain red, he whispered to the youth, 'Have we lost the connection?'

The lad whispered back, 'It's still working.'

Jonathan cast a cursory glance over the rows of seated retirees, having no expectation of receiving any bids from that quarter at this level; many appeared invigorated by the unexpected excitement of such an expensive painting being sold at their country auction, and especially one by a local artist. He looked again at Graham. 'I'm selling to your buyer, Graham.' He took a final look around the hall. 'If I have no further bids, this item will be sold for forty thousand pounds.'

He looked again at the online bidding screen, checking the panel still showed red. In turn, he aimed a careful gaze at each of the other three people employed to accept telephone bids, receiving shakes of their heads in response. 'I have forty thousand pounds on the telephone for the Piscaro.' He slowed his words as though savouring them. 'Forty thousand pounds going once, forty thousand pounds going twice, forty thousand pounds going three times.' He brought the hammer down sharply. 'And sold; a record auction price for a work by Milo Piscaro.' Many of the retirees burst into spontaneous applause; he smiled at them. 'I need to take a short break after all that excitement.' The regulars tittered. He beckoned Graham to come with him. 'Hell of a price, that.'

Graham nodded. 'Yes; Bill will be chuffed.'

The two walked into the entrance hall where a heavily made-up woman was handing over a debit card transaction receipt. She was dressed in non-matching designer clothes: a brown suede skirt that had become fashionable again; and a black blouse decorated with large red blooms, now faded. 'Andrea, I'd like you to check something for me; there's a painting that went for a higher price than I'd anticipated.'

The young man standing by the table smiled at him as he put his debit card and receipt into his wallet. 'Yes, it was a battle between the artist's Norfolk descendants and the Shawton ones; my family owns the cottage in Norfolk, and we were determined to have it.'

Realising the young man's incorrect assumption, he pretended he had indeed been referring to lot 175. 'I'm very pleased you were able to secure it; there must be something really satisfying about taking it back home to where it was painted.'

Jonathan walked to a side table and examined an uninteresting stack of Victorian prints that were awaiting collection. A young helper arrived with lot 175 and carried it outside in the young man's wake. Jonathan turned to Andrea Carter. 'I'd like you to check the bona fides of the telephone bidder for one seven six. What's his name, Graham?'

The words tumbled out. 'Um, sorry, I don't know. She only gave me her bidding number; it's three.'

Andrea made a few key depressions to select the appropriate inquiry option, then entered "3" and scanned through the "Bidder Details" screen. 'There's nothing filled in; it just says to refer to Mr Campbell.'

Jonathan frowned. 'Who's listed as the seller? Is it Bill himself, or is it him acting for Milo's estate? Either way, he ought to have put his name into the catalogue.'

Andrea hit a few more keys. 'No details; it just says refer to Bill. It does say there's no seller's premium.'

Jonathan tapped the table several times with the two middle fingers of his right hand. 'Bill had better not be running some sort of a scam; I don't want my name brought into disrepute.'

Andrea looked alarmed. 'I'm sure he wouldn't do anything like that.'

Jonathan looked unconvinced. 'My mother always told me, "Never trust a Campbell"; but then, she was a MacDonald. Tell Bill to let me know the background; it wouldn't do for us to fall out.'

Andrea coyly fluttered her extended eyelashes. 'Yes, of course Jonathan, if I see him before you do.'

He repeated the rumour that had been circulating. 'I thought you and Lewis had moved in with him?'

She dropped her voice to a whisper. 'I didn't know it was common knowledge.'

CHAPTER 2

Detective Chief Inspector Priestley, nestling into the black leather chair in his office at Midshaw Police Station, stared at the dirty white ceiling in search of inspiration. He had started that Monday morning by delegating all his own mundane tasks, and now found he was left with only the administrative work that had been passed down to him; he would have shared this out, too, had it not been for the restrictive maxim *delegatus non potest delegare*, one cannot delegate powers that have themselves been delegated.

He considered taking back a few cases, though knew that risked upsetting whichever officers were currently assigned, as they might infer he believed they were failing to make sufficient progress with them. As though to interrupt his boredom, the telephone rang. Recognizing Superintendent Richard Yelland's number on the caller display, he made an effort to sound alert, barking out "Priestley".

'It's Richie. You know that artist chappie who topped himself? Well, maybe he didn't.'

'You mean Milo Piscaro, aka Miles Percy?'

'Yes, that's the one. There's something suspicious in the toxicology report. They're not doubting the immediate cause of death was the inhalation of ether, but they've raised a moot point: would the amount of alcohol and diazepam he took earlier have knocked him out? If so, someone else would have had to have been there to administer the ether. Are you busy at the moment, Marcus? Could you take a look?'

Priestley had no intention of admitting he was at a loose end. 'I'll pick it up right away, Richie, though I'll need to put in some extra time to keep other things moving forward.'

Priestley immediately fetched the toxicology report and began to peruse it.

"Head-space chromatography was used to test the blood. Toxicological analysis reveals the presence of diethyl ether at 128.4 mg/dl. Indicates death due to asphyxiation rather than an anaesthetic-type death."

Priestley accepted this part of the report was consistent with the deceased having been found with a plastic bag over his head, inside it a small towel soaked in ether. As there was an ether bottle nearby with the deceased's fingerprints on it, the conclusion would normally be suicide; however...

"Oxazepam was identified in the urine. Oxazepam is a major metabolite of diazepam (Valium), together with nordazepam and temazepam." Priestley scanned lower for the interpretation. "The diazepam was ingested approximately one hour before inhalation of the lethal dose of ether."

He looked for the time of death and found several competing preliminary estimates. "Rigor mortis was almost complete... Stiff jaw but softer thigh muscles indicate death had occurred between nine and twelve hours earlier."

"Livor mortis indicates death occurred between four and twelve hours earlier and is consistent with the deceased having been in a seated position at the time of death." He considered the implication for a moment. The normal interpretation would be that the body had not been moved, though an alternative was that the body had been transferred from one place to another and from one seated position to another. He put that thought aside for now, classifying it as probably irrelevant.

"Algor mortis:

(1) Rectal temperature of *28°C* using the Glaister equation indicates ten hours forty minutes since death.

(2) Liver temperature ... Mallory equation... eleven hours and fifteen minutes since death."

"Tardeau's spots suggestive of asphyxia."

"Ocular Changes:

(1) Corneal opacification was observed at a low level, indicating the eyes were closed at the time of death and that there was no additional corneal cloudiness due to exposure to ether. This suggests time elapsed between death and the examination to be at the low end of the twelve to twenty-four hours range, say, ten to fourteen hours; however, if the eyes had initially remained open, the indicative time would be very much shorter, perhaps as little as two hours.

(2) Vitreous potassium based on a leak rate of 0.14 mEq/L/hr indicates sample taken eleven hours after death; however, this is close to the reliability limit of twelve hours, so has a raised uncertainty factor."

Priestley scanned to the bottom line and calculated backward. Eleven hours plus or minus two hours; body examined at 9:56 a.m., so time of death was between about 9 p.m. and 1 a.m. Taking off an hour for the diazepam, the time of ingestion was in the range 8 p.m. to midnight.

He made a mental note that the two critical events involving diazepam and ether had occurred about an hour apart, and that the investigation needed to focus on what Piscaro was doing from about eight in the evening until one in the morning, up to the moment he died.

He put down the file and settled into the chair, closing his eyes. Reminding himself that when in doubt, proceed as though a crime has been committed, he imagined various scenarios and attempted to place them in descending order of probability.

Option one: Milo was murdered by someone who slipped him enough diazepam to render him unconscious, or at least to make him too drowsy to resist the plastic bag they then put over his head.

Option two: Milo made himself drowsy so as to lower his instinct for survival, before self-administering a fatal dose of ether.

Option three: Milo, either alone or with others, was experimenting with altering his perception of reality by taking diazepam and then sniffing ether.

Option four: Some weird sex thing.

Priestley found himself thinking of sex with Helen, his wife; a smile played on his lips.

'Marcus! What are you looking so happy about?'

The shock of having his reverie interrupted by Chief Superintendent Barbara Watt brought a film of sweat to his forehead. He squeaked a strangled, 'Nothing ma'am.'

Watt offered a rare smile. 'People don't normally look pleased about nothing, Marcus. When you say "nothing", that must mean you don't want me to know, which narrows the field. My guess is it was something to do with sex. Am I right?' He was too slow in responding. 'I'll take that as a "yes". I'm surprised men ever get around to doing any work, thinking about sex every hour of the day. Or is it every minute?'

Priestley decided it would be politic to agree with her in some part, so ignored her reference to the officially discredited belief that men always have sex on their minds, despite personally finding evidence to support the hypothesis. He settled for a reply close to honesty. 'You're right, ma'am, I was thinking about sex, but it was to do with a case; I was trying to put myself into the mind of an artist just before he died, and considering if there was a sexual angle to the death.'

She nodded twice. 'Ah, the Milo Piscaro case. Well, if your method produces results, I'm not going to interfere. Is it Helen's influence, this psychological approach?'

'She does sometimes act as a sounding-board; within the rules of confidentiality, of course.'

'Of course. Well, everything's on file, so you can assess this one on your own, can't you? Until we know whether there's anything to investigate.'

'DS Whittington was only recently promoted, ma'am, so I was thinking he might benefit from the experience of seeing how I perform an initial assessment.'

'I agree. It could be good for him to see how you work, before putting him with someone more, um, conventional, perhaps.' As though completing a discussion with herself, she nodded again. 'Right. Keep me informed of progress.' She rushed away without waiting for a final response.

Priestley made a few notes, then went into the main office to look for DS Neil Whittington, finding him sitting on the edge of DC Linda Plummer's desk. He looked at her surreptitiously: young, slender, blonde, pretty, with large, bright, deep blue eyes. And surprisingly unattached. He automatically smiled at her. 'Hello Lin; do you mind if I drag Neil away?'

She responded with a wider smile. 'Be my guest.'

Witty followed him into his office and stood to attention at the desk, waiting for instructions. He felt slightly uncomfortable with Witty's altered persona; before, he had been the office joker, even close to the point of insubordination. Priestley pointed to the stack of steel-framed, plastic-seated chairs by the wall. 'Grab a pew, Neil, and I'll fill you in.'

Witty sat facing Priestley across his desk, looking earnest. 'Something come in under the radar, has it sir?'

Priestley picked up a buff file and opened it at the autopsy report. 'You remember that artist who killed himself? I'm going to be taking a closer look at it. Something's shown up in the tox. screen; someone may have given him a helping hand, with or without an invitation. I'd like you to shadow me on the initial investigation. We'll have end of day meetings where you can ask me anything you're unsure of. Make the most of it, because I'd like you to know how I think. Then, in future, I'll expect you to anticipate what I want rather than waiting to be asked. You can start off by familiarising yourself from the online documents; I'll hang onto this file for now. Any questions?'

'No sir, I'll get right onto it sir.'

'Neil, you've gone from hardly ever calling me "sir", to doing it all the time. You can call me "Marcus" when it's just the two of us, you know; I'm sure you're not wanting me to think you're sucking up to me. You need to relax a bit when you're around me, otherwise you'll make me nervous. What say you we go to the pub after work today and chew the fat?'

'Sounds good to me Sir Marcus.'

Priestley was laughing like a ham actor when Yelland stopped at the open door. He called from the doorway, 'You're far too happy today, Priestley.' He had addressed him using his surname rather than his first name, as a junior officer was present. 'The Chief Super mentioned she found you smiling, earlier, and reckons you have sex on your mind all the time.'

'That was a misunderstanding, sir.'

'Or was it an understanding Miss, eh? Eh?' He marched away down the corridor, the laughter at his own joke eventually dying away.

Priestley turned back to Witty. 'Don't look at me like that! I was attempting to get myself into Milo Piscaro's mind just before he died.'

Witty grinned. '*I* believe you, sir.'

Priestley interpreted the emphasis on the "I" as implying the remainder of the expression: "Thousands wouldn't." He decided not to plead his case further, dismissing Witty with backhanded flicks suggestive of shooing away a fly.

CHAPTER 3

Priestley opened the file labelled "Miles Percy". On seeing the Major Incidents log had been started by PC Elias Dunn, the first officer at the scene, he grimaced and looked at the first Witness Statement instead. Against "Age" and "Occupation" were entered "over 18" and "parcel delivery woman". "I rang the bell and rattled the door knocker but received no reply, so walked around to the side of the end-terrace property and peered through the window, where I saw a pair of feet at the foot of a chair, as though someone were sitting facing away from the window. When I tapped on the glass, I observed no reaction. Assuming they were ill, I dialled 999 and requested an ambulance." Noting use of the subjunctive, he assumed the woman had dictated every single word to Dunn.

He returned to Dunn's account in the log. "I got there just after the ambulance. I smashed the door down and ran inside. I saw the body. I ripped the plastic bag off the head. The paramedics said he was dead. I put the lid back on a bottle of ether, because it smelled strong and I thought it might be dangerous stuff."

Priestley opened a computer file and typed notes on follow-up actions.

One: have someone re-interview the parcel delivery woman in case she had noticed something else unusual and failed to mention it.

Two: ask Dunn if he had deliberately set out to destroy as much forensic evidence as possible, or whether he was just naturally talented that way.

Two, revised: try not to show annoyance with Dunn; he probably imagined he was doing the right thing.

Two, second revision: ask Dunn if the deceased's eyes were closed when he ripped off the plastic bag.

Three: arrange house-to-house enquiries in the immediate neighbourhood. Establish whether anyone saw Milo or anyone else going into or coming out of his house at any time from early morning on his final day right up to the time the following morning when the ambulance arrived. Also, ask what were the normal patterns of behaviour in and around Milo's house on a typical day and compare with what was actually observed.

Four: create a Family Tree and an Associates Network.

Five: go through Milo's family and known contacts and note when each last saw or spoke to him; if on his last day, follow up with a detailed interview.

Six: check CCTV in the vicinity. Identify anyone passing by on foot, by cycle, on a bike or in any type of vehicle. Use facial recognition software to check against records for this region; extend to other regions and the Web if necessary.

Seven: examine phone records for recent contacts. Include landline and all mobiles. Arrange for call logs and transcripts of voice messages to be put on file, as well as texts. Locate any computers and have their recent browser history checked out. Track down e-mail accounts and examine recent activity. Check paper mail already delivered and make sure all future items are intercepted.

Eight: do full background checks against the names

Milo Piscaro and Miles Percy, including criminal convictions, financial status, debtors and creditors. Find out if he had any enemies. Check for prior contact with the police, e.g. receiving threats, being watched, complaints about stalking by him or against him.

Nine: learn about Milo as an artist and research his style. Look for artists with similar styles who may benefit from having one less competitor.

Ten: *cui bono*? Check what happens to his estate. Life insurance? See if someone is getting a big pay-out.

Priestley looked though his top ten list, much of it common to many cases, except the art aspect.

The implication of the toxicology report meant there were sufficient grounds for opening a homicide inquiry. He telephoned Superintendent Richie Yelland who confirmed the launch of a full investigation, with Priestley as SIO and Witty as his deputy. It was agreed there were no special circumstances warranting setting up a Major Incident Room near to the place of death, so MIR-1 would be used at the station.

Priestley stepped into the main office and located Witty, who was again talking to DC Plummer. 'Neil, come to my office, if you can bear to tear yourself away from Lin.'

Witty looked defensive. 'I was just saying to her she shouldn't believe every rumour she hears.'

'Well, there can be smoke without fire. The art is to believe the true rumours and disbelieve the false ones. Anyway, let's get on.'

In his office, Priestley read out his notes. Witty asked, 'Should I check the Murder Investigation Manual for anything else to go on the plan?'

Priestley shook his head. 'It'll be necessary to go

through the manual in due course, but at this stage I prefer my thinking to be unconstrained by standard procedures. What else should be on the list? You can suggest things that are not in the manual. It's your chance to use your imagination and "think out of the box".'

Witty looked like a man under pressure, concerned he would fail the initiative test. 'There's no mention of visiting the crime scene, if indeed it is a crime scene.'

Priestley nodded. 'That's right, it's essential. I was wondering if you'd spot that.' He added the action to the list. 'What would we need to do there?'

Witty smiled with relief, believing he knew the answer. 'Check for what's missing, and identify anything that shouldn't be there.'

Priestley reciprocated the smile. 'Quite right, Neil. Of course, that is in the manual.' He saved and closed the computer file, then swivelled the screen away from him in case Big Brother was watching. Speaking more slowly and softly, he asked, 'How's life treating you nowadays? How are things with you and Lily?'

Witty reported ostensibly positive news, but frowned nevertheless. 'After my annulment, I was all for marrying Lily straight away. But she said there was no need to hurry, and we'd get spliced when we start a family. She's got a three-month contract in Paris, so I'm only seeing her one weekend a month, which makes it quite hard...' He saw Priestley's wide grin. 'That wasn't meant to be taken as innuendo.'

Priestley wiped away his smile using the back of his hand. 'Sorry, Neil, though you have my permission to speak freely with me, and the odd joke won't hurt you.' Remembering his army days, he empathised. 'Sex just one weekend a month can be very frustrating; I know from personal experience.'

Witty inferred Priestley was also on short rations. He thought that may explain why he had been caught looking at porno magazines by the Chief Super, if the rumour was to be believed. Feeling uncomfortable to be in the office talking about sex, he put off any further discussion until later. 'We can chat about things down the pub, if you like.'

Priestley responded, 'Good idea.'

CHAPTER 4

A dozen officers were assembled in the Major Incident Room when Priestley strode in at 8:30 precisely. He glanced around and was pleased to see everyone had received the message and reported for duty on time. The background hum of chatter subsided, except for one unobservant constable who remained unaware of his presence. Priestley barked in his direction, 'Everyone, eyes on me.' Even breathing seemed suppressed as necks stiffened and the room fell silent.

Despite the prominence of the massive, movable, high-tech, clear Perspex display screen, and the wall-mounted computer projection screen that was almost as large, Priestley walked to an easel on which was hanging a flipchart of A0 paper, portrait-oriented. He wrote on the front sheet the names "Miles Percy" and "Milo Piscaro", using a broad-tipped red marker-pen. 'For now, we're assuming that Miles Percy, aka Milo Piscaro, was murdered.' He scanned the room to check everyone was paying attention.

'The working hypothesis is that someone dosed him up on Valium and then suffocated him with ether, with a plastic bag over his head. Ideally, the investigation would have kicked off straight away, as soon as the body was found, but it looked too obvious a suicide for anyone to take the murder option seriously 'til the toxicology report identified the diazepam connection. So we're going to have to make up for lost time, but we can't turn back the clock and collect any forensic evidence that's now gone forever. We haven't so much missed the Golden Hour as missed the Golden Fortnight.' He saw several officers manage a smile.

'DS Whittington has put all the tasks onto HOLMES, and allocated them as appropriate. Pick up your duties directly from the system.'

The oldest PC in the room called out, 'Can't we have them on paper, sir?'

Priestley had been expecting someone to raise this, so had a joke prepared. 'You have the option to print off your task lists, but think about the environmental benefits of online working; think of all the trees we'll be saving, not to mention the budget. Even the Action Book has gone virtual. You can choose the paper option if you wish, but you'll be required to re-use it in lieu of bog-roll.'

Many of the men laughed raucously, but all the women remained stony-faced, so he made a mental note not to re-cycle that joke in mixed company. Without waiting for the laughter to die down, he began again. 'I'm expecting to see rapid progress on all fronts; if you find you've a problem that's slowing you down, speak to Witty straight away. We're taking a blitzkrieg approach, so put aside all other duties until these tasks are complete. If there are other things you believe you really have to do, confirm in advance with him and he'll authorise overtime through me.

'There'll be a team meeting every morning at eight thirty. Attendance is mandatory, written reports are de rigueur.' A murmur reminded him to keep it simple. 'That means you have to do one, even if it's no more than a sentence. Remember, keep HOLMES informed.' He spotted a frown. 'I mean make sure everything's on the computer so everyone knows what you're up to. Any questions?'

A young PC raised a wavering hand, unsure of protocol; he accepted Priestley's nodded invitation to speak. 'On the Action Management screen I saw I'm down to do house-to-house enquiries. Should I just ask the questions on the list, or can I ask other things, or even ask people if they have anything else to say?'

Priestley nodded vigorously. 'I know you're new to this, but that's actually a very good question. The prepared questions are the essential ones, but if you think there's something else they might know, trust your own judgement and keep digging away 'til you think you've heard everything they've got. But that doesn't mean wasting time; if you reach a point where you're confident they've nothing relevant left to offer, move on to the next house, though leave them a card so they know how to give further information.'

Priestley's repeated invitation for questions received only blank stares; he gave a final sweep of the room to check for signs of reticence. 'I didn't really expect any questions at this stage; after all, we haven't started yet! If you do think of something, Witty is your first port of call, otherwise DC Plummer if it can be taken down a level, and me if it has to come up a level.'

DC Anthony Beresford muttered, 'Two levels.'

Priestley cupped his hand to his right ear. 'What's that, Tony?'

Berry looked uncomfortable to be correcting his boss. 'Strictly, it's two levels, sir: DS to DI to DCI.'

Priestley nodded to Berry. 'Accurate as always.' He turned to face the main body of officers in the centre of the room. 'We're one down on establishment numbers, so we'll shortly be getting a new DI. Until then, you'll have to make do with me.' Receiving an assortment of smiles and grins, he was pleased to have a positive response on which to close the meeting.

PC Dunn called out from his standing position by a sidewall. 'When do we get the new DI, sir?'

Priestley responded to the centre of the room. 'Someone has been appointed to join us; their arrival is imminent.'

Dunn asked, 'Do you know who he is?'

Priestley turned and looked directly at him. 'Why do you assume it's a "he"?'

Dunn looked down at his feet. 'So, it's a "she" then.'

Priestley allowed a sharp edge to creep into his voice. 'I didn't say that.'

Dunn looked up. 'Well, it must be one or the other.'

Berry muttered, 'Hermaphrodite.'

Priestley sighed audibly. 'The new DI will be joining us soon. There'll be an official announcement.'

Dunn commented, 'So it's someone who's just been promoted.'

Priestley stared at him. 'What makes you think that?'

Dunn shot back, 'Because you said it's a new DI.'

Priestley shook his head slowly and repeatedly to show his disapproval of Dunn. 'New DI can mean new to us. Now, that's enough idle speculation, so let's get on with our tasks. Give it your best shot, everyone.' He felt irritated that the meeting was closing on a sour note.

CHAPTER 5

Priestley walked with Witty back to his desk. 'You and I will take a look at the crime scene, if that's what it turns out to be. Do you have the keys?'

Witty fished a bunch out of a drawer. 'There's another set under a plant pot at the front of the house.'

Priestley frowned. 'You're kidding me.' Witty grinned to confirm he was indeed.

Witty drove them to the artist's home in Nethershaw, a depressed district of Shawton. The terraced houses throughout the area were largely divided into sections of six to ten dwellings by a criss-cross of small roads. Milo's property lay at the end of a row of seven and had a generous area of garden compared with those of his neighbours.

After pulling away the outer cordon of recently positioned blue-and-white "POLICE" tape, Priestley accepted the house keys from Witty and located the appropriate brand to match the lock. The door needed a continuous push to brush aside the accumulated post.

When Priestley had stepped past it, Witty bent down to deposit it all in a clear plastic bag he had brought in anticipation; he noticed most of it was junk mail.

Priestley looked around for anything out-of-the-ordinary. He thought the hallway seemed surprisingly normal for an artist, having expected art to permeate the whole house; all he saw were plain walls of oatmeal-coloured paper, though a few gold-coloured hooks suggested some hanging items had been removed.

Priestley opened a pine door and stepped into the kitchen. He initially thought the dozen labelled jars of herbs suggested Milo may have cooked extensively, until he noticed the stale brown thyme, blanched chives and yellow parsley which spoke of non-use; only the tarragon appeared fresh. Eighteen spice jars told a similar story, with the red cayenne pepper now lighter yellowy-brown than the mace, and both of them virtually full. Only a tall glass cylinder of long spaghetti suggested he had sometimes made an effort to rise above the lowest culinary level.

Cupboards revealed jars of passata and tins of kidney beans and tomatoes with future "best before" dates, and a large tin of peaches that should have been used by last year. There were more implements for opening, peeling and crushing things than there were different types of item to be opened, peeled or crushed. He felt saddened to see a rusting corkscrew, until he noticed a brighter one.

Ten dinner plates and twelve side plates were survivors from four sets, their widely differing designs unsuitable for combining to increase the number of compatible place settings. There were fewer saucers than plates, though they outnumbered the six assorted cups by three-to-two; his interpretation was of long, slow attrition rather than exuberant Greek weddings. He felt superficial as he drew a comparison with the perfect dinner-parties Helen gave; he recalled how her elegant guests' conversation inevitably sparkled from repeated self-polishing. He remembered how some of his happiest days were when nothing matched and all his friends lived close by. As he walked out of the kitchen, he hoped to leave behind his self-accusation, but found a dark cloud had settled on him.

'Are you alright, Marcus? Is it a migraine, or something?'

Priestley looked at Witty, recognising the concern writ large across his face. 'I was just trying to get myself into Milo's mind, to see if he was likely to have been happy here. In the end, I think it has to come down to character. Just because he's living in a small house with an almost empty kitchen doesn't mean he wasn't happy with his life; with the right friends, why shouldn't he have been happy?' He realised the sharp edge to his voice had made this last question sound like a rebuttal directed at someone who had suggested otherwise, though he knew that someone was himself.

He walked into the living room. The music system looked very dated, consisting of a silver-coloured cassette deck and a separate, matching tuner-amplifier, with the more recent addition of a black CD player. The large brown-sided black-fronted speakers were also vintage, though still represented good quality. He read through the racks of CDs and found an eclectic mix of outdated pop, timeless rock, Vivaldi's *Four Seasons*, concerti by Mozart, orchestral works by Beethoven, the more famous violin concerto by Mendelssohn, some popular Tchaikovsky and lots of Bach. He looked closely at the cases that were out of the racks, pondering whether this was music to die by, before remembering there had been no disc in the CD player. All of them named Messiaen as the composer: *Oiseaux exotiques*, double CD; *Réveil des oiseaux*, single CD; *Catalogue d'oiseaux* including *La fauvette des jardins*, three CDs; *Saint-François d'Assise*, four CDs. He collected them together. 'I'll take these with me and find out what they're like; they could be the last music Milo Piscaro ever heard.'

The police inventory had included a laptop computer that had been taken in for examination. A check of suicide-related websites had been considered non-urgent and so had remained on someone's "to do" list until it disappeared into the ether. This oversight had been remedied by inclusion in the Action Management task list, with the scope widened to include all websites irrespective of content. He turned his head and threw a question over his shoulder. 'How many computers would you expect at an artist's house?'

Witty considered the matter briefly. 'Without knowing him, it's difficult to say. Lily has a new one she takes abroad with her, and I have the old one. So when she's away our flat has one, and when she's at home it has two.'

Priestley brightened as he thought of his own family. 'We have four at home; Alice wouldn't have liked being left out when we bought one for Edwin. Milo lived alone, so I expect one was all he needed. Is there anything else that might be missing?'

Witty looked around. 'That's one of the hardest questions to answer; it's like proving a negative.'

Priestley glanced at the furniture and furnishings. 'He doesn't seem to have had much interest in possessions; some of his stuff is quite old and shabby, without the chic. Perhaps he was an ascetic by nature.'

'Or perhaps he didn't have the money for new stuff.'

'Yes, there is that, of course.'

Priestley took a final look around before heading up the stairs. He went first into the smaller bedroom, where he saw various artists' materials piled high, including a stack of old canvasses. 'I wonder why he didn't keep this stuff at his studio. And what was he doing with all these old daubs, anyway?'

He squeezed past Witty and continued into the main bedroom. The single wardrobe contained only men's clothes, their designs marking the passing of two decades. 'It looks like he may have kept his clothes 'til they wore out, rather than following the latest fashions.' Pressing down hard onto the bed several times, he heard a chorus of creaks and jingles. 'That would be noisy for entertaining, though it's an outside wall, so there'd be no neighbours to complain.'

Witty shrank his neck and sank his head between his elevated shoulders, turning up his nose as he spoke in a creepy, nasal voice. 'Or enjoy listening in.'

Priestley lowered his head and looked at him from under his eyebrows. 'That's sick, Neil.' Witty smiled at the appreciation. Priestley pointed to the door. 'Let's look in the bathroom.'

Witty backed out of the bedroom and went into the bathroom. White tiles covered the lower half of the walls, extending upward at the head of the bath where a chrome showerhead was fixed high above the taps. The matching white suite of bath, basin and WC looked to predate the former fashion for coloured suites.

Priestley reached past and opened the wall cabinet. 'Nothing interesting here.'

Witty saw an opportunity to shine. 'Perhaps that's interesting in itself; I thought an artist might have been more unusual in his choice of, uh, special medicines.'

Priestley shook his head. 'I'm not sure what we should expect of an artist nowadays. Andy Warhol was hardly a rôle model even in his own day.'

Witty only guessed at the meaning. As Priestley headed out, Witty spoke to his retreating back. 'Well, that's the lot apart from the loft.'

Priestley half-turned. 'Not quite; there's an airing cupboard. And what about the garden?'

Witty suffered his embarrassment in silence. He looked around upstairs but found nothing to help him access the loft space, not even a solid chair to stand on.

Seeing an arched bracket on the trapdoor, Priestley retrieved a wooden rod from the smaller bedroom, having noticed a metal hook at one end. 'Try this.'

Witty manoeuvred the hook into the arch and pulled on the rod; the hatch opened to reveal a few rungs of an aluminium loft ladder that was attached to it. He stretched up and took hold of the bottom rung, pulling down on it to extend the lowest leg of the ladder, before disengaging a catch to release two further sections. With the lowest end now grounded, he climbed into the loft. Visible just inside the entrance was a light switch; he depressed it and a bare bulb lit up. He called down, 'There's a lot of stuff up here, but it looks like old junk. Do you want to come up and take a look for yourself?'

Priestley knew to display confidence in his sergeant, though he would have preferred to check personally. 'You can do it. If there's anything you're not certain about, just give me a shout.'

Discovering only sheets and towels in the airing cupboard, he returned to the main bedroom and sat on the edge of the bed in contemplation. He thought to check below the mattress, but found nothing. Under the bed he discovered a mountain of fluff. Eventually, he heard the sound of the loft ladder being concertinaed, followed by the thud of the loft hatch closing.

Witty put his head around the bedroom door. 'I've made a full list, but it's really just old stuff that could have been thrown away. Plus an artificial Christmas tree; a small one.'

Priestley read through the list, finding himself in agreement with Witty's assessment. 'We'll take a look outside, then.'

The back door opened onto a small patio with a white plastic table and four stacked chairs. Behind it lay a postage stamp lawn flanked by narrow strips of turned soil, and beyond that a vegetable patch. Erected centrally at the far edge of the grass was a tall metal pole that split at the top into four orthogonal arcs, a bird feeder hanging at the end of each. Priestley inspected them and found they held different foodstuffs: sunflower seeds, sunflower-less mixed seeds, peanuts and fat balls. All were fairly close to full. 'Has anyone been topping up the feeders, do you know?'

Witty shook his head. 'Perhaps he'd just filled them before he died. Is that something someone would do if they're about to kill themself?'

Priestley reflected on this for a moment. 'If he was a bird-lover he might have wanted to make sure they didn't go hungry while the house was being sorted. On the other hand, he'd have had to have been very clear-thinking to remember about the birds while he prepared to take his own life. But maybe he had a routine and automatically kept filling them. In the end, I'm not sure we can really read anything into it.' He made a mental note to run it by Helen, then returned to the patio. 'Right, let's head back.'

CHAPTER 6

Priestley generally kept his office door open, but this afternoon he wished to discourage interruptions in order to focus on art and music in the hope of gaining an insight into the deceased's life. He searched the Web for "Miles Percy" but found nothing significant. In contrast, "Milo Piscaro" generated a relevant list. The first result linked to a website that on the home page had a picture of the artist and pointers to other pages; he tried a few of the options but each time received the message "Site under construction".

He went back to the list and selected the second result, which referred to an exhibition that was due to start the next day at the Graves Art Gallery in Sheffield.

Several other search results referred to English Geometricism and credited Milo as the originator of that art style; one even called it an art movement, though there appeared to be little evidence of followers.

A Web search for references to Olivier Messiaen revealed more than half a million results. Reading through several biographies, Priestley discovered he was an ornithologist as well as a composer. He was unsurprised to discover Messiaen was a Catholic, not only because he was born in France in the early twentieth century, but also because he had written an opera with the title *St Francis of Assisi*.

Recalling Thomas Percy was connected to the Gunpowder Plot, he searched the Web for the family names of recusants and found Percy on the list. He wondered if Miles Percy was himself a Catholic, and if so, would his faith have been strong enough to dissuade him from taking his own life.

Though he had always taken an interest in art, he accepted he would be unable to turn himself into an expert in a single afternoon, so considered where he should look for guidance. His first foray was within the police service, to the Art and Antiques section of the Metropolitan Police; the telephone conversation proved even shorter than he might have expected, as they were only interested in the London Metropolitan area.

His next call was to the Graves Art Gallery, where he navigated through a series of choice buttons before finding himself speaking to a curator, Anna van Honthorst. 'Hello, I'm Detective Chief Inspector Marcus Priestley from Midshaw. I see you're putting on an exhibition of paintings by Milo Piscaro. I'm trying to find an expert on him and his work; is there someone you could suggest?'

She responded quickly. 'The only real expert on Milo Piscaro was Milo Piscaro.'

He laughed lightly. 'I'm needing to talk to a living expert.'

There was a slight hint of Dutch in her bubbly voice. 'Well, I have some knowledge.'

'Then I'd like to talk to you, if I may. When would be convenient?'

'I am sorry, Inspector, but I have to work many hours at the moment. As Milo Piscaro was a local, we feel we have to put on an exhibition of his work straight away, so I have no time for anything else right now.'

Priestley switched to a different tack. 'I don't think you're a local though; are you from the Netherlands, by any chance?'

She giggled. 'Brilliant deduction, Inspector; was it my accent, or did the "van" in my name give it away?'

Priestley laughed down the telephone. 'Yes, Ms van Honthorst, it wasn't exactly a leap of the imagination on my part. Do please call me Marcus, by the way.'

'Call me Anna; it will be easier for you than trying to pronounce my family name correctly.'

'So, what can you tell me about him and his work?'

'He is credited with creating the movement known as English Geometricism, though it has not spread very far from here; perhaps it should be called South Yorkshire and North Derbyshire Geometricism. There are so many contemporary art movements, it is difficult to keep track of them all; lots of them disappear without a trace, and English Geometricism may be one of them.

'Now that Milo has died, I doubt whether anyone is genuinely an expert. Of the Sheffield curators, I am the one who has the closest knowledge of contemporary art, but we are all generalists to some extent. Perhaps you should look for someone else, who has more time.'

'That could take too long. A bird in the hand is worth two in the bush, you know.' Realising she may be unfamiliar with the expression, he added quickly, 'It's an old proverb to do with falconry.'

'We say, better than ten in the air. So, you wish me to be your bird in the hand.' Though her voice suggested no more than a correct interpretation, he nevertheless smiled inwardly. 'Did you know his final series is related to birds?'

'Yes; I saw it on your website.'

'And is that why you used the proverb?'

'Not deliberately; maybe I made a subconscious

connection. Anyway, are you happy to be my bird in the hand?' Hearing the expression again, she made an alternative interpretation and began to giggle. He decided he had pushed the joke far enough, so responded seriously. 'I'd like to meet you, and to see the paintings for myself. When could I come over?'

'The gallery will be open until six o'clock tomorrow evening, but the Birds in the Graves exhibition will only happen if I can arrange collections from the four owners today.'

'Does that mean there'll be just four paintings?'

'There will be five from one owner, three from another, and two each from two more. That makes twelve, if my maths is correct.'

'And you're busy arranging to collect them.'

'I need to do much more than that. First of all I have to decide exactly where they should go on the walls. Normally, Gallery Two or Gallery Three would be used for temporary exhibitions, but I am using this as an opportunity to revise the contents of Gallery Four. I have decided to use the twentieth century abstraction section. It currently contains works by Morrison, Hirst, Riley, Martin, Vaughan, Greaves and Quinn. The Quinn will remain in its current position; it is very popular. Others may be put away, either temporarily or permanently. The Riley was rated highly by my predecessor, but I do not find it sufficiently interesting to justify the amount of wall space it takes up; if I have my way it will remain in storage with the Martin and the Vaughan, to make room for several other items. I have not yet worked out all the details; that is why I am so busy today. Everything has to be ready for the morning, but I will still have lots to do tomorrow during the day, so I cannot see you then, either. I am sorry.'

'In that case, Anna, could I see the exhibition tomorrow afternoon...'

'Yes, of course; anyone can.'

'... and then talk to you after you've finished work?'

'Once I have finished, I shall be going home to have a nice meal... on my own.'

Unable to choose between alternative interpretations of those last three words, he tried another tack. 'Well, perhaps we could kill two birds with one stone...'

'We say, two flies with one smack.'

'What I mean is, could I take you to dinner tomorrow after work? You could then tell me all about English Geometricism over a nice meal.'

The lengthy silence was in marked contrast to her earlier rapid-fire conversation. Hesitantly, she asked, 'Are you allowed to do that, Marcus?'

Priestley chuckled. 'You're not a suspect, Anna, unless there's something you wish to tell me.'

Her giggle returned. 'How old are you?'

He wondered why she had asked, but answered anyway. 'In my thirties.'

'Could you come to the gallery at four o'clock?'

'Yes; and thank you for fitting me in.'

'I shall give you a brief explanation about the paintings, and then you can decide whether there is any point in grilling me further over dinner. Will you be wearing a uniform?'

He now assumed asking his age had simply been to assist with recognition. 'I'll be wearing a suit, unless you tell me I need to dress more like an artisan.'

Her giggles bubbled over. 'Yes; I think a black beret, a leather jacket, and a T-shirt splashed with paint. But if you are in a suit, how will I recognise you?'

'I'm six feet three inches tall...'

'What is that in metres?'

'About one point nine. I'm also quite fit-looking, muscular, and *very* handsome.' He waited in vain for the anticipated laughter.

'I am unsure whether I should believe you; perhaps you look like Rigoletto.' He laughed briefly to show he had understood the reference to Verdi's hunchbacked court jester. 'You will look out for me. I am in my twenties, a little above average height, with blonde hair in a ponytail; people used to say I am very pretty.' She gave him time to respond, but her use of the past tense had made him miss his cue. 'And I shall be wearing a badge with my name on it. I must go now.'

'I'll see you at four, then. Bye.'

After putting down the telephone, he replayed the conversation in his mind. The absence of elision was in contrast to her broad vocabulary and pace of delivery, suggesting the learning of English in a non-English environment. He wondered if that could have a bearing on how he should have interpreted "on my own"; perhaps she was asking he leave her severely alone, but maybe it was a *cri de cœur*. He thought her provisional acceptance of his dinner invitation suggested the latter, unless she had felt she could not refuse a request from a senior detective.

CHAPTER 7

Priestley was still cogitating on his conversation with Anna when there was a knock at the door. He immediately responded with a booming 'Enter!'

Witty stepped into the office. 'I was waiting 'til you'd finished on the phone.' After a moment, he added, 'I could tell you were speaking, but I couldn't hear what you were saying.'

Priestley thought Witty's uninvited denial could indicate he had been listening. 'It wouldn't have mattered if you had heard me. I was just arranging a meeting with an art expert. The only time they're available is tomorrow evening.'

Hearing use of the gender-neutral pronoun, Witty did his best not to register he had noticed the hint of subterfuge; he hurriedly moved onto the reason for his presence. 'I thought you ought to know, Milo sold all his work through a dealer by the name of William Campbell; he has that posh gallery at the top end of the High Street. If you think he'd be a good starting point for finding out about Milo, I could take you there now.'

Priestley paused to consider tactics. 'I'll pay him a visit tomorrow morning with Lin; could you send her in and I'll put her in the picture. Leave the door.'

Witty retreated, wondering why Priestley had chosen Plummer in preference to him.

DC Linda Plummer walked demurely into the office. 'You wished to see me, sir.'

'Yes, Lin. First of all, call me Marcus when it's just

the two of us, will you? Sometimes in CID we don't like to broadcast who we are; I wouldn't want you letting it slip tomorrow morning, for example.'

'Tomorrow morning, Marcus? What's it about?'

'We'll be visiting an upmarket art gallery. If we look like potential buyers, we might get inside information. I'd like you to dress up as a trophy wife, if that's alright. How do you feel about being my babe?'

Her attempted laughter faltered. 'Marcus, you really shouldn't say things like that; not even in private.'

He bit an edge of a lower lip. 'I was only thinking of the, um, what's it called, the syndrome, wealthy older man with attractive young woman. Am I going to have to go all Politically Correct with you, Lin?'

She still failed to force an authentic smile. 'Sorry, Marcus; it's just that, when I was in uniform, it was drummed into us to be ever so careful what we said.'

He nodded lightly. 'Yes, CID work can be more subtle, even underhand at times; but it may be essential for getting to the truth. I hope you don't have a problem with that.'

She smiled. 'I'll have to curb my natural honesty.'

He responded with a short speech he had made a few times before, designed to show they must be prepared to speak openly on any subject, however unpleasant. 'Actually, for our working relationship, I need you to be totally honest with me, and I'll be the same with you. That means we can always say what we think, without worrying about what's currently PC. It's the underlying attitude that matters, not the words we happen to choose. PC words change over time, and I don't want to have to be pre-thinking what I can say to you.' He looked her directly in the eyes. 'Look at the race question, for example. Agatha Christie didn't see any problem with writing *Ten Little Niggers*, but it was republished as *Ten Little Indians*, as even "negroes" had become unacceptable. What will the next reprint be? *Ten Vertically Challenged Native Americans?*' Seeing her look down on hearing the "N" word, he was convinced it now far surpassed the "F" word in its capacity to shock. 'In the past it was alright to say someone is "black", but then "blacklists" had to be renamed "referral lists", so now I don't know if the word "black" is alright or not for an IC3 or a B9. And "coloured" always used to be acceptable in the UK, even polite, but the preachy US media objects to the term. On a scale with white supremacist at one extreme and inverted racist athletics pundit at the other, I believe I'm squarely in the middle, treating all people equally and fairly; so it seems ridiculous I should have to be concerned about using the wrong word on that particular subject.' He observed how she only looked up after he had fallen silent.

Knowing it still lay with him to clear the air with his newest DC, he began again. 'What I mean is, if I say a word you don't like, such as babe, then it's alright to tell me. But for my part, I don't want to have to pre-think everything I say to you; it isn't a good way of working. Anyway, I was only talking in the general sense; I wasn't actually calling you a babe.'

To show she was comfortable with his attitude, she adopted a serious stare and played a game with him. 'So, are you saying you don't think I'm a babe?'

He reddened, his voice struggling to maintain pitch. 'That's not what I meant; of course I think you're a babe. Only...' He understood Plummer's broad smile.

'Oh, very good; you got me there. But why did you misinterpret in the first place? It isn't as though I've a reputation for improper behaviour.'

'You have now; haven't you heard the rumour?'

'No, Lin; if it's a rumour about me, I'd expect to be the last person to hear. So, what is it?'

'Something about you being obsessed with sex and having pornographic magazines in your desk drawers.'

'That's all a complete lie. It started with the Chief Super misinterpreting why I was sitting at my desk smiling; I was just trying to get into the mind of Milo Piscaro. And as to any porno magazines, I'll show you what's in my drawers right now if you like.' He looked into her big blue eyes for acceptance, but was unsure what lay behind them, and had to glance away.

Suddenly, she took on a mischievous expression. 'Are you doing a "I'll show you mine if you show me yours"? Are you hoping to look inside my drawers?'

He fought back with her earlier words. 'Lin, you really shouldn't say things like that; not even in private.' She looked uncertain, wondering if she had overstepped the mark. He let her suffer for a few seconds before breaking into unfettered laughter; she joined in straight away. 'I think we understand each other now, don't we, Lin?'

'I think we do, Marcus.'

'So, how do you feel about getting dressed up tomorrow?'

'I'm looking forward to it. I've got a really nice dress I could use. What about shoes; flats or heels?'

'Heels would be good; the higher the better.'

CHAPTER 8

At five o'clock, Witty went to Priestley's office, where they worked through the day's progress reports. The family tree made sad reading: no close relatives, no wife, not even an ex-wife. They looked at the network of associates; it was designed to illustrate connections with people, places, organisations, vehicles, et cetera, but showed very little for a man of forty-two. Priestley asked, 'How would you go about looking for more associates? Unless he's always been celibate, there must at least be an ex of some sort.'

He understood he was being tested, so took his time before answering. 'Grow it organically: interview the people he knew and ask them to tell us of any others. Also, come at it from different angles: other painters, art dealers, gallery owners, social media connections and virtual friends.'

'That's good, Neil; if it was murder, it's almost certainly someone he knew. I've just one more to add for now: check if he's known at the local churches, especially the Catholic one that's quite close to his home.'

Witty tried unsuccessfully to sound dispassionate. 'In order for resources to be allocated to checking out the expanding list of contacts, it would be necessary to know which ones should be kept back because they're on your personal list.'

Recognising he had chosen to use the passive voice, Priestley sensed an undefined concern in Witty's statement. 'Spit it out Neil; what are you thinking?'

'Well, you've decided to visit that art gallery tomorrow morning, and you're going with Lin, whereas I thought I'd be the one working closely with you.'

'It's horses for courses, Neil; we're going as a couple, to look like potential buyers. I feel there are so few angles at the moment, we need to follow the money and see if that leads us anywhere. I'm told the gallery has handled quite a few Piscaroes in the past, so I'm trying to find out what the market looks like from a buyer's point of view and work it back to the artist.'

Witty looked relieved. 'So I'm still your right-hand man, then.'

Priestley smiled. 'Yes, but sometimes I *really* need a right-hand woman.'

Witty wondered for a moment about the emphasis, before finally raising the matter that had been bothering him all day. 'What about when the new DI starts? Do they take over as deputy SIO?'

'If you haven't heard, it's Frank Cargill. He'll need time to settle in. I'll assign him to some tasks to get him involved in the investigation, but you can carry on as you are.' Priestley recognised the look of relief on Witty's face. 'Are you still alright for a trip to the pub?'

Witty was fully aware of Marcus's past drinking problem; after one such excess, Helen had informed Witty she expected him and his colleagues to keep Marcus away from temptation in the future. He therefore decided it would be best to set the parameters straight away. 'I've arranged to talk to Lily on Skype at seven on the dot, so maybe we could go over at six for a swift one.'

'I wouldn't want you to be late for her. Maybe better

if we go somewhere after. Just give me a bell at home if you're free.'

Witty left Priestley's office and worked through the reports again, checking and re-checking everything. This was his first opportunity to prove himself as a detective sergeant and he intended to make himself as visible as possible. By 6:30 p.m. the day-shift senior officers had all left the building, so he felt able to depart and drive back to his flat in Hope. It was in fact Lily's flat, which she had bought before Neil had left his wife and moved in with her. Shortly after, he had had his marriage annulled on the grounds that she had been pregnant by another man at the time of their wedding. He had outwardly agreed with Lily there was no need for her to marry him straight away, but inwardly he wished to tie the knot very soon; he had a worry gnawing away at him that she would find someone else.

He turned on the computer a little before 7:00; it was kept in the second bedroom which overlooked the road, unlike the main bedroom with its views over the beautiful Hope Valley, including the not-so-beautiful cement works. They often spoke to each other in the evenings, and seven o'clock was the agreed earliest time. He felt his lie to Marcus would be ameliorated if he did in fact call her this evening at 7:00.

Lily Martello had previously been a detective constable, but had left the service because she found the work too distressing. She was now determined to prove herself by taking freelance work as anything from a security advisor to a meet-and-greeter at public events. Her three-month contract with a fashion house in Paris was only just into its second month. From their chats, Neil had learned far more about clothes and fashion shows than he could ever have imagined, or wished to know. This did not stop him from asking her to tell him everything that had happened since their last conversation the previous evening.

'You won't believe who I saw today.' The name of the minor film actress was one Neil had first come across in a low budget, soft porn film. 'She was just out shopping for clothes, like an ordinary woman.'

Neil did believe it, being unsurprised the starlet wore clothes... well, some of the time.

Ten minutes later, Lily asked Neil for a blow-by-blow account of his day. He forced additional enthusiasm into his voice. 'We're getting a DI, but Marcus is still keeping me as deputy SIO.' Then, more subdued, 'Nothing much has happened yet, though.'

She was unsurprised, knowing how investigations often made little headway initially. 'How is Marcus? Has he been behaving himself?' She had been thinking of a time he had had too much to drink.

Neil's thoughts were on other matters. 'Actually, Lil, I'm not sure he has.' He paused, waiting for a response, before remembering how their conversations over the internet tended to flow better without the usual face-to-face short words of encouragement. 'Babs told him off about something; the rumour I heard is he was looking at a porno magazine. After that, I heard him making a dinner date with a woman. Then Lin told me he'd called her a babe. I think he may have hinted to me he isn't getting enough at home, maybe down to just once a month. I always thought he and Helen were a perfect match for each other, but I guess not everyone's happy to go without for a month at a time, like us.' He stopped, hoping she would confirm she was indeed going without.

Not thinking how anxious Neil might be, she missed her cue. 'Yes, it's too long for someone of his age; he's only in his mid-thirties. I think I'll send Helen a text; no, an e-mail. Maybe I'll even arrange a chat.'

Neil found himself regretting having been so candid. 'I'm not sure that's quite the thing to do, Lil. I wouldn't want Marcus thinking I've been gossiping about him behind his back.'

She unequivocally terminated that particular strand of conversation. 'Nonsense; I'll be discretion itself.'

After another quarter of an hour, Lily decided that had been enough for one evening. 'Right, got to go, things to do. I'll talk to you tomorrow if you're online.'

'Alright, Lil. Love you.'

'Love you too, Neil.'

He looked at the time displayed on the bottom right corner of the screen: 19:26. The General Strike, he mused. Was that Marcus's problem? Had Helen gone on strike? Well, it wasn't really any of his business, but maybe he'd reveal all at the pub.

He dialled Priestley's landline. Helen picked up the telephone and responded by reciting the number. He could never work out how she decided what to say; he had heard varieties such as "Hi", "Hello", "Helen", "Mrs Priestley", "Professor Priestley", "Speak", "Yes?", and probably some others, as well as the occasional total silence. He wondered if it was something to do with her being a psychiatrist.

He began, 'Hello Helen, it's Neil. I was wondering if Marcus can come out to play.' He shuddered with embarrassment at his infantile words.

She thought for a moment, and then a moment

longer, before deciding he was playing the part of a child in order to receive the protection generally afforded by adults. Had he been a naughty child, or was he planning to be? She began, 'Hello, Neil, how are you? How's Lily?'

He blurted out, 'We're both good. Great, I mean; never better. Everything's marvellous.'

'Well, I'm pleased to hear that. Now, what were you planning to do with my husband?'

'Oh, nothing really.' Her silence drove him to try again. 'I mean, I thought we'd maybe go to the pub. I could come over to Ecclesall, or he could come to Hope, or we could meet somewhere in the middle. If he's driving he'll only have the one, so maybe he should come over to my neck of the woods.'

'I'll bring him to the phone.'

A less hissy silence on the line suggested to him she may have pushed the "mute" button. Eventually, he heard a click and then Marcus spoke. 'Hello, Neil. Helen says you sound desperate to go t' pub. I know it was my idea, but could we postpone it for another time? Unless you're really keen.'

'Another time would suit me better; I've been Skyping Lily for half an hour…'

'Lucky Lily!'

'… I mean talking over the… Oh, you know what I mean. Anyway, I haven't had a bite to eat, yet, and I'll be in very early tomorrow morning, so if we could put it off 'til another day…'

Marcus interrupted. 'Yes; of course. We could go to a pub in Shawton straight after work, sometime; that'd be more convenient for both of us, really. Anything else? Developments on the investigation, perhaps?'

'Well, everything's up-to-date on the system, but nothing especially useful has come up yet.'

'Right. I'll let you go then. We've the team meeting at 8:30 to look forward to, and after that I'm taking Lin to Campbell's gallery, so you'll be in charge 'til I'm back.'

'Fine. I'll see you tomorrow then. Bye.'

He waited for any final words from Marcus, but there were none. A second later he heard a click; after another second the slight background hiss returned, and after a further short delay a continuous tone indicated the call had disconnected.

CHAPTER 9

The team assembled in the Major Incident Room ahead of the 8:30 start time, everyone knowing Priestley's views on being late for meetings. Priestley marched into the MIR at 8:28 and glanced around, noticing Plummer was missing. Sitting at the central desk, he stretched his left arm to make his shirt sleeve ride up and reveal his watch. To appear occupied, he made a show of looking through the critical decisions recorded in the Policy File, one of the few paper-based documents to have survived the office automation project.

With just seconds to go to 8:30, he jerked up in response to the wolf-whistles that had broken out from most of the men and one of the women. DC Linda Plummer had transformed herself into a trophy wife, adding to her height with silver-heeled six-inch stilettos that complemented her mirror-finish silvered fingernails. The matching silver-sequinned sleeveless dress hugged her figure so tightly it restricted her depth of breathing, and had the same effect on others. It revealed so much of her slender, tanned-looking legs that it barely covered her posited underwear, the reflective sequins masking any telltale lines. A string of three two-carat diamonds swayed in a narrow band of platinum below each delicate pink earlobe. On her left hand was a platinum wedding ring, nestling up against a matching engagement ring with a three-carat Passion Cut diamond. Her white eye make-up had been black-lined with precision in the style made famous by Cleopatra. Baby-pink gloss lay liquid on her lips. Her blonde hair had a flyaway, slightly tousled look, as though she had just slipped out of someone's bed.

Hearing someone gasp "'kin' 'ell", Priestley decided he must say something to professionalise the meeting. 'You've certainly taken your assignment seriously, Detective Constable Plummer; you look completely convincing.' He turned to Witty and spoke loudly for everyone else's benefit. 'We reviewed the status of activities yesterday evening; if there's been significant progress on any front since then, let me know after this meeting. Otherwise, the case is in your hands 'til DC Plummer and I have returned from our assignment.' He turned to Plummer as he headed for the door, harshly calling out, 'To my office; we need to discuss tactics.'

Once the door to the MIR had closed behind them, there was an eruption of noise, everyone loudly making their own assessment of their colleague's appearance, and someone asking what Priestley's tactics would be with her. Witty struggled to make himself heard. 'We all have our jobs to do, and DC Plummer will be doing hers this morning, professionally.' This triggered another round of ribaldry, with questions as to exactly what profession, and what her immediate assignment was, alone with Priestley.

Plummer followed Priestley into his office, where he pulled his chair out from under the desk. 'You'd better sit here; we can't have you using one of the tatty ones in that get-up.' As she carefully lowered herself, he tried desperately hard not to check whether her dress would ride up; he failed, catching a glimpse of silver knickers. Quickly, he jerked his head away, but was unsure whether she had seen him looking down. He blurted out, 'You look absolutely knockout, Lin, but too good for this time of the morning; we'll put off going to the gallery 'til eleven. And I don't think you should be seen out there before we go; I'm sure you were in danger of giving at least two of the blokes heart attacks. You'd better work in my office for now.'

Plummer looked concerned. 'I haven't overdone it, have I Marcus?'

He attempted to give her an "everything's completely normal" smile; it flickered for a moment and died. 'No, Lin, you haven't; you look absolutely perfect... for the part. I'm just wondering whether my get-up will look wrong with you. I've brought tatty jeans, a black T-shirt with a rock band's touring dates on it, and a leather jacket. When I was in London I found the well-off wore suits, but the really wealthy generally dressed down; only, that distinction might be lost on people up here. Do you think it'll work, or will they just assume I'm your bit o' rough?'

She thought of Lily, the expert on how to dress for every occasion. 'Lily would have known exactly what you should wear. And she'd have been so much better than me for today's visit. At five feet ten, she'd have really looked the part; I'm only five six.'

He was concerned at the suggestion of lack of confidence, so tried to bolster her ego. 'Lily certainly has that physical presence, but she never showed your perception. What's needed today isn't just someone who looks good, but who can put on a convincing performance, and can react and adapt to whatever happens at the gallery. I'm sure you're the best there is; I can't think of anyone else I'd rather be working with.

And you made a great entrance at the meeting earlier; you timed it to perfection.'

She retained her worried expression. 'I didn't try to time it; I was just putting it off. I was nervous about what kind of reception I'd get. It feels really strange, being the centre of attention; that never happened when Lily was around. And it feels weird to be wearing my sister's jewellery, especially her rings.'

Priestley's whole torso moved up to support his broad smile. 'Well, I don't think you should be in any doubt now about just how hot you look. You've every reason to feel confident when we step into that gallery.

'I've borrowed my wife's Range Rover to create a good impression; we'll be parking right out front, and I've arranged to collect a ticket from a traffic warden, just to show we have money to burn and we don't care about every little rule of law. I'll have to phone them to let them know our revised ETA.'

He realised he was still gazing at her. To break the spell, he added, 'Of course, it might all prove an anticlimax. It could be a dead end, but we only have one shot at making first contact.' His gaze became more distant. 'Unless we find some way of making a breakthrough, I can't see this case getting anywhere.'

He pulled up a cheap chair and sat at the visitors' side of the desk, picking up several items together from his in-tray. 'You have stuff you can do on the computer?'

'Yes; I'll go through my inbox.'

After he had made the phone call, they worked quietly for an hour, each determined to convince themselves there was no sexual tension in the air. He finally broke the silence. 'Would you like a drink, Lin?'

'Yes; I'll get them.'

'No, no, I'll fetch them; what would you like?'

'Strong coffee, a little milk, no sugar, thanks.'

He returned with a single mug of coffee. To avoid accidental spillage on her dress, he moved his mat away from her before placing the mug on it. Seeing her quizzical expression, he explained, 'So you don't knock it over.'

'No, it wouldn't do to make a mess on your desk.'

'I was thinking it wouldn't do to make a mess of your dress; I've never seen you looking this good before.' He realised he had perhaps said too much. 'I've a few things to chase up; I'll be back in an hour.' He hurried from his office, an inner glow warming and darkening his lightly tanned cheeks.

In the MIR, Witty gave him an up-to-the-minute progress report. He informed him that, according to the housekeeper at the presbytery, Milo had attended mass regularly at St Augustine's. Priestley asked who would be interviewing the priest. Witty hesitated. 'It was your idea, so I thought you might wish to follow it up yourself, or at least decide who should.'

Priestley rattled out, 'Then why didn't you ask me?'

Witty became more hesitant. 'I didn't want to disturb you.'

'Why on earth not?' When Witty made no response, he continued as though his question had been rhetorical. 'Well, put my name against the task.' He stalked away, preferring not to become embroiled in a discussion about the underlying cause behind Witty's reticence.

At half past ten, Priestley returned to his office and found Plummer sitting exactly where he had left her, though the missing mug indicated she had left at some point. 'I'll get myself ready, now. Do you need to freshen up?' He added quickly, 'Not that you look like you do.' He found himself wishing he had kept that thought to himself.

She responded, 'I'm raring to go, Marcus.'

He walked to the tall, wooden, narrow cupboard where he had left his undercover outfit. 'Right, I'll go and get changed.'

She looked him full in the eyes. 'Just go ahead; I'll turn the other way. You shouldn't be shy with me; after all, in half an hour we'll be a married couple.'

He felt he had been challenged in some way, and was never one to back down. Leaving the cupboard door wide open for extra privacy, he took off his trousers and put on the faded blue jeans. When he had his shirt off, there was a quick knock at the door, and the Chief Super walked in. She took one look and stepped back, closing it again.

He was fully dressed by the time Superintendent Yelland knocked and waited. Priestley hurriedly called out, 'Come in.'

Yelland looked at Priestley, flicked a quick glance at Plummer and then looked back again. 'We need to talk.'

'We're just about to go out, sir; can it wait?'

'It's better if we don't; I want this nipped in the bud.'

'That sounds like there's a problem, sir; let's deal with it straight away.'

Yelland dipped his head and looked out from under his bushy eyebrows. 'With DC Plummer here? Are you sure?'

'Of course; there's no time like the present.'

'Well, the Chief Super just bellowed down the office that she'd found you with your shirt off, and that I needed to get to the bottom of things.'

'I was just getting changed ready for a visit; we're going incognito.'

He turned to Plummer. 'Is there anything you would like to add, DC Plummer? Here, or in private?'

She gave her most innocent smile. 'Only that it's a good thing she didn't come in a couple of minutes earlier, when he had his trousers off.'

Yelland quickly failed in his attempt to look serious; his booming laugh ricocheted around the room and well beyond. He finally regained his composure, asking Plummer to confirm for the record there was no sort of incident to report. When she stated categorically there was no problem, he marched out of the room to report the non-incident to Watt.

Priestley frowned questioningly at Plummer. 'You seem very different this morning, Lin, and I don't just mean how you're dressed, but altogether in yourself. For a start, it wasn't like you to mention I'd had my pants off. What's got into you?'

Her smile exuded a confidence that had earlier been lacking. 'It's called Method Acting; I've been putting myself into the right mindset to be your bimbo babe.'

CHAPTER 10

Priestley stopped the Range Rover directly outside the gallery. Plummer waited for him to walk around the rear of the car and to open the door for her. He took her hand as she carefully stepped down to the pavement. As he locked the doors behind her, he glanced up and down the street and saw only a dishevelled-looking young man with a Laughing Cavalier beard and unkempt moustache, who was chaining his bicycle to a nearby railing. Then, around a corner, he spotted a traffic warden trotting toward them; clearly not a Method Actor, Priestley mused. Glancing at the gallery, he saw a figure standing inside, looking back at him.

As they stepped toward the door, William Campbell rushed to open it for them. 'Come in, come in; welcome to my humble gallery. Are you here to browse, or do you have something particular in mind?'

Priestley gave the response he had agreed with Plummer, making no mention of Milo Piscaro. 'We'll have a look around, see if something takes our fancy.'

'Please do, and if you'd like to know more about an exhibit, it would be my pleasure to impart any little knowledge I may have. Today, for discerning buyers such as yourselves, there's a ten per cent reduction on all artworks; what I call a courtesy discount.' There was a hint of a bow as he backed away from them.

The gallery had traditional representational paintings to one side and modern abstract to the other. They entered the contemporary section, looking closely at the first painting as though connoisseurs examining fine detail. She quickly moved down the line; he forced himself to stay for a minute, despite seeing nothing beyond a few blobs of colour and a line of paint that had dribbled part way down the canvas.

The cyclist, a youth of about twenty years, stepped into the gallery. Priestley noticed his welcome seemed less fulsome than theirs. Campbell addressed him questioningly, almost accusingly. 'Can I help you?'

'I'm just looking.'

'Are you intending to buy?'

'I'm here on behalf of a friend. She used to be interested in the YBAs, but now she prefers ones who are much more "Y". Perhaps it would be best if I look around for myself.'

Campbell's tone altered on hearing the loud, unselfconscious, plum-in-the-mouth voice that spoke of an expensive English education. 'I sense you are yourself an expert. Please feel free to perambulate.'

Campbell walked over to Priestley. 'I believe that young man may be descended from noble stock; appearances can be so deceptive. Now, is there a particular type of artwork that you and your lady would be interested in purchasing?'

Priestley called out, in a voice broader than his usual cultured tones, 'Lin, do you see anything you fancy?'

She floated over to him, despite the difficulty of walking in stilettoes. Putting her arm through his, she giggled, 'Only you, my love.'

Priestley turned to Campbell. 'Perhaps you could tell us what you think we might like.'

Campbell's face shone with delight. 'Certainly sir, madam. My star exhibit, if you will, is a painting by the local artist Milo Piscaro, who sadly died recently. Yet I fear it may be too expensive for anyone but the wealthiest in the land. If I could show it to you first of all, then perhaps we could progress downward, monetarily, until we find something that you would be pleased to welcome into your home.'

Campbell led the way to a portrait-oriented canvas that showed the planet Earth with England in the middle, set within concentric rainbow-coloured rings; over the planet there was a spiral of red discs centred on the North Midlands, and on the rainbow were various coloured shapes. 'This particular piece sold at auction recently for forty thousand pounds. The price paid was closer to fifty thousand when commission is included, and the dreaded V. A. T. Frankly, I think it was a steal at that price; there will be no more paintings coming from his sainted brushes. I have accepted instruction from the owner to offer it for fifty-six thousand pounds; with my personal courtesy discount, that would round down to just fifty thousand pounds to you, sir.'

Priestley raised an eyebrow. 'That doesn't seem to leave any profit; why would someone buy it at auction and then wish to part with it straight away?'

Campbell appeared to consider the question for a moment; he responded with raised eyebrows as though he had just thought of an answer. 'Perhaps it was simply for the thrill of having a beautiful work of art.' He cast an overt glance in Plummer's direction before smiling at him. 'I'm sure we can all identify with that.'

Priestley turned his head and began to walk crabwise to the next painting. 'Perhaps we'd better look at what else you have.'

Plummer tugged him back. 'If this is the best, isn't

that what you want to buy for me? Aren't I worth the best?'

Priestley grimaced. 'Of course, my love; you know I'd give you anything. It's just, well, I don't know anything about this artist.'

Campbell offered, with unseemly haste, 'If you would permit me to remedy that, sir, I should be delighted to give you more information; the artist was a close, personal, and very dear friend of mine. Many's the hour we whiled away together in his studio, discussing art and life.'

Plummer smiled saucily at Campbell. 'Go on then, tell us all about him, especially any juicy gossip.'

Priestley laughed lightly. 'You shouldn't say such things, Lindy-Lou.'

She put her arms around Priestley, placing her hands on his buttocks as she pressed herself up to him. He inclined his head slightly and accepted a moist kiss on the lips. 'It wouldn't be me if I didn't say such things.'

Overwhelmed by her performance, he was unsure he could speak evenly, so remained silent.

Campbell took the opportunity to respond to Plummer's inquiry with his prepared spiel. 'Milo Piscaro was a man of great depth, an artist with a vision of the world that was at the same time both simple and complex. His rainbow-coloured canvasses spoke of the beauty of God's sky.' He raised his eyes heavenward, then spoke with gravitas. 'I have set my bow in the cloud, and it shall be a sign of the covenant between me and the Earth.' He reverted to his usual voice. 'And yet, notice how the rainbow colours are behind the geometrical designs that, of course, represent planets and other extra-terrestrial objects; this is telling us that the observer of our planet is somewhere in that great cosmos. He is giving us God's view of the world.

'And what does he choose for us to see on God's Earth, or in God's sky? Birds! His Birds series consists of *Snipe, Bluetit, Wren, Pigeon, Wigeon, Plover, Tern, Curlew, Crow, Osprey, Merlin, Grouse*, and of course *Robin* which we see here. Most of them are in private ownership. Until yesterday afternoon I had five more of the series available on display, but a lady from the Graves Art Gallery in Sheffield has persuaded me to loan them to her for an exhibition.'

Priestley feigned ignorance of the other paintings. 'How many did he do, then, in this Birds series?'

'There are thirteen known publicly.'

'And did he sell them all through you?'

'Yes, I am pleased to say he had the confidence in me to allow all of them to be first exhibited in my gallery and for me to act on his behalf.'

'So who bought the other seven?'

'Just as I guarantee your anonymity, similarly I am not at liberty to divulge the identities of other buyers. Suffice it to say that one is a peer of the realm, another is a classical musician of outstanding virtuosity, and a third is a prominent businessman.'

'No rock musicians, then?'

'May I hazard a guess and suggest that there may be one in the near future?'

Priestley smiled at the apparent success of his ruse. 'It's like you said: confidentiality.'

Campbell leaned in conspiratorially. 'There are more paintings in the series, on loan with other friends of his. They will no doubt be delivered to me at intervals into the future, in accordance with his final wishes.'

Priestley looked closely at him. 'Did he tell you this right before he died?'

Campbell shook his head. 'Forgive me if I gave the impression he informed me with his dying breath; had I been present, I would of course have stopped him from taking his own life.' He paused just long enough to register his personal sense of loss. 'If I may be so crass as to speak of monetary considerations, we had a long-standing arrangement that I would sell his paintings at a rate that would avoid depressing the market in his work. To match supply and demand, he painted in advance and lent his works to friends, for return when they were due to be sold. I therefore confidently expect more to be delivered to me in future months and years.'

'He was very far-sighted then; I suppose he had to be to see things from God's point of view.'

'Oh, very droll, sir. He would have appreciated your jest; he had a well-developed sense of humour.'

'Now that he's dead, who will you pay for them?'

'You may recall I said he was a close personal friend; I am in fact the sole beneficiary of his estate. Therefore I already own them all.'

'But you don't know where they are, unless you know who the friends are. Do you know any of his friends?'

'Milo belonged to a small colony of artists at Green Lane Studios; I am sure they were all friends of his.'

'Maybe they're the ones who have his paintings?'

Campbell's smile disappeared. 'I cannot say which friends are holding his works; the arrangement guaranteed their anonymity. However, I am certain none of the local artists are involved, as they would be too obvious and so not anonymous.' His smile returned.

'Who are these other local artists, anyway? Are they anyone I might have heard of?'

'I fear fame has not yet touched them.'

'Can you give me their names?'

Plummer noticed Campbell looking puzzled at the interest in the other local painters, so interjected. 'Don't bother with them; it's this painting we're interested in. Just tell us about Milo Piscaro.'

Priestley recognised she had narrowly rescued their credibility; he leaned forward and kissed her lightly on the lips. 'Yes, you're right, my love; we don't want to buy just anybody's work.'

Campbell's countenance lost its puzzlement. 'I fear there is little else I can tell you about Milo, other than he led an ascetic life. He was more like a monk than a Bohemian painter, having minimal contact with other people. He really lived only for his art.' After the briefest of pauses, he continued, 'Now, should I put your name against this work? At least to earmark it? And a deposit of, say, ten per cent?'

Priestley knew this particular enquiry had reached its limit, as he had no authorisation to hand over five thousand pounds. 'I'll go away and think about it, but we're definitely interested.'

Plummer added, 'And I'll do my best to persuade him... in the nicest possible way.' She laughed coarsely, taking Priestley by surprise. He walked her to the door, giving Campbell a brief goodbye.

CHAPTER 11

Priestley released the car's locks and opened the front passenger door for Plummer, holding her hand as she edged carefully inside. He checked she was safely ensconced before closing the door gently. Removing the white- and black-bordered yellow missive from the traffic warden, he noticed Campbell was watching them, so threw it contemptuously into the back as he climbed into the driver's seat. 'Don't look around, but he's got his eyes on us. Just in case we need to play this again, we'd better put on a show. Am I alright to snog you?'

Plummer smiled coyly, 'OK, but no tongue!'

Campbell lost interest in their performance well before it had ended. When Plummer finally came up for air, she asked, 'How long do we stay in character?'

Priestley started the engine, waiting for a cyclist to pass by before setting off. 'While ever we're dressed for this rôle; so we'd better get you home straight away and out of those clothes.'

She sat in silence, wondering exactly what he had in mind. He also eschewed conversation, as he was fully occupied with processing various competing thoughts: Lin's performance, the investigation, Lin's pretty face, road traffic, Lin's body-hugging dress, Lin's body beneath the dress, Lin's kisses, …

He asked for detailed directions as they approached the area where Plummer's flat was situated, which she gave monosyllabically. As he parked up, she asked,

'Should I make my own way back to the station, or will you give me a lift? Are you in a hurry?'

He responded, 'Where's your car?'

She replied succinctly, 'At work.'

'Well then, I'll take you back when you're ready.'

She unlocked the door and invited him in. After stepping out of her high heels, she smiled sweetly. 'I'll be glad to get out of this dress; it's really tight.'

He looked her up and down. 'Yes; I'd noticed. It hugs you in all the right places.'

She turned her back to him. 'Could you unzip me? It's hard doing it for myself.' Priestley carefully pulled the zip down to the base of her back, observing her ribs under her creamy-white unblemished skin, and noticing there was no bra strap to interrupt the curve of her spine. She turned to face him again, holding her dress loosely at the shoulders. 'The loo's the second door on the right, just after my bedroom door.'

At the entrance to her bedroom, having checked he was watching her, she let her dress slip to the floor. After a moment, she pulled down her silver knickers and stepped into the room. Inside, she placed her clothes on a padded bench, slid in between the blush-pink sheets and waited for him.

He was transfixed by the brief rear glimpse of her naked body. Though he was virtually certain she had just invited him to her bedroom, he still had a lingering doubt; knowing there would be a presumption of duress between a DCI and a DC, he prepared to obtain her unequivocal consent. His head and torso angled forward, but his feet remained stubbornly immobile; he looked down at them, as though they had independently taken the decision not to move.

Years of living with a psychiatrist led him to consider the moral impediments consciously. He knew his superego was defeating his id, but his hormones desperately needed his ego to find a reason to override any constraints. He told himself he could continue to qualify as a moral man, providing his other behaviour was taken into consideration. His feet stayed planted firmly on the ground.

He turned the problem around, so he now needed a reason not to go to her. That failed to break the impasse. He argued that the situation was in the here and now, and that consequences only happened in the future. His feet remained unmoved.

He thought of using random chance: if only he had a couple of dice, snake eyes would mean no and the other thirty-five combinations would mean yes. He decided to leave it to fate: if there were no urgent messages on his mobile, he was free to go. He turned it on. There were three text messages, all from Helen, the last being: "Urgent! Call me as soon as you get this." He decided that that message probably did not really count as genuinely urgent, but deleted it anyway. He called up her number from the list, and she answered at once. 'I've been trying to get you for ages; where are you?'

He feared she could always tell when he was lying, so knew a variant of honesty was called for. 'I'm with a colleague.'

'Are you still at the gallery?'

'No; we left recently.'

'Recently? That's not very specific.'

'You said to call you; what are you wanting?'

'Will you be bringing my car back?'

'Can do; I have to go to Sheffield later, anyway.'

'Well, when will you be coming?'

He smiled inwardly at the sexual interpretation, before wondering if she had just laid a verbal trap for him; he knew there were no limits to her cleverness, but decided it was merely coincidental. 'I'm not sure; it's difficult to say.' He added with bravado, 'Something's come up; I can't say for definite how long I'll be.' The pause before her response left him worrying his bravery had simply been foolhardiness.

'I'm at uni. 'til three. If you're here before then, just swap cars; I'm parked in my usual spot. Up 'til ten past three, look out for me. After that you'll be too late.'

When Plummer heard Priestley on the phone, she assumed her invitation had not been specific enough. Flushed and embarrassed, she rushed to throw on her everyday clothes and remove her eye make-up.

After the call, he walked toward her bedroom; when only a few steps away, she dashed out, fastening the top button of her blouse. Improvising, he pointed down the corridor. 'I'll pop to the loo and then we'll be off.' He broke into a sweat at the thought of the massive mistake he had almost made, convinced he had earlier misread the situation.

They drove back to the station in an awkward silence. As he parked, he turned to her, trying to sound like a DCI. 'You did exceptionally well today, Lin; you're a natural as an actress. Would you be happy to work undercover with me again?'

She aimed to sound like a confident DC, but at the same time could not resist dropping another hint. 'I'd be happy to work undercover with you, anytime, whatever the situation. It was really exciting, being someone else. You know it was my first time, don't you? I'd like to do it again. There's no one I'd rather be with; working undercover, I mean.'

Priestley jerked his head around to the right to see who had just opened the car door. Witty was standing there, grinning. 'How did it go, then?'

Priestley pushed the door wider. 'Let's have a progress meeting straight away. And add Green Lane Studios to the Associates Network, will you.'

Priestley invited Plummer to join them for the ad hoc meeting. Witty reported that the groundwork on phone logs, e-mails and letters had been completed, though none of it had revealed anything pertinent to the inquiry. He then explained about the CCTV. 'The good news is there are some local authority cameras in the neighbourhood. The bad news is they were switched off. The council says it was due to budget cuts; they couldn't afford to employ anyone to monitor them.'

Priestley scowled. 'Put me down for an action. They should be recording everything, even if they're not being monitored, so we can do retrospective reviews. I'll push it up the hierarchy here; maybe the Chief Constable will put pressure on the council.'

Witty made a note of the action. 'We're checking out private CCTV. There are six million cameras in the country, so surely there must be one somewhere that will help us.' He went on to report there was no record of any criminal offence, or even a caution being issued, under the names Milo Piscaro or Miles Percy. No one was surprised there were no road traffic offences, as Milo had never obtained a driving licence and was believed only to have cycled. There were just four sets of fingerprints at the house, including Piscaro's, supporting Campbell's assertion he had had little contact with other people; none of the other fingerprints were in the system.

Priestley wound up the meeting. 'I'll be going over to the Graves Art Gallery later, and I don't plan to be back here 'til tomorrow morning. Neil, that means you're in charge again. Lin already stands in for you when you're not around, so I'd like to formalise that arrangement and make her your official deputy. From now on, keep her fully involved in whatever you're doing.' Turning to Plummer, he added, 'Lin, you were absolutely brilliant today. I can see you doing very well in CID.' He glanced at his watch. 'Excuse me, I have to be at another meeting.' As he headed out of his office, he called over his shoulder, 'Don't forget to close the door behind you.'

Witty turned to her. 'What did you do to earn his praise, then? You haven't let him roger you, have you?'

Plummer had a reputation for always being calm under pressure and never allowing any irritation to show. This increased the extent to which Witty felt the shock of her response, having accidentally triggered the release of the pent-up frustration which had been coursing through her veins and seeking an outlet. She flushed deep red, exploding in a torrent of words. 'No, I haven't; and isn't that just the kind of sexist assumption that men make all the time. I did a good, professional job, and I earned my praise, so don't you dare suggest anything like that, ever again, otherwise I'll be..., I'll..., well, just don't.'

He felt shaken. 'Sorry, Lin; I didn't mean it. I know you're not like that. I was only joking. I'm really sorry.'

CHAPTER 12

Priestley delivered the Range Rover to the university car park just before three o'clock. As there were no empty bays, he considered swapping cars and leaving before Helen arrived, but decided he ought to stay; after all, she would expect to see him there, waiting for her. He looked unseeingly as his mind wandered. Though she was very capable of worming every little secret from him, he had nothing to hide... except his deepest thoughts, which surely were his alone. But then, she had been his psychiatrist when he had left the army with his medals and his PTSD, and had known his mind intimately, long before she had known his body, so keeping thoughts hidden would not be easy. Anyway, she would have no reason to suspect that his mind kept returning to Lin, how she looked, how she kissed, ...

His reverie was interrupted abruptly by a tap on the passenger-side window. Helen opened the door and began speaking even before she sat down. 'Hello, love. How was your visit to that Gallery? Did it all go according to plan?'

To justify borrowing her Range Rover, he had had to mention how he and Lin would be visiting the gallery incognito and needed to appear wealthy. 'I think I made the right sort of impression.'

'And what about Lin?'

What about Lin, indeed, he mused.

'Well, are you going to answer?'

He thought she may have untypically given him

insufficient time to respond; but then, perhaps he had simply been too slow. 'Lin played her part very well. I don't know if it'll matter in the end, though; the case may have nothing to do with the money side. It's just so difficult to get this investigation going. All we really learned was where the artist had his studio; I would have picked that up earlier from his website if it had been working properly.'

'So, not a very successful trip, then.' She paused a moment. 'It sounds like nothing much happened.'

He noticed how intently she had been looking at him as she made that apparently innocuous comment.

'You could be right.'

'Exactly what did happen?'

Priestley had the uncomfortable feeling this was the start of the interrogation proper. 'I won't bore you with the details.'

'I won't be bored; you know I always find your work interesting. Go ahead and tell me all about it.'

'Well, like I said, the idea of us pretending to be a wealthy couple seemed to work alright.'

'How good were you at it?'

'I think we were quite convincing. She was dressed up and I was dressed down; the gallery owner probably thinks I'm a rock star.'

'And what does he think she is?'

'A trophy wife who likes to spend money.'

'What did she have to do to be convincing?'

'Basically, stand around and look attractive.' Helen's silence told him he was required to continue. 'She made a real effort to get into the part.' Feeling the oppression of the continuing silence, he made a faltering laugh. 'She even gave me a little kiss at one point.' Still silence. 'All in the line of duty, as they say.' What more did she want? Feeling as though she was still sifting through his thoughts, he blurted out, 'What sort of a day have you had, anyway?'

She ignored the attempted misdirection. 'We're talking about your day. Or don't you want me to know?'

'There isn't much more I can say, really.'

'Well, if you don't want to tell me, I can't force you. So, what are you doing now?'

'I'm going to the exhibition at the Graves. The curator is something of an expert on the artist.' He knew he had deliberately avoided mentioning the gender of the curator. Having only ever spoken to her on the telephone, he told himself she may have been joking about her age, and could be an old maid who cleaves to art in place of real relationships; except he knew her voice indicated a much younger woman. He wondered if Helen was smiling at him to put him off his guard. 'I may have to work late, so don't do anything for me; I might have to eat out.'

'Where will you go?'

Recognising she had said "will" rather than "would", he assumed she was thinking it was definite, so sought to undermine her certainty. 'It may not be necessary. I'll let you know if I'll be back early; otherwise, expect me when you see me.'

She recognised and appreciated his manoeuvre. 'Off you go then. Try not to wake me if you're very late.'

He wondered what that last statement had really meant. Though he loved her dearly, he did sometimes wish he could be the psychologically dominant partner.

They stepped out of the car in tandem. He held the

driver's door open for her; she climbed inside and closed it behind her in one movement, before calling through the window, 'Goodbye, love.'

As he walked away, he felt disturbed she had not given him the usual kiss. Was it because he had admitted Lin had kissed him earlier? A "little kiss", he had said, so that could hardly be the reason. Of course, if she had known about their final kissing session, it might have been a very different matter. He asked himself why he always imagined she was playing mind games with him; she was probably just in a hurry, to avoid being late collecting the children. Attempting to smile inwardly, he told himself everything was fine.

He drove the remaining mile into Sheffield and parked at Snig Hill Police Station, seeing no point in wasting the service's money on parking fees, or risking damage to his car by leaving a Police card in the windscreen. He called into the station and chatted to a few officers of his rank and above, knowing networking was as important in the service as elsewhere.

Fifteen minutes later he walked up the hill to the Central Lending Library, squeezing into the small lift after two women shoppers; he knew it had two doors at right angles, with the one to open being dependent on which level had been reached. It creaked and rattled slowly to the third floor, where the side door opened. The shoppers were now at the front; he followed them out. As they ducked left and into the lavatories, he turned right and into the Graves Art Gallery.

In the shop at the entrance a young man with bleached hair was seated at the cash desk. Priestley asked him to let Ms van Honthorst know her four o'clock visitor had arrived. She quickly came to collect him. He saw she fitted her description, providing he reinterpreted her use of the past tense: she was still very pretty, but nowadays no one was telling her so.

Van Honthorst led the way through two sets of double doors and into gallery four. By the painted sign "Abstraction, Pattern and Colour in 20th Century Art" were twelve Piscaroes arranged at two heights around three walls. 'There they are. I could tell you a little about them, though I think you can see as well as I can. It may be more use to you if I explain the background of the artist and the significance of his work within the context of contemporary art, but that would need more time than I can give you right now.'

He thought he detected an unspoken question, as she looked up at him with widened eyes. 'Yes, that would be best. You could explain it all to me over dinner, if you're still available.'

She gave a fleeting smile. 'I am available. See me here at six o'clock.' With a swish of her pony tail she disappeared back through the adjacent doors, leaving him alone with the twelve paintings.

Comparing them, he noticed similarities: the same bird in the top right corner; the Earth with North Derbyshire at its centre, surrounded by a thin layer of atmosphere and coloured concentric rings in rainbow sequence; and discs of decreasing size spiralling down to the area of the planet where the artist had lived and worked. Only the various coloured symbols positioned on the rainbow were substantially different in each painting.

He guessed the white designs in the top left corner were snowflakes, unless Campbell's interpretation of celestial bodies applied to them, in which case they were either comets, asteroids or stars. He noticed the signature in the bottom right corner had been painted into the picture rather than added later.

Though each painting was named after a different bird, he could see no direct connections between the titles and the contents. He wondered whether the black corners were accidentally or deliberately prophetic, and pondered on the significance of the small angel in the bottom left corner.

After ten minutes spent scrutinising the paintings in the hope they would convey something more to him, he noticed cards on the walls that named each owner. Five were identified as having been loaned by the Shawton Gallery, three by Mr George Chelmorton, and two each by Mrs Jessica Darley and Mr Samuel Elton. The names of the three private owners were unfamiliar to him. As he noted them down, he wondered which of them in Campbell's eyes was supposed to be the classical musician, which the prominent businessman and which the peer of the realm.

Having exhausted his appreciation of the Birds, he walked around the rest of the gallery and rediscovered his favourite artwork: a winter landscape by Joos de Momper the Younger, oil on panel. Having an hour and a half on his hands, he weighed the main options: more networking at Snig Hill; checking on progress with Witty; looking around the shops; or staying in the Graves. He decided to bolster his knowledge of art by viewing the rest of the gallery.

At a little before 6:00 a security guard approached him. 'Would you be so kind as to make your way to the exit; the gallery is now closing.'

He was taking out his warrant card when Anna

rushed through the nearest double doors. 'Marcus, I have found you; perhaps I should have guessed you would be here in the Impressionist section.' She scanned across to the painting he had been facing. '*Le Sidaner* has produced a subtle effect of a dim red light in the window, but you are standing a little too close to appreciate it fully.' She linked her arm into his and walked him two steps backward. 'Now do you see?'

He waited several seconds before recycling her words. 'Yes, the effect is much more subtle from here.'

Keeping her arm linked into his, she walked him through a half-circle before guiding him toward the exit. Looking up at him, she smiled, 'Dining out with a senior policeman will be very exciting for me; a curator's life can be quite *rustig*… um, uneventful.' She looked down at the brochure in her other hand as though she had just discovered it there. 'You might like to have this. It shows all twelve Piscaroes in the exhibition, with some brief notes about the artist.'

He unlinked his arm and took out his notebook. 'Could I have the contact details for the people who've loaned the Piscaroes? All except the Shawton Gallery; I know where that is. I could track them down myself, but you'd be saving me time. And it isn't as though they're wishing to remain anonymous; not with their names on the walls.'

'Yes, of course. The three private owners were all happy to be identified, which is not always the case. Mr Campbell, the Gallery owner, wanted a big plaque for each of his loaned artworks, but I had to insist on the standard display card. Come with me.'

CHAPTER 13

Marcus followed Anna down the stairs and into the office she shared with two colleagues, where she extracted a hanging file from a tall, four-drawer cabinet. She opened it onto her desk and put aside the front sheet that listed the twelve Piscaroes, then removed four pages each containing a single name and address, to reveal a stack of a dozen photographs, the topmost being of one of the paintings on display. She handed three of the four contact sheets to him; he noted down the details before handing them back to her.

'It is a little early for dinner, actually. Perhaps we should first go to a pub?' The way she had extended the gap between the two plosives in "pub" suggested an associated pleasure.

'Yes, a pub would be good.' He thought of one where he could enjoy performing his civic duty of supporting the local Abbeydale brewery. 'Do you have a particular place in mind?'

'I know one that has a good choice of wines. I like to drink white wine; we could have a bottle together.'

He tried not to let his disappointment show. 'Let's start with your pub, then, and we'll take it from there. I'm driving, though; so you'll have to have the lion's share.' He realised she may not understand the idiom. 'That means...'

She interrupted him. 'We have the same expression in the Netherlands: *het leeuwendeel van iets krijgen.*'

Knowing no Dutch, he happily believed her. 'Well,

practically, that means I'll have one glass and you can have the rest of the bottle.'

Her eyes locked onto his. 'Excellent!'

As they were leaving the building, she pointed out which three of the nine Portman stone carvings around the entrance symbolised painting, sculpture and architecture. He responded in kind by describing former uses of the various places they passed on their quarter-mile walk to the pub, and how Sheffield city centre had changed over the years.

The place was open and airy with plenty of tables for dining. Though it was successful during the day in welcoming parents with young children, it failed to provide an intimate atmosphere for couples later on, so tended to fill with large groups of students. At this time of the evening it was virtually empty.

Believing in equality of the sexes, he immediately passed her the wine list that the barman had just handed to him. 'You'll be having most of the wine, so you should choose.'

She scanned the list as though she were very familiar with it; her choice of a modest chardonnay came as a relief to him, as he had been unsure whether she was intending to have an expensive night out on his tab.

The barman was most insistent Priestley should try the wine before taking it away; he took a sip and nodded acceptance, rather than inviting her to perform the ritual. So that their conversation could remain discreet in the event of a sudden influx of customers, he carried the bottle and glasses to a table in an alcove.

Once they had settled into comfortable chairs, she took a mouthful of wine and held it there for several seconds to savour the moment.

Preparing for a didactic discourse, she pulled a sheaf of papers from her handbag. Looking at him intently, she asked, 'Which should come first, the painter or the paintings?'

He assumed this was not a philosophical question, so responded arbitrarily. 'Let's begin with the painter.'

'Very well, then. Milo Piscaro attended Shawton Art College more than twenty years ago, but he was too quiet to become famous.'

'Sorry, I don't understand what you mean by that.'

'Art nowadays is not simply about what can be seen on a canvas; it has much more to do with the legend.'

'What is that? I'm still not sure what you mean.'

'The legend, the story, is the route to fame. You have heard of the YBAs, the Young British Artists?'

'Yes; though only when one of them is in the news.'

'That is what I mean; it is all about the news and not about the art. It was their infantilisation that led to the stagnation of British art from the late nineteen eighties.'

She emptied her glass and waited for him to refill it. 'Self-publicists are focused on themselves; artists are focused on art. Some self-publicists become very rich, but that does not make them true artists. Publicity often counts for more than ability, I regret to say. For example, the Royal Academy appointed someone to be Professor of Drawing because she was famous, though she lacked qualifications in the subject. Milo Piscaro on the other hand would never have been given such an appointment, though he was a capable draughtsman and a talented artist. He was destined to become neither rich nor famous; he was not a self-publicist.'

'Isn't talent alone enough?'

'Talent for what? Too often, talent for painting

achieves less recognition than talent for telling a long and detailed story about the profound meaning behind their art and how only perceptive connoisseurs are able to appreciate the depth of their work. If such people wish only to tell their stories, they should write a book.'

'Do many go in for that sort of thing?'

'Yes; though others use a different trick. Some refuse to say anything about what their art means; they say the observer must read into it what they will. That is like producing a book with blank pages and saying, "Make up your own story." The age of art has been replaced by the age of stories and blank pages.'

'Do many people share your views?'

'How can one know what many people think? Those in the media push their own agenda by selecting whom to interview. Television programme makers need stories to broadcast, not art. You have an annual joke in this country called the Turner Prize, named after Joseph Mallord William Turner. He was a true artist of great genius, comparable with those from my own country, such as Hieronymus Bosch, Pieter Bruegel the Elder and Rembrandt Harmenszoon van Rijn. The Turner Prize often gives publicity to things that are not true art. Television presenters say, "You may not like it, but you cannot ignore it." Yet that is exactly what you should do; but it is difficult, as it is on your news programmes.

'I heard another joke on the radio. Someone was praising an unmade bed which had once been on the shortlist for the Turner Prize. He seemed to be quite serious, but then I realised it was *gekkendag*, the first day of April, so I knew it was an April Fool's joke. I wonder if everyone realised that?' She paused, but he offered no response. 'For authenticity, the creator of that piece of work should have to unmake the bed every time it goes on display; no one lives for ever, so I hope it will one day be consigned to the rubbish bin of history.' She took another large mouthful of wine, before asking him, accusingly, 'What do you think of such works?'

He squirmed under her steady gaze. 'I'm not qualified to know what's good and what isn't.'

She gave a flick of her mane, like a horse irritated by flies. 'Well, what about paintings? Everyone must have a view of paintings, so tell me some you like.'

He felt uncomfortable to be on the receiving end of an interrogation, so sought refuge in a "no comment" type of response. 'I don't know; I can't think of any right now.'

She became more animated. 'Then, what painters do you like? You must know some painters.'

'I do know some, but I don't know who's any good.'

She pointed a finger at his chest. 'That is the problem. Experts tell people what is good and what is bad. People fear to say something is rubbish because experts have said it is good. Tell me, when you walked around my gallery, which was your favourite painting?'

'I really liked the one by Joos de Momper.'

The tone of her voice indicated a correction. 'Joost de Momper The Younger.' Gazing inwardly, she recalled its details. 'Illumination of the church. Interesting ambiance and contrast. On the left, steep stepped gables rather than rounded Dutch or Flemish style. Two people in shadow walking with long rods in the foreground. The trees edged with shining silver snow.' Her focus returned to him. 'Why do you like it?'

'It reminds me of *The Hunters in the Snow*.'

She giggled. 'You should be a politician, Marcus, the way you selected one with parallels to a famous work by Bruegel, whom I mentioned, so that I cannot disagree with your choice. De Momper was of course heavily influenced by Bruegel. But be brave; tell me of a painter you like, without relying on what any expert may have said.'

'I like van Gogh. Well, his later works, anyway.'

'How late? Later than eighteen ninety? Did you know he became more prolific after he died?'

Priestley clamped his mouth shut, concerned he might offend her if she was into spiritualism.

She laughed, amused by his worried expression. 'You do not know what I mean. After he died, lots of forgeries were produced. Now, choose another painter.'

'I'm not sure I can think of any, off the top.'

'Then I shall name the painter and you will tell me what you think of their work. First: Pablo Picasso.'

'Very famous, very successful.'

'You see how you answered: fame and success. You must try again.'

'I believe he was self-indulgent in the extreme, and self-obsessed; he seemed to believe his own hype. In Sheffield we'd have called him "cocky". I'm not sure I'd have liked him as a person.'

'You still have not commented on his art.'

'His *Guernica* is very famous, but I don't know if it's any good. And I heard his *Women of Algiers* set a record auction price at Christie's in New York.'

'*Women of Algiers version O* was the last of a series of fifteen he painted from 1954 to 1955 as an *hommage* to his friend and rival Henri Matisse, who often painted *odalisques*; but such works hardly ever come onto the open market and so they appear to be rarer than they really are. It fetched a hundred and sixty million dollars before commission. And yet a couple of decades earlier it sold for just thirty-two million. The increase in price is a consequence of so many super-rich looking for ways to bank their wealth. I believe it was competition from perhaps fifteen such people that forced up the bidding; not just Americans, but also Chinese billionaires, Russian oligarchs and Arab Sheikhs.

'There are works by other painters that have been bought and sold privately for even larger sums of money; for example, a Tahitian Gauguin is reputed to have changed hands for three hundred million dollars. Museums are unable to compete with the spiralling prices, so people such as you and I do not often get to see them. There is one of the *Women of Algiers* series currently on loan in Liverpool; if you are interested, we could go there together and I would explain to you how I interpret it.'

'Thanks for the offer; that's maybe something to consider another time.'

She looked a little disappointed. 'You should not miss it. And there is another in Berlin; we could see that, too. A third is in New York, but that is too far away. Anyway, I can tell you something now. The subject of three women and a man is a reworking of *Women of Algiers in their Apartment* by Eugène Delacroix, which was painted in 1834. The Picasso is therefore conceptually unoriginal, but of course the cubist depiction is very different to that of Delacroix.

'As to Picasso's *Guernica*, which was his highest achievement, this also has unoriginal elements. Light has often been used in art to represent goodness, yet he used a searchlight as a harbinger of evil, an idea he may have taken from *The Third of May 1808* by Goya.'

He nodded sagely. 'I wonder if the idea of cubism itself is unoriginal. Perhaps it was triggered by a misunderstanding of the words spoken in the British parliament when they are having a vote: the ayes to the right and the noes to the left.' She stared at him, frowning. 'Aye means yes, so those who agree go right, and those who disagree go left.' He swivelled his eyes to look right, then pretended to pull his nose to the left with both hands. She now understood, and gave him far more of her laughter than he believed he had earned.

'So, you are the class clown. But you need to pay attention, as I shall be testing you later.' He returned some of her laughter, until she adopted a serious expression. 'Picasso painted *Guernica* in 1937, and then, in my opinion, his art declined to his death in 1973, though of course anyone who has paid hundreds of millions of dollars for a later work may disagree. Yet some of his earliest work showed he had talent, so his increasing abstraction was not for the usual reason; abstract art is too often the refuge of the technically incompetent. I admire some of his work, but there is much I do not like. And what was in his character to drive him to destroy beauty? A reaction to political events? Perhaps. Though I believe he was too self-focused for this to be an unchallengeable proposition.'

He found himself becoming increasingly fascinated by her: how her eyes shone, how her lips pouted, how animated she became when she spoke of art.

CHAPTER 14

Anna looked at Marcus a little sternly, like a teacher at a recalcitrant pupil. 'What I said was, it was unfair to ask you for a simple opinion of Picasso, as he was so complex.' He tried to focus on her words, rather than the sensuous way her lips moved when she spoke. 'Therefore we shall try another artist: Piet Mondrian.'

'He's supposed to be good, isn't he?'

'Marcus, you are a coward! Tell me what you really think.'

'His coloured rectangles might be better as a design for wallpaper. I don't believe his paintings have any real claim to being works of art.'

'Many of his rectangles even lack colour; they are simply two-dimensional boxes, more appropriate as the work of a draughtsman than a true artist. Finally, you are honest with me. Let us try another, an artist who shares your first name: Marcus Rothkowitz.'

'No, I don't know him.'

She responded with a giggle he found quite delightful. 'My first name is shared by his mother.'

'That's not much of a hint.'

She gave a sweet laugh. 'He was from Latvia when it was a part of Russia.'

'I still don't know.'

Her laughter effervesced. 'He went to America.'

'I'm still not there yet.'

She struggled to hold back her fizzing giggles. 'A famous Modern Artist.'

'Can't you give me an easy clue?'

Her laughter frothed over and infected him. 'You will know him as Mark Rothko, the American Abstract Expressionist, famous for his colour field paintings. Do you know his large panel, *Red on Maroon*? Or *Rust and Blue*? Perhaps *Magenta, Black, Green and Orange*? Or the various ones in inky-black on milky-grey?'

'I have some vague idea what they might look like, and I guess the titles are quite a good hint.'

She regained control, replacing her laughter with a smile that began with her eyes and encompassed the whole of her face. 'Perhaps you remember criminal actions more than paintings; did you know his *Black on Maroon* was damaged at the Tate Modern in 2012?'

'Yes, I remember the incident; it was on the news.'

'As a curator, I know it is very time-consuming to restore such damage. Now, tell me, what is your opinion?'

'My opinion of spending money on restoring it? I don't think they should have bothered.'

'So, you do not have a high regard for his work. Did you know he killed himself?'

'That rings a bell.'

'It is not uncommon for artists to take their own lives; some of them are very troubled. Do you know of the American Abstract Expressionist Jackson Pollock?'

'I know he was nicknamed "Jack the Dripper".'

'Ah, yes, from his "Drip" period, when he dribbled and squirted paint onto canvasses on the floor. He performed Automatic art, which followed on from Surrealism, which in turn developed from Dadaism, which was based on artists wanting their Daddy as though they were children, so they could ignore the horrors of the First World War.

'But going back to Pollock, you may know he died in a car accident, having had too much to drink; he was an alcoholic, I think. Now, would you believe me if I told you that that entire, barren art movement was backed by the CIA? They needed propaganda to make it appear the US had something to offer the art world, which is why the US Government funded people to become artists. You have heard of the GI Bill? Former American soldiers were paid to travel for art, but there was no requirement to produce anything; all they had to do was to register and claim the money.'

'Well, at least we don't waste taxpayers' money on would-be artists in this country.'

She smiled indulgently. 'You have not heard of the Arts Council? Some artists rely on funding because no one wishes to buy their work. How much does the taxpayer give to them each year?'

'I really haven't a clue.'

'Perhaps the way to improve the quality of art in this country is to abolish the Arts Council; then, only commercially viable art forms would survive. Instead, you have artists who do not contribute anything of genuine quality; they merely collect grants. Yet they are never mentioned when newspapers complain about people living off benefits.'

'You have some interesting opinions, Anna; why don't you publish them?'

'Opinions are one thing; peer-reviewed papers are another. Almost no one publishes academic articles expressing negative views about artists. If they were alive, they would sue. If they were dead, their estates would sue. People in the West do not realise the extent to which their freedom of expression has been curtailed by the use of lawyers. And what if I were to write that the CIA was behind a massive confidence trick? Would I be tracked down and assassinated by someone who is their equal to Mr James Bond, Secret Agent?'

She was clearly not waiting for an answer, but he interrupted anyway. 'You mean their equivalent. James Bond is British; he has no equal in the CIA.'

She cast aside his interruption with a toss of her head. 'That so-called art movement was to my mind a lie. It shows no evidence of anything being abstracted beyond coloured paint; perhaps the paint manufacturers should be given the credit for it.' She stopped for breath, her words having been rushing out with increasing vehemence.

He filled the pause. 'I hadn't expected you to be a conspiracy theorist.'

She began again, starting slowly. 'When you see a canvas covered in drips of paint that anyone could do, and yet it is claimed to be worth millions of dollars, do not ask yourself why you see nothing of merit, but ask yourself why anyone else sees merit where you do not. Perhaps, if you stare long enough, you will recognise some structure to the drips, but so what? It is still only infantile dribbling. Some people claim being the first exponent makes them special; they obviously confuse being first with the concept of genuine originality.

'However, you should keep your mind open to those abstract artists who create an effect that generates a strong and positive emotional response; for example, there are some local painters who achieve abstractions of Derbyshire landscapes that are almost Turneresque. On the other hand, there is a YBA sculptor whose work generates a strong emotional response, but it is only one of disgust; her work is an embarrassment to British art and makes your country look ridiculous in the eyes of other nations. And yet, what can one expect when teachers indoctrinate young people with ridiculous beliefs, such as art is only about generating a reaction.'

As she snatched up her drink, he sought to contribute to the conversation. 'I once heard some people in a pub discussing a novel; when one guy said he despised it, a woman claimed that must mean it's really good because it had evoked a strong emotional response. That type of specious literary argument is called doublespeak.'

'So, there are parallels in art and literature. Now, back to Milo Piscaro. What do you think of his work?'

'I quite like it, in a way. And owning an original artwork is much nicer than simply having a print; but I wouldn't pay fifty thousand pounds for one.'

She looked steadfastly into his eyes. 'So, this is all about the money. I know of a Piscaro that was sold recently at auction. When I was arranging insurance cover for the paintings in the exhibition, I had to make my own estimate of their true worth. I had intended to include all of them in our blanket policy, but Mr William Campbell disagreed with my estimates; he said all his paintings must be insured for fifty thousand pounds each. I had no choice but to agree to pay the premium.' She drained her glass again. 'You might think that the price of a work of art would go up when an artist dies, but for nine out of ten the price goes down at first. For those that do increase in value, sometimes the price goes up straight away, but it is more common for many years to pass before a deceased artist gains such recognition.

'Sadly, art is too often about the money. There are many inexpensive paintings that I would be pleased to hang in my home, but without a famous name they are destined never to appear on the walls of my gallery. And now that I have explained about the value, you no longer need me.' She put on a stylized unhappy face, pushing her lips forward and raising the centre of her mouth to produce an inverted smile, and suggesting tears by repeatedly running her fingers down both cheeks from below her eyes. 'So, no dinner for Anna.'

The unrelieved hormone surge he had felt earlier in the day with Lin was still playing havoc with him, and the effect was being multiplied in Anna's company; feeling the competing influences of pleasure and frustration, he considered the possible benefit of rushing home to Helen. Yet he knew he should at least stay to correct Anna's assumption that his interest was in the auction price paid for a painting. 'Could I tell you something in the strictest confidence?'

She stared at him. 'Ooh, that sounds interesting!'

'I'm investigating the possibility that Milo was murdered.'

Slowly and quietly she breathed a word, more to herself than to him. 'Fuck!' Her eyes stretched wide as she looked into his. 'How did he die?'

'A plastic bag over his head, with an ether-soaked towel inside it.'

'And you are sure it was murder?'

'Well, at least homicide. There are other factors, but it certainly seems likely.'

'Could it have been suicide? Or accidental?'

'It's possible.'

'Do you know the name Joshua Compston?'

'No; should I?'

'He was a *Wunderkind* in British Art.'

Noting the past tense, he deliberately asked a foolish question so as to invite her effervescent laughter. 'Should I put him down as a suspect?'

She explained in a serious, hushed tone, 'No; he died in nineteen ninety-six.'

'What's the connection, then?'

'The cause of death: ether on a towel, in a bag over his head.'

Priestley closed his eyes for a moment to consider this new information. 'I don't know what significance that has, Anna, but it's certainly given me food for thought, so I'll return the compliment; where shall we go for dinner?'

'We could eat here if you wish.'

Detecting a lack of enthusiasm in her voice, he picked up a menu. 'Hmm, burrito. *Burro* means butter in Italian but donkey in Spanish. The word-ending probably indicates a diminutive form. My guess is a burrito is a small Spanish donkey. Do you fancy that?'

She struggled to control her laughter. 'Maybe not. Let's go somewhere else.'

Her laughter finally subsided. 'Do you like Chinese?'

He gave a dead-pan response. 'I've nothing against them in principle. I believe only in liking or disliking individuals, rather than entire nations.'

As Anna's laughter bubbled over again, he realised just how attractive he found her.

CHAPTER 15

Anna chose a popular Chinese restaurant, just a short walk from the pub. As they waited to be found a table, Priestley asked her what she would like to drink.

Playfully, she shook her head from side to side. 'You are not trying to get me drunk, are you?' She became serious. 'I would not wish you to think I am an alcoholic; I am just a social drinker,' adding as an afterthought, 'Perhaps a very social drinker, this evening.' She noticed how grave he looked. 'Do you disapprove? You drink very little. Tell me what you think; should I drink less?'

Seeing the danger that the conversation would become weighed down with his own personal baggage, he tried to appear carefree. 'It really isn't for me to say. Just the occasional not-too-heavy session probably won't kill you. I'm driving, so I can't have much more, but I'll make sure you get home safely if you'd like another drink or two.'

Her mouth smiled, though her eyes appeared watery. 'In that case, let us have another bottle.'

They took the simple option of a set meal for two: crispy duck pancakes, shredded beef with black bean sauce, king prawns with Szechuan sauce, sweet and sour chicken, plus rice and noodles. As he poured her first glass of wine, she stated, 'We shall split the bill.'

He immediately responded, 'No, this is my treat; you've been so very helpful.'

She laughed a little too loudly. 'You did not say,

"We will go Dutch". Every time I share a bill, someone says we will go Dutch, and I say it is too late as I already am. But we will share the cost; no, I should pay more, as I shall certainly drink more.'

'Don't give it another thought; I'll get the police service to foot the bill,' he lied.

'Then I shall have to earn my food and drink.'

Believing she had already done so, he waited for clarification, trying not to jump to a certain conclusion.

She continued, 'You may ask me more questions.'

Though he realised she meant questions about art, he responded, 'Tell me about yourself, Anna. How did you come to be in Sheffield?'

She gazed at him silently for a few seconds. 'I should like to tell you something personal about me, as I think you are very sympathetic. Today is the first anniversary of the end of my marriage, and I should like to celebrate it. To celebrate the end of it, I mean. After it was over, I applied to some English Museums for work as a curator. I received several offers, including one from Sheffield, so I left the Rijksmuseum in Amsterdam and moved here.'

At the end of the synopsis, her gaze became distant. 'Like an artist, I looked at the world from my own single perspective, not a shared one.' She focused on his left eye. 'I am very happy with my freedom.'

Concentrating on her words and gestures, wearing the poker-face he had developed for listening to suspects, he found her last statement unconvincing.

Seeing no obvious reaction to her words, she was unsure whether she had evoked an empathetic response. She looked down at the table. 'Though I sometimes go out with the girls, my colleagues,' quickly she raised her head, her piercing blue eyes again looking intensely at his left eye, 'you are the first man with whom I have dined alone in England. Did you really intend to take me to dinner, or were you just being polite?'

He rushed to answer, believing she was desperately seeking support. 'I was delighted when you accepted the invitation, though you have to understand I'm an old married man, so it's a rare pleasure for me to have an attractive young woman for company.' He added, as an afterthought, 'I mean, apart from my wife.'

She turned her head away from him and viewed his anamorphic face with her watery peripheral vision. 'I think you are happily married; I am pleased for you. But you are not an old man.'

'I mean I've been married for quite a few years and I'm very settled in it. Besides, I'm well into my thirties, and you're only just into your twenties, I think.'

Smiling, she turned to face him directly. 'Thank you, Marcus, but I am now closer to thirty than to twenty.' She pointed to the lower edge of her right eye. 'Notice the first signs of *craquelure*.'

He leaned forward and examined the area indicated, finding only laughter lines. 'Without a microscope, Anna, I'd say you're perfectly unblemished.'

She felt an inner glow as she accepted the compliment with a modest smile.

The conversation was punctuated with silence whenever they picked up small or slippery morsels with their chopsticks. When she declined the included dessert, he hid his regret at feeling obliged to do likewise. Though the bottle was still more than half full, he asked if she would like a coffee, as he had no wish to encourage her to have more wine. She replied, 'Will you take me home now? We could have a coffee there.'

In response to his nod, the attendant waiter delivered the bill to him on a plain white porcelain saucer. He took it to the cash desk, paying by credit card. As they prepared to leave, the waiter handed her a small bag in which the stoppered wine bottle was just visible. She carried it casually, allowing it to swing by her side as they walked to the police station to collect the car.

The drive to her terraced house in Heeley took less than ten minutes. He stepped out of the car and walked around the rear; when he opened the door for her, she accepted the proffered hand and held it tightly. As she looked intently into his eyes, she asked, 'Will you come in for coffee?'

He hesitated, wondering if she really meant coffee.

She recognised the uncertainty. 'Do you think I am inviting you in for sex? It would not be correct.'

He felt confused. 'It would not be correct for me to think you meant sex when you said coffee?'

'No. Yes. I mean it is not correct for one to have sex with someone they have met only once.'

'Ah, not correct behaviour; not proper behaviour.'

'Not proper behaviour; I shall remember that expression. But it is proper to have coffee; it is Dutch imported coffee, and very good.'

'Then I'll be pleased to come in for coffee.'

In the kitchen she refused his offer of help. They sat at a pine rectangular table as the water percolated through the freshly-ground beans and filled the room with a rich aroma. He remained silent as she stood to pour the drinks; though her hand gave little indication of inebriation, he nevertheless feared any interruption to the process could lead her to spill it. In the continuing silence, he decided to invite her to talk more about art. Before he could speak, she asked in a steady voice, 'If I had asked to fuck you, would you have said yes?'

He took refuge in the word error. 'It isn't actually possible for you to, you know, to fuck me. The word comes from Latin, to bifurcate, meaning to split into two branches. So in theory I could, um, bifurcate you, but I don't see how you could, um, do that to me. Do you see what I mean?'

'But American actresses say it all the time in films.'

'Yes. I don't know which is worse, corrupting the English language or corrupting English sensibilities.'

'So now you will answer the question, please.'

He took a deep breath. 'No, I wouldn't have had sex with you, no matter how definite you appeared to be, because you've had too much to drink to be able to think clearly, and you might regret it in the morning.'

'And that is your only reason? Not that you yourself might regret it in the morning?'

'There's that as well, of course; it goes without saying. What with me being happily married.'

'So, you would regret having sex with me.'

He saw how unhappy she suddenly appeared and assumed it was due to the wine and the anniversary of her divorce. The need to respond quickly gave him little time to consider his words. 'That's not what I meant; of course I would like to have sex with you. You're very attractive, intelligent, interesting; any man would jump at the opportunity to be with a beautiful woman such as you. I just meant it isn't something we should consider right now, because you've been drinking and that may have impaired your judgement.'

Knowing he had overstated the rebuttal, he fell silent

and raised his coffee cup as a screen, holding it to his lips. He sipped a little more and found he had taken in some of the grounds; to avoid appearing uncouth, he swallowed them rather than spitting them out.

As he stood to take his leave, she rose with him and reached for his arm to keep him close, then stretched to kiss him lightly on the cheek. 'Thank you for making the day better for me; I did not wish to spend the evening alone.' She opened the external door and held it for him.

'It's been ever so nice, Anna. Goodnight.'

She responded, 'Goodnight.' As an afterthought, she added quietly, 'It is not proper behaviour to have sex with someone on a first occasion, but the rule does not apply to the second occasion.' After a mischievous smile, she added, 'I do hope I shall see you again.'

He drove away wondering which would rate as the more proper behaviour by him: not thinking about having sex with Anna or not thinking about having sex with Lin. Eventually, he dropped his resistance and allowed competing thoughts to jostle for prominence. He felt both appalled and delighted with himself as he identified the perfect solution: have both of them together.

After the short journey home, he parked on the driveway and fished the house-keys out of his jacket pocket. He saw the light from the hallway illuminate Helen as she unlocked the inner and outer doors. Unusually, she stepped outside, triggering the outdoor courtesy light. 'Hello, darling,' he breezed.

'Hello, love,' she immediately blew back. 'You've had a long day. Would you like a coffee? Or have you just had one? It smells like it, on your breath.'

He wondered what other clues she was picking up, and decided it would be wise to beat the retreat. 'It's been a really tiring day; I think I'll head straight upstairs.'

'Alright my love; I will as well, then.'

'You don't have to, if you want to stay up longer.'

'No, I am ready; I was just waiting for you.'

After an electric shave and a wash, he climbed into bed. Untypically, Helen was almost as quick. Rather than the usual silk pyjamas, she was wearing the short gossamery nightdress that he really liked because it left only just enough to the imagination. He deeply regretted having told her he was tired. As she edged into bed, he turned off the remaining light.

She ordered him, 'Turn it back on!' Then, in a lighter tone, 'I want to look at you while we're having hot sex.'

He stared at her; tomorrow was a working day, so why was she in her "vixen" mode? His eyes widened, as did his smile. 'Fantastic, but it isn't my birthday, you know. And we don't want to disturb them, do we?' He immediately wished he had not given her a possible reason to withdraw her invitation.

'It's alright, they're completely zonked.'

He felt a surge of relief that his faux pas had gone unpunished. 'Oh, Helen, you haven't been giving them Mother's Friend again, have you?'

She gave a light giggle. 'Very funny. An hour in the park works better than laudanum.' Her voice went deeper as she laughed dirtily. 'Now, whose turn is it to decide what we're doing?'

CHAPTER 16

As soon as the radio turned on automatically at 6:59, Helen was out of bed and into the shower. Marcus listened to ten minutes of the news before doing likewise. When he arrived downstairs, shaved and dressed, the breakfast table was already laid. He sat on the pine stool at his usual place, ready to eat his cereal. Before he could begin, Helen provocatively put her right leg over him, seating herself on his lap, facing him; after kissing him lightly halfway down his nose, she eased herself back in order to see his face, with her elbows on the table behind her to keep her weight off his thighs. Her opening salvo scored a direct hit. 'What have you been up to with Lin?'

Despite the intimacy of her position, he knew this was the start of an interrogation, so needed to be on his guard. 'I told you yesterday, we were acting as a married couple.'

'And you mentioned she gave you a kiss. Singular. Would you like to tell me where you were at the time: in the gallery, or in the front seat of my car.'

He realised she knew all about the kissing session. 'She kissed me in the gallery, and I pecked her back. When we left, the target was watching.' He had used the word "target" to suggest a professional operation. 'So we had to put on a show.'

'And how good was the show?'

'I think it was pretty convincing.'

'An observer thought it was Oscar material.'

'You haven't spoken to the target have you? It's all highly confidential at the moment.'

'It wasn't your target; it was one of my students. And before you suggest I was spying on you, just let me say, it was an entirely valid experiment to assess to what extent two people could take on different personae and convince a third party of their bona fides. I have to say, he gave you both top marks.'

He frowned. 'You really shouldn't risk my undercover work by putting someone at the scene.'

She replied defensively. 'Well, it clearly didn't affect the operation; you never mentioned him, so I assume you didn't even notice him.'

He snapped back, 'Aged about twenty, came by bike, looked like poverty, spoke like money, silly beard with a straggly moustache: is that who you mean?'

She was impressed, but masked it. 'That's quite accurate. Anyway, what happened after that?'

'I took DC Plummer home so she could get changed before going back to work.' Damn, he thought, I overplayed it.

'And when did Lin become DC Plummer when you're talking to me?'

He considered a "No comment," but settled for silence.

'And what about the evening? Why did you take her to dinner? Was that part of an operation as well?'

He sensed victory was his, so long as he played it cannily. 'Did you have another student watching me?'

'No; it was a colleague who phoned me to let me know he'd just seen you leaving the restaurant.'

'Who is he?'

'That isn't important.'

'Well, why did he call you?'

'You answer my question first. What were you doing there with Lin?'

This should be game, set and match, he thought. 'I wasn't there with Lin. I was actually with a woman who is a leading expert on contemporary art. It was the only time she could fit me in, to talk about the case.'

She recovered quickly, leaning into him and kissing the end of his nose. Her lips were not in his line of sight, but her voice suggested she was smiling at him as she offered playfully, 'So, you're kissing a colleague in the morning and you're wining and dining another woman in the evening. You're really far too young to be having a mid-life crisis.'

He felt his debating ability was being restricted by her sitting on his lap; nevertheless, he tried for a probing attack. 'Why did your colleague feel he needed to phone you?'

She leaned away again. 'He fancies me. Actually, he fancies anything in a skirt. I suppose he was trying to get into my good books.'

'Or into your knickers, more like. It sounds as though I should be the one spying on you, not the other way round.'

She angled her head and kissed him lusciously on the mouth, then whispered in his ear, 'You know I'll never go out for burgers when I have prime steak at home.'

He had to admit to himself that was a great move on her part. Accepting yet another honourable defeat, he gave a last show of defiance. 'Well, why don't you tell him to leave you alone or you'll report him?'

She sighed. 'He's almost untouchable; he's in a

wheelchair.'

'You mean he's incapable?'

'Not to hear him speak. One time, we were sitting together waiting for other colleagues to arrive for a meeting, and he whispered to me how women appreciate him sexually because he has great hands.'

Marcus bristled. 'I wish I'd been there to smack him for talking to you like that.'

Seeing how angry he looked, she tried to calm him with a soothing voice. 'And just imagine the newspaper headlines, love. Anyway, women have always had to suffer that sort of thing, though there's less of it these days, now that we're fighting back.'

His voice remained sharp. 'Well, what did you do?'

'I didn't think anyone else had heard him, so I couldn't do anything, really. I just stood up, walked over to the coffee flasks and looked out of the window; when another colleague came over, I poured for both of us and sat down next to her.'

'Has he ever spoken to you like that again?'

'No,' she lied. 'He's probably given up with the women in the department. I'm certain all of us have turned him down flat; that may be why he's started trying his luck at Open University summer schools.'

'Well, someone should warn them about him.'

She sighed. 'I suppose you're right; maybe I will. Anyway, it's hard not to feel sorry for people like him.'

'I thought disabled people object to being pitied.'

'It doesn't change the fact that we do, though; depending on the disability, some of life's pleasures are inevitably lost to them.'

'But disabled people like your colleague should be abiding by the same rules of behaviour as everyone else. If you and his other victims would give evidence, we could prosecute him.'

Helen cooed, 'Just forget him.'

He refused to be placated. 'When it comes to disabled people, nowadays no one's allowed to say what they think. Like with the Olympics and the Paralympics: if someone tries to point out the difference between being the best out of billions of able-bodied people, and simply being the best out of a small group with particular disabilities, they get the media after them like a pack of dogs. And bitches.'

She began to stroke his hair. 'Alright, love, that was a good bit of venting, but you can calm down now. And you know you support the Invictus Games, so it isn't all about numbers, is it?'

He shook his head to make her stop stroking him. 'That's different; they were my mates. Anyway, you'll have to get off; my legs are going to sleep.'

A small voice called from the doorway. 'What are you doing?'

She lifted herself off his lap, her voice switching seamlessly from lover to mother. 'We were having a face-to-face conversation.' She beamed a smile.

Edwin asked, innocently, 'Do other people do that?'

Her smile remained undimmed. 'Yes, sometimes.'

He walked away, calling up the stairs, 'Alice!'

She rushed to the doorway. 'Edwin, come back; I hadn't finished explaining.' He turned at the foot of the stairs. 'It's something only done by people who are married or in love. Brothers and sisters are never allowed to do it.' Marcus thought he had just seen a very rare sight indeed: Helen, flustered.

CHAPTER 17

The investigation team assembled in the MIR slightly ahead of the scheduled 8:30 start time. After the usual pleasantries, the status reports were reviewed and actions agreed. Subject to availability, Priestley and Berry would visit the priest in the morning, and the painters at Green Lane Studios in the afternoon. Plummer would work with Witty to collate updates and initiate further actions as appropriate. Unfinished work on other fronts would continue as before.

Priestley returned to his office to contemplate the overall shape and direction of the investigation. It had started late, but had made up ground. Disappointingly, results were largely unenlightening. The absence of CCTV footage in the immediate vicinity of the locus was particularly unfortunate. He asked himself why anyone listened to the shrill chorus of self-appointed protectors of civil liberties defending the rights of criminals to get away with murder so that innocent people would not be recorded going about their lawful occasion; if it were up to him, there would be CCTV everywhere. His internal rant was interrupted when the telephone began to ring. The incoming display facility revealed a mobile phone number that was unfamiliar to him. He responded in full to give them time to prepare to speak; it was not uncommon for callers to be so keen to inform him of something, their words would tumble out incoherently. 'Detective Chief Inspector Marcus Priestley speaking.'

'Marcus, I hope you do not mind my telephoning you this morning. I wished to thank you for an enjoyable evening, and to say how grateful I am to you for being such a gentleman.'

The hint of Dutch in her voice gave her a continental attractiveness he found appealing. He could smell the coffee she had made for them in her kitchen, which had had enough caffeine to keep him wide awake half the night; that had been fortuitous, as Helen had been determined to prove her youthfulness empirically. 'I should be the one thanking you, Anna; you gave me some very useful information.'

'And it was information you wanted, of course, to help with your investigation.'

Her voice betrayed her disappointment with his reply, so he tried again. 'Getting information was the reason I asked for the meeting, but what I had was a thoroughly enjoyable evening with you.'

She responded far too quickly. 'Then, if we both enjoyed it, I hope we can do it again sometime soon.'

Though he felt a certain frisson, he nevertheless attempted a neutral response. 'If there's ever a need for another discussion with an art expert, you'll definitely be my first port of call.'

Again, she responded quickly, suggesting she had pre-thought the conversation. 'I think I was enjoying your company so much, I did not give you anywhere near enough information. There is so much I have to offer you; just let me know when you would like us to get together again.'

He knew he was playing with fire, but his hormones drove him to keep all options open with her. 'I'm sure something will come up that needs your expertise; I'll call you when it does.'

'Thank you, Marcus; I hope to hear from you soon.'

As the line went dead, he asked himself whether it was wrong of him to give her any encouragement; after all, he really did love Helen, so why was he wondering how he might justify seeing Anna again.

He tried to focus on the investigation, but found memories of recent events repeatedly interrupted his train of thought. Eventually, he telephoned the number for Father O'Clery. A housekeeper relayed messages to and fro and a meeting was arranged for 10:30.

His thoughts returned to Anna. Applying male hormonal logic, he decided the best way of avoiding thinking of her was to switch to a different attractive young woman, and Lin fitted the bill.

He went into the MIR and walked over to Lin. 'Is Neil keeping you fully informed of developments?'

'Well, I suppose so.' Her smile was far too generous for a senior officer. 'I mean, I wouldn't know if there's something he hasn't told me.'

He reciprocated the smile. 'Not every day is as interesting as yesterday. You're down for working in the office all day today, aren't you?'

She gazed at him steadily. 'Yes, though I'd drop everything at a moment's notice if you asked me to. If you want me in a hurry, just blow your whistle.'

'I'm sure it won't be long before you're the perfect partner in crime, again. See you later.' He tried to untangle their conversation, wondering whether coded messages had been passing each way.

To assuage his feelings of guilt, he returned to his office and telephoned Helen. 'Are you busy? I just called to say…'

'I love you.'

'It's ever so nice to hear you say so.'

'No, I mean I do, but I was just continuing the lyric. So, why were you calling?'

'It's like you said, to say I love you.'

'Anything else to say?'

'Not really.'

She considered for a moment whether the call had been triggered by feelings of guilt, but decided it probably originated from a diffcrent reason. 'Are you after another performance tonight?'

'No; I'm too knackered.'

'Should I take that as a compliment?'

'Definitely. I'll see you later, then.'

'Bye, love.'

He asked himself why he still kept thinking of Lin and Anna when he had Helen, but could find no logical answer.

CHAPTER 18

Berry drove Priestley to Father O'Clery's presbytery, close by St Augustine's church. Introductions were delivered formally. 'I'm Detective Chief Inspector Priestley and this is Detective Constable Beresford.'

'And I'm Father O'Clery. Should I address you by your full title?'

O'Clery's Southern Irish accent was unmistakable. 'Detective or Mr Priestley will do fine.' O'Clery was short and of a portly build; combined with his glowing red cheeks, and the small spectacles too far down his nose, the effect was of a jolly, Dickensian character. Priestley was determined not to be unduly influenced by his appearance. He continued sharply, 'And do you have a shorter form of address, yourself, sir?'

O'Clery smiled, wrinkles adding to the jovial impression. 'I think you are, perhaps, uncomfortable with addressing me as "Father". May I assume you are not of the faith?'

Priestley chose the Kipling response. 'I'm a God-fearing Christian atheist.'

O'Clery's eyes twinkled. 'But a Protestant atheist, I think; not a Catholic one.'

Priestley found himself warming to the man, but knew it threatened to undermine his plan of attack for the interview. 'You're quite right, Father. Now, I'd like some information about someone who was of your persuasion.'

'Is that "was" in the sense of they have lost their

faith, or "was" as in they are no longer alive?'

'The latter. When I phoned earlier, I did mention it was about Miles Percy, or perhaps you knew him as Milo Piscaro.'

'Ah, poor Miles. Mrs Brown will have taken it upon herself to filter the communication.' He took on a mischievous look. 'Someday I expect to find her in my side of the confessional box, saying not to trouble myself and she'll tell me later what I need to know.'

Priestley laughed out loud, as not to have done so would have appeared boorish, and could have lost him the moral high ground he was striving for. Berry echoed with a quieter laugh. 'Now that Miles is dead, are there any secrets of the confessional you can disclose that might have a bearing on how he died?'

'Would you have me suffer *latae sententiae*? Automatic excommunication? I can't even inform you whether or not he took confession.'

Priestley knew he was softening to the singer, but not to the song. He shot back, 'So, the Catholic Church places itself above the law.'

O'Clery sighed. 'I'm sure you know the situation as well as I do. I'd be happy to tell you anything I can, unless I'm bound by the seal of the confessional.'

Priestley remained unappeased. 'Except you might lie to me if the truth is dependent on information obtained in the confessional. So you could mislead the investigation and yet your own Catholic conscience would remain untroubled.'

O'Clery put on his calmest face. 'Rather than worrying about what limitations may or may not apply to the answers I give to any of your questions, perhaps you could just ask me something specific and see if my answer helps at all. But before you begin, would you tell me something about the underlying reason for the investigation? Miles's death was reported in the newspapers as suicide, which I'm sure you know has implications for his mortal soul. Is the fact that you're investigating his death an indication it was not suicide?'

Priestley set his face hard against the priest. 'That's not something I can respond to; I'm bound by the seal of the Constabulary.'

O'Clery took on a troubled frown. 'Did someone in the Catholic Church hurt you when you were young?'

Priestley refused to play along. 'The Catholic Church does something to undermine all humanity, every time it declares its views are superior to those of other faiths. Just look at the world today and see how religious extremism is at the core of so much inhuman suffering. So, I'm against all religious extremism; and more than that, I'm against any religion if it claims at any level the right to restrict the freedoms of others. But, most pertinent to my work as a police officer, I object to the Catholic Church's refusal to allow disclosure of criminal acts obtained in the confessional. I see your Church as an organisation that undermines the law, and its priests as the tools that spread that subversion.'

When O'Clery and Priestley fell silent, Berry asked, 'Does that mean Father O'Clery can't say anything, sir? Are we finished here, then?'

Priestley snapped at Berry, 'No, we're not finished; we haven't even started.' He turned to O'Clery and asked him, just a little less sharply, 'Now, Father O'Clery, what *can* you tell me about Miles Percy?'

O'Clery shook his head slowly from side to side. 'I

knew he had become disillusioned with his work as a painter, but I know of nothing to suggest he would ever take his own life.'

Priestley refused to take even this simple statement at face value. 'Barring anything you heard in the confessional.' He continued after a pause. 'How well did you know him?'

'He attended mass regularly.'

'And frequently? Regularly as in once a year?'

O'Clery acknowledged the distinction. 'I'm sorry, I see you're needing facts. Miles attended mass every Sunday, religiously.'

Priestley smiled inwardly, but frowned outwardly to suggest this was not an occasion for levity. 'And was he spiritually committed, or simply paying lip-service?'

'I believe he was naturally disposed to seek spirituality in all things; certainly in his faith, but also through his painting. We sometimes spoke of God. He told me his last series of paintings was of God looking back at us on Earth.'

'But he became disillusioned.'

'Yes indeed. I had always assumed he was naturally positioned at the ascetic end of the spectrum of unworldliness, but he hinted his simple lifestyle was more a consequence of never having earned much money out of painting. So he was planning to find work that should pay more, though he recognised it would be less rewarding, spiritually; specifically, he was intending to work as a painter and decorator. I asked him if that might not crush his soul, but he replied he needed to keep body and soul together.'

'That must have been disheartening for him. Would you say he appeared depressed?'

'Only slightly. I would say he was accepting of his situation. I certainly would not say he was, um, what would you call it, clinically depressed. I can't reconcile my knowledge of the man with the idea that he took his own life. And I can say that without any connection with the confessional, so you can put aside your earlier misgivings on that particular score.'

Priestley felt he had obtained what he came for. 'Thank you, Father O'Clery. If the police wish to ask you any further questions, we'll be in touch.'

Priestley hastily left the room and the presbytery with Berry trailing in his wake. When they reached the car, Berry put the key into the ignition but held back from starting the engine. When Priestley had fastened his seat belt in the rear, he asked, 'Are you in the back because you've some work to do? Do you want me to keep quiet?'

Priestley knew he should have a proper conversation with Berry, but decided to deliver a monologue. 'Here's the problem with interviewing a Catholic priest: it can be like interrogating a sociopath. It's difficult to read someone who doesn't give the usual indications of lying, or of being troubled by conscience. A priest may be lying to you, but it's difficult to tell because he may himself believe he's saying the correct things in accordance with his religious rules. For him, his first duty lies to the Catholic Church.'

Into the silence, Berry risked, 'Not to God then?'

Priestley responded without hesitation. 'No, not to God; or at best, only to their Catholic God. And certainly not to the members of their congregation. Imagine a priest being told by a young girl that she's been raped by a man she can identify, and that man had previously confessed to the priest that he was a child rapist; so the child suffered the abuse because the priest didn't report the man to the police. You can blame the perpetrator of course, but to my way of thinking you could also blame the priest and the entire Church hierarchy right up to the top. The only sanction available to the priest is to refuse to grant absolution, but that doesn't help the poor, damaged child.'

Berry frowned. 'Your logic may be correct, but how does that have a bearing on this case? He said specifically he didn't believe it was suicide, and that that view had nothing to do with the confessional.'

Priestley smiled. 'And that was what I was waiting for him to say. I gave him a hard time about keeping secrets, so his conscience may have been looking for a way of revealing the truth without breaking the seal of the confessional. One interpretation is that he spoke simply and honestly when he said he was confident Miles didn't kill himself. Another is that he knew something from another person's confession that he wasn't allowed to disclose, but he had been able to convince himself he could justify telling us without taking that into account.'

Berry thought long and hard before responding. 'Either way, he wants us to believe it wasn't suicide.'

'Yes, so we have two main possibilities to consider: Miles took his own life and O'Clery was mistaken or lying; or Miles was killed by someone else. If the latter, then who did it? I don't believe it was O'Clery himself, but could it have been another of his parishioners? And might it be someone who admitted as much in the confessional box?'

Berry had no wish to disagree with his boss, but felt

an imperative obligation to be true to his own god, logic. 'Or was it someone else entirely, and it's nothing to do with St Augustine's church or any confession.'

Priestley knew Berry had made a valid point, but remained stubbornly with the Catholic theme. 'Yes, Tony, this line of inquiry could prove to be a dead end, but if you don't look, you don't find. Seeing as Miles attended Mass every Sunday, we should include the Church with a capital "C" on the Associates list; that's the priest and all the members of the congregation. And remember your ABC of Detection if you end up interviewing any of them: Assume nothing, Believe no one, Check everything.'

CHAPTER 19

Priestley sat in his office in front of the computer screen and moved the mouse to click on a search engine icon. He located Green Lane Studios, recognising the address was of a former industrial building on the edge of Shawton. The studio's website enabled searching by type of artist; the long list of options included Metalworker, Silversmith, Jeweller, Sculptor, Mixed Media. He selected Painter and found five artists were listed, each with links to their own website. Choosing Milo Piscaro, he discovered it called up the web address he had tried previously; this time, the front page indicated Milo had died. The site no longer claimed to be under construction, so he delved deeper and found examples of his work dating back over fifteen years.

He repeated the process for the other four artists, Tom Derwent, John Doe, Peter Erewash and Lisa Wye, noting down their names and contact details. Looking at the second name on the list, he wondered if it was a pseudonym or whether the parents were responsible.

Priestley preferred to make his own telephone calls, as the time taken was often little more than would be expended on delegating the task. Besides, he reasoned, initial contacts were sometimes quite informative. He called the mobile numbers and spoke to Tom, John and Peter, arranging to see them at their studios in the early afternoon. There was no reply from Lisa, so he sent an e-mail asking her to make contact.

Priestley called Berry into his office. 'Tony, we'll be

seeing three painters this afternoon, and perhaps a fourth. What do you know about contemporary art?'

'About as much as I know about making ice cream.'

'What do you mean?'

'Liquids go in and solids comes out.'

'Right, well, here's their names. Find out everything you can about them, and report back if you discover anything that might give us cause for concern.'

Berry took the list and read through it. 'John Doe? I can guarantee that's going to produce millions of false positives. Do you know anything more about this particular John Doe?'

'Start with the Green Lane Studios website; that applies to all of them. Anyway, it could be worse: what if it was John Smith?'

'Don't worry; I'm sure I'll find the real McCoy.'

'No, not McCoy; it's Doe.' He waited for Berry's dutiful laugh, but received only a pulled face. 'We'll be off at ten to one; that's time of day, not gambling odds.'

Berry gurned again. 'You're really trying today, sir. Though when I say "really trying", I mean "really trying", not, "really trying".'

'Well, thank you, Tony, for that entirely unhelpful clarification. Now bugger off.'

Berry chortled as he headed out of the office.

Priestley reflected for a moment on Berry's development since his recruitment as a maths graduate with fast-track potential; he now not only understood what jokes are, but recognised inferior quality ones, and even attempted some of his own.

Priestley checked his watch: almost time for the Senior Officers' 11:45 meeting to discuss the latest crime figures. He imagined himself searching with increasing desperation through desk drawers for anti-bullshit pills. Steeling himself for yet another discussion of the impossible high-level targets now being set by the Police and Crime Commissioner following the recent assessment of their collective shortcomings by Her Majesty's Inspectorate of Constabulary, he trudged to the main conference room.

Chief Constable Charles Coker was seated at the head of the table. Deputy Chief Constable Dorothea Forbes-Smythe was at his right hand, with Assistant Chief Constable Archie Cameron at his left, and next to him Philippa Hatchette, Head of Human Resources. With so many of the Great and the Good collected together at that end of the table, Priestley pondered on whether their proximity represented a threat to the service; what if another von Stauffenberg planted a bomb at their feet and killed them all? He played in his mind an insincere self-reprimand for that thought, before concluding it would make not the slightest difference if they were all wiped out. He knew some of them had once been good officers, but as they had progressed through the ranks they had transmogrified into politicians. He prayed to God the same decay would never happen to him; then he asked Allah, Brahma, Vishnu and Shiva, just to be on the safe side.

'Priestley!' Chief Superintendent Barbara Watt had hissed his name in the hope of gaining his attention without attracting that of the high-ranking officers at the other end of the table.

He looked in the direction of the sound and saw Watt glaring at him; half-a-dozen other officers seated near her were also staring in his direction. 'Ma'am?'

She whispered loudly. 'Mind elsewhere again? Sit

next to me so I can keep an eye on you.'

A pile of status reports were passed around, everyone taking a copy and looking at the first spreadsheet. Forbes-Smythe raised a question. 'Yesterday's pile-up involved nine vehicles, all of which must have been driven carelessly, otherwise the drivers would not have found themselves in an RTC. So, there were nine offences, but all stemmed from the same incident. Therefore, would it not be appropriate for a single entry to be added into the statistics?'

Coker sighed audibly. 'I understand where you're coming from, but HMIC insist we crime them all.'

Forbes-Smythe responded, 'Then we must use targeting to reduce our red numbers; I suggest we revise every officer's personal target so as to double their achievement level. We need improvements and we need them now.'

Hatchette asked, acidly, 'And how do you propose we achieve that improvement in real terms? What strategy? What tactics?'

Forbes-Smythe turned and smiled at Coker. 'Strategy is the responsibility of our Chief Constable.' Her smile faded as her eyes skipped roughshod across the other senior officers present. 'And tactics are the responsibility of the rest of you.'

Priestley realised his muttered "Christ Almighty!" had been picked up by Watt's keen hearing.

She leaned in closely. 'Try to see these meetings as a form of battle-hardening; what doesn't kill you makes you stronger.'

Feeling so much better for knowing she understood his suffering, he gave her a nod and a smile.

After the most senior officers had finished

displaying their command of jargon and buzzwords, the lower-ranking officers were invited to propose some Practical Policing Policies, or PPPs. Priestley kept his head down in the hope that no one would ask him any questions.

As the meeting was nearing its natural death, Forbes-Smythe called out sweetly, 'Marcus.'

He looked up and saw she was smiling warmly at him, as she so often did; he worried about that, and why she always addressed him by his first name. He knew he had strayed accidentally into her good books, but could not recall how. 'Yes, ma'am?'

'You reclassified a suicide as a suspicious death by revising the statistics for an earlier time-period; to the date of the death, in fact. Well done. That makes the current reporting period look better.'

He smiled back at her. 'Thank you ma'am.' He had not the slightest idea who was really responsible. When he considered the morality of accepting unearned praise, he remembered it was common practice in the service for the innocent to be punished and the uninvolved rewarded.

When the meeting finally came to a close, he felt like an unacademic schoolboy escaping from the classroom at the end of the last day of term.

CHAPTER 20

While driving Priestley to the studios, Berry briefed him on his investigation into the painters. He had found no evidence of any criminal activity, which, ironically, he deemed disappointing. On the other hand, John Doe was proving interesting, having apparently sprung into existence several years ago; he therefore became the automatic first choice to be interviewed.

Priestley pressed the button that was dangling loose to one side of the solid metal door and spoke into the intercom. A woman answered. 'You're expected; just push.' The loud buzzing sound indicated the door could now be opened.

They walked into a reception area and asked to speak to John Doe. The woman seated behind the reception desk ran her index finger down a list of names on a sheet of paper, then traced a line across to the right. She informed him, 'He's in studio seven. I'll take you there; it's just along the corridor.'

He responded, 'There's no need to trouble yourself; I'm sure we can find it.'

She looked at him severely under a furrowed brow. 'People aren't allowed to go wandering around on their own; security, you know. Follow me. And when you're finished with...' she snickered, 'John Doe, make sure you come back to reception; I can't have people walking around unescorted.'

She walked ahead of them to the fourth room on the left, which had the name "John Doe" displayed prominently on the wall at the near side of the door. She knocked and waited, explaining to Priestley, 'There's dangerous chemicals and stuff, so you have to wait to be invited in.'

Doe came to the door and opened it for them. 'You can go now Margaret, thank you.' Turning to Priestley, he asked, 'Would you prefer to talk somewhere more comfortable?'

Priestley wished to see inside the studio, in the hope that it might provide him with some insight into the character of the mysterious John Doe. He held out his warrant card as he responded, 'Let's start off in here, shall we? I'm Detective Chief Inspector Priestley, and this is Detective Constable Beresford.'

Doe apologised, 'There's only one chair and a stool. I sometimes sit on the stool to work, and in the chair to relax a bit. If I have a model in here, she generally uses the stool with a cushion and a sheet on it.'

Priestley wondered if it was Politically Correct for artists to have only female models. 'You said "she"; does that mean you have just the one model? Or do you have several models and they're all female?'

Doe smiled comfortably. 'I find most women's naked bodies to be attractive to varying degrees. I don't find men's bodies attractive, though of course that doesn't mean they aren't interesting from an artistic perspective. But in the end, I do life drawing and painting for enjoyment, so I always choose women who look good naked. By the way, your detective constable is displaying symptoms of shock; perhaps he should sit down before he faints.'

Berry considered denying the suggestion, before seeking an alternative way out of the awkwardness. 'I think it's the smell of paint that got to me a bit, but I'm fine now, thank you sir.'

Doe scrutinised Berry. 'If you say so. But do feel free to sit.'

Priestley turned to Berry. 'You sit in the chair, Tony.' Berry did as instructed, trying not to touch the paint on the arms. Priestley remained standing, turning to observe the dozens of paintings arrayed on the walls.

Doe gestured with a sweeping hand. 'Do feel free to look around. The impressionistic landscapes are better seen from a distance, whereas the figurative works, especially the nudes, are best seen from much closer.'

Priestley promenaded around the room, feeling obliged to take as much time over viewing the landscapes as examining the nudes; he eventually looked at their faces and realised there were just three different women. Trying to sound casual, he asked, 'Who does the modelling for you?'

Doe responded brightly, 'There's an agency who supplied two of them. The third is an actress I met a few years ago.'

Priestley saw an avenue of investigation open up before him. 'I'd like their names and addresses.'

Doe smiled mischievously. 'Why, Inspector? Are you intending to become a painter yourself?'

Considering they were investigating a suspicious death, Priestley felt Doe appeared to be far too much at ease, until he realised Doe had probably accepted the version of events reported in the local newspaper. 'It's possible the young women also modelled for Mr Piscaro, so I'll need to check them out.'

Doe dropped his smile. 'That suggests Milo's death may not have been suicide.'

'There is some evidence to suggest he may have been unlawfully killed.'

'Really? How did he die?'

'How do you think he might have died?'

'That's hardly a question for me, is it, Inspector?'

'Humour me, if you will, sir. If you were intending to kill an artist, how would you do it?' Priestley wondered if the technique used by Joshua Compston was well known to artists and if Doe would suggest it.

'Well, if you're looking for a method that might employ materials widely available to painters, then there is one that springs to mind.'

'And what would that be, sir?'

'I'd smear a bit of cobalt blue in his sandwiches. He wouldn't notice the taste, and it would get him eventually. Cadmium yellow would be an alternative, mixed with mustard.'

'And what about a more instantaneous death?'

'A palette knife through the heart would be very effective for someone with the strength to push it in, though I can assume that isn't what happened to Milo, as it would have been fairly obvious to your forensic people. So, what you're fishing for is a method that is, if not undetectable, then at least ambiguous.' He closed his eyes for a second or two. 'Hypervitaminosis A could easily be missed in a general toxicity screening. A venous air embolism, that's a bubble of gas in a vein, might not be picked up by a busy pathologist. Suffocation of an unconscious patient can be difficult to recognise, depending on circumstances. I'm sure you have specialists to give you this sort of information.'

Priestley was taken aback by Doe's level of knowledge. 'Have you spent much time thinking about how to kill someone, Mr Doe?'

Doe's smile returned. 'I'd better come clean. I'm not Mr Doe, for two reasons. One: I adopted the name "John Doe" for reasons of privacy; my real name is Michael Paderewski. Two: I'm not a Mister. I was a Mister, then a Doctor, then a Mister again when I became a consultant surgeon, and finally a Sir when I was awarded a knighthood for services to medicine.' Priestley pondered over how best to continue. 'Not what you were expecting? Actually, quite a few of us, medics I mean, take up painting when we head into retirement. The steady hand of a surgeon is definitely an asset when it comes to representational painting.'

Priestley sensed he was not dealing with a murderer. 'I'll still need to do a full investigation into your background, sir.'

'Do call me Michael, Inspector. I've had a lifetime of formality, so I'm happy to lose the "Sir" whenever it isn't relevant.'

'Well, thank you, Michael. As to Milo's death, it was from diethyl ether.'

'But you don't think it was suicide?'

'It's the diazepam that entered his system an hour earlier that troubles me.'

'Ah! A death played out in two acts. It certainly sounds like it was carefully planned. Though, unless Milo was actually unconscious, can you be certain he didn't self-medicate?'

'The working assumption is that it wasn't suicide, but the investigation still has a long way to run. Anyway, I'd like the names of your models, as I said before, and I may need to get back to you once all the background checks have been completed.' Berry noted down the women's names and contact details. 'Do you have any skeletons in the cupboard you'd like to tell me about, right now?'

'Only surgeons who restrict themselves to the easiest operations are ever going to achieve a one hundred per cent success rate. I'm confident my personal performance was well above average, taking into account the complexity of each operation and the state of health of each patient, but it wasn't a perfect record. So, yes, sadly there are some skeletons, but certainly no more than should be expected, and I believe, far fewer.'

'Any skeletons away from the operating theatre?'

'No, neither metaphorical nor literal.'

Priestley's final questions were ones that would have been his first under different circumstances. 'What did you know of Milo? What did you think of him? What was he like? Just tell me anything that comes into your head.'

'Well, he knew who I really was, and to use an old-fashioned word, I'd say it made him shy of me, though I think he was naturally shy of most people. His ex-girlfriend, Lisa Wye, was the exception. I was probably the last to know they'd broken up; on the rare occasions I saw him talking to her this year, I'd say he still displayed all the signs of being besotted with her, and she appeared to be still fond of him. Neither of them had anyone else, as far as I'm aware, so I don't know what led to the break-up.

'Probably the most I've ever spoken to him was last year, when I took it upon myself to organise the Christmas dinner. It's a tradition that all the artists here at the studios make an effort to dress up for it; we spend so much of our time dressed down, it makes it quite an occasion for us. I like parties. I have to admit I accept almost every party invitation I receive, nowadays; well, you're only young once, aren't you?' Priestley smiled, guessing he was probably into his seventies. 'But Milo said he wouldn't be going, and refused to say why. In my experience, most people would just make up a lie and try to sound convincing, but Milo wouldn't do that. So I challenged him to admit it was because he was short of cash, and he agreed that was the reason. When I offered to pay his share, he didn't take it as an insult, which I suppose some people would have done, but he still wouldn't budge. I said the occasion wouldn't be the same without him there, and I insisted he go. Perhaps I was rather bossy, but he then said he would go, only it seemed like he was taking it as an order from a superior, which isn't how I meant it.

'Anyway, I then came up with an idea for paying for the do. I e-mailed everyone on the studio list, saying that amongst artisans there are always good years and bad years, and so the Christmas festivities would be funded on a voluntary basis according to their feelings of success. I said I would leave my studio unlocked for a quarter of an hour each day starting at midday, and people wishing to contribute should place their donations in the black drawstring bag under my easel.'

Priestley felt intrigued. 'How did that work out?'

Michael smiled. 'I'd no sooner sent out the e-mail, than a certain female responsible for the administration of this building came knocking at my door to complain how irresponsible it was of me to tell everyone I would be leaving my studio unlocked! Nevertheless, I persevered with the plan; I was fully prepared to fund the whole shebang myself if I had to. I'd had years of high earnings but never the time to spend it, so I could afford to pay for us all quite comfortably. But I didn't need to; the total collection came to almost twice the usual cost. So I upgraded the festivities to spend the lot, and some more besides, and we all had a marvellous time of it.'

'Including Milo and Lisa?'

'I suppose so; I'm fairly sure they were still a couple then. But I can't honestly say I noticed for certain.'

As Priestley found himself wondering what would happen if someone tried to organise a Christmas party back at the station along those lines, Michael offered one last observation. 'Milo always seemed as though his mind was in another place, as though he was thinking deep, philosophical thoughts. Now that it's too late, I really regret never having taken the trouble to get to know him better. He was a true artist who genuinely believed in his work.'

They took their leave and headed for the door, until Priestley turned abruptly. 'Where were you at the time of Milo's death?'

Michael answered immediately, 'That evening and into the wee hours I was at a large, formal dinner.' He provided the details, before adding, 'I thought for a moment you'd forgotten to ask your key question; I realise now you were doing a "Columbo".'

Priestley shrugged. 'It sometimes works.'

Michael asked who else they intended to see; he then directed them toward Derwent's studio. Berry reminded Priestley of their instruction to return to reception first. Michael grimaced. 'Never let matron think she's in charge; it took me a long time to learn that lesson.'

CHAPTER 21

After creeping silently along the corridor, keeping close to the wall to minimise visibility, Priestley stopped at Tom Derwent's studio door and looked through the glass panel. He watched and waited as the painter bent close to a canvas and carefully applied a few thin strokes of a narrow, flat brush. When Derwent sat up on his stool, Priestley knocked quietly. Seeing a face peering at him, Derwent navigated a route with studied care through his jars of brushes, pots of paints and stacked canvases. Priestley thought his movements reminiscent of a *matador de toros*, a killer of bulls.

Derwent opened the door and noticed the second visitor. 'Greetings, gentlemen.' He waved away the warrant cards being held up for his inspection. 'Now, what can I do for you?' After formal introductions, Derwent waited for Priestley to begin.

'I'm investigating the death of Milo Piscaro, but could I take a look at your work, first?'

'Please do.'

'Are all these yours? There are two different styles.'

'I like to keep my hand in by doing some technically demanding, representational work. Though, if you look closely, you'll see I sometimes include impressionistic overtones. But mostly I create abstract works. Look at these two.' He pointed to an almost photographic image of a scene from the local Dark Peak, and then to a canvas with a mass of variously-coloured streaks of paint in a pattern that had its clearer equivalent in the first painting. Priestley noticed what appeared to be sand embedded in the areas that equated to the rocks in the first painting. 'Which do you prefer? Be honest.'

'I'd be happy to have either of them on my wall at home. The first one looks really good, but then I suppose I could have had a photograph blown up and framed instead. The second one certainly creates a dramatic impression; I'm sure it would make for a more interesting talking-point at dinner-parties.'

'It sounds to me you're one of that rare breed who genuinely appreciates abstract art.'

Priestley looked again at the two paintings. 'Actually, I think they work best as a pair. Do you ever sell your paintings as pairs?'

Derwent frowned in concentration. 'The most interesting ideas can come from those who know least.'

Priestley pretended to bristle at the response, over-emphasising his words and gestures to make clear it was all in fun. 'Are you saying I'm ignorant? Insulting a police officer is a serious offence.'

Derwent laughed so much his eyes watered. 'I only meant you're someone who's not in the business; not contaminated by our collective belief set. I think you've actually come up with a brilliant idea, Inspector; I may well use it.'

When Berry's quieter laughter came to a halt, Priestley allowed his own smile to fade. 'Anyway, I need to ask you some questions about Milo Piscaro.'

'Why me? Because I'm also a painter? I hardly knew him. You should ask the people who knew him better.'

'You're quite right. That leads me onto my first question: are you able to give me the names of the people who knew him well? His closest friends?'

'To the best of my knowledge, only Lisa Wye knew him intimately. I doubt whether any of the rest of us here knew him well, with the possible exception of Sir Michael; you may know him as John Doe. I believe they had a few long chats in the run-up to Christmas.'

'Tell me about last Christmas, if you will.'

Derwent's eyes twinkled. 'The snow lay clean and crisp upon the ground, the hunters' boots leaving a trace of corrupted humanity as they stalked their defenceless prey; the silvered trees sparkled in the moonlight, as the world lay bedded down for the night in a womb of goose-feathers.' He scanned the small audience for appreciation but received only looks of surprise. 'What exactly do you wish to know, Inspector?'

'What happened with the Christmas party?'

'Well, Sir Michael sent an e-mail to everyone saying we should each decide how successful we felt we had been and contribute to the party fund accordingly. That triggered some interesting conversations. I remember Peter and I considered the question together from a philosophical perspective, deciding that success was not to be measured only in monetary terms, and so we concluded we had both been successful.'

'Peter...?'

'Peter Erewash. We decided the half of us who felt successful should contribute double the anticipated rate to support the other half of our little community.'

'And how did that work out?'

'I suspect Sir Michael doubled the entire fund so that we could all have a good time, though he denied it. We had champagne to start, port to finish, and decent wines in between.'

'And the food?'

'Yes, I'm sure we must have had food as well, though I don't remember much about it.'

Priestley nodded. 'We've all been there.' Glancing at Berry, he remarked, 'Well, nearly all of us.' He looked closely at Derwent. 'You mentioned Sir Michael may have known Milo better than most people, but when we asked him, he said he didn't feel he knew him especially well.'

'It's all relative, Inspector. I don't believe anyone here really knew Milo very well, but some may have known him a little better than others. In the end, you could probably question the entire cadre of artists and receive a similar response from all of us. You see, he was so very quiet, so absorbed in his painting. He didn't teach, do demonstrations, go to craft fairs, sell prints; he just painted. He was the antithesis of an entrepreneur, not doing any of the things the rest of us have to do to make our fortune.'

'So you do make a fortune, then?'

'That's just a figure of speech. I make enough to get by, living the simple life that I do. Fortunes are those things accumulated by dealers, not by we painters.'

'I understand some artists have made massive sums of money.'

'Ah, you speak of the lottery winners, though not the lottery with random numbers and prize draws. Do you know how the art world operates, Inspector?'

'No, not really; do tell.'

'Well, I'll give you one perspective. You need to recognise there are two types in this country: those who're in London, and those who're not. The London art market is for those who wish to play the roulette wheel of life; I'll start with them.' He walked backward to the window, perching himself on the sill above the radiator. 'If someone in London is not picked up by a major dealer, they remain in obscurity until they leave the scene, one way or another. But if someone does become the chosen one, riches await. Mr Big buys everything they have, assigning huge prices to every artefact. Other dealers follow suit and the artist becomes a prized asset; everyone wants a piece of their work. Prices no longer bear any relation to the genuine worth of the artworks. Life is good for the artist while ever this lasts.

'The most astute start to operate independently of Mr Big, and so become multi-millionaires. But the others discover one day Mr Big has dumped all their artworks, selling through auction houses before the market recognises the consequence of oversupply, which is to say, plummeting prices. Other dealers follow suit, and the prices fall through the floor. The artist is now a worthless commodity, and may be unable to sell anything at any price from that point onwards. Some may have put a stash aside from the seven years of plenty to fund their continuing lifestyle, whereas the less astute worshippers of Mammon realise they will never rediscover their own personal Oz, and so they drop off the bottom of society, sofa-surfing for a while on their descent to street level; broken by Mr Big, they die in obscurity.'

'You make it all sound like a Dickensian tragedy. Surely, if their work is any good, there'll always be a market for it.'

'There's a big problem there, Inspector: what if their work never was any good, and the prices only rocketed because of market pressures when Mr Big was manipulating the system upward? In the real world, how much would you pay for a bed, made or otherwise? But if everyone around you is saying it's worth a fortune, can you resist the pressure and stick with your own judgement? How would you rate Mark Rothko or Jackson Pollock if others say they are great?'

'I know something about Rothko's work; big areas of colour, except when he preferred black.'

'Quite right, though some of his early paintings of New York subways were fun, unless you make a darker interpretation. Ignoring other people's opinions, what do you think of his big blocks of single colours?'

'A total waste of space.'

'Precisely. Therefore innate quality is not a reliable measure of financial worth.'

'Well, that's London and New York dealt with. But what about up here in Derbyshire?'

'If anyone wishes for riches beyond the dreams of avarice, they have to go to London. Seeing that in reverse, if an artist does not go to London, they're unlikely to be seeking to make a fortune. Instead, they wish to ply their trade as jobbing artists, because they believe in what they do. Their fear is not so much that they'll fail to make a fortune, as they'll fail to generate enough income to pay their bills.'

Priestley nodded to indicate outward acceptance of Derwent's analysis, though inwardly he maintained his professional scepticism of uncorroborated testimony. He manoeuvred to bring the discussion closer to the investigation. 'Does the name Joshua Compston mean anything to you?'

'Indeed it does. Suicide by someone who had tried and failed to make it onto the London scene.'

'And what about Milo Piscaro?'

'The northern equivalent; suicide by someone who was unable to make ends meet.'

'What if I were to say Milo may have been murdered?'

'Then I would say you're misguided, Inspector. Why would anyone wish to murder an unassuming, shy, poor, committed artist?'

'Did he have any enemies?'

'He was a painter; with the exception of Caravaggio, we're hardly the type of people to have murderous antagonists.'

'Could there be a motive away from art? You mentioned Lisa Wye: how well did they know each other?'

'I would say, intimately.' Derwent was unsure Priestley had taken his meaning, so clarified his testimony. 'Milo knew Lisa biblically, carnally, globally, repeatedly. She was his muse, his lover, his obsession, his salvation.'

'He must have been distraught when they broke up.'

'And there you have your motive for his suicide: he couldn't bear to live without her.'

'She's obviously someone I need to speak to; do you know where I can find her? I tried her phone but it's been turned off, and I've sent an e-mail but had no response. Do you happen to know where she is? I've heard people mention St Ives is something of a magnet for artists; do you know if she has friends down there?'

'I'm sure we all have friends down there, or at least friends of friends, but I've no reason to believe that's where she's gone. Besides, she now focuses on jewellery, which has closer connections to other parts of the country, such as Birmingham. But then, if she isn't answering her phone…' Suddenly, the blood drained from his face, leaving him ashen. 'My God, I hope she hasn't killed herself in some fit of remorse at having driven Milo to suicide.'

'I hope so too, Mr Derwent, though I've no evidence at this time to suggest she has. We'll leave it there for now, but I'll be in touch again if I think of something you might be able to help me with. Many thanks for your help, and especially for your insights into the art market.' As he reached the door, he turned and asked, 'By the way, where were you on the evening that Milo died?'

Derwent returned Priestley's fixed gaze. 'I was home, alone.'

Outside, Priestley led Berry a few steps back down the corridor away from Derwent's door. 'What did you think of that performance?'

Berry hesitated. 'I didn't know what to think, really. He spoke eloquently, but I'm not sure about the content.'

'Precisely. He seems to see the world as some sort of melodrama. But I think we can drop him right down the list of suspects; I'm convinced he's convinced Milo killed himself. Let's try the next guy, Peter Erewash, studio twelve.'

CHAPTER 22

Priestley glanced in through the glass panels as he walked with Berry past four even-numbered studios from twenty down to fourteen. Though they all contained artefacts of artistic creativity in various forms, no one was present in any of them. He looked into studio twelve and saw a middle-aged man seated at a stool in front of an easel, a paintbrush motionless in his right hand. After several seconds, Priestley knocked quietly. A few seconds later the man turned and looked in his direction, though gave the impression his mind was elsewhere; he beckoned for them to enter.

Priestley made the formal introductions, Peter Erewash responding in kind. 'I'm investigating the death of Milo Piscaro; do you mind if I ask you a few questions?'

'I'm not sure I knew him well enough to be much help to you. Have you asked anyone else?'

'I've just been talking to Tom Derwent.'

'Did he have much to say? He usually does.'

'Not so much about Milo, though he did explain his view of the art market.'

'Which view was that? He has quite a few different ones. Was it about how the London market has lots of posh painters who lack talent but have wealthy friends they can sell their dross to at inflated prices? Or was it how the taxation system for companies distorts the market by enabling them to pay less tax which means other taxpayers have to pay more?'

'It was neither of those. He explained how Mr Big can buy and sell to create or destroy artists at his whim.'

'Yes, I know the one. All his theories have at least a grain of truth in them.'

'Well, tell me about the taxation scam; as a taxpayer myself, I'd quite like to know.'

'It isn't really a scam; it's playing by the official rules. Let's say someone owns a chain of hotels, or some other buildings with public spaces. They buy lots of paintings from a chosen artist, and then write off the cost in their accounts over the following seven years. At the end of that time, they may quite literally dump the stuff into a skip. So the artist will have been pleased to have made a lot of sales, but it can be quite soul destroying to discover their work is eventually deemed worthless. You could argue the companies are being supportive, but in the end, if the tax rules didn't allow them to write off their purchases against profits, would they have the same attitude? I'd say they're being generous with taxpayers' money.

'There's also a tax avoidance scheme that's used by wealthy individuals. Imagine a painting that by any sensible measure is worth, say, two million at most. Behind the scenes, the owner claims it's worth twenty million. The museum that's due to get it as a gift to the nation doesn't quibble, as they may not get it otherwise. The tax man accepts the museum's valuation of twenty million, because they're experts. So twenty million is set off against their tax liability, but they've really only paid two million in tax.

'Of course, whenever the exchequer loses out, ordinary taxpayers such as you and me have to pay more to make up the difference. Well you, anyway.'

Priestley allowed a hint of humour to enter his voice. 'So, what tax avoidance mechanism do you employ? Or is it tax evasion? Should I be cautioning you?'

Erewash smiled. 'I use the simplest of all tax avoidance mechanisms: some years I don't earn enough to reach the minimum net income to qualify. If it wasn't for my wife having a proper job, I doubt I'd be able to keep going.' He shrugged his shoulders.

In the silence that followed, Priestley looked around at the paintings on display; they were largely architectural, including many of the insides of churches with shafts of light illuminating tombs or pulpits or groups of sightseers. 'I see you paint church scenes, Mr Erewash. Are you religious yourself?'

'Not anymore; now, I'd describe myself as a proselytising atheist, or maybe a humanist. I'm painting these church interiors to order. I'd paint the devil himself performing a naked virgin sacrifice on an altar if someone commissioned me, though I can imagine it might just lose me some repeat business from certain Christians. Nevertheless, it would be good for provoking a reaction; you may be aware that's something many artists try to achieve in lieu of producing anything of artistic merit.'

'And there I was, thinking your church scenes are so convincing they must come from some inner spirituality. Your work seems very good, to me; how is it you're not making much of a living out of it? Does it take a long time to paint each one?'

'It certainly takes much longer to make an accurate representation of something than simply to throw some paint around on a canvas and wait for some cretinous critic to declare it a work of genius. Nowadays, if someone just wants an image, they use a camera; I aim to represent a place in a way that makes it identifiable, but at the same time shows some aspect of it that isn't simply a copy of a moment in reality. One complaint levelled at my work is that it's too close to a straight image, but that's usually made by someone who can't recognise confidence tricks masquerading as art.'

'Such as American Abstract Expressionism?'

Erewash frowned. 'A lucky guess? Or have you been doing your homework?'

'Something I heard recently. So, what sort of prices do your paintings fetch, Mr Erewash?'

'If you're a potential buyer, I'll say two grand. If you're intending to check my tax returns, I'll say less than half that. I once sold a particularly fine painting for sixteen hundred, but generally I take what I can get.'

'How do you sell your paintings? Do you use an agent or a dealer? Or do you do your own marketing?'

'I usually put them through auction with a fixed reserve, and then sometimes they sell and sometimes they don't. In the summer I do the odd craft fair, though more for the enjoyment of the occasion, really. I'm not one to go for a hard sell, so some people have walked away with real bargains, if they did but know.'

'You don't sound especially interested in the money side of things, if I may say so.'

'I certainly don't get too excited about it. My wife's happy to fund us both.'

'What does she do?'

'She's an accountant. Yes, I know what you're thinking, we must be like chalk and cheese. The cliché about opposites is certainly true with us; I'd call it the magnetic attraction of poles.' His voice lightened. 'That's funnier than you might think; she's Polish. Well, second generation.'

Priestley smiled briefly before adopting a serious expression. 'May we talk about Milo Piscaro, now?'

'Why the interest? He killed himself, didn't he?'

'We're treating it as a suspicious death.'

'Is that code for you think he was murdered?'

'Not necessarily, but we do have to consider all possibilities. So tell me, what was he like?'

'Quiet, reserved. Your average painter can be quite gregarious, whereas Milo didn't socialise much. He was so timid he didn't even try to sell his paintings himself; he just passed them on to that friend of his. Just a minute, his name will come to me.' A frown creased his brow for a moment. 'Bill Campbell. He owns a gallery on the High Street; he's someone you ought to talk to.'

Priestley avoided reacting to the name. 'And they were friends, you say?'

'Yes; he used to visit Milo in his studio. Actually, he used to pop in on several of us; he saw us as potential clients, I think. Bill's alright if you can ignore his smarm. He probably knew Milo as well as anyone; except Lisa Wye, of course. You do know about Lisa?'

'I've heard something, but I'd appreciate your take on her.'

'Well, she's a real cracker, but don't tell my wife I said that. Lisa makes jewellery in her studio here.'

'Really? I looked on the website for this place and she came up as a painter.'

'It needs updating. My impression is she was a struggling painter who did a bit of jewellery-making on the side, and then found the jewellery business suddenly started to take off, so she stopped painting.'

'What was Milo's view of her stopping? Did he feel she was selling out?'

'I don't know what he thought about that, but I do know he was broken up when they, um, broke up. They shared a large studio for their painting, and she had a tiny studio for her jewellery work. Once she dropped the painting side, it wouldn't have made sense to continue to share with Milo, so he ended up with it all to himself, and she moved into a largish studio to do her jewellery. The charges are quite reasonable here, but for Milo his monthly rental will have doubled when she moved out, which must have been a strain for him.

'Up 'til then, I don't think Milo would have objected to anything she did. He always went all doe-eyed whenever he looked at her; he was such an innocent, she could have led him like a lamb to the slaughter.' He suddenly looked shocked, realising the implication of his own words. 'Christ, no! I never meant to suggest she had anything to do with Milo's death. Just because they split up, that doesn't mean she didn't still have feelings for him. If I hadn't been told, I'd have thought they were still a couple. I recently heard a rumour something happened at the party last Christmas that drove a wedge between them.'

'Do you have any idea what that might have been?'

'Perhaps that's when she told him she was planning to concentrate on jewellery in the future. Or maybe he discovered she'd been giving it away elsewhere.'

'Do you have any evidence to support either of those suppositions?'

'That sounds very legalistic. I have no knowledge of either; I'm just speculating, trying to be helpful.'

'And I appreciate it. So, is there anything you know for definite about last Christmas?'

'I remember we had a great party, but I thought Milo didn't seem to be enjoying it as much as the rest of us; he looked uncomfortable, as though he didn't want to be there, but like I said, I don't actually know what was wrong. He spent a lot of time talking with Lisa, so I think she's the one you'd better ask about that.'

'Do you know where I might find her? I sent her an e-mail because she wasn't answering her phone, but she hasn't got back to me.'

'I know she's always gone to Antwerp several times a year. She chooses her own gems there; some of her stuff is quite expensive. She's very confident and independent-minded; maybe that's what attracted her and Milo to each other. Opposites, again, you see.'

'Do you know how she travels? Plane, ferry, maybe Eurostar or Eurotunnel?'

'Always by car ferry, I think.'

'What route would that be?'

'I remember one time she mentioned going Hull to Zeebrugge overnight, but she normally went Dover to Ostend.'

'If she only recently started to put a lot of effort into her jewellery work, why has she been travelling regularly to Antwerp in the past?'

'No mystery there; she comes from Belgium. Didn't you know? Her family lives somewhere near Antwerp.'

Priestley took a moment to digest the information. 'That explains a lot. Thanks very much for your help.'

At the door, he turned and asked, 'Do you recall where you were the evening Milo died?'

He nodded. 'Home with my wife.'

'Someone will need to interview her. Could we have her contact details?'

After Berry had noted down the wife's particulars, they headed back to the entrance, where Priestley spoke to the receptionist. 'We've finished here …'

She interrupted him in mid-sentence. 'You didn't remember to come back to reception every time you wanted to see someone else, did you?'

He went for the hangdog look. 'Sorry, I forgot.'

She kept them waiting at the locked door for a moment, before calling out, 'Well, make sure you remember next time.' When she jabbed her middle finger at the release button on her desk, a buzzer sounded, and Priestley pulled the handle to escape.

As they walked away, Priestley remarked, 'Do you think they should have a notice saying "Beware of the Dragon"? Are you familiar with the 2014 amendment to the Dangerous Dragons Act?' Berry chortled as they headed back to the car.

CHAPTER 23

Gloria Naylor was on reception when Priestley returned to the station with Berry. 'Frank Cargill is in the canteen waiting for you. Aren't you the lucky one.'

DI Cargill was widely believed to have been promoted to Inspector more as a consequence of his involvement with the Police Federation than his competence as a detective. He was now on the Inspectors' Branch Board, which met regularly to consider issues affecting their electorate. Priestley tried for a neutral look. 'Has anything been circulated about him today from HR, Gloria?'

'Not yet, though we all know he starts tomorrow.'

'Could you get them to send out an official notice.'

'Will do. It isn't in my job description, though.' She smiled at him, always willing to do whatever he asked.

Priestley instructed Berry to try to locate Lisa Wye, then went to his office to check his correspondence. Twenty minutes later he went to the canteen, where he found DI Cargill sitting with a mug of tea, the used bag on a plate nearby. 'Frank, it's good to have you on board.'

Cargill accepted the proffered hand, pressing his thumb on Priestley's second knuckle. Priestley pressed his own thumb further around, stretching to reach the area between Cargill's second and third knuckles, believing it signified his higher status amongst Free and Accepted Masons. Ever since Anthony Ashbourne, now a Conservative MP, had played at being a Freemason when shaking Priestley's hand, he had found it amusing to do the same when first meeting other police officers. He wondered whether his handshake had appeared authentic enough, or whether Cargill had recognised Priestley was just messing with him.

Cargill bowed his head to Priestley, who gave a curt nod in return, hoping his Masonic pretensions would not be examined. He looked into Cargill's empty mug. 'I see you've finished your tea.'

'Yes; I've been here a while. I was looking out at the car park and saw you arrive.'

Priestley wondered if that was intended as a criticism; if so, he chose not to take the bait. 'Let's go to my office and I'll put you in the picture; you'll be working on the Milo Piscaro case. Have you read about it in the papers?' He set off and immediately became irritated by Cargill rushing to walk ahead of him.

Cargill looked over his shoulder. 'Yes; they claimed it was suicide. Do we know it wasn't?'

'We've evidence to suggest otherwise. Read through the autopsy report and you'll see what the problem is.'

'Will I be SIO?'

'No, I'm staying with the case.'

'So I'll be deputy SIO?'

'No, you need time to settle in.'

'I don't need time, sir; I've done it all before. When it comes to starting in new places, I've plenty of experience. I always hit the ground running.'

Priestley believed he knew exactly why he had had so many new starts. 'Call me Marcus when it's just the two of us; I find it makes for a better working atmosphere.'

'In my experience, sir, lack of regard for proper rules

of address leads to falling standards on other fronts.'

Priestley remained silent. He felt all his worst fears about Cargill had been confirmed, and they had not yet reached his office for their first proper meeting.

He saw Witty approaching them along the corridor, so raised his hand to signal him to stop. 'DI Frank Cargill, meet DS Neil Whittington. Neil is my right-hand man on the Piscaro case; he's deputy SIO.'

Witty gave a brief smile. 'Good to meet you, Frank.' As they shook hands, he looked down at Cargill's right thumb, wondering what he was trying to do with it.

Cargill responded curtly, 'You can address me as Inspector, or sir.'

Witty looked at Priestley but found he was avoiding eye contact.

Priestley set off quickly without warning, to get ahead. 'Come on, Frank; it's this way.'

Witty wondered whether he had addressed Cargill as "Frank" for Witty's benefit, to show a degree of support.

Priestley walked into his office, around his desk, and sat in his black leather chair. Cargill picked up a guest chair off the top of the stack and prepared to sit on it. He froze when Priestley addressed him quietly. 'Don't sit down, DI Cargill. I mean for you to start out the way I wish you to go on. We have a choice. I can be awkward with you. You can be awkward with my DS. He can be awkward with the DCs. But they have no one to be awkward with, so they go home and kick their cats. I'm not especially an animal-lover, but I have no wish to see small furry animals being abused.

'The alternative is that you adopt a different attitude. We're a good, effective team; a happy team, if you will, where there's no favouritism of any sort and everyone's treated fairly. If you don't recognise the ethos I've worked to engender, then that's a failing in you. So, you need to fit in, for your own sake as well as everyone else's. Can you do that for me, Frank?'

Cargill looked shocked. 'I'll try, sir.'

Priestley responded with a smile. 'That's good, Frank. And call me Marcus when it's just the two of us. And do sit down.'

Cargill gave a forced, 'Yes, Marcus.'

'Right. Now that's settled, let's take a look at the Piscaro case together.'

'What should I be focusing on? What's the MLOE?'

Priestley picked up the file from his desk. 'There are several lines of enquiry at the moment, but it's too early to identify any as the main one. The autopsy report is on the system; have a read through it. He took diazepam an hour before he died of ether inhalation, which suggests to me the involvement of another party. The one who appears to have been closest to Milo is William Campbell; he has a gallery on the High Street. I want you to go and see him. Find out if he has an alibi, and if he has, check it out and make sure it's kosher. Take DC Beresford with you; that's Tony.'

'If he's the closest person to the deceased, I'm surprised no one's spoken to him yet.'

Priestley wondered if this was deliberate criticism of the investigation. 'Actually, I've already seen him once; it's on file. I went with DC Linda Plummer to try to find out what kind of a person he is. We went in mufti.'

Cargill shook his head. 'Mufti?'

'Plain clothes; well, we're always in plain clothes, really. I mean incognito. Lin was dressed up to look like a million dollars; I wore a leather jacket and black T-shirt, pretending to be a rock star or something. Anyway, it gave us an insight into what he's like. Just in case we need to do it again,' he had intended to say "reprise the rôle" but was unsure Cargill would understand, 'we need to avoid him discovering who we really are. So leave Lin off your list of potential helpers; I'll personally be assigning her to tasks, so that we don't blow our cover.'

'Should I go and see Campbell straight away?'

'You don't officially start here 'til tomorrow morning; that'll be soon enough. You need to read through the file first, anyway. Any questions, Frank?'

'No, nothing… Marcus.'

'Alright. We begin every day with an eight thirty team meeting in MIR-1, so be here for that. Oh, and make sure you log all your investigations without delay; everyone on the team's expected to keep themselves up-to-date at all times, and we don't want any cock-ups because someone else hasn't put them in the picture.'

After Cargill had left, Priestley wondered why he had been lumbered with him. The decision had not only been taken without his approval, but even without his knowledge; obviously they knew he would have objected vociferously, but in the end it was outside his control. Anyway, he reasoned, an extra body must always be useful, so what harm could it do to have Frank on the team.

CHAPTER 24

Priestley was preparing to conduct a last check of his team's progress before finishing for the day, when his telephone rang. He was surprised to hear the plummy voice of DCC Dorothea Forbes-Smythe. 'What can I do for you, ma'am?'

'Come and see me right now, Marcus, unless you're in the middle of something.'

Unable to think of any reason why she would wish to see him, he felt a little uneasy as he walked to her office and knocked at her closed door.

'Come in, Marcus. Take a seat. I don't get to see enough of you, so it's a pity the reason for this meeting is a bit, well, awkward, really. DI Frank Cargill hasn't officially started, and yet he's already raised some complaints.'

'Who has he complained about, ma'am?'

'Well, you, actually.'

Priestley shook his head in disbelief.

'He's brought me quite a list. Shall we go through them one at a time?'

'Please do, ma'am.'

'Right then. Complaint number one. You kept him waiting for twenty minutes.'

'I believe it's my prerogative, ma'am, to prioritise my work and meet people when my schedule facilitates my availability.'

'Yah, absolutely; anyway, it's almost obligatory to keep subordinates waiting. So, complaint number two.

You called him Frank.'

'Guilty as charged, ma'am; I did indeed call him Frank. Though that is actually his name.'

'Yes, but he likes to be called by his title. That links to complaint number three: you didn't reprimand DS Whittington when he called him Frank.'

'On my team, for short, personal interactions, we like to call each other by first names. We find the informality works very well, ma'am, for making a good atmosphere where everyone pulls together.'

'And you don't see a downside to that? Informality leading to indiscipline?'

'I don't believe one necessarily leads to the other, ma'am.'

'Very well, then, Marcus. I shall try it out with you, right now, and we'll see how this meeting goes. You must call me Dotty; it's my nickname from childhood.'

Priestley hesitated. 'Are you sure, ma'am?'

She smiled sweetly. 'That's "Are you sure, Dotty?" Go on, give it a try.'

'Yes, Dotty.'

'Now, where were we, Marcus?'

'DI Cargill being called Frank; he didn't like it, Dotty.'

'Indeed. Well, we've dealt with that. Complaint number four is that DS Whittington is your deputy, whereas Frank outranks him and argues he should be.'

'DS Whittington is only my deputy on the Milo Piscaro case, which is how it was agreed with Superintendent Yelland before DI Cargill appeared on the scene. Keeping the structure unchanged is not only good for continuity, but also gives DS Whittington the opportunity to consolidate his experience of working at his new level of responsibility; he was only recently promoted and has a lot to learn, so this case provides a context for him to develop while I'm personally available to keep a close eye on him and to check on his performance. Also, DI Cargill is new to the team, so I'm giving him time to settle in, for his benefit.'

'Excellent, Marcus. Now complaint number five is that you would not let him sit down.'

'That's true, Dotty. I felt he was in danger of failing to comprehend the nature of the team into which he would shortly be immersed, and that by keeping him standing I was enabling him to remain more focused on my short introductory speech.'

'That's absolutely tremendous, Marcus. So, onto complaint number six. DI Cargill alleges you failed to interview a suspect properly, by getting dressed up and not disclosing who you are.'

'The facts, Dotty, are not in dispute. The underlying reason, however, may have been too subtle for DI Cargill to comprehend. In the absence of an obvious MLOE, I attempted to find an opening by having an off-the-record conversation with someone who may have been more willing to disclose insights when speaking to potential customers of his business, than to police officers. I believe it worked very well.'

'I suppose only time will tell on that one, Marcus. And finally, complaint number seven. DI Cargill gained the impression that DC Plummer is unavailable for general duties, as you have claimed her for yourself. Is there any truth in that? Are you bedding her, Marcus?'

Priestley reddened. 'No ma'am. No, Dotty, I absolutely swear I am not in an inappropriate relationship with DC Plummer.'

'Well, that's all of those issues dealt with satisfactorily. Now, what should we do with DI Cargill? I can't have him complaining and wasting our time.'

'May I suggest, Dotty, you lay down the law to him. Tell him any further unjustified complaints will reflect very badly on him. You might also like to say that any attempt to circumvent your personal authority will be deemed a serious breach of protocol, and that any complaints must be brought to you and not to anyone else, under any circumstances. I think if you don't do that, he'll look for ways of using other senior officers to bypass you. Maybe you should let them all know the situation; that way, he might be kept in check. I'd say, don't give him an inch, because he'll take a mile.'

She nodded deeply. 'That's exactly what I was thinking; I'll do that.' She scribbled herself a reminder. 'Now, what about all this dressing up you've been doing? It isn't exactly normal procedure. What will you be up to next, I wonder? Do I need to keep you under control? If I gave you an inch, how much would you take?' Priestley reddened to a deep puce. She realised what she had said, and began to laugh like a horse. 'One hears rumours, you know. Are all those hormones of yours keeping you up at night?' She laughed giddily.

Priestley tried to laugh a little, before seeking an exit line. 'If that's all, Dotty...'

She eventually quietened, wiping the tears from the corners of her eyes. 'I understand DC Plummer looked a real knockout; it reminds me of my early days. Did you know I used to do deep undercover work? When they needed a certain type, the right voice, the right manners, that sort of thing. Are you surprised?'

'No, Dotty; I can imagine you were very good. I'm

sure you played your parts brilliantly.'

'Well, I did, even though I say so myself. And I was very attractive back then; does that surprise you?'

'Not in the slightest, Dotty.' He stroked her ego a little more, as she appeared to be expecting it. 'I'm sure you were crackerjack.' And still more was being asked. 'You're still very attractive.' That should do the trick, he thought.

'Do you really think so?'

He offered one final piece of ego massaging. 'Absolutely, Dotty. You still turn heads at this station.' He thought she seemed satisfied with that.

'You know, if ever there's a need for you to go undercover with a, shall we say, slightly older woman, I'm still game for anything. Don't be afraid to speak up. I'll be very willing to do something exciting with you; anything, really. You only have to ask.'

'That would be great, Dotty. I'll definitely keep you in mind if something comes up. May I go now? I have an urgent meeting.'

She presented him with her most becoming smile. 'Yes Marcus, away you go. But don't forget where my door is.'

He tried not to break into a run as he exited her office.

CHAPTER 25

Priestley returned home after a final check on progress. He eventually remembered he had intended to ask Helen about Milo's bird feeders, so raised the topic over the lasagne and salad.

'I have a question for you; it's to do with birds.'

She responded quickly before he could elaborate. 'No, you can't; I should be enough for you.' They laughed fondly into each other's eyes. 'Go on, what's your question.'

'You know the Milo Piscaro case; my instincts tell me he didn't kill himself. I'm trying to interpret some evidence; he had four large bird feeders in his back garden, and they were all quite close to full. Does that suggest he topped them up just before he topped himself? I'm not sure anyone in a suicidal frame of mind would think to do that. But maybe not many birds come to feed in his garden.'

She looked pensive. 'Are you sure no one filled them up after he died?'

'I don't know for definite. There were some unused picture hooks on the walls, so maybe someone's been to take some paintings away, and they could have filled them up. Apart from that, there's the forensics team, but I don't think they'd risk contaminating any evidence.'

'If his garden doesn't attract many birds, the feeders could take months to empty. You could always monitor the four levels of feeding activity from now on, to get an idea of consumption rates in the recent past, and then project back to calculate the dates when each feeder was last filled to the brim. If they weren't filled right up the last time feed was added, the consequent actual dates would be more recent. But if the earliest possible date of all four is after the date of demise, someone must have added more feed. Of course, you'd have to take into account recent weather, statistical variance, and expected feeding rates based on life cycles of the actual species of birds and availability of insect life.'

He pretended to look smug. 'That's exactly what I was thinking.'

She tittered, knowing he was not genuinely claiming to understand the details. 'The four projected dates wouldn't be very accurate, but it could be interesting if they pointed to him having filled them up around the day he died.'

He frowned. 'I suppose so, but in the end I'm not sure it's really worth the effort of investigating that line. He was very much into birds, so for now I'll just assume he always made sure they had plenty of food.'

'What do you mean, very much into birds?'

'He was an *ornithophile*. His last ever series of paintings had a bird theme; he named each one after a British bird. The Graves Art Gallery has twelve of them on display; they're what I went to see. I've a brochure with pictures of them, if you're interested. They're abstract; I can't see any connection with birds, myself.'

'Show me when we've finished.'

After the lasagne, while the coffee was percolating, he fetched the brochure and handed it to her.

She peered closely at the twelve small images. 'I can't see them clearly enough. I'll pop into the Graves sometime soon and take a look. How many are there in the whole series?'

'There's another one in that gallery I went to on the High Street; the owner hinted there are more to come, but he wouldn't or couldn't say how many.'

'Wouldn't he lend his one to the Graves?'

'He actually lent them five others; maybe he kept one back so he'd have something to sell.'

'That does make sense, I suppose.'

Marcus grinned. 'Actually, there's thirteen birds in the Graves, if you count the curator I had dinner with. She's cute with a capital "Q".'

Helen gave him an inquisitorial look. 'So, have you been made an offer for your body?'

He decided to avoid an outright denial in case she read his thoughts. Choosing misdirection, he replied with apparent heavy deliberation. 'Yes, I think I have.' He smiled before continuing. 'By a police officer.'

She responded immediately. 'Lin.'

Realising he was heading deeper into the mire, he fired off a rapid response that implied denial. 'Try again.'

'Not Babs, surely?' She saw the shake of the head. 'There are so many women who fancy you... in your mind! You'd better just tell me.' Despite her fixed smile, she always had a concern about women being attracted to her husband: those who liked masculine men, rather than the effete variety.

'Well, it's just possible I misunderstood, but Dorothea Forbes-Smythe said she'd be game to do something exciting with me, and I only had to ask.'

A relieved laugh escaped unbidden. 'She must be fifty if she's a day.'

'Yes, but she hasn't entirely lost her looks. They're

probably what got her to where she is now; that, and her posh accent. I'm pretty sure it wasn't her brain; I think she must have more between her legs than her ears.'

'Marcus! You're disgusting!' She tutted several times before finally smiling at him.

After coffee, Marcus moved the dishes to the kitchen and Helen slotted them into the dishwasher racks. She filled the "Soft Water" powder section, moved the water cut-off tap by ninety degrees, flicked the electricity switch and turned the machine's control knob. An initial click was followed by the sound of running water as the machine filled, which changed to a low hum half a minute later. Having wiped the work surfaces, she joined him in the living room. 'Shall we watch the news?'

He shook his head. 'Later.' The news programmes were set to record as a series on their satellite receiver, so each day they could view them after transmission, speeding through advertisements and uninteresting topics. 'Milo had lots of recordings of music by Messiaen to do with *les oiseaux*. Would you like to listen to some with me? I'm still looking for insights into the case, trying to get into his mind.'

She nestled against him on a leather settee, her legs tucked up to one side. He knew he loved everything about her: her smell, her warmth, her touch, her brilliance, even her hint of Northern Irish accent. He chastised himself for finding other women attractive, regretting men had no "off switch" to stop their testosterone from forever pressing them to check out other women. As he put his arm around her shoulder, he told himself he wished never to be unfaithful to her.

Holding the CD case in front of them, he read the

title of track one, '"*Réveil des oiseaux: Minuit.*"' He offered a translation. 'Awakening of the birds at midnight.'

She suggested an alternative. 'Dawn Chorus?'

He countered, 'That would be *chœur de l'aube.*' The music started shortly after he pressed a button on the remote control. Though it was an orchestral version, the piano was predominant. A repeated note prompted him to whisper, 'Birdsong, but in a lower register.'

They listened in silence. He paused the CD at the end of the first track. 'What do you think of it?'

She countered, 'What do *you* think of it?'

'I can imagine it's what birdsong might sound like if it was slowed down.'

She shook her head slightly. 'Some time ago I listened to recordings of birds at half-speed and quarter-speed when I was researching subliminal messaging through audio signalling; at quarter-speed, wrens sound like *The Clangers.*' He gave a short, nasal laugh. 'People have different temporal resolution capacities; Messiaen may have been at the more sensitive end of the spectrum, but no human is in the same league as the birds themselves.'

'You never cease to surprise me, love. Did your research turn up anything of wider interest? Anything that might be relevant to the case?'

'Well, where an average human can only hear a trill or a blur of sound, a bird can identify individual notes and cadences. The most perceptive humans have the capacity to hear birdsong played at full speed and hold it in their minds, then replay it internally at a slower speed so they can reinterpret what they heard and break it down into its constituent parts. I doubt whether any of this will help your investigation, though.'

'No, I can't see it giving me any sort of an angle; I'm still chasing shadows.'

She smiled. 'Not chasing birds, then?' He gave a short, deep-toned laugh. 'Anyway, did you like it?'

'I'm sure it's really good.'

'So, shall we hear some more? You've got the remote.'

He made no move to pick up the control box. 'Maybe another time. I'd rather listen to something…'

She interrupted to complete his sentence. 'More enjoyable?'

'Something with a lyric. What about "Chasing Rainbows"?'

'What about "Chasing Cars"? Reminds me of my youth.'

'Reminds me of my work.'

'"Chasing Pavements", then?'

'Yes; Adele's brilliant.'

'Reminds me of *my* work, in a way; sometimes, people can give too much of themselves.'

He changed the Messiaen for Adele's *19* album. As "Daydreamer" began, she put her arm around his chest and cuddled up closer to him, kissing the crook of his neck. After again placing his arm around her shoulder, he lifted his hand and stroked her hair, as he remembered another song: if it's magic, why can't it be everlasting?

CHAPTER 26

Priestley delivered some carefully chosen words to begin the 8:30 meeting. 'Good morning, everyone. Let me start by introducing our new team member: DI Cargill. That's Frank, to his friends. And we're all friends here, so make him welcome.'

There followed various greetings with a common theme. 'Hello, Frank.' 'Welcome, Frank.' 'Hi, Frank.'

Priestley had checked the progress reports prior to the meeting, so asked for anything that had not yet been recorded. Berry responded, 'The artist, Lisa Wye. A uniform went round to her house yesterday afternoon, but there was no one in. After trying the neighbours, he left a note through the letterbox. As of five minutes ago there was still no response.'

Priestley acknowledged Berry with a nod. 'Alright Tony, but we need to do more now. Frank, would you like to pick this one up? You'll see from my report she's been known to visit Antwerp for her work, but also has family out there. She was born in Belgium, so I expect she'll have travelled on a Belgian passport, but don't assume anything. And I'm suspicious of the coincidence that her surname is the same as a local river, so her passport may well be in a different name.

'It's a pity Immigration doesn't keep track of all movements. You'll have to check car ferry records; Dover to Ostend is her usual route, but she's also been known to travel Hull to Zeebrugge. If you draw a blank with those two, keep searching for ferries, and then expand your search to other modes of transport. In the end, we need to know if she's out of the country. Let me know as soon as you have anything.

'Tony: Frank will be interviewing Campbell as soon as poss. You'll be working with him and doing any additional investigations he needs. Prove to him you're as good as we all reckon you are.

'Anyone not know what they're doing, today?' Silence reigned. 'Right. Keep the reports coming in. I'll be incommunicado all day…'

Someone called out, 'Is that in Mexico, sir?'

He gave a wry smile. 'I'll be in a brainstorming session on target setting. If something comes up you think I should know about straight away, run it by Neil and he'll relay it to me as appropriate. I'll see you all Monday morning, if not before.'

Cargill rushed to be the first to leave the MIR, beckoning with a curled index finger for Berry to follow him. When they had reached a corner of the main office, he turned to face him. 'Right, DC Beresford, let's get this investigation moving.'

Berry responded earnestly. 'I'm up for it, Frank.'

Cargill considered demanding he address him formally, but knew Priestley had already undermined that position. 'I've been given the two likeliest suspects, that's William Campbell and Lisa Wye. You need to arrange an appointment for us to see Campbell, and to track down that Belgian woman. Any questions?'

'No; I'll get right on it.'

'I want to see some rapid progress; tell me as soon as you have anything. The clock starts now.'

Berry wondered what work that left Cargill to do. Shortly afterwards, he noticed him standing in a corner of the car park, smoking a cigarette.

Berry sat at a computer and used the internet to look up the gallery's opening time for that morning, making a mental note to telephone them shortly after. Then, he used the constabulary's electoral roll search facility; though he specified all categories, he found nothing relevant under Lisa Wye. Local authority records proved more useful: the only occupant listed at her home address was Lisa de Cock. A search of Companies House data revealed Lisa de Cock was the sole director behind Lisa Wye Jewellery Ltd. On Facebook, a search for Lisa de Cock found a dozen entries, but none of them relevant; however, a search for Lisa Wye found fewer entries, and in very little time he had located the relevant woman.

A few minutes later he established that Lisa de Cock had travelled on a Belgian passport from Dover to Ostend five days ago. He rushed to the car park to inform Cargill, feeling the type of pleasure he had known throughout his school days when he had been the first to finish maths questions. 'Frank, I've got something for you.' He relayed the information, as Cargill drew hard on his cigarette to squeeze every last microgram of carcinogen into his lungs.

'What about Campbell? Have you phoned?'

'The gallery isn't open yet.'

'Well, call them anyway; I want to get started.'

Berry bristled at having orders barked out at him. Cargill rushed past and led him to his desk, where he loomed over him while he telephoned; Campbell answered and agreed to meet them without delay.

As Berry was driving them to the gallery, he noticed Cargill take out a pack of cigarettes. 'We'll be there soon, Frank, if you want to hold on; cigarette smoke makes the car smell for ages after.'

'Just remind me what rank you are.'

Berry understood this was intended to subjugate him. 'Detective Constable.'

'Well, Constable, I'm an Inspector. So you don't tell me what I can and can't do.'

'It's Health and Safety rules, Frank. Sorry, but I can't do anything about it. The car counts as an enclosed place of work, so it's covered by the Tobacco Smoking Prohibition regulations.'

Cargill scowled as he put the cigarettes back into his pocket; having received an early morning reprimand from DCC Forbes-Smythe, he anticipated any complaints about his behaviour would be seized upon by his superiors.

As they approached the gallery, Cargill growled, 'Pull up outside. Stick a Police notice in the window.'

'Sorry, I don't have one.'

'Why not? You need to be better prepared than this.'

Berry drove past the gallery and found a legal parking place close by.

Cargill climbed out of the passenger seat as soon as Berry had applied the handbrake, striding to the gallery without waiting for Berry to catch up.

Campbell was standing at the door, waiting to welcome Cargill. 'Good morning.'

Cargill stepped inside and held up his warrant card, as Berry hurried to join them. 'I'm DI Cargill and that's DC Beresford. I'm here to ask you about Miles Percy aka Milo Piscaro.' He had made the "aka" sound like an accusation of criminality.

Campbell adopted an expression of concern. 'I knew

Milo was a very troubled individual, but I was as shocked as anyone to learn he had taken his own life.'

'I'm investigating exactly what happened to him. First of all, where were you on the day he died?'

'When the gallery was open, I was here, as always. After the gallery closed, I went home for the evening.'

'And can anyone confirm your alibi?'

'My alibi, Inspector? If you mean was there anyone at home to confirm I was there, then yes there was. Andrea Carter was at home with me all evening, as was her fourteen-year-old son, Lewis.'

'Does Andrea Carter live with you, sir?'

'We're in the early stages of a relationship, so I would say she lives with me but not in the common interpretation of the expression.'

'And where might I find Ms Carter?'

'She's probably at home.' He extracted from his wallet a handwritten piece of paper which he handed to Cargill. 'Here's the address and home telephone number, plus her mobile number.'

Berry copied the details into his notebook as Cargill terminated the interview. 'If your alibi checks out, there may be no further need to contact you, so thank you for your time.'

As they walked to the car, Berry asked, 'Did you consider asking him what he knew about Milo?'

Cargill sneered. 'There was no need; DCI Priestley has already bled that one dry.'

CHAPTER 27

Once outside the gallery, Cargill instructed Berry to telephone the landline number Campbell had given them. 'Am I speaking to Andrea Carter?'

'Yes, that's me.'

'Good morning, I'm Detective Constable Tony Beresford. William Campbell gave us your details. I'm with Detective Inspector Cargill. We'd like to interview you in connection with the death of Miles Percy. Would it be convenient to come to your house straight away?'

'Yes, of course; I was expecting you to call.'

As Berry closed the conversation, Cargill gave a 'Pah!' which triggered a dry cough. 'I'll be doing the interviewing, not "we". Make sure you don't say anything that might screw it up.'

Berry attempted to head off any further conflict. 'Shall we go straight away, Frank? Or would you like a ciggy, first?'

Cargill sought and found a negative interpretation. 'I hope you're not suggesting I'd let smoking get in the way of my investigation. Let's get going right now.'

Berry decided silence was the best policy, so said nothing until he had drawn up outside Campbell's house. 'That's the one. This is an upmarket area, so it must be worth quite a bit.'

Cargill stepped out quickly and stood at the end of the long path that wound its way to the house, looking up at the large, mock-Tudor property. His gaze moved down and to the right, failing to register the incongruity of the attached double-garage. 'Big place for a bloke on his own; I'm not surprised he's got a bint moved in with him.' He nodded in the direction of the front door for Berry to go first. Berry pressed the doorbell. Cargill pushed him aside, knocking loudly and repeatedly on the door's central panel. 'We're not neighbours calling in for a chat; we're the police. Let her know it's us.'

A woman hurriedly opened the door. Though Berry thought she was probably in her forties, he found the way she had trowelled on her make-up reminiscent of his elderly grandmother. He felt slightly uncomfortable with the amount of wrinkled cleavage her dress was revealing. Her smile never quite materialised as she stood back and beckoned them in. 'Come in, officers; through here.' She opened the door to a small room that may have been designed as an office but now had a settee and an armchair crammed into it. 'Can I make you a drink? Tea? Coffee?'

Only when Cargill had requested coffee did Berry feel able to speak and ask for the same. With Andrea out of the room, Cargill commented, 'Bit of a squeeze, isn't it? What's that tell us? I'd say we're unwanted guests.'

Berry nodded in agreement but said nothing.

Andrea returned quickly with three mugs of instant coffee, the milk already in them. 'This is my sitting room; cosy, isn't it?'

Cargill responded, 'Yes, Ms Carter, very cosy.' He glanced around for her benefit, before looking directly at her. 'I'm investigating the suspicious death of Milo Piscaro; you may have known him as Miles Percy.'

'"Suspicious", you say; does that mean he was murdered? Fancy that!'

'I only said "suspicious"; we in the police force are trained not to jump to conclusions, so I'm keeping an open mind about what the circumstances were that led to his death. Now, I have some questions to ask you. How long have you lived here?'

'About a month.'

'And are you in a relationship with Mr Campbell?'

'It's early days yet, but I think it'll become a proper relationship in due course.'

'Let me be straight.' For the thousandth time he regretted his name stopped him from using the obvious adjective. 'Is your relationship sexual?'

'It's a loving relationship.'

'What does that mean?'

'Bill is behaving as I expected he would; he's an absolute gentleman. He makes no demands on me, but I'm sure in the fullness of time our relationship will blossom and grow into something more.'

Hearing how she had responded, Berry wondered what sort of novels she usually read.

Cargill remained silent, so she began again. 'Apart from that side of things, we're very close. We have all our meals together, and I do his washing and ironing. It's almost like we're married, but without the other. And he's just like a father to my Lewis.'

'Understood. Now, you remember the day Milo Piscaro died?'

'Of course I do; I'll remember it to my dying day.'

'Can you tell me exactly what you did in the time leading up to that night? Start from the morning and talk me through it.'

'I got up and made breakfast for us all. After Bill had gone to the gallery and Lewis had gone to school I put the washing on and then I cleaned the house. When the washing was finished I put the clothes in the tumble dryer; then I went out. I walked to the shops and had a look around, but I didn't buy anything apart from a cup of tea in a café. After that, I walked back home and made myself a sandwich and had another cup of tea. Then I did the ironing in the kitchen, with my little TV on. After that, I put the clothes away. Then I watched some more telly, and then I came in here and read a book.' She reached over to a small bookshelf and picked out a dog-eared paperback; on the front of it was a sketch of a blonde woman with bouffant hair, looking at a tanned, clean-shaven man wearing a striped blazer over an open-necked shirt with a cravat. 'It was this one.' She held it out for Cargill to inspect; he glanced fleetingly at the title, then waved it away.

'And what time did you stop reading?'

'About five o'clock, when I went to make tea; I did bolognaise. Bill came back at about quarter past five, which is when I put the spaghetti on.'

'Had Lewis not come home by then?'

'Yes, I'm sorry, you're right; I sometimes hardly notice him. He goes straight up to his room and puts on his headphones; he does his homework listening to pop music. I couldn't work like that; it would put me off.'

'Alright, so you did the spaghetti, and then what?'

'We all ate together in the dining room. Then Lewis went back upstairs and Bill went into the lounge, while I did the tidying up. At six, I watched the BBC national news with Bill, and then the local news. When that finished, he turned off the TV and picked up his paper, and I came in here to listen to the radio.' She pointed to the micro-stereo system. 'It was about twenty past nine when Bill came in to see me; he said there was something on telly I might like to watch with him. We'd missed the start, but it was easy enough to pick it up; it's that new murder mystery serial on ITV. Funny, isn't it, us watching a murder on TV when there's a real one happening not far away.'

'There's nothing funny about murder, Ms Carter, but I only said Mr Piscaro's death was suspicious. Now, what were you doing from twenty past nine onwards?'

'We watched TV together. The program finished just before ten o'clock and then we watched the BBC news again; it was just the same as the earlier news. After the weather forecast, just after half ten, I said goodnight to Bill and went upstairs. I called into Lewis's room and gave a little tug on his shoulder; he hadn't heard me go in. He took off his headphones and I told him he needed to go to bed so he wouldn't be tired in the morning. I tried to kiss him but he wouldn't let me. He always used to let me; it's all part of growing up, I suppose. Then I went into the bathroom. And then I went to bed.'

'Did you hear Mr Campbell go to his room?'

'No; his bedroom's at the other end of the corridor, so I never hear him.'

'Did you not hear him in the bathroom?'

'He has an en suite; he doesn't use the main bathroom.'

'Did you hear anything else that night? Anything at all?'

'Lewis used the bathroom straight after me. Then I fell asleep and didn't wake up 'til my alarm went.'

Cargill twisted his neck and looked at Berry. 'Have you got all that written down, DC Beresford?'

'Just about, DI Cargill; I'll be finished in a minute.'

Cargill turned back. 'I just need you to sign to confirm everything you've said, and then we can leave you in peace, Ms Carter.'

When the formalities had been concluded, Cargill and Berry took their leave. Once outside the door, Cargill gave his assessment. 'That looks all very normal on the outside; Mr Campbell comes home and spends the evening with his live-in partner. Except, to me she seems more like a housekeeper. She's pleasant enough, and maybe a bit younger than him, so why isn't there something more going on?'

Berry assumed the question was rhetorical, so maintained his silence.

'Well, haven't you got an opinion? You need to learn to assess people and not just rely on what they say. Why share your home with a woman and not get the benefits? Seems a little queer to me.' His attempt to laugh at his own pun was lost in a chesty wheeze.

Berry remained silent, refusing to join him in his out-dated humour.

CHAPTER 28

Priestley returned to his office in the afternoon and found a note from Superintendent Richard Yelland, requesting he call him as soon as possible. He telephoned Yelland to check he was available, and then walked to his office, knocking firmly at the closed door and waiting to be invited in.

'Come in. Marcus, how's the investigation going?'

'I've come straight from an all-day meeting, so I haven't had time to check on progress yet.'

'Well, I've had a look at today's updates, and DI Cargill seems to think he knows where it should be going; he came to see me. He said he would have spoken to you about it, but what with you being in a meeting and this being urgent...'

'Should I take a look at the progress reports myself, and see you after?'

'Yes, do that. Cargill says the prime suspect is a Belgian woman by the name of Lisa de Cock, who's living under the alias Lisa Wye. He believes she's scarpered back to Belgium where she has family. Rather than sticking with the formal route, he's asked me to authorise him to travel to Antwerp tomorrow so he can spend the weekend familiarising himself with the place, and then he'll press the local police into starting an investigation there on Monday morning.'

Priestley looked stunned. 'Don't authorise anything, Richie; not 'til I've had time to give the case some close scrutiny.'

'Don't take too long, Marcus; we don't want to miss a trick on this one.'

Priestley headed back to his office and checked through the status reports. He telephoned Berry and called him into his office.

Berry knocked at the open door.

'Come in and close the door behind you. I need some more detail on what's been happening today with you and Frank. Start off with your visit to the gallery.'

'He asked only the most basic questions; they're included in my report. After we'd left, he told me there was no point in going any deeper into what Campbell thought of Milo, as you'd already done that.'

'Did he let slip he already knew enough not to need to ask anything else? Did he blow my cover?'

'Not really. I suppose Campbell might have wondered why he asked so few questions, but it would probably only mean something to someone who knew what to expect.'

'Alright. What about tracing Lisa de Cock? I assume you checked she hadn't returned to this country.'

Berry flushed crimson. 'I haven't actually checked, no; DI Cargill was telling me exactly what to do, and I suppose I stopped thinking for myself.'

'Right. Sit here at my desk and do it now. I'm going to see Superintendent Yelland and give him an update. Did you know Cargill was intending to go to Antwerp tomorrow, by the way?'

'No, I hadn't heard a word.'

Priestley called on Yelland again. 'I've set DC Beresford onto tracing if Lisa de Cock has returned to this country. Cargill told him to check outgoing journeys only, and he's too worried to do anything that he isn't specifically instructed to do. Cargill's undermining my work of getting officers to think for themselves. How long do I have to put up with him?'

Yelland raised his hands at the wrists to suggest pushing back rather than surrender. 'Everyone moves him on as quickly as they can, but he's unsackable; no one wants the Federation on their backs. Can't you just give him tasks where he isn't able to do any harm?'

'He's a liability and he doesn't accept boundaries. He's already been to DCC Smythe with trumped-up complaints about me, though I believe she's now clipped his wings on that front.'

'Yes; she put me in the picture about that.'

'And now he bypasses me to come to you with a request for a "jolly" to Belgium.'

'He said you weren't available to discuss it.'

'Did he also say I'd left instructions that everything should go through DS Whittington, who'd then get in touch with me if necessary?'

'Yes, he did tell me that, but he said he assumed that didn't apply to him as he's more senior.'

'I made it clear it applied to everyone. He's certainly putting the "ass" into assume.'

Yelland laughed more than was deserved, trying to reduce the tension. 'You've certainly got your work cut out there, keeping him in check.'

Priestley felt a vibration in his pocket. 'Excuse me a moment.' He peered at the small screen. 'Lisa de Cock came back to England yesterday by Ferry.'

'I'd better scrap his travel request, then... unless you'd rather send him to Belgium, anyway?'

After laughing together comfortably enough, he left Yelland's office and returned to his own. Berry jumped up and asked breathlessly, 'Did you get my message?'

'I did indeed, and very timely it was, too. You need to try and track down where she is now; you can go back to your own desk to do that. But before you do, talk me through the interview with Andrea Carter. Tell me what isn't written down.'

'Well, I'm hardly an expert on relationships…'

'Aren't you seeing Susan…'

'… Newhouse? Yes, but one swallow…'

Priestley quickly raised a hand and pushed the palm through the air at him. 'Don't go any further; I know I asked for an oral report, but…'

Berry blushed like a schoolboy, managing a forced smile as he hastily completed the proverb. '… doesn't make a summer.'

'Or a spring, if you're French. Carry on.'

'Frank asked her about their relationship, and she said it was still early days yet. Afterwards, Frank said she was more like a housekeeper, and I think he's right; they don't seem like a couple.'

'But do you believe her testimony?'

'Yes, I do. I didn't get the impression she was lying, only she seemed a bit too ready with her answers.'

'As though she'd been coached?'

'Or at least been asked the same questions before.'

Priestley looked through her testimony again. 'The two of them appear to have been in different rooms for much of the evening; could either of them have left the house without the other one knowing?'

'It's a large house and her little room downstairs is well away from the main one, so it isn't impossible.'

Priestley sighed. 'Someone may need to have another go at her, but I wouldn't want Frank to be the one; it needs someone who can read people and think on their feet, spot weaknesses in stories, explore side issues. And what about her son, Lewis? He should be interviewed to find out if he heard or saw anything; that could give us an opportunity to interview Mrs Carter again without it looking too obvious we didn't get it right the first time. I'd like to talk to her myself, but she'd probably tell Campbell all about it, and if she described me accurately enough he might put two and two together, which would blow my cover. That disallows Lin as well, of course.'

There was a lull. 'Do you wish me to volunteer?'

He smiled. 'No, Tony; I was just thinking who might be the right person. It's a second attempt, which can be tricky; people often dislike repeating themselves, so they don't open up with more detail. We need someone very experienced, very reliable.'

'Maybe it won't be relevant, anyway. Frank says Lisa de Cock is now the number one suspect, especially as she's living under an alias.'

'Hang on a minute; just put yourself in her position. Would you really want to be known by that name in this country? And choosing a local river as a surname could make perfect business sense. You get back to tracking her down. And be thankful you're not the one wasting, I mean "investing", your time exploring target setting and efficiency measures.'

As Berry walked to the door, Priestley called out to him. 'And tell Frank I'd like to see him. Now.'

CHAPTER 29

Ten minutes later, DI Cargill came to the half-open door of DCI Priestley's office and pushed it fully open. He called from the doorway, 'You wanted to see me, Marcus?'

Priestley looked up. 'Come in, Frank. Close the door behind you and pull up a pew.'

'A pew? Am I going to get a sermon, then?'

'Do you think you should?'

'You tell me.'

Priestley adopted a neutral voice. 'I'd like you to tell me how you think things have been going so far.'

'I've been putting a lot of effort into trying to make it all happen, but I haven't had a result yet.'

'That's a very positive way of seeing things, Frank. Now try again, but this time seeing things negatively.'

Cargill maintained an unruffled expression. 'I began by looking for things that could, I mean might, be improved, and I made a list of them. As you're running the investigation, I couldn't very well bring them to you; it had to go upstairs. I thought it needed someone sufficiently remote from the case to take a look at my findings; out of the people available, DCC Forbes-Smythe seemed the likeliest contender, so I arranged to talk to her. She listened to everything I had to say, so I thought I was getting somewhere. But then this morning she pretty much tore me to pieces. I don't think she's genuinely displayed an open attitude to my ideas.'

'So, she's failed you. Alright, carry on. What about your interviews with Mr Campbell and Mrs Carter?'

'You'd already spoken to Campbell, so there wasn't much I could do with him. Anyway, when he told me his alibi, I knew you'd been barking up the wrong tree.'

'So I made a mistake when I talked to him and failed to establish whether he had an alibi?'

'No, that's not what I meant. You could have been right to do things your way.'

'But nevertheless I was wrong. Alright, carry on.'

'Ms Carter confirmed Campbell's alibi, so that was the end of that line of the investigation, which left this Lisa woman top of the list. Your man Tony only did half a job of tracking her movements, which made me waste my time putting together a travel request for Antwerp.'

'What about that request? I'd said everything on the case had to be referred to me through Neil, but you went direct to Yelland.'

'Yes, but you couldn't have meant anybody above DS, could you? I mean, that would have been disrespectful of people's rank. You weren't available, so I just went up one level.'

'I agree it would have been disrespectful to have you report to someone of lower rank, but this was just an administrative mechanism for relaying messages, so you should have done as I'd said. As it is, you've made yourself look a fool by asking to travel to Belgium when the woman has already returned to the UK.'

'I don't see why you say that makes me look like a fool; if your man had done his job right, I wouldn't have made the request. I've just explained that to Yelland, so he won't be blaming me for the mistake.'

'You say it was Tony's fault, but he was only doing exactly what you said, so it all comes back to what your orders were. And you didn't check to see what he had done, so your supervisory skills are also lacking.'

'Well, I've come to expect people to do their jobs properly, so I shouldn't need to be forever checking their normal, everyday work.'

'When you say "come to expect", where exactly have these expectations of yours been satisfied? You don't seem to have stayed long enough in any one place to develop expectations.'

'That's because I'm not appreciated. Everywhere I go there's people who object to me trying to improve things; they get settled into their own ways and don't want to change. Each time I move I try harder and harder to make an impression, to get myself noticed; but it doesn't seem to matter what I do, it just never works out. Is that what this is all about? You want to move me on? I've only been here a day; surely I need to be allowed more time to make an impact.'

Priestley noticed Cargill's stony-faced expression had started to show a small sign of crumbling; he judged this the moment to explain the error of his ways. 'I'll tell you how I see things. You begin from a completely false premise: the belief that you need to make a visible impact. That's actually the opposite of what you need to do in a new place at your level; you need to enter the water smoothly without making waves. Have you ever watched divers in the Olympics? They try to make what they call a "rip entry", where there's barely a ripple after they've entered the water. But for you to believe that's how you should really be operating, you first of all have to believe in the person who's giving you the advice. You've already suggested you think I've been getting it wrong, which will have made you resistant to accepting advice from me. So, whose advice would you accept? To hear you speak, everyone is wrong except you. You're like the squaddie who's marching out of step with everyone else but claims he's the only one in step.' He paused to see if there was any evidence of his words being accepted, but saw only Cargill's hard face trying to reassert itself.

Priestley picked up a sturdy brown rubber band, which he stretched a little before allowing it to regain its shape. Then he stretched it again, this time taking it to the limit of his strength, before placing it back on the desk in front of him. 'You see how this rubber band hasn't quite gone back to its original shape; it's looking a bit white in these two places. Think of it as a person that gets pulled about. If the stress isn't too much, they end up back where they started. But if there's too much stress, they end up distorted and deformed.'

Cargill was unable to keep the sneer from his voice. 'And you think I've become affected by too much stress.'

Priestley shook his head. 'No, Frank, I'm talking about me. I used to suffer from stress, and I was in danger of ending up out-of-shape, mentally. Then I met someone who proved over and over again they really understood me, and that gave me the confidence to believe in them so that I could accept their advice without question. They rescued me, and what you need is someone to rescue you; someone you can believe in. Because, right now, the only person you seem to believe in is yourself, and frankly, Frank,' Priestley smiled briefly, 'you're the last person you should be putting your trust in, because you're always getting it wrong.'

Cargill looked at him closely, curiosity etched on his face. 'Do you normally have this sort of conversation with people?'

Priestley held his gaze. 'I've lived through some experiences that could have left me broken. Someone found me and put me back together. What I've learned from that process is something I willingly share with other broken vessels. What it comes down to is this: to start to improve, you have to believe in someone. I believed in my psychiatrist, and I'm inviting you to believe in me; that means seeing me as someone you respect, not someone you're trying to undermine to make yourself look better.'

'Perhaps I should see this psychiatrist of yours myself, if you think I'm a headcase.'

'I don't think you're a headcase, Frank; I just think you need a lot of guidance on how to rub along with people. Anyway, you can't see her; she's too busy looking after my children.'

Cargill looked confused. 'What?'

Priestley gave a broad smile. 'It's like the line from that book: "Reader, I married him".' As Cargill looked more confused, he spelled it out. 'She's my wife.'

'Oh, I see.' He asked, meekly, 'Can I go now?'

Priestley nodded assent. 'Yes, but do give some thought over the weekend to what I've said.'

CHAPTER 30

Susan Newhouse, a young solicitor, felt the need for a defensive telephone call screening procedure that ensured she would never be faced with an unwanted caller. She had entered every one of her contacts into the telephone's directory so that she could identify any caller before answering; no calls were ever accepted unless the caller was already on her list. If a previously unidentified number was displayed, she noted it down and used the internet to try to find its origin. If that search proved unsuccessful, she entered the name as "UNKNOWN", followed by a number; she was currently up to "12". A successful Web search would result in an entry being made on the telephone's directory, with acceptable contacts being entered with a personalised description, and unacceptable ones with an "X" followed by a brief identifier. Repeated calls from unknown or unacceptable contacts would receive the ultimate sanction of being placed on the "Blocked" list. She never answered calls from "Number Withheld" sources, except by appointment.

As there were currently no time-critical strands to the Piscaro investigation, the core team were taking the weekend off. The exception was DC Tony Beresford, who had requested permission to try to track down Lisa de Cock in Birmingham where her car had been seen; he was still smarting from his earlier failure to check for her return to the UK, despite Priestley offering him the get-out clause of "Acting under orders."

Susan Newhouse was Tony's girlfriend. He had met her while investigating her brother's suspicious death. They had entered into a very restrictive relationship, the rules of which were defined by her; one of the rules was that he was never permitted to question her rules.

Many of the young women Tony came into contact with in a professional capacity were in the business of selling themselves for sex. In contrast to working girls' rules, Susan had made it quite clear sex would never be allowed under any circumstances, though kissing was permitted.

They saw each other most days, always returning at night to their separate homes. His very limited success with girls at any level of intimacy had left him willing to accept Susan's ground rules. When he had once suggested she perhaps cleaved to imagined attitudes of a bygone era, her response was to tell him to take them or leave them. As she had then cried intermittently all day, he had reassured her he was happy always to abide by her rules, though inwardly he remained optimistic they may change, given time.

He telephoned her landline at 8:30 on the Saturday morning to check she was still available, as it was not unknown for their weekend plans to be cancelled without notice due to one or other having to work on a case. Seeing "Tony Beres" displayed on the telephone's small screen, she answered, 'Hello, Tony.'

Despite the lack of physical intimacy, he nevertheless felt close to her, and empty when they were apart; the brightness in his voice was therefore entirely genuine. 'Hello Susan. Are you all ready to go?' She insisted on Susan, not Sue: another of her rules that she would not explain.

'I'm ready, but do you know exactly where we're going? You were acting all mysterious, yesterday. Birmingham's a big place; a bit more than a village.'

'I've a few places to start with, and we'll see where we get to from there.'

'What sort of places?'

'Jewellers.'

Her apprehension was immediately reflected in her quavering voice. 'You're not thinking of doing something stupid, are you, Tony? We don't know each other anywhere near well enough, yet.'

He laughed happily, as he inferred hope for their future from that final word. 'My stupidity will have to wait a while; I need to be on my game today. We're going to be tracking down a fugitive.'

The reciprocated laughter was grounded in relief. 'Is it someone dangerous? Are you sure we'll be safe?'

He tried for laid-back. 'No worries. Actually, she isn't strictly a fugitive; she probably doesn't even know we're looking for her. I just need to ask her some questions.'

'Will she need a solicitor?'

'Because if she does, you're ready and willing.'

Tony drove to Susan's flat and rang the bell; she buzzed him into the building and he walked to the lift that was already waiting at ground level. When he exited on the third floor, he found her standing at the doorway, looking out for him. She prepared to close the door behind her.

'Hang on, Susan; I had another think. I don't know how far we'll get today with tracking down this woman, so I've brought an overnight bag with me. We could stay somewhere and start again tomorrow if needs be.'

The suspicion in her voice was palpable. 'Are jewellers open on Sundays? Anyway, you should have said. You need to go on your own if you're not coming back tonight.'

He read the extent of the worry on her face. 'It'll be OK, honestly. We could have two rooms, if you think twin beds isn't, um, ...' His voice trailed away.

She read the panic and fear in his expression, which gave her confidence she would be safe with him. 'You'd better come in while I throw some things together.'

He followed her into the flat. Though he had been in before, it was only ever as a brief stopping-point on the way to somewhere else. Whenever they had an evening in, it was always at his flat, even though it was less pleasant than hers. He suspected that was so she always had control of when they would part in the evening, knowing it was easier to leave someone else's place than to press someone into leaving one's own.

She hurried to collect together the things necessary for an overnight stay; her pink gym bag was bulging by the time she decided she had everything. 'I've just got ordinary stuff; do I need anything else? Anything special? What about shoes? Will this coat be alright?'

'It's only Birmingham we're going to; it isn't as though we're leaving civilisation.'

She quipped, 'Are you sure?'

He smiled. 'If you've forgotten something, I'll buy you another.'

As he drove them the motorway route, M1, M42, M6, he felt as happy as though they were going on holiday together; this overrode his apprehension at being under-prepared for the investigation, having so far failed to make any progress from a whole series of telephone calls.

Lisa de Cock's mobile phone appeared to be dead, and she had not responded to her e-mails, so he was left with tracking her down by other means. The ANPR system had located her car, or at least a car bearing her registration number, in Birmingham's Jewellery Quarter; but that was yesterday, so she may already have moved on. Though he doubted his search would be successful, he nevertheless felt pleased to be attempting to contribute something substantial to the investigation.

They were well into the two-hour journey before their chitchat started to flag. He thought of something to say, to avoid any suggestion of awkwardness between them. 'Shall I tell you about the toxicology report?'

She stopped him immediately. 'It's always going to be a problem between us, isn't it? You're not supposed to divulge confidential information to me, though I'm sure husbands and wives are a special case. But, as well as that, if you give me inside information, as a lawyer I'm ethically bound not to take the case.'

He knew there were lots of messages to unpick, but they were just approaching a motorway interchange and he needed his wits about him. 'Just hold onto those thoughts a moment.' When they reached a clear section of road, he replayed her words to himself, then looked for a logical route through the tangle. 'There are plenty of cases to go around, so I'm sure we could avoid working on the same ones. If necessary, I'd ask to have myself taken off a case if it comes your way. If there isn't a conflict of interest, I could disclose information to you on a strictly confidential basis, and you could give me legal advice in return. I'm sure I know of at least one senior officer who shares information with his wife, and benefits from hearing what she has to say. We could co-operate in the same way, if we were married.'

She shook her head in disbelief. 'If that was a marriage proposal, I have to say it sounded more like an offer to join a firm; whatever happened to romance? Anyway, we hardly know each other, so you shouldn't talk like that.'

'You were the one that mentioned husbands and wives, so I just followed your lead.'

'You've confused an offer to enter into a contract with an invitation to treat.'

He flashed her a quick smile. 'An "invitation to treat" sounds good to me.'

She held her smile in place so he would notice it if he again turned his attention from the road ahead. 'I can see I'll have to teach you something about contract law. The expression describes an invitation to commence negotiations.'

His peripheral vision caught her smile. 'In that case, let's thrash out the terms. And let me tell you right away, I'll agree to all your proposals.'

Her smile faded and her countenance darkened. 'You don't know anywhere near enough about me to be thinking of any kind of proposals.'

CHAPTER 31

Tony drove on in silence, wondering if there was some dreadful skeleton in her cupboard. Suddenly, Susan put on a showbiz smile and an excessively happy voice. 'We're going away together, so let's enjoy the weekend.' When she saw he had seen her smile, she removed it just as quickly.

As they entered the outskirts of Birmingham, he asked her to handle the navigation. 'First stop is Birmingham Central Police Station; their code begins B4 6.'

'It begins before six? Does that matter? It's nearly eleven now.'

'Very funny. I'm expected, but I still have to make myself known to them, seeing as I'm on their patch.'

She wrinkled her nose. 'Their patch? Do coppers still talk like that?'

'I suppose not. Codes are the thing nowadays. Anyway, we should be close to the POLSTA by now.'

'The Pole Star? That must be hundreds of light-years away.'

'Look, if you get us lost, we won't have time for a Code 99.'

'An ice cream with a flake in it?'

He turned quickly to smile at her and saw she was already smiling back. 'Not narcotics; a tea break.'

At the station, he drew into a designated parking bay. 'Come in with me; I can say you're helping the police with our enquiries.'

At reception, he gave the name of his contact. Sergeant Jerry Edgbaston appeared through a side door, and the three of them introduced themselves. Tony added, 'Be careful what you say; she's a solicitor.'

Jerry responded, 'Thanks for the warning.' He continued, 'The Jewellery Quarter team's been briefed to look out for that woman. There's four of them on duty at the moment, two PCs and two PCSOs, to help you with your manhunt.'

Susan corrected him. 'Womanhunt.'

Tony countered. 'Personhunt.'

Jerry grinned at Tony as he nodded his head in Susan's direction. 'She's sharp, this one.'

She laughed self-consciously, embarrassed at having spoken out of turn; the two men quickly joined in.

Jerry asked Tony, 'What's this woman done?'

'We really don't know if she's done anything, but she's a known associate of someone who died in suspicious circumstances.'

Susan butted in. 'Calling her a "known associate" makes it sound like she's part of a criminal conspiracy. You told me she simply used to be his girlfriend.'

After grimacing at her, Tony handed Jerry a list of jewellers known to have had contact with Lisa Wye in the past six months. 'We're just going to go walking around, asking if anyone knows where we might find the...' he turned to Susan, '...suspect.' She threw a playful punch toward his left biceps, pulling back from making actual physical contact.

Jerry pointed at Tony's arm. 'I witnessed that, if you want to do her for ABH.'

Susan retorted, 'It's good to see the police here are just as honest and accurate as they are back home!'

After the men had responded with a burst of rapid-fire laughter, Tony and Susan took their leave.

Tony had prepared a route that enabled the six jewellers to be reached without back-tracking, taking in Spencer Street, Vyse Street and Warstone Lane. The first on the list was Breakfast Diamonds. Tony showed his warrant card to the older assistant, a small, stout, clean-shaven, balding man of well over sixty. 'I'm Detective Constable Beresford; this is a civilian associate, Ms Newhouse. I telephoned yesterday and spoke to Solomon Gilder.'

He tilted his head back and looked up. 'That's me.'

'I was asking about someone who previously supplied some jewellery to you: Lisa Wye. I'm trying to locate her to help with our enquiries.'

He looked closely at the identification. 'You're not from around here. Does that mean she's done something serious?'

'No, sir. She lives local to my area. She hasn't been heard of for a week or so, and we need to ask for her help with a case we're investigating. We've reason to believe she was in this area yesterday. Do you know exactly when you last saw her?'

'I'll need to check my records.' He disappeared behind a solid metal door.

Tony and Susan looked at the various locked display cases together. Most of the price labels on the items were face down, making it impossible to read them without asking for assistance. They were poring over an impressive array of engagement rings, reading out the few visible prices to each other, when Gilder emerged with a brown leather-bound ledger.

'It was over two months ago when she delivered a

pair of earrings to us. They were for a regular client of ours: a woman who likes to have unique pieces made, based on her own ideas.'

Tony looked at the entry in the ledger, noting the invoice price. 'That looks expensive for a pair of earrings; not that I know anything about it.'

'There's a world of difference between a ready-made pair of earrings and something specially designed and produced by hand. The six diamonds were selected by Ms Wye from her own sources, though I would have been pleased to provide them myself. She's a qualified gemmologist, so it wasn't for me to press her on the matter. In the end, the client was delighted with them, Ms Wye received her payment and we took our commission, so everyone was happy.'

'Are there any other orders for her in the pipeline?'

'Bespoke jewellery is only for the most discerning; as you rightly pointed out, it commands a substantial premium. There haven't been any more requests since then for the type of high quality work Ms Wye undertakes, and we generally pass lower-premium commissions to various local people.'

'OK, well, thank you for your help. Could I leave you my details? If you see her in the next few days, please get in touch with me straight away.' He handed over his card and turned to leave.

The jeweller called him back. 'Have you perhaps forgotten something?'

'Not that I know of. What were you thinking?'

'You may be trained to look at faces, but I look at fingers as well. Are you not interested in seeing our engagement rings?' Seeing Tony looking stunned, Susan began to giggle. 'Forgive me if I've said the wrong thing; my instincts are usually right when I see two people together.' He smiled. 'I always give a discount to members of the constabulary, in appreciation of the excellent support they give us here in Birmingham, unlike at Hatton Gardens!'

Tony remained dumbstruck, so Susan responded. 'It's rather too early to be thinking about engagement rings. We're really more like good friends.'

He smiled at her. 'Well, if the situation changes, be sure to come back. I can imagine several of our rings would sit handsomely on your elegant fingers.'

She giggled again as she looked at Tony. He turned to the jeweller, not wishing to continue that discussion thread. 'If you see Ms Wye, don't forget to call me, will you? Thanks again for your help.'

Once outside and out of sight of the jeweller, Susan was no longer able to suppress her laughter. 'You looked mortified, Tony, but earlier you were the one talking about marriage. I know it's not going to happen, but you could at least have pretended. What's he going to think of us, now?'

Tony found his own words blocked his attempt to smile. 'What do you mean, "It's not going to happen"? What's stopping us?'

Susan's laughter died suddenly. 'Come on, let's go to the next one.'

As they approached "Engaging with Diamonds", Tony touched Susan on the shoulder. She flinched, and knew it had registered with him. 'I'm sorry, Tony; I just wasn't expecting you to …'

'No; *I'm* sorry. I was just wanting to say, before we go in, what about, um, …'

She saw how troubled he now appeared. 'Come on,

Tony, you can say it, whatever it is.'

He was thinking of Marcus and Lin on their recent escapade, which was now circulating the station and growing at every turn. 'Well, sometimes in CID we keep it hidden that we're in the police. What about us not telling them straight away who we are? Well, who I am. We can see what happens.'

'You mean, behave like we're actually looking for an engagement ring?'

'Yes. Let's see how convincing we can be.'

Tony held the door open for Susan to enter the jewellery shop. A comprehensively made-up young woman came over to them straight away. 'Good morning. Do you have a particular ring in mind, or perhaps a certain gemstone? If you suggest a price range, I'll show you the trays that may be suitable.'

Tony now felt slightly uncomfortable with the deception, though he intended to continue with it a little longer. 'You think we're a couple, then, looking for an engagement ring?'

'This is "Engaging with Diamonds", so it's fairly obvious. But you're not, are you? Are you the plod?'

'If you mean am I a police officer, then yes. I telephoned yesterday.'

'Just a minute.' She opened a rear door and called out, 'Mr Thompson, there's someone to see you.'

A middle-aged man appeared and took the warrant card from Tony, scrutinising it closely with the aid of a magnifying loupe. 'Is it work, or are you after a discount?'

'Strictly work. I telephoned yesterday about Lisa Wye; she made some bespoke jewellery for you a while ago. Could you tell me when you last saw her?'

He answered immediately. 'Three months back.'

'And do you expect to see her again soon?'

'No; her work's too pricey for most of my customers. It is good, I'll give her that, but no one likes to pay top whack nowadays, and she doesn't do "cheap". If I got the right customer in, I'd get in touch with her, but I'm not holding my breath.'

'OK, well thanks anyway. Let me give you my card, and if she shows up in the next few days then do let me know straight away.'

Susan and Tony set off for the next jeweller on the list. She remarked, 'That was very different to the first one. If I'd been a genuine customer, I don't think I'd have been impressed with them; too business-like.'

He nodded in agreement. 'The woman didn't take long to suss us out, though; perhaps we didn't act the part well enough. We'll have to try harder, next time.'

At the street corner just before the third jewellers, Tony deliberately put his hand on her arm, knowing it was against the rules; she stiffened, but suppressed the shudder her body had expected to deliver. He looked intently at her. 'Let's have some lunch, shall we? There's plenty of time to see the others.'

She turned sharply away from him so that his fingers lost their grip, then pointed in the direction she was now facing. 'Good idea. There's a caff in this direction, I think.'

Tony interpreted her reaction correctly, knowing she was unfamiliar with the area. He avoided any awkwardness by following her unquestioningly, though he realised it was leading them away from various pleasant-looking pubs that were advertising meals.

After circling around, they ended close to where they

had started. He suggested, 'What about that pub over there?' They crossed the street and read through the menu; it was displayed in alternating white and yellow chalk down one side of an A-frame sandwich board that stood at the road's edge. Checking the other side for more food options, he found only beers; a glance at the three blackboards leaning against the whitewashed wall revealed yet more beers. He pointed to an item on the meal menu. 'I fancy Cumberland sausage and mash with peas and onion gravy.'

She responded, 'I'll have the same. At least that way we should be served together, so neither of us is kept waiting.'

He wondered if that was a tacit acknowledgement she had just wasted his time by heading off blindly in the wrong direction. Though he recognised he may be over-thinking her choice, he nevertheless felt pleased at how much more discerning of other people's feelings he himself had become since joining the police service.

CHAPTER 32

In the pub they found a dining area with an empty table; as she settled in, he noticed the "7" on the brass disc inlaid near a corner. 'What would you like?'

'You're on duty, so I suppose that means soft drinks.'

He answered with bravado. 'I'll be having a pint of bitter.'

'I'll have half o' lager, then.'

He went to the bar to place their order, returning with their drinks. 'Two down, four to go.' He saw her questioning look. 'Jewellers, I mean.'

She looked him in the eye. 'Couldn't your enquiries have been made over the phone?'

He knew the evidence supported her implied criticism. 'Meeting people face-to-face can be better; sometimes you get a vibe.' He hoped her laughter was not meant unkindly. 'You think I'm too inexperienced to have a gut reaction? Well, maybe you're right, but I'm sure I'm improving.'

'And what has your gut told you so far?'

'That I'm hungry.'

They chatted about Birmingham's Jewellery Quarter: what they had seen and how much of its history had been preserved. By the time the food arrived, they had moved onto a broader discussion of jewellery and gemstones.

After their meal, Tony drained his glass first. 'I just need to pop to the loo. Do you want to stay here?'

'I'll pay a call as well. See you outside.'

He was the first to leave the pub. As he stood waiting for her, he saw two PCSOs walking down the street in his direction, so took out his warrant card and held it up for their inspection. 'Hello, I'm Tony. I believe you're keeping a lookout for a woman from my area.'

The female officer looked at the card before responding in a singsong, Welsh voice. 'I'm Carys Evans and this is Owen Davies. So, you're the mysterious invader from up north. Well, we're keeping an eye out, but the photo was quite small, and it looked a bit fuzzy when it was blown up, so don't expect too much from us.'

Owen asked, 'You couldn't get a better photo, could you?'

Tony responded. 'Sorry, though it's actually a passport photo; it was either that, or one from a Christmas party where she's wearing a Santa hat.'

Owen continued. 'What's she done then?'

Tony shook his head. 'Probably nothing, but we're struggling to get a lead on a suspicious death; it's someone she used to know very well.'

Carys responded. 'OK, we'll do our best, and we have the car reg. as well. We need to be going now, so best of luck, and let us know if you need help with anything or anyone.'

Owen jerked his thumb at her. 'Yes, she's very good at subduing females, aren't you?'

They laughed conspiratorially at their private joke. As they headed off, Tony noticed how they checked out their reflections in the first two shop windows.

When Susan emerged, Tony mentioned having met

the two PCSOs. 'Carys Evans and Owen Davies. I'm sure they're both Welsh, so we're not the only aliens.'

He looked on his list for the third jewellery shop, noting it was just a short distance away. 'Anne Chor Engagement. That's C H O R.'

She observed, 'Unusual name; maybe another alien.'

'Perhaps it's code; Birmingham's hallmark is an anchor. Anne Chor, anchor.'

'Yes; you didn't have to spell it out for me. Don't forget, it's you who're the policeman.'

He responded defensively, 'Not all policemen are thick, you know.'

'It was just a joke, Tony.'

Realising his laugh had been delivered too late, he apologised. 'Sorry.'

'You need to be more relaxed when you're with me.'

He recalled the expression involving the kettle and the black pot. 'I am relaxed, really. Let's do the "couple" thing again, shall we? And I'm looking for a solid performance this time, with full engagement into the part. Do you know, one of the married senior officers kissed one of my colleagues in public, when they were acting like a couple.'

'Where?'

'At a shop; an art gallery.'

'No, I mean, where did he kiss her: cheek, lips, …'

'Lips. Rumour has it they just about sucked each other's faces off.'

'Well, I hope it wasn't under duress; women are often forced against their will, you know, even though they don't realise it at the time.'

'I shouldn't have told you; it's only a rumour. It was a traffic warden who started it, so you can draw your own conclusions. If it's true, they were very believable... so the story goes.'

'And you don't think we could do "believable"? Well, we'll see who can act and who can't.'

Tony held the door open for her. As they stepped inside, he gently took hold of her fingers; she passed the first test by not snatching her hand away. He saw the only assistant was a woman of about thirty, standing behind a counter. Scanning the shop, he identified a battery of security cameras positioned all around the walls, suggesting to him someone else was watching.

She greeted them warmly. 'Good afternoon; should I bring out the engagement rings, or do you have something else in mind?'

Susan looked up at Tony as he responded for them. 'Engagement rings, please.' She brought out two red cushions into which were embedded several dozen rings. He looked at the prices, identifying the most expensive. 'What would we need to do if we wanted something even more special? Something made specifically for us, to a unique design?'

'We do provide such a service, though I have to tell you it's really rather expensive. There's a Belgian lady who buys gems from her father's company in Antwerp; she creates quite exquisite pieces. But you could easily be looking at twice the price of our most expensive ring, here.' She picked up the three-diamond ring Tony had previously identified as having the highest price.

She looked directly at Susan. 'I'd be happy to put you in touch with her, but, you know, love isn't measured simply by what your engagement ring cost. Perhaps I shouldn't say that, considering the business I'm in, but I do think young couples such as yourselves should only spend what you can afford.'

Susan's eyes watered; a tear escaped, meandering down her right cheek. 'That's what I told him, but he's always wanting to lavish whatever money he has on me.' She turned to Tony. 'We should go away and have a proper think about it.'

Tony was rooted to the spot, unsure what had just happened. When Susan took his hand, he smiled at her before turning to the woman. 'Yes, we need to think about it.'

'When you've decided, come back and see me; I'm the proprietress, Sarah Cohen.'

'Not Anne Chor?'

'That's just a made-up name; anchor, you know, the Birmingham hallmark.'

Tony obediently allowed Susan to lead him by the hand to the door; outside, his eyes were dazzled by the brightness, like cameras with the apertures set too wide.

Inside the shop, a door opened and a young man put his head around the corner. 'What was all that about, Sarah? Are you trying to put us out of business?'

'It was his shoes, David. He's out looking for an engagement ring with the girl he obviously adores, but he's wearing a pair of old, heavy brogues, which must be his best shoes, so he really can't afford to be spending much. Maybe they'll come back when they have a sensible figure in mind.'

Tony walked in silence toward the next jewellers on the list, quite disturbed about what had just taken place. Susan eventually spoke, which made him jump as though woken abruptly from a dream. 'How did I do?'

He failed to comprehend. 'How did you do?'

'How did I do with my acting? Admit it, I was

brilliant.'

He stopped and looked directly into her eyes. 'You were too convincing; even I believed you. Let's take a break and just have a wander around.'

She saw the new moon in his eyes, but was unsure whether she wished to stray so far into this unknown emotional territory. 'No, Tony, you need to finish your tasks, first. We can have a wander tomorrow.'

'Tomorrow? So we're staying overnight? Shall I book two rooms, or a twin room, or something?'

'A twin will do fine.'

'You have a look in some shop windows then, while I book it.' He knew he had just lied to her, but felt it was more of an organisational bending of the truth. As she peered at another jewellery display, he walked out of earshot before cancelling two bookings and confirming a third, having been covering all options.

When he returned to her side, he took hold of her hand and she returned his grasp. 'It's all arranged; one night, twin room, including breakfast. Let's go to jeweller number four. I'd like to play it straight from now on, if that's OK.'

"Park Lane 4 Diamonds" proved to be a top-end jewellers who had had the latest meeting of all with Lisa Wye at just three weeks, but their contact details were simply those on the police file. "Bull Ring Jewellery" was more down-market; they had only ever had one contact with Lisa Wye, six months ago. "Brum My Sparkle" was a young woman's outlet for her own creations; four months ago she had passed on one expensive commission to Lisa Wye, for fear of failing to produce a sufficiently high-quality piece herself and thereby risk her reputation.

As they left the final shop, Tony took Susan's hand. 'That's work done for today. What shall we do now?'

'Get our things and check into the hotel. If it doesn't come up to expectations, we'll be out again sharpish.'

He suspected "expectations" was code for "two separate beds". Having cancelled the double bed option, and the two separate rooms, he hoped she would find no reason to object to the surviving booking.

CHAPTER 33

As they entered the hotel room, Tony saw how cramped it was. He noticed the two beds were positioned with just a narrow gap between them, which would enable them to be put together without much physical difficulty if the occupants so desired.

They took it in turns to empty the contents of their toilet bags, with toothbrushes, toothpaste, et cetera, being distributed equitably on the available surfaces. Susan folded her next-day clothes into a neat pile and placed them on a low shelf in the single cupboard. He followed suit, choosing a higher shelf. As they would be going out later to eat, she decided not to hang up her coat; she threw it down casually onto the single armchair, though with less abandon than she had intended. He imitated her, ensuring his coat did not lie directly on top of hers. Having completed the minimal unpacking, suddenly their close proximity within the small room introduced an air of tension that they both felt keenly; she translated it into words. 'I don't know why we're both so nervous. You know the rules as well as I do. That's your bed and this is mine, and that's how it's staying, isn't it?'

He recognised the pleading edge to her voice. 'Of course. I wouldn't ever do anything to upset you; you know that.' He looked at her closely for signs of acceptance of his reassurance. Satisfied the tension had largely dissipated, he suggested they take a walk and explore the area.

Heading out through reception, he picked up a slim brochure of canal walks. After glancing at it briefly, he handed it to her. 'Fancy a walk by a canal?'

They followed the signposted route to the canal, then headed along the towpath, passing several attractive pubs of differing styles.

She stopped immediately when he took her hand in his. Making no move to extricate it, she looked at him with sorrowful eyes. 'It's nice walking here with you, but don't imagine it's more than it is.' He would have demanded clarification if she had been a suspect; instead, he just smiled, in the hope that that was an appropriate response.

Having walked for half an hour and seen more than enough prettily decorated narrowboats, she suggested they turn back. As they re-passed the pubs, he asked if she would like to eat at one of them. She chose the largest and most open; he would have preferred the smallest and most intimate, but readily accepted her decision. She chose a table by the front window with a clear view of the canal basin; again, his choice would have been quite different.

He pulled two large menus from the stand in the centre of the table and handed one to her. She glanced down the choices: fairly standard fare. She assessed the prices: only a small premium, considering the location. 'This shouldn't break the bank, unless you go for the beluga caviar.'

'We can go somewhere else if you'd like something classier.'

'You're forgetting, this is my turn to pay.'

'No, Susan; I'd like to treat you.'

'It's like I said in that jewellers: you're always

wanting to spend money on me. You know I believe in equality, and that includes taking it in turns to pay for meals. Besides, I'd especially like to treat you this evening; who knows what tomorrow may bring.' He received the words with a sense of foreboding.

As they drank nondescript red wine and waited for the cannelloni and salad, he found her conversation was especially bright and gay. Her arms moved like an Italian as she laughed far too loudly for her usual restrained self. She spoke of a holiday she had taken in Italy with a girl from school, and how the sea in the Bay of Naples is so much bluer than the sea at Cromer. He suggested the sunlight and the sky could be factors, but she waved away such science with a dismissive sweep of her hand.

She frowned as she compared the local youths of the two places, the former being so much darker in appearance and character. He felt she should be hosting a glittering dinner-party rather than directing all her energy toward him alone. Though he enjoyed her performance, just as a member of an audience might appreciate that of an actress at the theatre, he nevertheless retained an undefined, niggling worry.

The bottle had yielded three glasses each; as he finished his share he realised she was holding back one last mouthful in her glass. 'We could have another drink, if you like. Or should we go back?'

She knew they never had more than the one bottle between them, and had no wish for either of them to have more alcohol, but neither did she like the idea of going back to the hotel room with him. 'Let's go for a coffee somewhere.'

They walked along the towpath, holding hands,

something that had previously been against the rules. He smiled at her. 'It's nice, isn't it?'

She withdrew her hand from his. 'I'm sorry, Tony, I think you may be getting the wrong idea. It is nice, but it doesn't mean any more than it is.'

He decided to press for disambiguation. 'Holding hands is OK now, isn't it? And touching you on the arm, that's alright as well? I've never really understood why it was OK to kiss you, but not to touch you.'

She stopped to look at him. 'Kissing was always OK. But touching can lead to more touching, and that's never going to lead to anything but your frustration. That's why I think we need to stop seeing each other.'

He felt her words as a blow to the pit of his stomach, leaving him nauseated. 'You mustn't say that. You always have the right to set the rules, and I'm not trying to push back your boundaries. I'm just trying to understand where they're coming from.'

'It's a lose-lose situation for you. If I don't tell you, you're frustrated by the limits of our relationship; and if I do tell you, you won't want to know me anymore.'

'I'm sure if you told me what the problem is, we could work through it together.'

'And I'm sure it's too big a problem for that, which is why I don't want to burden you with it.'

His words were choking in his throat. 'I can't bear to lose you, Susan. So let's just go back to how we were.'

'That wouldn't be fair on you, to keep you holding on when I know I can't have a proper relationship.'

He saw a glimmer of hope, in that the limitation was not directed at him alone. 'You're too precious for me just to walk away.' They continued in silence, as it had been her turn to speak but she had chosen not to.

Stepping into the hotel ahead of him, she asked for their room key at reception, electronic locks not yet having spread to this particular corner of Birmingham. She chose the stairs rather than the lift, and he followed in silence, desperately hoping she would speak to him again. After unlocking the door, she hesitated before walking inside and placing the key on the nearby table. She waited in a corner of the room until he had closed the door behind him. 'Don't look so glum, Tony; believe me, it's for the best.'

He looked mournfully into her eyes. 'I do wish you'd trust me, Susan; I'm sure I wouldn't let you down, whatever the problem.'

She went to her bed and pulled out her plain cotton pyjamas from under the pillow, taking them into the bathroom. He sat on his bed, looking out of the window at the grim view. Five minutes later she emerged with her pyjamas on, buttoned to the top, and holding her clothes in front of her chest. She spoke almost in a whisper. 'Your turn now; we need to be up early.'

He obediently picked up his new pyjama set of two-tone blue T-shirt and shorts from on top of his pillow. After he had entered the bathroom, she put down her clothes and eased herself between the sheets. When he emerged, he saw she was looking away from him, her face close to the wall.

CHAPTER 34

He had lain awake in the darkness for almost an hour when he heard the sound of a distant church clock chiming eleven; he would normally have still been up and about at this time, but their separate beds had made for early refuges. It was then he heard the first quiet sob. He would have liked to have offered her a shoulder to cry on, but not knowing the reason, and fearing he himself was the reason, he waited for her to make the next move. There was a second sob, a little louder, and then a whole flood of them. He risked speaking into the darkness. 'Susan; Susan, my love, you need to tell me what's the matter.'

She registered he had called her "my love", which had not previously been part of their joint lexicon. 'If I tell you something, do you promise never to breathe a word of it to anyone?' He switched on his bedside light. 'Turn it off. I'll only talk to you if you can't see me.'

He quickly flicked the switch. 'I promise to keep your secret, whatever it is.'

She held the silence for several seconds. 'Just listen; don't interrupt.' There was another brief pause. 'I'm not a virgin.'

He responded immediately. 'No one is nowadays; it's not a big deal.'

She snapped back. 'I said not to interrupt. And anyway, I believe *you* are, but don't answer because men always lie about that sort of thing.' She waited long enough to ensure he would abide by the instruction to remain silent. 'I haven't told you what I need to say.' He tried not to breathe too loudly. 'On my sixteenth birthday, Monday the seventeenth of July two thousand and six, someone told me I needed some practical sex education to help me develop into a mature woman and become more confident when I'm dealing with other adults.' He breathed out noisily, not having realised he had been holding the air tightly in his lungs. 'I said I could wait 'til I was older, but he said I needed that confidence right away to see me through sixth form. He emphasised it was for my benefit, and said he could just teach me what I really needed to know. I said if it's all about teaching me, then he didn't need to kiss me because I was already experienced at kissing. It's true, I was; lots of the girls in my year used to practise kissing with this really handsome boy, who liked demonstrating in public how good he was, like a professional actor. Looking back, I think we liked him because we sensed he wasn't a threat; he came out as Gay a few years later. Anyway, we agreed there'd be no kissing; that's why it was alright for you and me to kiss.

'I also said, if it's all about educating me, then he couldn't touch my breasts either because that's not part of the education; at least, not the way he'd explained it to me. He didn't like that idea, but I said he had to agree. So that's why I always kept a T-shirt on, and a bra as well so he didn't get the wrong idea. But I knew in some ways it was the wrong idea, because I shouldn't have let him have sex with me. I think it was all my fault, for encouraging him to see me as a woman; you see, when I was in my mid-teens and my breasts started to develop, I was so proud of them I used to wear low-cut tops to show them off.

'Anyway, he said he'd educate me, and he certainly did that. He educated me at least once every day for the next three weeks in the school holidays. That first time, he made it seem like it was a school lesson, starting with, "This is a condom and here's how it works." Except I already knew about condoms. All the girls learned about them at school; not in the lessons, but in the changing rooms. He said we'd begin with the missionary position; that means me on my back and him facing me on top. He even told me it would hurt the first time; he was right, it did.

'For the next two years he must have had me at least half a dozen times a month, long after he'd run out of anything new to teach me. He had me from every position and angle you could think of, though I refused to do any oral stuff or to let him bugger me. But I never enjoyed what we did together because it just wasn't right, even though I knew he was doing it because he loved me.

'When I was coming up to eighteen, I decided it should stop, so I went away in the summer after my A-levels to do some temporary work with another girl from school. At the end of the summer I went to university, and I stayed in a shared house instead of halls so that I didn't have to come back home at the end of each term. When I did come back for Christmas, he told me how upset he was at not seeing me anymore, and he asked me if we could have sex again. I told him he couldn't because it wasn't right, but I wouldn't have sex with anyone else either because I knew he was the one who really loved me.

'I kept my promise to him all through university, though at first there were quite a few lads who showed an interest in me. Then someone started a rumour I was a lesbian, and that led to some girls making advances. To put them all off, I joined the Methodist Society, as the girls all had a reputation for abstinence from the sins of the flesh, as well as the demon drink.

'Straight after university I began my training to become a solicitor. I worked a lot of hours for three years, and whatever spare time I had I spent in the gym. I'd no interest in having a boyfriend, but you came along when I was vulnerable, and you didn't push the sex thing, so I thought we'd be alright together. Only, you're wanting to move things on, so you have to understand why you shouldn't be wanting to have sex with me, because of my past. Now you can speak, Detective. Do you understand what I've told you, or do I have to spell it out?'

Tony realised the word "Detective" was intended to be significant, but dared not utter his theory in case he was mistaken. 'Everyone has skeletons in their cupboard, Susan.'

'My particular skeleton was cremated.'

He now knew his awful theory was correct. 'It was your brother.'

'Yes, it was. And that's why you won't want to know me anymore.'

Having heard her revelation, he was amazed to find himself overwhelmed with relief bordering on happiness. 'Susan, my love, nothing you've said has put me off you, though I do think we need to talk about what really happened to you. May I turn the light on so we can discuss things face-to-face?'

'No, Tony, because by the morning you'll feel very differently about it all. I expect you to change your mind about me, so all I ask is you remember it's a secret that you promised you'd keep. I need to sleep now; I feel exhausted.' Her voice began to fade away. 'I've never told anyone about it before.'

Five minutes later, Tony heard the steady breathing of someone who had fallen gently asleep; in marked contrast, he was now thoroughly wide awake. Feeling deeply ashamed of his physical reaction to her revelations, he crept quietly to the bathroom to give himself some traditional manual relief. Afterwards, he flushed the lavatory automatically, unable to stay his hand as he realised too late it might wake her. Feeling his way back to his bed in the darkness, he stubbed a little toe on something solid, but uttered no sound beyond a sharp intake of breath. Peeling open the sheets in the dark, he edged in between them. Soon, the hypnotic rhythm of her steady breathing lullabied him to sleep.

CHAPTER 35

Susan was still sleeping like an unburdened, innocent child when Tony became aware of the early morning traffic. In the dim light he located the kettle on the dressing-table and stealthily took it into the bathroom, berating himself for failing to anticipate the need for water. He noiselessly closed the door and turned on the shaving light above the mirror, wincing at its click. Choosing the more distant water source relative to Susan, he dribbled water quietly into the kettle from the bath's cold tap. After turning off the light, he opened the door and crept out, placing the kettle back in its original position. Silently, he pressed the plug into the socket, before easing the other end into the kettle. As it began to heat the water, it seemed so noisy to his ears he was certain it would wake her; he cast around for some way of dulling its sound, straining to see in the semi-darkness. As his eyes readjusted to the dim light, he could see her eyelids remained closed, though perhaps too tightly shut for someone who was genuinely sleeping.

Turning off the kettle before the water reached boiling point, he made two cups of coffee, emptying three tiny cartons of UHT milk into one and the remaining carton into the other. Carrying the cup of milky coffee to the small ledge affixed to one side of the top of her bed, he placed it carefully on a disposable coaster. As he knelt down beside her, he wondered whether he might kiss her, and if so, should it be on the forehead or the lips. He was unsure how she would react, so settled for whispering in her ear. 'I've made you a cup of coffee, love.'

Her eyes blinked open as though a spring had been triggered, and she delivered the line she had prepared a couple of minutes earlier. 'In the children's version, the handsome prince awakens sleeping beauty with a kiss.' He accepted the invitation, kissing her lightly on the lips, avoiding anything more intimate as his mouth had not yet been freshened for the day with toothpaste or mouthwash. 'Turn my light on, will you?' He turned on her bedside light.

As she prepared to sit up, he quickly turned away and walked to the table where his own coffee was waiting. He sipped it but found it too hot, so told her 'I'll have my shower now.' He took his pile of clothes from the cupboard to the bathroom, closing the door behind him. When he emerged, fully dressed, she was sitting up in bed. 'Right, your turn.'

She made no move to get out of bed. 'Should we have that conversation now, or would it be better if I'm dressed first?'

A wave of panic spread over him, a response to the flatness of her voice. 'What conversation? What do you mean, Susan?'

'The conversation where you say you're really sorry for me but I'm too screwed up and it's better we don't see each other anymore.' As she received no immediate response, she added, 'We can still be friends, Tony, but you've every right to move on and find someone undamaged; someone without my baggage.'

He felt this could be the most important conversation of his life, so wanted more time to prepare, being afraid of saying the wrong thing if he began too hastily.

'Your silence says it all, Tony, and believe me, I understand perfectly. It's what I would do if I were you, so don't feel bad about it.'

He needed yet more time. 'Just be quiet, Susan, and don't put words into my mouth.' She smiled serenely, dissembling her feelings. He thought her intention was to put him at his ease so that he could give her the hard word and she could show how she was still calm and placid. 'Right, I do have something to say to you.' At that moment her smile flickered and died, and he thought he glimpsed a fleeting micro-expression that betrayed her true emotion. 'I'm going to try to express things in your language, the law; and in my language, logic. What happened to you was wrong, but it was not your fault; you are not culpable. He was in a dominant position. You were a minor. He used undue influence to coerce you. He should have loved you like a brother, and not taken advantage of you. When you made a promise to him, it was given under duress, and therefore has no validity. Also, as he is no longer alive,' he had carefully avoided using the word "dead", 'any sense of an agreement is extinguished. Therefore, there is nothing to stop you, legally and morally, from entering into a complete relationship with someone in the future.'

He paused before switching themes. 'It would be illogical for a victim of abuse to apply a self-imposed constraint on their future potential happiness. Why should the innocent suffer? And, believe me, Susan, you are not only innocent, but *an* innocent. You have every right to live a normal life with anyone you choose, if they're willing. Well, I'm willing, and I hope

I shall be the one you choose, because I love you so much I don't ever want to be without you.' His words died in the sudden arid desert of his mouth; he felt his declaration should have been less academic, less structured, less logical, more eloquent, more sensitive, more emotional, altogether a much more accurate expression of his depth of feeling.

She looked dispassionately at him as she spoke steadily. 'Perhaps you should have been a lawyer; that would have made a highly convincing closing speech.'

'And are you? Highly convinced, I mean?'

Suddenly, her face relaxed. 'I've read all about this subject, but it's difficult to accept anything written by someone who doesn't know me personally. I know how logical you are, so for you to say such things gives much more weight to the arguments. I needed someone to say the words, someone I could trust, someone to give me permission to begin again.'

'And will you choose me? Can we become a couple? I mean a proper couple?'

'A proper couple?' She stepped out of bed, walking up to him and kissing him lightly on the lips. 'I am screwed up, I know that, but if you're patient with me, maybe we can get there.'

'We can go as fast or as slow as you like; there's no pressure from me to hurry things along, so long as we're moving in the right direction.'

Though she wished to give a brave smile, she found her face muscles had set rigid as she prepared to take the first step. Unbuttoning her pyjama top, she held his gaze with a stare into his unblinking eyes that begged him not to look down too soon. When all the buttons were unfastened, she opened the front and revealed her breasts. 'You can look down now, Tony. Tell me honestly what you think of them.'

He took a deep breath and let the air out slowly. 'They're magnificent.'

Abruptly closing the show, she discovered a long-lost cheeky grin. 'That's what I thought.' She grabbed her clothes and rushed into the bathroom, proud of herself, and pleased to discover in the mirror she still had the innocence to blush.

When she came out of the bathroom fully dressed, Tony was drinking cold coffee, standing looking out of the window, oblivious to the view of the car park and the roads and the concrete buildings beyond. She called over to him, 'Shall we go down to breakfast?'

He turned to her and put down his cup. 'In a minute. I have something else to say to you.' He held himself back from walking toward her, in case she imagined him to be in some way threatening. 'I think we should get engaged.'

She laughed delightedly. For the first time, she felt confident enough to be ever so slightly crude with him. 'So, one flash of my tits is all it took.'

He was encouraged by her tiny descent into vulgarity. 'To me, you've always been perfect, and nothing's changed; I would have asked you ages ago, but I was sure you'd say no.'

'And what about all that stuff I did in my teens? Doesn't that spoil me? Spoil us?'

'For me it's almost a relief you're experienced; at least it means one of us will know what we're doing.'

Reading the sincerity in his face, her emotional dam burst. As the tears flooded down her cheeks, she made no move to brush them away. He quickly stepped over to her and pulled several pastel-coloured paper hankies out of a box that lay on the table close to hand. She accepted them and began delicately to mop up the tears that were now dripping from her chin. Wishing to regain some of her lost dignity, she raised a point of law. 'Contracts require offer and acceptance; you haven't yet made an offer.'

He began a formal declaration. 'Susan, will you...'

She stopped him with the raised palm of her hand. 'Hold it right there.' Pointing to the floor with her right index finger, her thumb raised in imitation of a gun, she commanded, 'Down on one knee!'

He found himself overcome with an unmanly fit of giggles, but nevertheless obeyed quickly, though no longer fearing rejection. 'Susan, will you marry me?'

She raised an index finger to her lips and tapped them several times. 'Let me think about that; it doesn't do to hurry these things, you know.'

Laughingly, he spat out, 'You bitch!'

She joined in his laughter, but found that triggered more tears. Struggling to control the two faces of the same emotion, she finally regained enough composure to answer without her voice quavering too much. 'Oh, alright then, if you put it like that. I accept.'

CHAPTER 36

Over breakfast, Tony checked his notebook. 'I don't have any more definite leads to follow up, so we could just walk around and talk to people in the jewellery business and see if anyone knows anything.'

Susan responded brightly, 'Or we could just enjoy ourselves and take in the sights.'

'Or, and I think you'll agree this is the best option, we could go and buy an engagement ring.'

She found she was unable to control her rediscovered ability to blush. 'Not so loud, Tony; everyone will stare at us.'

He looked around at the two couples occupying tables in the furthest corners. 'I don't think I said it loud enough; shall I say it again?'

'Don't you dare. It's a nice idea though; we're certainly in the right place.'

'We could go to that first one we went to yesterday; Breakfast Diamonds. They live up to their name; they're about the first to open on Sunday mornings.'

'Yes, and the old man even offered a discount.'

'That's not why I said it; I don't want you to think I'm a cheapskate.'

'Don't worry about that; I know you'd bankrupt yourself for me if I asked you to. We could start there and then try another one; the woman at Anne Chor seemed very nice.'

'Sarah Cohen. The trouble with that is we didn't say who we are or why we were there. And having asked about bespoke jewellery, it's going to look bad picking something, um, from stock.'

'Were you going to say "something cheap"? I hope that isn't a reflection on how you see me!'

'I was thinking, something cheaper than hand-made, but not cheap; I want you to know just how much I love you, so I'll spend everything I've got.'

'Tony, you're too soppy. It's like Sarah Cohen said, love isn't measured by how much the engagement ring costs. Maybe we should settle for something out of a cracker, and have brass curtain rings instead of gold wedding rings.'

'How do you come up with ideas like that?'

'Sorry, Tony, they're not original; I'll have to take you to the theatre sometime.'

After breakfast, Tony phoned the station to see if there had been any developments on the case. Receiving a negative response, they sat in the hotel lounge and talked about their impressions of Birmingham. To them, grim concrete had become authentic sixties architecture, the canals were clear, the narrowboats attractively decorated, the pubs charming.

As they meandered toward Breakfast Diamonds, Susan took hold of Tony's hand; he turned his gaze to her and found she was examining his face minutely, as though she had never seen it before. Neither of them felt any wish or need to speak into the silence.

Solomon Gilder, the proprietor of Breakfast Diamonds, had been born in Poland a few years after the war. His mother, a nurse, had left her first husband's bones in Auschwitz. When she had returned home, she had found her former friends and neighbours had suffered collective amnesia concerning the few possessions left with them for safe-keeping. A brief liaison with a man of apparent wealth had led to the birth of Solly, though no escape from her abject poverty as he had denied paternity, unjustly claiming any one of many men could have fathered the child.

Solly had grown up quickly and become an expert in the art of self-sufficiency. Before he was even out of his teens he had brought his mother to England to begin a new life; she chose to see nothing of her new country beyond the small area of Birmingham where they lived. She would venture out to visit the nearby synagogue on Pershore Road, or to argue with some local shopkeeper or market trader who refused to give her a discount. Whatever the weather, she could be seen in long sleeves, determined to hide the black numbers tattooed on her arm that screamed out her survivor's guilt.

He never asked her what she had experienced, knowing there were no words in any language that could adequately describe the horror, and unsure whether there were any a son would wish to hear concerning what she had had to do to stay alive. He recognised one consequence of that time, however: for six days of the week she would argue against the existence of God, and on the Sabbath she would curse Him for failing to protect His chosen people.

Her compulsion to negotiate the cost of foodstuffs led to the more astute local shopkeepers asking initially higher prices of her, so that they could be haggled down to the same level that everyone else paid. Her first encounter with a supermarket led to her being declared *persona non grata* when she insisted on negotiating reductions for milk and apples. After that, Solly generally did the shopping, returning home to suffer lengthy interrogation; he thought she may have been disappointed to learn no goods had been stolen and all had been paid for in full.

Having lived through poverty, every day Solly rejoiced in his financial good fortune, certain he had earned the success and sure it had not been given to him by God. Nevertheless, he did sometimes wonder how it was that his Hungarian next-door neighbours always drove harder bargains, yet somehow made less profit, both by their official and unofficial book-keeping.

His greatest treasures were his many children and grandchildren. Almost half of them had entered the legal profession and the rest had gone into business. Success had cascaded down through two generations, and none of his descendants were financially dependent on his jewellery business; yet he enjoyed being at the shop and had no intention of ever retiring from it.

When Solly saw Tony and Susan enter the shop, he waved them over to him. 'Good morning to you both. And are you still pursuing your enquiries? Or are you here for another reason?' His dark brown eyes were as inviting as chocolate as he looked from one to the other.

Tony responded self-consciously. 'It's the other reason; we're looking for an engagement ring.'

'Then I have to begin with a difficult question: what sort of price range are you aiming for?'

'I can stretch to one thousand eight hundred and fifty pounds... if I don't eat for the rest of the year.'

Susan interjected. 'But love isn't all about how much an engagement ring costs, so let's look for something up to, say, half of that.'

He pleaded, 'But I've got it all ready in my account.'

She frowned at him. 'How did you know you'd need

it? It seems to me you've taken me for granted.'

'There's nothing wrong with being an optimist.'

'Well, half of one thousand eight hundred and fifty pounds is…'

'One thousand five hundred.'

'No it isn't, Tony; it's, um, nine hundred and twenty-five, so that's my limit.'

'Well, at least round it up to a thousand.'

Susan slapped her hand on the counter. 'Done!'

Solly smiled at Tony. 'Her worth is far above jewels.'

Susan cut in. 'Don't, Mr Gilder, he's soppy enough without you encouraging him.'

He smiled at her benignly. 'Do call me Solly.'

'I'm Susan.'

'Tony.'

'Now, what type of gemstone were you thinking of? Diamonds are the most popular, but there are others you could consider.'

She responded, 'I think diamonds; after all, this is "Breakfast Diamonds". By the way, why did you call it that?'

'I didn't. The name was chosen by my wife, Emily.' He added more quietly, in idiomatic Yiddish, '*Olov hashoolom.*' [May she rest in peace.] As he raised his head, he smiled at Susan and translated across languages and religions. 'God rest her soul.'

She offered a sympathetic frown. 'I'm sorry, Solly, I didn't mean to ask an awkward question.'

Tony unnecessarily attempted to rescue her. 'No; she saves those for cross-examining people like me.'

'Ah, you're a lawyer; the law is such a noble profession.'

He turned again to Tony. 'You are indeed fortunate.'

Tony smiled to the ceiling, encouraging the two of them to take discussions forward.

She began, 'Single diamonds look nice, though three diamonds look good, too. How much might they cost?'

'It depends on many factors, and not just the size of the stone. For two similar stones, half a carat could cost quite a lot more than point four of a carat; so many people ask simply for half a carat, there's a premium that goes with the higher demand. The same applies even more with one carat. Then there are the cuts to consider: Round, Cushion, perhaps for you it should be Princess or Heart.' He pulled out a long card from a drawer. 'Here are ten popular cuts. Perhaps it would be easier to show you what rings we have and you could look through them.' He turned to Tony. 'Together.'

Tony replied, 'Yes, that's probably best.'

'Come and sit over here.' He called over to the young woman who was standing near the door, where she was looking outside and pretending not to listen. 'Rachel, we need trays G1 and G2.'

She responded. '*Zaydeh*? [Grandfather?] Are you sure you don't mean F1 and F2?'

'No, no, G1 and G2.' Looking up at Susan, he muttered, 'My granddaughter, she thinks I'm *meschigeh*.' [foolish.]

'But they're…'

'I can give *a metsiah* [a bargain] if I wish, can't I?'

'You're not trying to *schmier ehm* [bribe him] are you?'

'*Schah*! *Redt nischt azoy viel*.' [Shush! Don't talk so much.]

Susan examined the rings on the two trays, turning

over the hidden prices. She looked up at Tony and whispered, 'Perhaps we should go halves on the ring.'

He shook his head. 'You bought the last round, so this is my shout.'

Aware both pairs appeared to be masking their conversations by using foreign words or speaking in code, she explained his joke to Solly. 'He's saying we should take it in turns to pay. I bought yesterday's evening meal at the pub, so he buys the ring.'

Solly gave Tony a genial smile.

Susan finally put the problem into words. 'These are very nice, Solly, but they're outside the price range.'

He tipped his head and held out an upturned hand. 'I said yesterday there's a discount for members of the police force; it should bring them just within range.'

Tony spoke up. 'I can't take a discount; it would be unethical, unprofessional.'

'Nonsense, my boy. Everyone gets a discount, unless they want to show off they come from the real *hoicher fenster*.' [high window, meaning wealthy family.]

'Well, if everyone gets one, that makes it OK.'

She tried on one ring after another, feeling special to be the centre of attention. For a third time, she picked up an eighteen carat gold single-stone round-cut diamond ring that fitted her finger perfectly; checking the price tag again, 1,395 pounds, she reluctantly placed it back into its slot. Picking up a similar ring with a smaller diamond, and a price tag 250 pounds less, she held it up to Solly. 'Does this come close to a thousand pounds, after discount?'

Solly examined the ring minutely, using his loupe for effect. 'The setting on this one is not quite right for you.' He took out the earlier ring. 'This one suits you much better. And after discount it comes to exactly one thousand pounds.'

She looked up at him. 'That is ever so generous of you, Solly.' Suddenly, her smile dissolved in tears.

Tony put his arm around her shoulder. 'Don't worry about her, Solly; her emotions have been all over the place this weekend.'

Once the ring was again on Susan's finger, she insisted it stay there. Tony completed the formalities with Solly: payment made by debit card, receipt and certification forms written and signed. As they left the shop, they exchanged warm goodbyes.

When they were out of earshot, Rachel turned to her grandfather. With a stern face and her hands held forward, palms upward, she asked accusingly, '*Farvoss, zaydeh, farvoss?*' [Why, Grandpa, why?]

'*Azoy, Rucchelle, azoy.*' [Because, Rachel, because.] '*Seht ois wie dein bubbe hot ojsgesehen ven zi iz g'ven jing.*' [She reminds me of your grandmother when she was young.] '*Un mir machen a bissel gelt oichet, sorg dich nischt mein bubbelle.*' [And we still made a little money, so don't worry my dear.]

'*Yeh, a bissel mer vi gornischt!*' [Yes, a little more than nothing!] She smiled warmly at him so that he would be certain her apparent annoyance was only a pretence. '*Di bist nischt azoy gitt in gescheften meer zaydeh. Eftsher zol ich sichen a mojschiv zikainim far dir?*' [You're losing your touch at selling, grandfather. Maybe I should look for a care home for you?]

CHAPTER 37

Tony smiled at Susan when she took hold of his right hand. He stretched his index finger and just reached the diamond. Suddenly, he let go and stared closely at his finger end. 'Damn! A glass splinter.' She laughed unrestrainedly.

He beamed at her, pleased his joke had gone down so well. 'Let's just have a wander around, shall we? Maybe call in at some of the classier jewellers; they're more likely to have had dealings with Lisa Wye. It'll have to be formal; it isn't as though we can claim to be looking for an engagement ring anymore.'

As they meandered, gazing in windows, Susan frequently held up her hand to look at the ring, each time surprised to see it there on her finger.

Tony's mobile rang. The caller's number was unknown to him, though he recognised the area code for Birmingham. 'Detective Constable Beresford.'

'Hello, I'm David Cohen at Anne Chor jewellers. You telephoned on Friday to say you'd be calling in to see us sometime this weekend. Something to do with Lisa Wye.'

Tony felt uncomfortable, unsure how to handle the call; after all, they had visited the shop, but he had not identified himself to them. 'Do you have some information about her?'

'Yes; she was here thirty minutes ago. I told her you were looking for her and gave her your number. She said she'll be in touch with you tomorrow; you didn't say it was urgent, so I assume that's alright.'

He sighed; this was not an outcome he had anticipated when they had performed their little charade. 'Do you know where she went?'

'My wife spoke to her, but she's busy right now. Are you in the neighbourhood?'

He saw no good reason to lie, beyond some possible embarrassment. 'Yes; I'm close by.'

'Well, maybe it would be best if you called in and spoke to Sarah yourself; she might be able to give you some more information.'

'Right. We'll be there in five minutes.'

Susan looked up at him enquiringly. 'Where are we going?'

'Anne Chor jewellers. Lisa Wye was there just half an hour ago. Bugger it!'

'Tony, just because we're engaged, that doesn't give you the right to use bad language with me.'

'But you used the word when...'

She cut him short. 'Stop! Stop right there! You don't seem to understand the rules. Whatever conversation we had, you do not have permission to make any reference to it without my specific approval. Clear?'

'Yes, clear. I'm sorry. It's just that ...'

Again she interrupted. 'When you've put all traces of that earlier conversation into the deepest recesses of your mind, you can start again. And no swearing.'

The lack of a smile told him she was in deadly earnest. 'It was Sarah Cohen's husband, David. I said we'd call in straight away and speak to them.'

'Right. And start with formal introductions.'

As they entered the shop, Sarah noticed them straight away and gave them a welcoming smile.

'You've had a think, have you, about what sort of …'
As she was about to say "engagement ring", she
glanced down and noticed the ring on Susan's finger.
'Is that an engagement ring you're wearing?'

'Yes; I'm sorry.'

'Don't be; getting engaged should never be
something to be sorry about.' She smiled warmly at her.

'It all happened so quickly.'

'Let me look then; you'll have to get used to
showing your ring off to everyone.' Susan held up her
hand, and Sarah examined the ring with an expert eye.
'It's very nice; I hope you didn't pay over the odds for
it. May I ask how much?'

'Would you like to guess, first?'

'I'd have to know the exact size of the stone, but I'd
say about fifteen hundred.'

'We got it for a thousand.'

'Really? That's what you might call a fire-sale price.
So, what can I help you with?'

Tony interrupted. 'I'm sorry, we're doing it again. I
was meant to introduce us. I'm Detective Constable
Tony Beresford, and this is Susan.'

'Ah, looking for Lisa Wye. So, are you really
engaged, or is this all an act?'

Susan responded for them. 'We're really engaged, as
of this morning.'

Sarah turned to Tony, applying the rules of etiquette.
'Congratulations, Tony.' She paused long enough to
separate two incongruous statements. 'And now tell me
why you didn't introduce yourself yesterday.'

'I didn't mean to deceive you; not really. Let's just
say I wanted to experiment; I'm still quite new to police
work. I do apologise if I've caused you any offence.'

'You said that like you meant it, so no offence taken. But I'll offer you a word of advice, if I may.'

He sensed his acceptance would reduce the likelihood of an official complaint being raised. 'Please do; I need all the advice I can get.'

'I've had professional dealings with quite a number of police officers, and you're not in the same mould as any of them. You're too open and honest, admitting it was an experiment and that you're a novice, and now you've said you need advice. Are you usually like this? Or is it getting engaged that's affected you?'

'If I say I'm usually like this, that would be committing the same offence again; so I'll say it's down to getting engaged, which implies it'll never happen in the future.'

'You sound like you're a quick learner. So, you're looking for Lisa Wye. Well, let me advise you again: whatever you think she's done, forget it, because I'm sure she hasn't.'

'I'm not saying she's done anything; I'm just needing her help with an inquiry. I keep trying her number but I'm getting no response.'

'I can explain that. When she goes to see her family in Antwerp, she switches her UK sim card for a Belgian one; I don't know exactly why, but she says it's more convenient. It's probably something to do with call charges; she's clever about things like that. But she left her UK card in Antwerp; so, not quite so clever, there. Anyway, it's being posted back to her.'

'It sounds like you know her very well.'

'Certainly; we're old friends. Well, not so old; she's just thirty. I used to be a bit older than her, but not now I'm going in reverse.'

Tony gave a very generous show of appreciation of her humour, still a little anxious about possible consequences of the earlier deception. Eventually, he asked, 'You wouldn't happen to know where she might be right now, would you?'

She checked his face for any sign of mendacity. 'If she hasn't done anything, why are you so anxious to talk to her?'

'I'd just like to return home having achieved something.'

Susan spoke to him sharply. 'I agreed to marry you; isn't that an achievement?'

Sarah exchanged smiles surreptitiously with Susan before turning back to Tony. 'She has a point. If you'd like some more advice, I'd say go out and enjoy yourselves. You can rely on Lisa to contact you in the morning.'

Susan added, 'Yes, you should be taking me somewhere nice, in celebration of your immense good fortune.' Tony accepted the suggestion, convinced resistance would be futile.

CHAPTER 38

As Priestley walked briskly into the incident room right on time, he discovered Berry was several paces behind him, rushing to avoid being late for the 8:30 meeting. Priestley reached the front and turned sharply. 'Not like you to be late, Tony. Well, the last shall be first, et cetera. Let's have your report on the weekend. Have you made contact with Lisa Wye?'

'Not yet; I was just making a final check before I came in here. I'm optimistic I'll hear from her soon.'

'So, nothing actually achieved from your jaunt to Birmingham.'

'I wouldn't say that, sir.'

'Well, tell us what have you achieved.'

His cheeks started to glow as he blurted out, 'I got engaged.'

There was a stunned silence as heads swivelled to face him. Priestley spoke first. 'Congratulations, Tony. This is unexpected news; very welcome, but unexpected.' There followed a torrent of hearty felicitations as everyone now vied to be heard, in overcompensation for their initial reactions.

'Thank you. Some of you know Susan; she's a wonderful girl. We haven't set a date yet.'

'Right, well, we'll have a chat about it later. For now, we need to get on with the investigation.' He directed his gaze to the centre of the room. 'I've read all the reports up to Friday evening. Has anyone had anything significant since then?' He jerked his head to the side. 'Tony, you don't have to answer that.'

The room erupted into a variety of hoots and whoops; Priestley held up a hand to quieten them. 'Frank's in charge of house-to-house enquiries; if we don't get a lead elsewhere, odd sightings may be all we have to work on, so look out for anything the least bit unusual. The rest of you should know what you're doing today; if you don't, ask Neil. If there's nothing else to report,' he quickly scanned the room, 'let's get going.' He turned to Berry. 'Come to my office, young man, and you can tell me all about it.'

Berry followed Priestley to his office, accepting the invitation to take a chair off the stack; he felt apprehensive as he waited for the questions to begin.

'Well, Tony, you took everyone by surprise. So, you're getting married. Not a shotgun wedding, is it?'

'I knew to expect that sort of question, but really, we have a special relationship that goes beyond the physical. Our love has a purity that...'

'Hang on, Tony. You're starting to sound like a women's magazine. I don't wish to know the details of what you've been up to, or haven't; I just want to know how things are with you. I get the impression you're deeply, madly, et cetera. So, if you'd like a chat sometime, it's up to you.'

'Thanks, Marcus. What Susan and I have isn't something I want to talk about casually; it's too special for that.'

'Alright, understood. So, tell me about your investigation in Birmingham.'

'Well, one of the jewellers I contacted turned out to be a friend of Lisa Wye. She explained the problem about Wye's mobile phone not working: the sim card was left behind in Antwerp. It's been posted to her, so she should be contactable on her old number fairly soon. The jeweller told her I'm trying to contact her, and has given her my details, so I think there's a good chance she'll be in touch this morning.'

'Right. If and when she does make contact, let's you and me interview her straight away; I'll keep my morning free of appointments. If there's no contact by midday, you'll need to revisit her home and studio, and try to track her down. Now, anything else I need to be aware of?'

'Not really. I've put some detail into my report, but it doesn't amount to much in the end.'

'Alright then, off you go. And congratulations, again; though try to keep your mind focused on your work, won't you?'

'I'll do my best, but it's a very strange feeling, being engaged.' Berry put on his serious, professional face as he left the office, but found a smile kept breaking out.

Witty intercepted him in the MIR. 'Congratulations, Tony. You're a dark horse, aren't you?'

'I don't know what you mean; you knew about me and Susan. If I remember rightly, you were the one who brought us together; I can't thank you enough for that.'

'Well, I have to say, I didn't really expect it'd lead to this. When do you think you'll be getting hitched?'

'I don't know; Susan hasn't decided, yet.'

'Susan hasn't decided? So she'll be the one wearing the trousers in your house, will she?'

'Well, it's the same in yours, isn't it?'

'No, it isn't! Lily only wears elegant dresses.'

He laughed appreciatively. 'Seeing as you started it off, would you be my Best Man when the time comes?'

Neil smiled warmly. 'I'd be absolutely delighted.'

Lin walked over to chat with Tony. 'Well, who'd have thought it: you went away single and came back engaged. What happened?'

'We were just talking and then suddenly we realised we were made for each other, so I asked her and she accepted. When you're sure you're in love with someone, you just have to make your move.'

She found herself wishing it were that simple. 'Well, when you come down from cloud nine, there's a message on your desk; Lisa Wye's been in touch.'

He went and read the message. 'Lisa Wye's mobile phone is now on and she's waiting to hear from you.'

Before he could make the telephone call, PC Brandon Bullock came over, rested a hand on his desk and leaned in close to him. 'Good on yer, Tone. Have you been shagging her all weekend?'

Tony repeatedly shook his head slightly from side to side. 'Our relationship is above such things.'

Brandon offered a sympathetic look. 'Not getting any yet, then. Well, it's like buying a new car; you need to give it a trial run before you can be sure it's the right make and model for you.'

Tony felt intensely annoyed that his pure relationship was being brought down to this level of conversation; nevertheless he tried to take it with good humour. 'Thank you for those words of wisdom, Brandon; who says you lack sense and sensitivity!'

'Always glad to give a bit of advice where it's needed; if you'd like some on practical stuff, just ask.'

'Thanks, Brandon, but I'm sure we have enough expertise on that front.'

'Don't tell me; you read all about it in a book.

Anyway, congratulations, mate.'

'Thank you.' He picked up his telephone and began to dial. 'I've an urgent call to make.'

Lisa Wye answered immediately. 'This is Detective Constable Tony Beresford at Midshaw Police Station. I'm investigating the death of Milo Piscaro, and your name has come up in the course of our inquiries. Detective Chief Inspector Priestley would like to interview you as soon as possible. When could you come over here?'

'Well, if it's urgent, right away. Does it have to be at the station, or could you come to me? I'm at my studio, and I'm working to a deadline.'

'We'll come straight over.'

In the car, Priestley asked Berry what plans he had for organising an engagement party.

'I hadn't thought about it.'

'Well, everyone at the station will be expecting something; Friday evening in the pub, at the very least. Considering your reputation for planning in meticulous detail, you don't seem to be making much of a job of this engagement lark. And you know it'll cost you, don't you? How are you fixed for readies?'

'I'm flush at the moment; Susan wouldn't let me spend as much on the engagement ring as I'd intended.'

'I hope you haven't come over as tight, Tony; women can say one thing and mean another.'

'No; she decided the maximum I should spend, and the jeweller gave us a big discount to match the limit.

Priestley looked troubled. 'Why did he give you a discount? You need to be very careful about accepting discounts. Did he say it's because you're in the police? Are we going to have a problem? Is he expecting something in return? You can't be too careful; what you think is a discount can look like a bribe to someone else. What size of discount are we talking about?'

'Thirteen ninety-five down to a grand.'

'That's a hell of a lot; you've got me worried, now, Tony. We'd better put the details on your personnel file, so it's all above board. Why do you think you received such a big discount?'

'It was just an old guy who took a shine to Susan. I'm sure there'll be no comeback.'

'I knew a senior officer in the military, stationed abroad, who was buying artefacts at bargain prices; he thought he was simply being astute. What he didn't realise was they were being fed to him so that the local criminal fraternity could build up a dossier on him. It was only when they asked a favour and listed all their so-called bribes that he understood what had been happening. He told his superior, and it was investigated officially. They decided he'd been naïve, but was innocent of any wrongdoing. End result was, his tour was terminated; but it could have been much worse if he'd tried to cover it up. So, all I'll say to you is, if you're offered a gift horse, do look it in the mouth and check its teeth, because it might come back to bite you.'

They travelled in silence for the remainder of the short journey; while Priestley recalled his military days, Berry thought through the encounter with the jeweller and concluded everything was fine.

CHAPTER 39

Berry parked close to Green Lane Studios. The receptionist escorted them to Lisa Wye's studio, but then blocked their way and wagged her finger at Priestley. 'You remember what I said last time? No wandering around on your own.'

He answered with apparent sincerity. 'No, ma'am.'

'And you come back to reception when you're finished here.'

'Yes, ma'am.'

She knocked at the door and it was quickly opened by a tall, powerfully-built woman. Priestley stole a glance at the Amazon; her skin was golden-brown and her chestnut hair shone in cascades of ringlets to below her shoulders. 'Lisa, it's the police. When you're finished with them, make sure they come back to me.'

'I'll take good care of them, Margaret.'

Following introductions, Priestley began. 'I have to give you some news that may trouble you.' He looked closely at her face, ready to gauge her reaction. 'The evidence is pointing us in the direction of Milo Piscaro having been unlawfully killed.'

Lisa's eyes widened. 'You mean he was murdered?'

'The law recognises a number of different criminal offences relating to homicide; we'll only know the exact offence when we have a full understanding of precisely what happened.'

'But not suicide?'

'No, Miss Wye, not suicide.' He waited for any

further comment, but none was forthcoming. 'I have to ask you, where were you around the time of his death?'

'I came home early in the evening and I stayed there 'til morning.'

'Was anyone with you at any time?'

'No, I was on my own.'

'Did you make any phone calls?'

She considered the question at length. 'I don't recall making or receiving any calls, but can't you check that for yourself?'

Berry looked down to avoid eye contact, knowing they had already checked and found no activity.

Priestley continued. 'We have a landline and one mobile number for you. Do you have any others?'

'No, just the two.'

'I understood you use a different mobile number in Belgium.'

'That's correct, but I wouldn't use it in the UK.'

'May we have that number?'

'Yes, of course.' She read out the series of numbers and Berry noted them down.

Priestley glanced around the studio. 'Before we talk about what you knew of the deceased, would you like to give us an idea of what you do here? I can see a lot of equipment; is jewellery-making quite complicated? I'd always imagined someone using hand-tools, sitting at a bench.'

'There are so many techniques, what equipment to use depends on exactly what's being made. If someone was using an engraving tool, say, to put grooves in silver, then they'd sit at a bench just as you imagined.' She pointed to a small, sturdy piece of wood attached to the nearest bench; he noticed it had several V-shaped indentations. 'This is called a bench peg; I can sit at this stool and use it to hold a piece of jewellery in place while I work on it.' She pointed to a tool that was held tightly in a vice. 'That black moulded device is a Delrin anticlastic stake. I have a set of them; they're designed to enable me to shape flat metal into very precise curves.'

'It looks like stretched-out antlers from a very small moose. You hammer the metal onto the stake to create the same shape?'

'Essentially that's right, though not a metal hammer; that would damage the finish. I use a Delrin mallet.' She pointed to a dozen mallets of various sizes. 'I choose the one with the appropriate weight, depending on what I'm doing.'

He scanned the room. 'You have a lot of benches.'

'When I give classes my students each need their own bench. I've attached different sizes and types of vice to each one; when I'm working on my own, I just go to any bench that has the right vice for the job.'

He looked at the various electrical devices, including saws and drills, and what he thought was a high-powered microscope. Spotting a tall green gas canister, he asked, 'What would that be used for?'

'It's argon gas for arc-welding.'

He homed in on the items of direct interest to him. 'You've a lot of chemicals as well.'

'Yes. There's nitric acid for etching copper. I combine it with hydrochloric acid to make aqua regia for etching gold. I'm trying to go green, so I'm testing out a pickle that's less damaging to the environment; that's why the place smells like a fish-and-chip shop.'

Priestley made a show of sniffing the air. 'Vinegar?'

'That's the acetic acid.'

'Do you have any particularly dangerous chemicals?'

'Even more dangerous than the concentrated acids?'

'Well, what about cyanide, for example?'

'Yes, I sometimes use a cyanide bath.' Recognising his lack of comprehension, she elaborated. 'It's for gold plating: I sometimes plate silver with gold. I don't use it for plating copper with silver; I only use sterling silver. Actually, I use Argentium silver; it contains germanium to stop it tarnishing.'

'Do you have any chloroform?'

'A small amount; it's good for welding acrylics.' She saw his uncertainty again. 'Gluing pieces of plastic together.'

He tried not to look too interested as he asked the key question. 'Do you have any ether?'

'It isn't something I use.' Seeing no reaction, she fetched a clear plastic container from under a bench in a corner of the room. 'The nearest I have is five litres of butanone. Well, a bit less; some of it's gone. I use it when I'm micro-welding.' She checked Priestley's face for comprehension. 'That's soldering.'

He read the chemical's name. 'Methyl ethyl ketone.'

'Yes; some people call it MEK.' As she put the container back under the bench, Priestley gave Berry a surreptitious shake of the head, indicating it was not the same chemical as had caused Milo's death.

Priestley smiled at her as she stepped back to him. 'Have you *ever* used ether?'

'Only when I was at the Royal Academy in Antwerp. I did some wet gilding using ether and gold chloride. But not since then.'

He glanced around again. 'It's all very interesting; I've never been inside a studio like this before.' Continuing to engage with her eyes, he cleared the smile from his face. 'But now we have to talk about the reason for our visit: the circumstances surrounding Milo's death.'

She frowned. 'Are you allowed to tell me exactly what happened to him?'

He appeared to concentrate hard for a few seconds. 'You were a very close friend of his, weren't you?

'Yes, I think it's fair to say that.'

'Then you have a right to know. He was found with a plastic bag over his head, and inside was a cloth soaked in an anaesthetic that's fatal in high doses.'

She looked at him suspiciously. 'And the chemical was...?'

'Diethyl ether.'

'Which is why you were interested in what chemicals I have here. You could have just asked me. Or am I a suspect?'

'We don't have any clear suspects at the moment.'

'So everyone's a suspect, including me.'

'I'd rather see you as someone who's helping us with our enquiries. May I ask you some personal questions?'

'Yes, go right ahead; ask whatever you like. Perhaps we should go somewhere and sit down; there's an area near the kitchen that has some comfy chairs.'

CHAPTER 40

Priestley and Berry sat in easy chairs while Lisa brewed fresh coffee in the adjacent small kitchen. She brought out three mugs, sat herself in a chair, and began speaking immediately. 'You're wishing to know the details of my relationship with Milo, but I have to say it wasn't anywhere near as close as you might imagine.'

Priestley had not expected her to take the lead, but was more than happy to let her do so. People with something to hide would often prepare carefully crafted responses to questions; in contrast, words that simply flowed out were generally less premeditated. To make it clear he was not about to speak, he picked up his mug and held it to his lips, though it was too hot to drink.

'I'll begin at the beginning, so that you can see how things developed. I wished to be a watercolourist, so I came to England, where the humidity is ideal. Do you know about the use of watercolours?'

'Only what I can see in a finished painting.'

'And you never wondered why people generally don't go to the South of France to do watercolours?'

'It wasn't a question I ever asked myself.'

'Then you'll have to take my word for it.' She waited for his nod of acceptance. 'I was rebelling against my father's invitation for me to go into the diamond trade. He runs a small company in Antwerp, and he wanted one of his four children to inherit his position. I have three brothers, but he said he wanted the most ballsy of us all, which was me. When I refused, he had to make do with my eldest brother.'

She took a sip of coffee. 'I struck a deal with my father for him to pay for my education. I had to go to the Royal Academy in Antwerp to study silversmithing and jewellery-making, before I could come to England to take a Fine Arts degree.' She smiled and shook her head at the recollection. 'You wouldn't believe the stupid things some of the students were doing at the college, like painting a canvas in just one colour and leaving a small white rectangle; I mean, come on, what's the point of that? There's a lot of pretentious rubbish in art colleges, you know.

'Anyway, I spent my time there learning how to draw accurately, and how to paint using pastels, acrylics, oils, and especially watercolours. When I moved to Shawton, I rented a small studio and set myself up as a watercolourist. That was when I changed my name. Have you any idea how juvenile some of the people are around here? "I'd like a Lisa de Cock." And then they'd laugh themselves silly. So I took my new surname from the nearby river.

'After that, I came here and rented a bigger studio. Back then, I was mostly doing watercolours, plus some life drawing and a bit of jewellery making. In fact, my male nudes earned me more than my watercolours; the pink pound was rising, you might say. Not that making money or not making money mattered too much to me: my father was bankrolling me. But I wished to make my own way in the world, so I decided to put more time into my jewellery business, because that was more profitable than the painting side.'

Priestley put down his coffee mug. 'Back when you were mostly painting, is that when you met Milo?'

She nodded. 'I'd exchanged a few words with Milo, but I didn't really know him; he was so quiet. And then one time my life model didn't arrive, so I knocked on his door and said, "Milo, I need a model. Are you up for it?" He was petrified; actually, up until then, he used to look terrified every time I spoke to him, to be honest. Well, he finally managed to nod "yes", so I told him to come into my studio sharpish and get his kit off. When he was ready, I told him how he was to stand. After a short while, he committed the sin that male models get sacked for; but then, he was only an amateur.'

Berry asked into the lull, 'Ahem, I'm taking notes, but I don't understand what the sin was; would you mind explaining?'

She looked at him. 'Yes, of course. He got a great big erection.' His face coloured bright crimson. She turned to Priestley. 'Look, Chief Inspector, if I'm going to give you the lowdown, I think it would be better if you and I talked together, alone. Yes?'

'Yes, of course.'

She spoke to Berry. 'I ought to take you to reception, but do you think you can man up and face Margaret on your own?'

Berry nodded, scurrying through the door like a frightened rabbit. She continued as soon as the door closed behind him. 'Milo was so embarrassed, I felt sorry for him. He tried to cover up, but it was too late for that. So I said to him, "You look pretty desperate there, Milo. Shall we forget the life drawing and go back to my flat for sex?" I remember he blinked a few times, and finally said, "Yes please." I mean, honestly, who says "Yes please"? Anyway, I took him back for sex, and I thought that was that. But he seemed to think it was a big deal, so I let it run for a while.'

As Lisa had paused, Priestley asked, 'Let it run? You mean, you became a couple?'

'I suppose you could describe it that way. We never lived together, but we did share a large studio for painting. It worked out well enough, as I like to paint in silence, and he liked to be quiet. We had sex quite a lot over those months; I think he was making up for lost time. He wanted to do the romance thing as well. It was all a bit of a novelty for me; up until then I'd always treated men simply as functional objects.'

'Functional objects?'

'Yes. Whenever I wanted sex, I'd just ask someone. If I enjoyed it enough, I'd consider asking them again, but there was never anything more to it than that.'

'What if there wasn't anyone available?'

She combined a smile and a frown. 'That was never a problem; no one has ever turned me down.'

'No one?'

'No one. Why? Are you thinking of becoming the first?'

'Well, you haven't actually asked me.'

'OK. Would you like to have sex with me? Mutual satisfaction guaranteed.'

He tried to appear calm as his heart began to pound. 'I'm not allowed to enter into a relationship with a suspect; it would be unprofessional.'

'Well, get in touch once I'm off the suspects list. I'd quite like to examine your rippling muscles; I can imagine what you'd be like with your kit off.'

'I'm going to have to disappoint you, Miss Wye. For now, because you knew the deceased intimately and don't have an alibi for around the time of his death; and in the future, because I'm a happily married man with no intention of straying. We'll leave the interview there; I'll find my own way out.'

'Well, if you change your mind, the offer's firmly on the table.'

Priestley reached reception and found Berry sitting close by. Margaret looked up as he arrived. 'Still walking around on your own, I see. I might not let you into the building, next time.'

Priestley snarled at her. 'And I might charge you with obstruction. Now, hit the door release before I grab the handle, otherwise I'll arrest you for false imprisonment.' Hearing the instant click of the release mechanism, he yanked the door open forcefully and stepped outside. As they headed for the car, Berry had to break into a trot to keep up with his extended strides.

CHAPTER 41

In the car on the way back to the station, Priestley looked out of the side window, determined to maintain silence. Berry finally asked, 'Did I miss anything?'

'Not to speak of.'

'Will you be writing up the interview?'

'You can do that up to the point you left us.'

'And what about after that?'

'There was nothing of any significance.'

'But what about her relationship with Milo?'

'They had a lot of sex.'

Berry decided he had to press for a proper answer. 'If you don't want to tell me about it because it's all to do with sex, I'm sure I won't be too shocked; or are you afraid you'll corrupt me?'

'Look, they had a relationship, but she didn't take it that seriously.'

'It was all a bit of a laugh for her, then?'

'Not a laugh, as such.'

'Well, what was it then? I've never known you to keep details from me before. Were the two of you just having a laugh yourselves?'

'What are you suggesting, Tony?'

'Oh, no, I didn't mean that; of course not. Well, were you having a proper laugh with her about something and you don't want me to know?'

'No, Tony, we didn't have a laugh about anything; this is an inquiry into the death of her former partner, so having a laugh would be entirely inappropriate.'

'But you do sometimes have a laugh with people in interviews. How do you decide when it's OK?'

Priestley looked through the front window so that Berry would not be tempted to make eye contact with him; he preferred drivers to keep their eyes fixed firmly on the road. 'If it's, say, a murder inquiry, or it involves the death of a child, then you never, ever, joke with family or close friends, unless they make it completely clear they're wishing to behave as though everything is normal; and even then, you never make jokes that are anything to do with the actual death itself.

'But, and it's a big but, the guilty may disclose information accidentally if they're feeling relaxed, such as when they're having a laugh. So, sometimes, you have to weigh up the pulls in the two directions. What I would say to you is, if in doubt, remain serious.'

'I've known Neil make jokes with both witnesses and suspects; would you say he understands just when to be serious and when not?'

'He's your sergeant, so it wouldn't do for me to express an opinion to you. I will just say that, in the past, he may have made jokes because he thought of something funny, and may not always have considered how appropriate they were.'

After giving Berry a minute to absorb the advice, Priestley began again. 'Joking with colleagues is different to joking with suspects or a victim's friends or family members. Your peers ought to accept a bit of humour so long as it isn't offensive, but I've come across a number of cases where an ambitious female has complained about a male colleague of the same rank, alleging inappropriate behaviour, as a way of doing him down. It can be a bitch-eat-dog world.'

Berry remained silent until he had manoeuvred around a parked lorry. 'If there's inappropriate behaviour by a civilian directed at a police officer, we do sometimes take action on that, don't we?'

'Providing there are witnesses, or it's recorded.'

'It's quite difficult for me to put together a single set of rules and procedures to follow so that I know when to be serious and when I can be more relaxed. I suppose it's something that only comes with experience.'

'One way to develop is by thinking through various scenarios. Then, when you're in a situation that's close to one you've thought through before, you'll have a better idea of how to react to anything that happens.'

'Have you ever found yourself in a completely new situation you hadn't thought through in advance?'

Priestley considered what he might disclose and what should remain hidden. 'For the sake of your education, hypothetically, what would you do if a gorgeous suspect invited you to have sex with her?'

Berry responded immediately. 'I'd say no; Susan's the only girl in my life.'

'In that case, you can interview Lisa Wye next time.'

A grin spread slowly across Berry's face. 'So that's why you won't be writing up the interview. You did say no, didn't you?'

Priestley turned and bellowed into the side of his face. 'Of course I said no; what do you take me for?' He reduced the volume close to normal. 'I can't imagine ever saying yes; I'm far too happily married to have any wish to go playing away.' His voice became more subdued. 'As it is, I'm wondering if Miss Wye has something to hide, and she was just trying to get close to me to find out how the inquiry's progressing.'

They continued in silence for a few minutes. As they approached the station, Berry asked, 'Is Lisa Wye now top of the suspects list?'

Priestley considered the question at length before responding. 'We're struggling to find any genuine suspects at this stage, so she's certainly on the list. But I think she may simply have an uninhibited attitude to sex, so I don't believe her offer in any way implies her guilt. All the other indicators point to her innocence. We just need to keep an open mind.'

He glanced at Priestley for a moment. 'Were you serious about me interviewing her next time?'

'Maybe not. I think Neil would be the best choice; he only has eyes for Lily, and he's more experienced.'

Berry parked the car. Priestley stepped out and waited for him by the entrance. 'I'll put Neil in the picture about Miss Wye, but I'm not going to document her offer; if I did, I could imagine half the station wasting time trying to find a reason to interview her.'

Inside the main office, Priestley spoke briefly to Witty. 'Give me five minutes and then come and see me; you can update me on progress and I'll put you in the picture about an interview I've just had.'

Seated in his office reading through a file, Priestley recognised Witty's rat-tatta-tat-tat. After calling out 'Come in,' he realised Plummer was following him.

Witty read the uncertainty on Priestley's face. 'You told me to keep Lin fully involved; I assumed you'd want her in this meeting.'

Priestley recognised he could not ask her to leave without her feeling side-lined. 'Of course, Neil. Lin, would you like to brief me on the state of play, to prove you're up-to-date with everything?'

'Yes, of course, Marcus; not that there's much to report. We're extending the CCTV search to include any activity within a mile of the locus, but all that will prove is which vehicles came into or left the general area. No one's optimistic it'll produce a good lead.

'Frank's coordinating the house-to-house. He's defined an expanding radius in terms of streets and houses; he's actually quite good when it comes to that sort of organisation.'

'That's great, Lin; I do love the way you find the positive in people.' He tried not to show he had accidentally allowed the word "love" to replace the "like" that was common parlance, and realised he had unintentionally given it extra emphasis.

Plummer also pondered on the word-choice, causing a hiatus in the dialogue. Witty broke the silence. 'You said you'd put us in the picture about the interview.'

Priestley looked for a way out that would not make it appear he was excluding Plummer. Finding none, he put on his most unemotional visage. 'Tony will be writing up the interview to the point that he left at Miss Wye's request; she suggested she would be more forthcoming if she spoke to me alone. Miss Wye then explained to me she had been in a sexual relationship with the deceased.'

'Not exactly a surprise. Was it a big thing for them?'

'My impression is that it was much more important for the deceased than for Miss Wye, who appears to have a fairly casual approach to relationships.'

'That sounds intriguing; come on, tell us what she actually said. Was she having another relationship at the same time? If we follow that line of inquiry it could lead us to a suspect, or several. What happened next?'

'I cut short the interview.' They looked at Priestley with surprise. 'I felt it would be better if the interview were reconvened with two people present.' They continued to stare. 'Look, something happened that derailed the interview, alright?' Witty and Plummer both recognised silence remained the technique most likely to yield results. 'Basically, she invited me to have sex with her.'

Plummer asked, sharply, 'You didn't, did you, Marcus? You'd better not have!'

Priestley was taken aback by her vehemence. 'No, Lin, of course I didn't. Anyway, she wasn't meaning there and then. And I am a DCI, you know, so I do know not to do anything as unprofessional as that.'

Plummer realised her face had reddened. She was still struggling to regain control of her voice when she suggested, 'Perhaps a woman should pick up where you left off; or does she swing both ways?'

He responded to Plummer while gesturing to Witty with an open hand. 'Actually, I believe Neil is above such temptations, so I think he should interview her with Tony.'

Lin snapped back. 'Why not with me?'

He gave her a fulsome smile. 'Because, Lin, I think you might be tempted to give her a telling-off, and that could make her less forthcoming with information.'

She smiled back. 'You could be right, Marcus.'

CHAPTER 42

Witty telephoned Lisa Wye. 'This is Detective Sergeant Neil Whittington; you spoke to my boss this morning, Detective Chief Inspector Priestley. He'd like you to come to Midshaw Police Station to give a statement; how soon could you make yourself available?'

She responded rapidly, 'Is it urgent? I'm just trying to finish off a piece of jewellery.'

He replied less hurriedly, 'Not exactly urgent, but we believe you may have information that would help with our inquiry. Could you come in this morning?'

'Would twelve o'clock be OK?'

'Yes, thank you. Come to the main entrance and make yourself known to someone at the front desk.'

At ten past twelve, Witty received a call from reception. 'There's a Lisa Wye asking for DCI Priestley, but he's not available. She said you phoned her earlier; are you expecting her?'

'Yes; Marcus passed her to me to interview.'

'That was very generous of him.'

He responded impassively. 'I'll be right there.'

Witty pressed the door-release button and walked into the reception area. 'Miss Wye?'

'Yes, Lisa Wye.'

'I'm Detective Sergeant Neil Whittington. Thank you for coming. I'd like to ask you some questions.'

'Isn't your man Marcus around? He interviewed me before.'

'I'm sorry, he's unavailable; he asked me to

interview you this time.' When he waved at the receptionist, she pressed the release button to let them through the security door. 'Just follow me, please.'

He led her to a door that displayed an acrylic sign: "PACE INTERVIEW ROOM 2 0.012". As he was following her through, he saw Berry turning the corner into the corridor, so poked his head out and called to him, 'We're in here.'

Berry rushed in, closed the door and stood to one side. Witty seated himself opposite her, refusing to be affected by her striking beauty. 'You're not under caution so this isn't a formal interview, but I'd like to record it for possible future reference. Is that OK?'

'Yes, of course.'

He pointed to a sign that read, "Please switch off mobile phones as they could interfere with the recording equipment." 'Could I ask you to switch off your phone, please.'

She took her phone from her handbag and held down a small button until the display faded. As she returned the phone to her bag, she commented to Witty, 'It must be very sensitive equipment.'

He nodded. 'I suppose so, though it's better not to have interruptions, anyway.'

The old-style "Press the Red Button" tape machine had recently been replaced with digital recording equipment that produced CDs and DVDs on demand. Witty deferred to Berry as the official "computer nerd". 'DC Beresford, would you like to do the honours?'

Berry walked across the room and seated himself in front of the black box. He touched the small screen and waited for a virtual keyboard to display on the lower half. Another touch, and a form appeared above it with white words on a black background. The software had prefilled Derbyshire Constabulary under "Force". He entered Witty's details under "Primary Officer": "Collar Number", "Rank" and "Surname". Then he added his own details under "Secondary Officer". He looked questioningly at Witty when he reached the choice of "Suspect", "Witness" or "Victim".

Witty resolved his dilemma by asking Lisa a question. 'We're just recording your name on the system as a witness; which surname would you prefer?'

'My real name is Lisa de Cock, so, if this is official, I suppose that's the one you should use, though I prefer "Lisa Wye" for anything else in this country.'

Berry clicked the "Witness" option and typed in her real name, then touched the virtual "Start" button. Witty introduced himself again, for the recording, and Berry followed suit. Witty then addressed Lisa. 'Would you mind stating your name, for the record.' After she had done so, he followed the traditional procedure of stating the date and time, even though the new recording equipment rendered it technically unnecessary.

At Witty's invitation, Berry reiterated the information from the earlier interview, stopping just short of the point that he had left Priestley alone with Lisa. Witty then took over. 'Now, if I understand correctly, Mr Piscaro displayed what might be called an unprofessional response to the situation of being your life drawing model. Would you like to continue from there?'

She hesitated. 'Am I supposed to phrase everything delicately like you just did?'

'I was only trying to avoid putting words into your mouth, Miss Wye. If you'd like to speak plainly, I'm sure that would be best for our understanding.'

'OK. Milo got an erection that just about lifted him off his feet; then he tried to cover it up with a piece of cloth. I was quite impressed with his tackle, so I suggested we go back to my place for sex. We were both pleased with the performance and I was toying with the idea of booking him again, when he came out with some very touching words. It seems he'd been in love with me for ages and hadn't dared say. He obviously wanted a relationship at an emotional level, rather than simply having occasional sex. That had never been my way before, so I thought I'd give it a try. It was quite nice, really, while it lasted. I think the biggest problem for him was that he struggled to make any money, so I usually had to pay if we did anything like eating out or going to the cinema. I made it absolutely clear it didn't matter that I was the one with the money, but I could see it troubled him.

'Then, last Christmas, he told me he had a plan to start making enough money to support us, or at least to pay his share, when we got married. I had to tell him I was never going to marry him. I mean, a bit of romance is one thing, but I'm really not the marrying kind. And Milo was a sweet guy, but if I ever did consider getting wed, it wouldn't be to someone like him. I'd want some big strong handsome bloke like your boss.'

Witty kept a straight face as he spoke into the machine. 'For the record, would you confirm that was a reference to DCI Marcus Priestley?'

'Yes. Why? Have you any more like him?'

'No, I don't suppose we have. Now, could I ask you, during the time you were in a relationship with Milo, were you seeing anyone else?'

'You've gone all polite again, haven't you? Anyway, the answer is "no". I was getting enough sex from Milo.'

'Was it at Christmas that you broke up with him?'

'The Friday before, at the Christmas party. I told him he'd had the wrong idea about me, and he should simply have enjoyed it while it lasted.'

'So, there wasn't anyone else at that time who came between you?'

'No; no one. In fact, I felt a bit bad about how upset he was when it finished between us, so I decided to give sex with men a bit of a rest after that.'

Witty repeated, 'With men? So, women, instead?'

'No, I'm not into women.'

'You chose to do without sex.'

'I chose machine over man; you know, sisters are doing it for themselves. Are you wanting more details? Though I don't see what it's got to do with you.'

'I don't wish to know any more details than you've already furnished, thank you Miss Wye. I was only trying to establish if there might be someone who could have seen Milo as a rival, his having been a recent lover.'

'Well, I'm sorry to disappoint you, but there really wasn't anyone. I've always been self-sufficient when I needed to be, so I felt no urge to go rushing to find another man. Though, having said that, man is superior to machine in one way. Like it says in the song, it ain't nothing like the real thing, baby.'

'Does this mean you're again on the lookout for a man, Miss Wye?'

'Not for the likes of you, Detective Sergeant.'

Witty froze for a moment. 'I'm sorry, I didn't mean

to imply a personal interest; I was just trying to establish if your position had changed.'

'Well, it hasn't.'

'Then let's go back to something you said earlier. Milo mentioned to you he had a plan to earn money; do you know what form it took?'

'Essentially, it was decorating people's houses, but with artworks applied directly onto walls; like Rex Whistler's murals at Plas Newydd on Anglesey, if you know it.' Witty shook his head. 'I told him to go for it, but not be too disappointed if he didn't get any takers. I mean, how many people would give that sort of commission, nowadays?'

'Do you know if his plan made any progress?'

'I bumped into him one time and asked how it was going; he simply said it was early days yet. Then, probably for want of something else to say, he mentioned he'd turned down a different money-making plan last year. Something to do with his dealer boosting the price of his paintings, but he wouldn't go along with it because it was immoral.'

'Immoral? Could it also have been illegal?'

'I really couldn't say, because he didn't explain anything more about it.'

'So, he had just the one plan.'

'I'm not even sure he was serious about that one. I think his original reason for wanting to earn money was all to do with me. Once I'd told him I wasn't an option, he might not have had a reason to go on.' She shook her head. 'I mean a reason to go on with the idea; I didn't mean suicide.' She looked intently at Witty. 'You're absolutely sure it wasn't suicide, aren't you?'

'The evidence points to someone else having been

involved.'

'Could it have been assisted suicide? Some friend helping him with the actual process?'

'We're keeping an open mind at this stage. Would you say he could have been suicidal at the time you broke up?'

'He was certainly very unhappy. It was as though I had become his *raison d'être*, so he suddenly had no reason to carry on. But he did carry on, so he must have been getting over it really, mustn't he?'

Witty recognised her voice had lost its confidence for a moment, taking on a pleading note as though seeking his assurance she had not been indirectly responsible for his death. 'It's often said that time heals all wounds. Did you gain the impression he became less unhappy over time?'

'I didn't really see much of him, though we did sometimes bump into each other at the studios. I thought he was back to being how he was before; that's to say, very quiet, very serene.'

'Did you see him on the day he died?'

'Yes.'

'What time?'

'Three, maybe three thirty.'

'Where?'

'In the kitchen.'

'What did he say to you?'

'Just hello.'

'You said?'

'Hello, Milo. How are you doing? I'm making a pot of coffee; would you like some? Something like that.'

'And he said?'

'Thanks.'

'And then?'

'I may have said something about I hoped he was OK, and if there was anything I could do for him sometime then he just had to ask.'

'What did you mean by "anything"?'

'Nothing in particular.'

'Sex?'

'Possibly.'

'Help with suicide?'

She looked closely at Witty. 'Is that what you think? Is that why you wanted to talk to me? You think I helped him kill himself?'

'Did you?'

'No! Certainly not!'

Witty remained silent, waiting for anything further she might offer. She pressed her lips together tightly, a clear indication she had nothing more to say. Witty finally accepted he would have to be the next to speak. 'Well, thank you, Miss Wye; you've been very helpful. If you think of anything else that might assist our investigation, do please let me know straight away.' Turning to face the recording equipment as though it were a human being, he concluded the interview and informed the machine of the date and time, before inviting Berry to switch it off.

CHAPTER 43

Priestley was Managing By Wandering About when he spotted Witty. 'How did the interview go?'

'OK, but no breakthrough.'

'Bring Lin and Tony to my office for a brainstorming session, will you; we need to think about where we go from here.'

In his office, Priestley removed four chairs from the stack and arranged them close together in an inward facing box, leaving a narrow entry point to the inner square; this was to support the concept that in brainstorming sessions all participants are equal, thereby facilitating the liberation of ideas from lower ranks. The other three joined Priestley, and they sat together with knees almost touching. Priestley began the session by addressing Berry. 'What was your impression of the way Neil conducted the interview?'

Berry began without hesitation. 'He started by telling Miss Wye she was a witness, which implied not a suspect, thereby putting her at her ease. After I'd reminded her of the details of our earlier interview, he asked her an open question to find out what she thinks, rather than using a closed question that tends to bring yes or no answers but often fails to unearth any facts we don't already know.

'When he asked about sexual relationships, he kept the language formal so as to suggest a dispassionate interest; she stated there's been no one since Milo, by the way.

'He then asked about her perception of the deceased's state of mind at the time they broke up, which was last Christmas, and whether she had observed any subsequent changes. He also questioned her on whether the deceased had financial plans, in an attempt to gain an insight into his intention to continue to work, and to live, into the future.

'Finally, he switched to shorter questions and spoke quicker, so she didn't have as much thinking time to prepare her answers, in the hope of catching her out in a lie or getting her to let slip something she hadn't intended to tell us. At the end, he asked if she had had any involvement in the death, which she denied.'

'Well done, Tony. When you started last year you admitted you were weak at understanding people. Now it seems like you've become an expert overnight.'

Witty turned to his right and pointed an accusing finger at Berry. 'OK, I don't know who you are, but tell us what you did with the real Tony Beresford.'

After a ripple of laughter, Witty spoke again. 'He makes me sound really good, but all I did was to do what comes naturally.'

Berry explained, 'I've always been good at analysing things, but that doesn't mean I could have done the interview anywhere near as well as Neil did.'

Priestley held up a hand. 'That's enough from the mutual adoration society. Neil, did he miss anything?'

'He didn't mention we recorded the whole thing, which was your idea, or that she thinks I'm not handsome enough to have sex with, unlike you. Clearly this indicates she has poor judgement or an eyesight problem.'

Priestley and Berry tittered, while Plummer scowled.

'Apart from that bit of unreliable testimony, do you believe her answers and explanations were truthful?'

Witty responded emphatically, 'Yes, I do.'

'What about you, Tony?'

'I do too. I think she's really, um, very open and honest.'

Priestley noticed the hesitancy in his voice. 'But?'

'Her attitude to sex is rather... Well, I don't know how to describe it.'

Plummer spoke up. 'You mean she's a tart.'

The others laughed throatily. Priestley responded, 'Let's not be judgmental, Lin.' After the two had exchanged warm glances, he asked Witty, 'Do you believe she had any involvement in Milo's death?'

Witty responded without hesitation. 'No, I don't.'

'Tony?'

'Not directly. It's just possible the break-up led indirectly to his death.'

'That was very carefully worded, keeping your options open.'

He looked first at Plummer, as she had been largely excluded from the conversation so far; then he circulated his gaze among all three to keep them fully engaged. 'It seems unlikely Lisa Wye deliberately caused Milo's death, so we need to identify other suspects.' To discourage speaking and encourage thinking, he closed his eyes for a moment as though in deep contemplation. 'I don't know how this fits in, but I'm concerned about the painting that was auctioned shortly after his death. As Campbell owned it, that made him the likeliest candidate, but Frank checked out his alibi and says he's in the clear. I have to say I'm not entirely happy about the depth of that particular investigation, but for now I think we need to cast our net wider.'

Witty asked Priestley, 'What about other painters? Could the motive be professional rivalry?'

Priestley responded, 'I can imagine that sort of extreme back-stabbing if we were talking about estate agents or lawyers.' He quickly turned to Berry. 'Sorry, Tony; Susan excepted of course.'

Berry leaped to her defence. 'Why pick on them?'

Priestley shrugged. 'Because they're an easy target; people can often relate to the accusation if they've ever sold a house. Perhaps a better choice for most people nowadays would be newspaper reporters; it can be illegal for one of us to accept a bribe from them, but they're not necessarily regarded as guilty of any offence for doing the bribing. It's as though there are such low expectations of reporters, the courts accept that someone from the gutter press can't be blamed for acting like someone who lives in the gutter.'

Plummer noticed he appeared to be becoming slightly agitated, though she was unaware of him having had any direct involvement in attempted bribery. She discreetly gave him a two-handed "Slow Down" signal: palms down, hands repeatedly pushing an imaginary brake pedal.

He noticed the signal but glanced away, wishing to vent a little more frustration on the media. 'Personally, I suspect the most back-stabbing group of all could be those professionally pathological radio and TV interviewers who don't let politicians' answers get in the way of their own self-important questions.'

Plummer knocked her knee against his, then pressed it against him; he accepted her implied restraint.

Knowing Plummer was observing him keenly, he presented a calm visage to Berry and Witty. 'Anyway, the local artists I've met so far are too gentle and sensitive to look like serious contenders for this case. If they're all like that, I'd say the odds of one of them ever being a murderer are about the same as for a poet or a Tibetan monk.

'Milo doesn't appear to have had any involvement with artists beyond this region, but we need to keep a lookout for associations. If we find a link to London, we'll need to make different assumptions. I suspect there are über-egocentric London artists who could have a pathological hatred of competitors. I heard of one famous artist who was arguing with someone in a restaurant and they ended up scuffling on the floor; the waiting staff just looked on, claiming they were powerless to intervene. That type of behaviour suggests someone who's out of control, which is only one step away from thinking they're above the law. But we should see London artists as a million miles away from our local ones.' He smiled at Berry. 'I expected someone to correct my estimate.'

Plummer suggested, 'What about sexual rivalry? Tony mentioned she hasn't had any lovers since Milo, but what about her former lovers? They could be jealous he had a longer relationship with her.'

'Good point, Lin. Put it on the pending list; we've already interviewed her twice, so we don't want to look like we're hassling her. Any ideas, Tony?'

'Wouldn't we normally expect to interview his immediate family? Except he doesn't appear to have anyone close. Maybe there's someone out there we're not aware of.'

'It's certainly possible; for now, put that one on the back-burner.'

Plummer spoke again. 'What about Milo's past lovers? Or don't we believe he had any? Then there's unrequited love, male or female.'

'Yes; more good suggestions for the pending pile.'

As there was a lull, Priestley began again. 'Perhaps we should consider it from a different angle, the one made famous by my namesake, Marcus Tullius Cicero.' He turned to Witty to offer the relevant Latin phrase.

'*Cui bono*? I looked it up, the last time you said it.'

'So, who benefits? Let's start with the latest sale and work backward. That painting fetched a lot of money at auction, but it was sold by Campbell, who has an alibi. There are three more owners of paintings from his final series, plus some anonymous friends who have some as well, according to Campbell. Then there are all the owners of earlier works; considering how many years he was painting, it should be a long list. In the end, how much someone benefits may be related to how many paintings they have, except I don't know if the high price paid at auction would only affect the Birds series. To start with, I think we'd better interview those other three Birds owners, before considering earlier buyers.' He noticed Berry looking pensive. 'Tell us what you're thinking, Tony.'

'No, it's just me being too anal; people used to joke I put the "anal" into "analyst".'

'Come on, man, don't put yourself down. What was it that came into your mind?'

'Well, what if that last painting wasn't by Milo Piscaro? I mean, the auction happened after he'd died, so he wasn't around to stand up and say it's a forgery.

But it's just me, doubting every little thing. I don't think there's any evidence to suggest it isn't genuine.'

All three stared at Berry in silence. After several seconds, Priestley spoke. 'If it isn't genuine, that puts an entirely different slant on the case. We need to check it out. There's a curator at Sheffield's Graves Art Gallery who should be able to spot a fake. I'll give her a call right away.'

The others prepared to leave. 'No, don't go; it'll only take a minute if she's in.' Though he had previously entered her direct number onto his mobile phone contacts list, he nevertheless dialled her number in full from his desk telephone. When Anna answered, he responded immediately, before she could say anything that might embarrass either of them. 'It's DCI Priestley. I'm sitting with colleagues; you're on speakerphone, so we'll all be listening to your words of wisdom. Would you be able to spot a fake Piscaro if you saw one?'

'Do you mean, could I identify if a painting had been produced by the hand of someone other than Milo Piscaro, with the intention to deceive?'

'Yes.'

'Then you mean "forgery" rather than "fake". I believe I could identify a bad forgery, but I could not guarantee to identify a good forgery. None of the tests available to check the authenticity of older works of art have any relevance to something created very recently using widely available modern materials. All that is left is a physical examination, looking for consistency with the brushwork of an authenticated painting. I can tell you right away, all the twelve paintings in my gallery have comparable brushwork, each displaying a confidence of movement of the hand that created them;

if one of them is a forgery, I am unable to identify it.'

'There's a thirteenth painting at a local gallery here in Shawton. Would you mind checking it out?'

'I should be pleased to help; you know you only have to say when you want me, Marcus.'

'Thank you, Ms van Honthorst. I'll phone you later.'

He replaced the handset. 'Just sit quietly, will you. I need to get into my other voice to call Campbell's gallery.' He cleared his throat and dialled. 'Mr Campbell, you showed me a painting last week by Milo Piscaro; I was there with my wife.'

'Of course, sir. I do recall having the pleasure of meeting you both; I recognise your voice.'

'Well, I'd like to take another look.'

'Regrettably, sir, that particular bird has flown.'

'What do you mean?'

'I sold it to the *Alexandre de Caen* gallery in Paris, a bijou establishment on the *rue des Beaux-Arts*. They telephoned me just this morning to confirm its safe arrival and to say how pleased they are with it. I do have five more paintings in the series which I would be happy to make available to you at a comparable price. If you insisted on an immediate purchase and delivery, I am sure the Graves Art Gallery could be prevailed upon to return one or other to me.'

'There's no hurry; I'll be in touch sometime.' He pressed the call termination button immediately so that no unintentional sounds from the others in the office would be relayed. 'It's going to be a bit harder to check out your theory, Tony; the painting's been sent to Paris. But, I think it has to be done, so I'd better see when that curator woman might be available to go there.'

He called her again. 'Hello Ms van Honthorst,

you're on speakerphone again. We're wondering if you could check that painting for us sometime soon.'

'I could do it tomorrow if you wish.'

'The only problem is, it's now in Paris.'

There was a pause, so Priestley spoke again. 'We realise it will take up more of your time, but the team here would like to know if you'd be willing to make the journey, and if so, when would be your earliest date.'

'Will you be travelling with me?'

'Yes, that would make sense.'

'Then let us go there tomorrow. I could examine the painting on Wednesday, and we would travel back on Thursday.'

'I'll need to get that authorised, but it sounds good to me. I'll phone you to firm up on details. Bye.'

Plummer spoke as soon as Priestley terminated the call. 'What's she like, this Ms van Honthorst?'

Priestley laughed nervously. 'Oh, a little wrinkly old woman in her sixties who's spent her whole life looking at paintings.' He saw Plummer's questioning glance, and guessed she may be about to remark on Anna's youthful voice; to block any comment from her, he turned to Berry. 'Check out that French gallery, will you; opening hours and so forth. But don't simply contact them directly; I need to find out if they're kosher, without them getting wind of what's behind the visit.' He glanced quickly around all three of them. 'We'll reconvene when the plan's firmed up. See you later.'

CHAPTER 44

The three of them left Priestley's office, Berry walking briskly and the other two dragging behind. Witty turned back after just a few paces, commenting for Plummer's benefit, 'Something I forget to mention to Marcus.'

Witty knocked at the open door. 'What is it, Neil?'

He closed the door behind him. 'I'd like to volunteer to be your bagman. And while we're over there you could maybe give me a bit of time off to see Lily.'

'I suppose you are the obvious choice, though you're quite key to the investigation at this end.'

'I've kept Lin completely up-to-date; I'm confident she could pick up the baton and run with it, so to speak.'

'I'm sure she could, but nothing's been agreed, yet; Yelland might give it the thumbs-down.'

'Well, you know I trust you to do your best, boss.'

'Alright, Neil; I'll talk to you later.'

A moment after Witty had left the office and turned right, Plummer arrived from the left. She walked in without knocking, and closed the door quietly behind her. He looked up but said nothing.

'Marcus, I'd really like to go to Paris with you. I'm sure I'd learn a lot from the experience; I've never been abroad on duty before.'

'Thank you for volunteering Lin, but nothing's been agreed yet; it might not even happen.'

'Well, if it does, you will take me, won't you?'

'I'd certainly be pleased to have you there. But

Yelland may not give approval for two people to go.'

'Surely he would never expect someone of your rank to travel without a junior officer.'

'He's pretty tight with the budget. I wouldn't put it past him to say he'll only pay for one of us to go.'

'Well, they charge by the room in Paris, so the two of us could share to save on expenses.'

'I'd have thought a twin room would still cost more than a single.'

She attempted to give him a broad smile, but it lacked confidence at the edges. 'You could book us a double.'

Priestley gulped. 'That's quite an offer, Lin; let me talk to Yelland.'

He stood up and ushered her from the room, then continued directly to Yelland's office. After knocking and being invited to enter, he stepped inside and closed the door behind him.

Yelland signalled for him to sit. 'So, what's the problem, Marcus? Something hush-hush, I take it.'

'I don't know if this'll prove to be the breakthrough we've been looking for in the Piscaro case, or whether it's a wild-goose chase, but the team think it's worth checking out whether that painting which sold for forty grand is actually a forgery.'

'Then go check it out.'

'There's a curator at the Graves Art Gallery who's willing to give it a professional examination.'

'Well, get on with it then.'

'It's going to cost a bit.'

'We've plenty in the kitty for that.'

'But the painting's now in Paris.'

'That's not so far, is it? You could spend a few days

and see the sights. When were you thinking of going?'

'Tomorrow morning.'

'Not letting the grass grow under your feet. Who are you thinking of taking with you? DS Whittington, I suppose?'

'He volunteered, but he's a key player back here.'

'Well, who then?'

'DC Plummer has also volunteered.'

'I'm starting to see the picture now, Marcus. I hope you know what you're doing; you're playing with fire, there. But, so long as no one gets burned, let it not be said I'm one to stand in the way of true lust.'

'That's not how it is, Richie. I'm actually wanting you to take the fall for something.'

'Not for that; if Helen comes gunning for you, I'm the other side of the barricade.'

'No, it isn't like that. I want to be able to say that neither of them can go because you wouldn't authorise it; otherwise I'm in the bad books with one of them.'

'But it isn't true. Oh, I suppose it's the best way out. So it's just you, then?'

'And the curator.'

'Of course. You organise it and I'll authorise it. Who is this curator, by the way?'

'Van Honthorst.'

'Male or female?'

'Female.'

'And what's she like?'

Priestley's attempted misdirecting laugh died too quickly. 'DC Plummer just asked me the same question. I said she's a little wrinkly old woman in her sixties.'

Yelland had observed him closely. 'And how would you describe her when you weren't lying through your teeth?'

He hesitated before accepting he had to give at least a distant approximation to the truth. 'She's about thirty; typical divorcee, man-hater.'

'Try again, and this time assume I'll be checking out your statement personally.'

'Alright. She's blonde, very pretty, charming, intelligent, amusing; but I only want her there because she's a real expert.'

Yelland laughed throatily. 'A real expert in what, I ask. Just make sure you leave your room forensically cleansed.'

Priestley went to Plummer in the MIR and motioned Witty to join them. 'I've just seen Yelland; he's only prepared to authorise one officer to make the journey, and it has to be me. He's a tight bastard, isn't he?'

Witty sighed. 'Oh well, if that's the way it is.'

Plummer said nothing as she stared at her desk despondently.

Priestley signalled to Berry. 'Come and join us. We'd better reconvene the meeting in my office.'

Watching them file in, Priestley felt a twinge of guilt as he recognised two of them were struggling to hide their disappointment. 'I'm going to Paris in the morning and should be back on Thursday, sometime; I won't know exactly when, until the booking's been processed. So, Neil, you're going to be running the show for the next three days. Lin, you need to take over whenever Neil's unavailable. I've every confidence in the both of you, so just keep things moving forward, and don't let Cargill push you off course.

'Now, about those three owners of paintings in the Birds series: arrange for someone to interview them before I'm back, if at all possible. I'm not optimistic it'll lead us anywhere, but you never know 'til you try.

'Push the guys to keep checking out the CCTV; I know it's a boring task, but we need a definitive list of everyone who entered and left the area. Of course, it's perfectly possible the perp. lives locally, so won't figure on any CCTV.'

Berry asked, 'The perp.? Is that what we're supposed to call them, now? Is that on the list of standard terms? Where can I get the full list?'

Witty commented to Priestley. 'Now we've got the real Tony Beresford back.' He turned to Berry. 'He only said it because he thinks it sounds cool.'

Berry murmured, '"Cool" isn't cool anymore.'

Priestley glowered with mock-sternness at Witty. 'I'm clearly held in such high regard, it's probably a good thing I'll soon be out of your way.' He glanced around all three. 'Speaking of which, get back to it; I've plans to make.'

Once his office had been vacated, he closed the door and dialled van Honthorst. 'Hello, Anna. I'm on my own now. It's been authorised for the two of us to travel to Paris tomorrow and back on Thursday. Have you any preference for mode of transport?'

'I enjoy travelling by train.'

'So do I. How early do you feel like getting up? If you could be at Sheffield Midland Station in time for the seven twenty-nine Master Cutler, we'd get into Paris around two o'clock their time. In the afternoon I'll be making contact with my French counterparts; they probably make it back from lunch around three.' He paused, but heard no laughter. 'I'll be free in the evening, if you're interested, or would you prefer to make your own plans?'

'I would very much like to spend all evening with you, Marcus.'

'Well, it's a working trip, so I'll have to look like I'm hard at it. I'll need to send e-mails late enough each evening to suggest I've been beavering away all day.'

'You sound like a master of deception.'

'It comes with the territory.'

'Perhaps, when you are finished working, we could have dinner together at the hotel?'

'Yes, let's do that.'

'I shall make sure I am not late tomorrow.'

'Look out for me; I'll be wearing a red carnation.'

'Why?'

'Sorry, it's a cliché. Two people who don't know each other are meeting somewhere; they both wear a red carnation to be recognised.'

'But we do know each other, so it was a joke.'

'Yes, Anna, but not a very good one.'

She spoke her laughter with laboured insincerity. 'Ha, ha, ha. I shall remember to laugh at all of your jokes, if you warn me they are jokes.'

'I could have a little sign made up that says "This is a joke." Then I could just flash that at you.' She laughed lightly. 'I'll see you in the morning.'

He called up the on-line application form and entered the details of the travellers and the journey; for accommodation, he specified two separate non-smoking rooms at an hotel close to the gallery. Then he made an e-mail request to arrange a French contact.

Rather than waiting until he was home, he decided to telephone Helen and tell her about his journey plans. 'Hello, love. Someone had to volunteer to go to Paris tomorrow, so…'

She interrupted. 'Someone? Anyone I know? Give us a clue.'

'Someone you sleep with.'

'Well, that narrows the field a little. Come on, don't keep me in suspense; who is it?'

He laughed appreciatively. 'It's to do with the case. I won't be back 'til Thursday. Hope you're not going to miss me too much.'

'You're not travelling with an attractive young blonde woman, are you, by any chance?'

He worried she had a sixth sense. 'Why do you ask?'

'Are you going with Lin?'

'No, I'm not; you're far too suspicious.'

'Well, who are you going with?'

'The budget only stretches to one officer, so I'm on my own, apart from an art expert to check out a painting; we have to make sure it isn't a forgery.'

'That wouldn't by any chance be the same one you met before, would it?'

'Yes; there was no choice, really. It's hard to get hold of a proper expert, you know.'

'Well, make sure you don't get hold of that one.'

He laughed nervously. 'Surely, you know me better than that.'

'Sorry; I know I can trust you. You'll have to tell me all about her. And all about the last time you met her.'

He hoped her ability to read his mind did not operate quite so well over telephone lines. 'Sure; I'll tell you everything this evening.' Or not quite everything, he thought, knowing the dangers of too much honesty.

CHAPTER 45

Marcus arrived home to find his children in the conservatory painting pictures. Helen was with them, a streak of orange paint across her cheek like a film version of a native American. She sang out, 'Daddy, look what we're doing.'

He bent low over their daubs, first Alice's, then Edwin's. 'These are very good. What are they?'

Edwin answered. 'This is a train, like the one you're going on tomorrow. And this is the Eiffel Tower in Paris. And this is you and Mummy.'

'But Mummy isn't going with me, sweetheart.'

'She said it would be nice for you to take this picture with you so that Mummy's there as well.'

Marcus recognised the moral pressure being directed at him. He turned to Alice. 'And what's your painting about, my little love?'

'It's you and Mummy and Edwin and me, but it wasn't very good, so I covered it with blue paint.'

'Well, it's still very nice to know that we're all in the picture, even though we're hidden.'

Helen smiled. 'You do like them, don't you, Daddy?'

'Oh, yes. And Alice's painting may have helped me appreciate American Abstract Expressionism; just because it's all one colour on top doesn't mean there isn't a masterpiece underneath.'

He watched Helen doing her cute puppy look with big eyes and a head that struggled to stay upright.

She eventually stopped and smiled at him. 'Now, my love, do I need to get things ready for you for tomorrow? My toothpaste is nearly empty, but there's enough for a few days, so you take that instead of wasting space in your sponge bag with a full one. I'll do all your packing; you'll just be needing the essentials.'

'It's only three days; I'll be back by Thursday evening. There's no need to fuss.'

'Just leave it to me; you sit and relax. They've already eaten; we'll be having salmon soufflé later.'

'My favourite.'

'And there's a bottle of white Burgundy in the fridge.'

'I'm starting to feel like a condemned man.'

He sat with his children, talking to them about styles of painting. Sensing they were being favoured with grown-up conversation, they hung on his every word. Edwin decided to try his hand at Cubism, though the result was more akin to Constructivism. Alice painted green rectangles within brown lines; she declared it abstract fields with hedges and fences. When the painting session was over, he took them upstairs and put them to bed at the same time, despite Edwin's protestations about his age-related right to stay up later. He read to Alice until she fell asleep, then read to Edwin until they agreed it was now quite late.

As Marcus descended the stairs, Helen intercepted him in the hallway and proffered a glass of wine, holding it carefully by the base of the stem so as not to disturb the heavy condensation. Where he touched the bowl with two fingers and a thumb, the nusp turned into rivulets that became droplets at the base and splashed onto the polished parquet floor. 'I put your glass in the fridge to make sure the wine would be chilled enough.'

He took a sip. 'This is nice! Where's your glass?'

'In the kitchen. Food will be ready in nine minutes.'

She called him into the dining-room eight minutes later. He saw in the meantime she had lost the war paint and was now in a pretty dress she had last worn for a visit to the opera with him, the long, thin lines of purple, red, green and yellow creating an impression of a jungle or a rainforest. 'I do love that dress.'

'And the girl wearing it?'

'Even more so.'

After fetching bowls of salad from the kitchen, she brought in the bottle of Burgundy and plunged it into a silver wine-cooler that was half-filled with ice. 'It'll save me having to go back to the fridge every time you'd like another glass.'

'I do appreciate what you're doing for me, but isn't it all just a little OTT? Two nights away isn't much, really. I mean, what would you do if I was going to be away for a whole week?'

She gave him a dirty laugh. 'I'd think of something.'

Hearing repeating tings from the kitchen, she fetched the soufflé and presented it for his close inspection, pleased with the way the crusted top towered above the oatmeal-coloured dish. 'I'd say it turned out just right.'

'You're a damn fine cook, woman.'

'A damn kine…?' She gave another dirty laugh.

After the soufflé, he prepared to stand to clear the table, but she signalled him to stay seated. 'There's another course.' She took the salad bowls, plates and used cutlery into the kitchen and returned with two warmed ramekins, each containing a hot chocolate sponge. A dark brown viscous liquid lay atop the truncated cones and more dribbled down the sides, reminiscent of volcanoes with molten lava.

'Fantastic. But not good for my calories.'

'Don't worry; you'll be burning a lot off later.'

'I should go away more often.'

He thought she was really overdoing things when he saw she had pressed into service the antique silver coffee set they had bought at an auction several years earlier. She had decanted strong filter coffee into the warmed pot and now presented it on a tray, together with a milk jug, a matching sugar bowl filled with dark brown crystals, two small hand-painted Italian cups and saucers, and a pair of tiny silver spoons. Leaving him to pour, she brought out two brandy glasses and the bottle of thirteen-year-old *Ferme du Lieu Bill* Calvados they had bought on holiday in *Blonville-sur-mer*.

After finishing their coffee and apple brandy, she insisted on doing all the tidying, leaving him free to go and watch the news. When her chores were finished, she stepped daintily into the living-room and peeled off her red leather slippers, seating herself close to him on the settee and placing her feet on his thighs.

He looked down at her toe-nails. 'You've been doing some painting of your own, I see; what colour are they?'

'Coral pink.'

'That's so much nicer than the dark red toe-nails some women go for. What about your finger-nails; have they had the treatment as well?' She extended her slender fingers for his inspection. 'The same colour?'

'I know what you like. Do you remember that time I tried black? You said it just made me look like I'd been playing in the dirt and hadn't washed my hands.'

'Well, it was only an opinion. If you want black fingernails, it's up to you.'

'I only want what you like. Is pink still your favourite colour?'

He recalled Lin's silvered nails, which bizarrely reminded him of the inside of a test tube in a school experiment he had conducted half a lifetime ago. 'Yes, pink is my favourite, though I'm sure there must be other colours that are nice sometimes.'

'Well, if you think of one, just let me know and I'll get some.'

A little after nine, Helen stood up and put on her slippers. 'Turn the TV off; you need an early night. You go up first.'

As he went into his bathroom, he heard the set of beeps that indicated the burglar alarm system was being activated. Before he had finished in his bathroom, he heard her in hers; she had taken the long route via a bedroom to avoid intruding on him. He climbed into bed, leaving his side-light on. She took the normal route from her bathroom, entering the bedroom via his bathroom. He looked over at her, expecting to see her in the very short nightdress she knew he liked. Instead, he saw she was wearing nothing but a lacy red bra and matching skimpy panties. As she arched herself backward to make her breasts more pert, he wondered if the delicate bra would withstand the strain.

She placed her thumbs inside the front edge of her panties and suggestively peeled them a short distance down and back several times. 'I bought them this afternoon; what do you think?'

He jumped out of bed. 'Very nice. Now get your kit off; I'll give you a hand.'

CHAPTER 46

Priestley had occasionally suffered from taxis arriving late, so elected for a squad car to take him to the railway station, as a quick burst of blues and twos would generally overcome any unexpected delays. Having been collected early, he reached the station a full quarter of an hour before the Master Cutler was due to depart; in his experience it was invariably punctual, unlike some of the later London trains. As he looked around platform one, he saw Anna was standing close to a hanging basket of red flowers, one hand on the extended pulling-arm of the small-wheeled case that was by her side. He wheeled his own case toward her, smiling as she saw him approach. 'I thought *I* was early; have you been here long?'

'A little while,' she responded obliquely. She pointed up at the flowers. 'Here is my red carnation.'

He laughed quietly with wrinkling eyes that still had the sleep in them. Stretching up a hand toward the flowers, he moved as though to pluck one. She grabbed his arm and pulled it back. 'Stop that. What if you were arrested before we had even set off?' She clung to his arm. 'I see I shall have to hold onto you.'

Shortly after the cleaning staff had exited the train, they heard an announcement that it was now available for boarding. When he moved to take her case, she put her hand on his to restrain him. 'I shall carry my own case; it is too difficult getting on and off with two.'

'Follow me then; I know where our seats are.'

She settled into her reserved place while he stowed their cases in the gap behind their seats. As he sat beside her, he asked, 'Have you had breakfast? There's a dining car for first class passengers, but if I flash my warrant card I can probably persuade them to let us in.'

'The journey has yet to begin and that is the second wrong thing, the second improper thing, you wish to do. What other improper things should I expect?'

Priestley wondered if she was already dropping hints, or whether this was merely friendly conversation. Having barely had time to recover from the pleasure of Helen's delightful performance not much more than an hour ago, more sex was the last thing he wanted to think about right now. 'I'll behave myself. There's a buffet car, anyway, if you don't want a sit-down breakfast.'

'I had something to eat before I set off. You did not? Then you should go to the buffet car.'

'Yes, I will. Anything for you? Coffee, perhaps?'

'I brought my own flask of coffee; you may share it with me.' She saw his uncertain look. 'Once, on an English train, I had a liquid which they claimed was coffee; that is why I now bring my own supply.'

'Yes, I know what you mean. I'll go and get myself a bacon butty. That means...'

'I know the word "butty"; I am becoming familiar with the local vernacular.'

He fetched two baps, one containing bacon and tomato, the other sausage and tomato; she declined either. While he ate them both, she poured coffee into the deep beaker-like cap that she had screwed off the top of the vacuum flask. 'We shall share this; do you call it a "loving cup" when people share?'

Again he asked himself, polite conversation or hint. 'They normally have two handles, so it doesn't really count.' He finished the two baps and shared three beakers of coffee with her.

She asked, 'What do you usually do on the train?'

He gave the question some thought. 'Sometimes, I read. If I'm weary, I just look out of the window.'

'Do you see interesting things on this route?'

'There's a late-sixteenth century lodge where everything is built in triangles. It was designed by the father of one of the Gunpowder Plotters; they were men who wanted to blow up our parliament building, along with the King and all the politicians. For Catholics, the number three symbolises the Holy Trinity: God the Father, God the Son, God the Holy Ghost. If I see it, I'll let you know, but it'll be ages yet.

'Speaking of parliament, I once saw a Labour MP travel first class from London to Chesterfield. To me, it didn't square with the image he projects as a rebel and a rough, working-class type.' He shook his head. 'The politicians in this country are something else.'

'Something else?'

'I just mean their behaviour often doesn't match their words.'

'That does not apply only to this country, I think, though I do not know much about politics.'

'But you do know a lot about art. How'd you like to improve my education while we're travelling?'

'I have nothing prepared.'

'Then just talk about whatever you like; I love hearing your voice.' He realised he had accidentally used the "L" word, and resolved to be more careful for the remainder of the trip.

She began by talking of her time at the Rijksmuseum in Amsterdam. He closed his eyes and listened, before drifting off to sleep, only waking when she gently tugged at his arm. 'Sorry, I must have nodded off for a moment. Where are we?'

'Between Renaissance and Romanticism.'

When he heard her give an unreasonably light giggle for this hour of the morning, he added his own laughter, though it was heavy and mucus-laden. 'I meant where are we on our journey.'

She gazed into his eyes. 'As I said, we are between rebirth and romance.'

He laughed it off. 'How close to London?'

'Ten minutes.'

'I'd better pay a visit.' He saw her puzzled look. 'To the loo.'

They exited the train and headed for St Pancras International where they would be catching the Eurostar. On the way he bought three large packs of sandwiches and two bottles of orange juice for them to have later, being unsure what availability, standard and cost to expect from a Eurostar buffet car.

They continued the short distance to the Eurostar terminal and passed through security. Sitting waiting, he realised a comfortable silence had existed between them for fully twenty minutes; he wondered how they had bonded so easily, having met only once before.

They boarded the train and sat in their reserved places, which were adjacent at one end of a carriage. Though the seats were comfortable, she twisted and turned as she sought the perfect position to rest. Finally, she angled herself with her head on his shoulder, mumbling, 'I shall try to sleep.'

Within minutes, he thought she sounded as though she were sleeping, but wondered if her arm that now lay across his chest had moved there unconsciously or by design. Soon, he was certain her sleep was authentic.

When she woke for the first time, she continued to pin him to the seat, whispering, 'You have a comfortable body for sleeping against.'

Having established her optimum position, when she again prepared to doze she adopted the pose she had held previously, this time with no suggestion of going to sleep first.

He told himself he was being no more than a friendly pillow, though nevertheless hoped no one he knew would see her resting against him in this way.

Long before they reached Paris she shook herself awake for a final time and straightened her clothing. 'It would not do to arrive in Paris looking shrivelled.'

'I think you mean dishevelled.'

'Oh, that is the word, is it? Dishevelled.'

Giving her the choice of the three packs of sandwiches, she chose prawns, having the least calories. He took out the two bottles of juice. 'Have one of these, unless you'd rather get a drink from the buffet.'

'If the coffee here is as good as British Railway's coffee, I think I would prefer the orange juice.'

As the train approached the suburbs of Paris, with its high-rise flats and graffiti-laden low walls, she asked, 'Will you contact the French police straight away?'

He shook his head. 'First, I think we should check into the hotel. Then I'll go and see *Capitaine Dubois*.'

They took line four of the Metro from *Gare du Nord* to *St-Germain-des-Prés* in the *Sixième Arrondissement*. Exiting onto *boulevard Saint-Germain*, they headed toward *rue Bonaparte*, stopping for a moment while Marcus consulted the map, a one-page print of the area provided by Berry. As they were about to set off again, two young women rushed by with a noisy swarm of thirty children at their heels, all excited about being on a school trip; several more responsible adults bobbed along in their wake, trying to keep up.

Turning a corner, they located the hotel. As they approached, the doors opened automatically and they entered. Priestley asserted his linguistic credentials by addressing the receptionist in what he assumed to be her native tongue. '*Bonjour. Nous avons des réservations en noms de Monsieur Marcus Priestley et Mademoiselle Anna van Honthorst.*'

The receptionist looked down and hit a few buttons on her computer. After a few moments she raised her head. 'Ah yes, Mister Priestley and Miss van Honthorst. You are due to stay with us for two nights. Two single rooms have been reserved for you; is that correct?'

Marcus hurried to respond, concerned Anna might make a suggestion about changing to a double room. 'Yes, that's right.'

They completed the booking formalities and took their plastic credit card-shaped door keys. Outside her room, Anna observed, 'We are next-door neighbours.'

He asked if she intended to explore Paris on her own, as he would have to visit the *gendarmerie*; she expressed her wish to go there with him. When she entered her room, he avoided any invitation by closing the door behind her, before continuing to his own room at the end of the corridor.

After several attempts, his plastic card eventually released the lock and allowed him to enter; inside, he slipped it into an electronic slot that turned on the lights. He unzipped his case and took his sponge bag into the small bathroom. As he carefully emptied the contents, he noticed Helen had omitted to include any aftershave; he chastised himself for imagining this could be anything other than a simple oversight.

After putting away his few items of clothing, he checked his watch. Realising he had not yet adjusted it for the hour difference, he pressed the tiny buttons and corrected it for local time.

Shortly after, he knocked at Anna's door; she opened it and invited him in. He took a few steps forward and looked around. 'It's a mirror image of my room.' He stepped back out. 'Are you ready, or shall I see you in reception in a bit?'

'I shall be down in two minutes.'

He took the stairs rather than waiting for the lift. As he arrived in reception, the woman looked up at him and smiled; *à propos* nothing, he commented, 'Earlier, when I spoke to you in your native tongue, you responded in mine.'

Her smile widened. 'It was not my native language; I am Romanian. But your French is very good. You have a room to yourself; do you wish me to arrange some company for you? Any type.'

Anna appeared from around the corner by the lift. 'He will have all the company he needs, thank you very much!'

CHAPTER 47

Anna and Marcus set off walking in the direction of the *gendarmerie*. She linked her arm into his and looked up at him. 'So that I do not go missing among the crowds.'

He glanced both ways along the almost deserted street. 'Yes, it's very busy, isn't it.' They exchanged smiles.

She realised her window-shopping was slowing progress too much. 'I should like to go into these galleries later; but first, you must see your policeman.'

'You can look at them now, if you like; all except the one we'll be visiting tomorrow. I could see you back at the hotel.'

'Are you trying to be rid of me?'

'I just don't want you to be bored.'

'The galleries can wait. I wish to walk with you.'

Their arms were still linked as they reached the steps of the *gendarmerie*; he forced her to release her grip by choosing that hand to push open the door. Seeing a line of chairs in the reception area, he invited her to sit and wait while he spoke with his designated contact. He continued to a desk where a young man in a dark blue uniform was sitting, leaning forward while reading. *'Bonjour, je m'appelle Marcus Priestley. Je viens pour voir Capitaine Jean-Luc Dubois.'* The officer looked up momentarily and pointed to the man who was already approaching from the direction of the main entrance.

Dubois gave Priestley a firm handshake. 'I saw you arriving; I was just behind you. It is your intention to visit the gallery tomorrow, is that not so?'

'*Oui, c'est le plan.*'

'And do you wish to be accompanied by a member of the *gendarmerie*?'

'*Non, à moins que vous ne pensiez que c'est essentiel.*'

'You do not intend to do any more than you explained to me yesterday? You will simply look at a painting? That is it, is it not?'

'*Ouai, c'est ça.*'

He nodded in the direction of Anna. 'And you have brought your expert with you. I would have invited you to see Paris with me this evening, but I think you will have lots of work on your arms.'

Priestley recognised the literal translation of *avoir beaucoup de besogne sur les bras* and understood Dubois thought he would have his hands full with Anna. He remained determined not to give way in the battle of the linguists. '*Nous allons manger à l'hôtel ce soir et vous seriez le bienvenu si vous nous y rejoigniez.*'

'I would like to come and join you; however, I do not wish to have the gooseberry.'

Having walked toward them, Anna caught the tail end of the conversation. 'You are joining us for dinner? I saw the menu in the hotel; I do not think they have gooseberry, anyway.'

Priestley responded to her for his benefit, 'Captain Dubois was concerned that he would be in the way; he mistakenly imagined he would be a third person with a couple.' He turned to Dubois. '*Vous ne vous trouveriez pas en tiers.*' Turning back to Anna, he continued, 'Of course, he would be very welcome and not in the way.'

Anna smiled briefly at Dubois. 'Yes, you would be very welcome.'

Dubois recognised Anna was unable to mask an underlying reluctance. 'Thank you, but I regret I must refuse on that occasion; I do not have the time.'

Priestley felt he should press the matter further, not just for the sake of Anglo-French *entente* but also in recognition of the protection that a *chaperon* may confer. 'At least come and have a drink with us.'

'Yes, I could do that, perhaps.'

Priestley and Dubois exchanged contact details and agreed procedures for calling up assistance tomorrow if that should prove necessary. They took their leave of Dubois, whose eyes lingered on Anna as she walked away.

As soon as they had left the building, Anna took Marcus's arm again. 'What shall we do now?'

'What would you like to do?'

'There are many galleries near here that I would like to visit. But you may prefer to do something else, so I shall do anything you wish to do.'

He wondered if she had intended her closing invitation to sound quite so emphatic. 'Visiting the galleries would be useful experience for me; it would be good practice for tomorrow. I don't intend to say who I am; would it be too difficult for you to seem like an ordinary tourist?'

'But I am an ordinary tourist, today.'

'Ordinary tourists don't have your expertise.'

They wandered from one gallery to another; in each of them she provided an assessment of the paintings. Interpreting a glassy look to his eyes as an indication his interest had begun to wane, she suggested they take a walk by the river. As she hung on his arm while they proceeded along *rue de Seine*, he told her he wished to walk past their target gallery, though not to enter it. On *rue des Beaux-Arts*, they glanced surreptitiously at the *Galerie Alexandre de Caen* without slowing their pace. At the end, they turned right onto *rue Bonaparte* and headed for the river.

As they swung onto *quai Malaquais* and began to walk toward *quai de Conti*, where *pont des Arts* spans to the *quai des Tuileries*, she looked over the river, past the gardens and toward the *Musée du Louvre*. 'I would like to go to the Louvre before we return to England.'

'We have to earn our corn tomorrow afternoon, but the rest of the time is yours to do with as you wish.'

'I was hoping we could go together.'

'Yes, I'd like that too, but if our painting's a forgery I'll have to spend time liaising with my colleagues.'

They continued on *quai Conti*, looking at the bridges and the water and watching the occasional *bateau mouche* full of sightseers, before crossing to Île de la Cité via *pont Neuf*. He asked, '*Quai des Orfèvres*, do you know what it's known for?'

'No, though it sounds familiar.'

'The office of a famous detective.'

She smiled. 'More famous than you?'

'A fictional one.'

'You will have to tell me.'

'Inspector Maigret.'

'Ah yes, I know the name.'

'When I was young, I read lots of Maigret novels, though the French in them is quite dated. I had to switch to more recent novels to learn the current vernacular and idioms; that is, to keep up with modern usage of the language.'

As they reached *quai du Marché Neuf*, he pointed to the left. 'The *Préfecture de Police* is up that way; perhaps I should call in and ask for Maigret.'

She laughed more than his weak humour deserved. 'And then they would lock you away in an asylum.'

They continued to the cathedral that stood majestically on *rue du Cloître de Notre Dame*. He checked the opening times. 'Shall we go in?'

'We can take a look around, if you wish. I could tell you about some of the murals.'

'You're giving me a marvellous education, Anna.' After another series of short lectures, he asked if she wished to go up to the roof.

She responded, 'Have you been up there before?'

'Yes, a while ago.'

'I have also been up. May we save our strength? There are so many steps. I would go up if you wish. The gargoyles are very, um, I cannot think of the word.'

'Impressive? Frightening? Threatening?'

'Like creatures from nightmares.'

'Monsters from the id. I think you probably mean the grotesques: fantastic animal statues. Gargoyles are water spouts.'

'So, now you are educating me.' Her smile was followed by a weary sigh. 'Perhaps we shall go up another time.'

As they headed for *pont de l'Archevêché*, she indicated the *Mémorial des Martyrs de la Déportation*, which was shaped like a ship's prow. 'Two hundred thousand people were deported from France to Nazi Germany. I do not wish to go in there; not today. I think it would be too upsetting, like visiting the Anne Frank

House back home.'

When they had again crossed the Seine and were walking on *quai de Montebello*, she looked back at the Cathedral. 'It is a beautiful building.'

He pointed to the roof. 'Look! Esmeralda and Quasimodo.'

She laughed gently, though a little wearily. 'May we catch the Metro back to the hotel? It has been a long day and I wish to be bright and gay when we dine together this evening. You will have to tell me if I am not bright enough or gay enough.'

He perceived a hint of concern emerging from her emotional depths. Knowing how people often betrayed their true feelings when they were close to exhaustion, he wondered why she should feel it so important to maintain her façade. Recalling how the need to encourage his troops had been drilled into him in years past, he gave her a broad smile. 'I'm absolutely certain you'll be wonderfully bright and gay; you always are.'

They continued along the quay until they reached the corner with *rue Danton*. 'The *Métro* is just up here.'

As they took the short ride from *Saint-Michel* to *Saint-Germain-des-Prés*, he noticed just how tired she looked. 'I think you could do with going to bed for a while. What time did you get up this morning?'

She answered indirectly. 'I did not wish to miss the train.'

They made the short walk back to the hotel, passing through the lobby and taking the lift to their floor. As they were approaching her room, he thought she was about to speak, so began quickly to avoid any uncomfortable misunderstandings. 'I have some work to do, checking e-mails and so forth. What time would you like to go to dinner?'

'You are sure you have to work?'

'Positive.'

'Shall we meet in an hour and a half?'

'That would be ideal; it should give me just enough time to get my work done.'

He continued to his room, intending to nap for ninety minutes.

CHAPTER 48

Marcus used the internal telephone number to call Anna; there was a delay before she answered. He asked, 'Are you ready to go to dinner?'

'I went to bed; I was asleep. I shall have a shower first. Come to my room and we can talk while I dress.'

He saw the danger and headed it off. 'I'm not quite finished working, yet; I was just checking on you. Give me a call when you're ready to go.' He ended with a higher-pitched, 'Bye-ee,' before quickly replacing the handset.

Anna telephoned a quarter of an hour later. 'I am ready now; are you ready?'

'Yes. I've finished my work, so I'm yours for the evening.' He felt slightly guilty about lying to her, having spent less than ten minutes on the computer and the rest of the time dozing on the bed.

She opened the door almost the moment he knocked, remaining hidden behind it as she sang out, 'Come in.'

He looked down as he stepped into the room, careful to avoid tripping over anything that may have been left lying around. As he checked behind the door, he saw her pretty feet in delicate, orange strappy sandals; he worked his way up past her slender, tight-muscled bare legs to the light orange dress that hugged her slight figure, and the diaphanous shawl that emphasised her fragility. He wondered if it was the matching orange lipstick that made her mouth pout so temptingly.

'Well,' she demanded, 'how do I look?'

Detecting some uncertainty in her voice, he sought to boost her confidence with an unrestrained response. 'Absolutely gorgeous, Anna.'

Her smile, with bright white teeth displayed up to her pink gums, gave an unmistakable signal. For a moment he wondered if he should deflate the palpable sexual tension that now hung between them, but reasoned it might undermine her enjoyment of their evening together in the restaurant.

He had reserved dinner for two, in accordance with the hotel's policy of booking in advance. The waiter ushered them toward the side of the room with the best views, then directed them to the cosiest corner table. Seeing it was already occupied, Marcus turned questioningly to the waiter. *'Où se trouve notre table?'*

'Celle-ci. Vous avez une invitée.'

The woman who had had her back to them now stood and turned to face them. In her high heels she was about the same height as Marcus. She put her arms around him and squeezed him tightly before holding herself away a little, offering first one cheek to be kissed, then the other, then back to the first. He complied, making the third kiss linger longer. 'What a fantastic surprise!' He turned to Anna and saw how shocked she looked. 'Anna, this is Lily, an old colleague; Lily, this is Anna. We're here on a case; Anna is an art expert.'

Anna eyed Lily warily, making no movement. Lily put out a hand, which Anna held briefly, not waiting for a shake. Marcus found the action reminiscent of two boxers at the start of a bout. He could see Anna's disappointment writ large, as though she were recovering from a knockout blow delivered by the mismatched opponent who towered above her. He tried not to sound overjoyed at the surprise encounter, in order to empathise with Anna. 'Well, Lily, this is unexpected. How did you know we'd be here?'

'Helen told me where you're staying. I checked and found you'd booked to have dinner here, so I came along to surprise you. Are you pleased?'

'Yes; it's marvellous to see you.' Diplomatically, he turned to Anna. 'This is great; it's far better than you having to put up with only me to talk to all evening.'

Anna nodded, remaining silent.

'So, Lily, what have you been up to lately?'

She launched into a detailed description of her work as a special security adviser to a fashion house, which sounded to him as though it consisted almost entirely of looking good and welcoming VIPs. He encouraged Anna to talk about her work as a curator, but she remained stubbornly reticent. Even an invitation to choose the wine did little to lighten Anna's spirits. At the end of the main course Lily checked her mobile phone for messages and found there was one that required a call-back; she excused herself and stepped away a short distance. He stretched underneath the table and gave Anna's hand a squeeze, then leaned in closer and whispered, 'I know it isn't what you had in mind.' She shook her head in confirmation. 'Do you remember asking me to say if you're not being bright enough or gay enough? Well, you don't really need me to tell you. Why don't you show off that sparkle you have? I really love it when you're all bubbly.' He hoped the "L" word would have the desired effect.

Lily completed her call and returned to the table. Anna asked, 'Do you find you are never off duty? It must be worse than when you were in the police. Or do you love the job so much that you are happy to make business calls even when you are eating out with friends?'

Marcus knew she had just made by far her longest contribution to the evening's conversation, and though the ending suggested they were all friends together, he nevertheless recognised the implicit criticism. He encouraged her to speak again. 'You can't fool me, Anna; I know you love your job just as much. The moment you start talking about art, you just light up. Tell Lily something of the things we saw today. What about at *Notre Dame*?'

Anna accepted the invitation and delivered a pastiche of her earlier lectures, though to Marcus her animation seemed a little *faux*. Lily asked questions in all the right places, showing how far her social skills had progressed since her days as a detective constable. When the waiter came over and suggested another course, the two women shooed him away in concert, both keen to retain their slender figures. Marcus wondered about calling him back, but decided it would be bad form for him to continue eating after they had finished.

He was watching the two women, now in competitive, conversational full flow, when a hand touched him on the shoulder. Turning and looking up, he found Captain Dubois standing behind him. 'You invited me to come for a drink.'

Marcus stood to shake his hand. '*Jean-Luc*, I'm so glad you were able to make it; I'm not able to get a word in edgeways.' Seeing *Jean-Luc* looking puzzled, he elaborated. 'I mean, they're talking so much, I don't get the chance to say anything.' When he turned to Lily, she stopped speaking in mid-sentence. 'Lily, meet *Capitaine Jean-Luc Dubois* of the *gendarmerie*. *Jean-Luc*, meet Lily, formerly Detective Constable Martello, now security adviser to one of your famous fashion houses.'

Lily held out her hand; *Jean-Luc* attempted to turn it to the horizontal and to bring his lips to kiss it, but she twisted it away and grabbed his fingers, crunching them in a handshake. Marcus saw the performance and smiled inwardly, reminded of the young woman he had worked with. He tried not to show he had witnessed the refusal, as he asked *Jean-Luc*, 'Coffee? Or shall we have something stronger?'

Jean-Luc took a chair from an empty adjacent table and then signalled to the waiter. As he approached, *Jean-Luc* responded to Marcus. 'A coffee and a brandy would be a good way to end a meal.'

Marcus nodded. 'That would suit me. Girls, what would you like?'

When they both answered 'Just coffee,' they were so close to being in unison that they laughed to each other, as though the ice had finally broken.

Jean-Luc and Marcus talked shop; Anna and Lily talked shopping. *Jean-Luc* took coincident lulls as an opportunity to ask Lily about her previous work in the police. She answered factually before reverting to her explanation to Anna about the shops around *boulevard Saint-Germain*; which end for the expensive boutiques, which for the cheaper, more *Avant-garde*. *Jean-Luc* motioned with his hand for Marcus to listen to him closely. 'Could we talk in private?'

They walked to a balcony. As all conversation at the

table had been in English, Marcus refrained from now speaking in French. 'What's the problem, *Jean-Luc*?'

'Not a problem, but I am wondering. There is a joke about the number three: three Italians makes a political party, three English makes a club, three French makes a happily married couple. You are here with two beautiful women; that may be the French way, but it is not usually the English way. Do you intend to take them both to yourself?'

Marcus laughed throatily before speaking with a softened voice. 'I don't intend to take either of them. Lily is engaged to my sergeant and is definitely unavailable, to me or to anyone else for that matter. And Anna is just a friend.'

'I do not think Anna knows she is just a friend; I saw the way she held onto you earlier today.'

'Oh, I'm sure she's just a naturally friendly young woman. Anyway, with a wife like mine at home, I would never risk my marriage by looking elsewhere.'

'But this is Paris, and what happens in Paris stays in Paris.'

'I thought that was Vegas.'

'Paris is the same, but with more sophistication and fewer gaming machines.' He gave a stereotypical yet authentic Gallic shrug. 'Well, if you find you have one too many, I am available to help you out, my friend.'

Marcus laughed briefly, refusing to suggest he had taken the offer as anything other than a joke. He headed back to the table before *Jean-Luc* could press him further. When they were again seated, he disguised the nature of their conversation. '*Jean-Luc* was just wondering what plans we all have for the evening. I had a very early start to the day, so I'll be wanting an early night. I suspect Anna may be the same.' Anna smiled at Marcus and nodded repeatedly. 'What about you, Lily?'

She responded abruptly. 'That won't do, Marcus. I haven't seen you for ages, and this is Paris; no one goes to bed early in Paris. I'm going to stay up with you all night and look at the river and the bridges and the stars, and we'll talk about old times.'

Anna looked steadfastly into Marcus's eyes. 'It has been a very long day. I had a short sleep earlier, but now I wish to go to bed for the night.' She stood up, and Marcus immediately did likewise. For a moment, she thought she had made the better offer, but quickly realised he was merely preparing politely to bid her goodnight. She looked around. 'Goodnight, everyone.'

Jean-Luc had also stood up. 'May I accompany you to your room, to make sure you are sound and safe?'

She gave him a withering look. 'I am sure I will be entirely safe without you.'

After goodnights from the other three, Anna left the restaurant. *Jean-Luc* waited until she was out of sight before adding his own farewell, giving a small, polite smile to Lily and a broader one to Marcus.

After a minute of looking out of the window, Lily stood up from the table. 'Right, well, I need to be going. I have to look my best, you know. It's been great seeing you again.'

Marcus frowned. 'What happened to all that stuff about gazing at the river and the stars? You made it sound enchanting.'

'Oh, that. It's just what Helen told me to say if I thought you needed help getting rid of someone so you could go to bed... on your own!'

'So, I've been stitched up! Doesn't she trust me?'

'As far as any woman would trust their husband, if he was some big handsome bloke like you. That means she trusts you about as far as she can see you.'

Marcus grinned. 'Well, you've successfully scared off the opposition, so what are you really doing tonight?'

'It's like I said: I need my beauty sleep. So I'm going to bed as soon as I can, and I don't mean yours!'

They laughed into each other eyes, comfortable in the certain belief they would never be more than just good friends.

CHAPTER 49

A little after midnight Marcus was wakened by a gentle knocking at the door. Hearing 'Room service' spoken in English, he instantly became hypervigilant, before realising it was probably just Anna. Determined not to invite her in, he made no move to get up. His suspicions were confirmed when he heard the voice quietly call out 'Marcus'; he decided his best ploy was to remain silent and leave her to go back to her own room. When she called out 'Lily? Lily?' he wondered if there was a valid reason for Anna to be disturbing his sleep, such as the staff having given her something that Lily had left behind in the restaurant.

He switched on his bedside light, climbed out of bed and went to the door, opening it just a little way. 'What is it, Anna?'

'Is Lily there?'

'No, she went back.'

'Really? She said you would be talking through the night.'

He opened the door wider and saw she was dressed in the clothes she had worn to dinner, whereas he was now wearing only a pair of short pyjama bottoms. 'No, that was just a joke.' She eyed him suspiciously; he felt he had to prove his innocence. 'Come in and see; she isn't here.'

She walked into the room and glanced at the bed. 'Then I have brought too many glasses.' Carefully lifting two bottles of champagne and three fluted glasses from a bag and placing them on a small table, she smiled warmly. 'You will have a drink with me.'

He heard this as an instruction, not a question. 'But it's very late; we both need to catch up on our sleep.'

Her smile faded, replaced by an anxious expression. 'I wish to sleep with you tonight, Marcus. I like you very much, and I know you like me at least a little.'

He believed the unequal strengths of "like" indicated a depressed ego, and the hesitancy in her voice suggested she was in unfamiliar territory. He sought a way of boosting her self-confidence while keeping himself faithful to Helen. 'I like you very much, Anna, but I'm happily married, so I never sleep with anyone else.' He saw her lower lip quiver and thought she may be close to tears.

'I never sleep with anyone.'

'You're just waiting for the right man.'

'I believe you are the right man.' She read his concern. 'I would always keep this a secret.'

'You mean, what happens in Paris stays in Paris?'

'Yes, though I thought that was Las Vegas.'

Marcus smiled momentarily as he remembered his earlier conversation with Dubois. He tried a different strategy. 'Anna, you're far too beautiful to want to waste your time on someone like me; you deserve so much more than I could ever offer.'

She held his gaze as a sea of brine washed over her light blue eyes and cascaded down her cheeks. 'You say nice things to me but you do not want me.'

Seeing her chin begin to wobble, he had a sudden flashback to a time at Sergeant Jones's stag party when a young woman barely out of her teens had exhibited similar signs of distress. She was a novice who had been hired to do a striptease, and had performed a fan dance like an amateur, finally stopping when she was down to a G-string and two large feathers. The all-male private audience had consisted of police constables, two sergeants and one inspector, himself. The other men, disinhibited by alcohol, had demanded she lose every last vestige of cover. He had seen how ugly and contorted their faces had become as they bayed at her. She had clearly looked frightened, so he had stepped onto the stage to offer her some support, standing next to her and bellowing to the onlookers, 'Well done; you did great.' She had then spoken so quietly to him he had not heard her words, so he had leaned toward her as she repeated, 'It's what was agreed: down to my G-string.' At that, he had turned to his colleagues and shouted out, above the whistling and the catcalling that was being led by Mick Jones, 'She did very well, so show your appreciation in the usual way; especially you, Sergeant Jones.' The inclusion of his rank had had the desired effect, and he had followed Marcus's loud applause by leading the others in doing likewise, knowing, come the morning, Marcus would revert to being his boss.

Though that old memory came flooding back to him in all its detail, the recall time was just an instant. His response therefore appeared to Anna to have been delivered almost without hesitation, as he made one last attempt to walk the tightrope of boosting her ego while still declining her offer. 'I do want you, Anna; you're so lovely, how could any man not want you. But you might regret it in the morning, when you wake up with a married man and not with the love of your life.'

She looked into his eyes, blinking away two final tears from her own. 'I used to wake up with the man I thought was the love of my life, but I divorced him when I discovered it was all a lie. Now I just want to wake up with a lovely man. Please say yes to me.'

Short of destroying her self-confidence, he knew he was out of options. He gazed at her as he breathed his response. 'Yes, Anna; yes, yes, … yes.'

Having received the green light, she quickly brightened and smiled, though the streaks of her tears remained visible on her cheeks in contradistinction. 'I remember very clearly our conversation back at my house. So that you have no concerns about duress, I shall be the one to open the champagne.' As she held the bottle by the neck, she stripped away the gold foil and pulled open the wire cage. Grasping the cork firmly in her left hand, she expertly turned the bottle with her right, until a loud pop announced its ejection. The first cascade of yellowy-orange bubbles filled two glasses before fizzing down to one-third volume. After repeatedly topping them up in turns until they almost reached the brim, she announced proudly, 'And not a drop spilt.'

She picked up the two drinks and handed him one. He clinked his glass carefully against hers. 'Here's to a beautiful friendship.'

'And beautiful love-making,' she responded, as she clinked back. After just a few sips, she placed her glass back on the table, before taking his glass from his hand and putting it down next to hers.

Slipping off her sandals and dress, he saw she was wearing nothing but a pair of plain white knickers. She reached forward and stretched the elastic waistband of his shorts, easing it over his projection. After she had pulled the shorts to the floor and he had stepped out of them, she fished in her handbag and transferred several small foil packets to the table. Picking one up and holding it tightly, she tore across it, pulling out the condom which she then rolled down onto him, before wriggling out of her knickers. 'It would not be proper for me to become pregnant.' Looking into his eyes, she breathed, 'Now give me a fuck I will never forget.'

After a heavy sleep, Marcus woke an hour before his seven o'clock alarm. He lay on his side facing her, with one arm over her back and the other under her neck; she in turn had one arm around him, the other tucked down between them. He reasoned inwardly, 'Having sex with Anna for a second time makes me no more unfaithful than just the once; the principle is the same.' Easing her onto her back, he began to kiss her body. He found her nipples quickly hardened in the warm bed; knowing he should not simply assume she wanted him again, he whispered, 'Shall we?'

Anna opened her eyes and gave an extended, 'Yes.'

His kisses started low and meandered slowly up her body, enjoying lengthy, soft detours before culminating in a tender kiss on her lips. He offered a corny line. 'We'll always have Paris.' Her contented 'mmm' indicated she had not recognised the humorously intended reference to *Casablanca*. He felt guilty, but only for making light of something he was certain she was feeling far more deeply.

CHAPTER 50

When the alarm rang, Marcus quickly stretched over to turn it off. Seeing Anna was awake, he asked, 'Shall we go and have some breakfast?'

She sighed contentedly. 'Yes; you need to keep your strength up. After breakfast we shall come back to bed.'

He thought through his essential plans for the day. 'We need to be up by midday, so that gives us a few hours, unless there are e-mails I have to attend to.'

'And will you sleep with me tonight?'

'Yes, I'd love to.'

After breakfast, they returned to his room; as he held the door open for her, he checked that the multi-lingual "Do not disturb" sign was still facing outwards. He logged onto the hotel's Wi-Fi and checked for e-mails, while she slipped out of her clothes and into bed. When he joined her shortly after, he was surprised to find her turn away from him. She pulled his arm around her, so it nestled between her breasts; he placed his fingers on the curve between her shoulder and her slender neck. Within minutes, she was breathing slowly and steadily, and he soon drifted off to sleep.

The midday alarm woke them instantly. She turned to him. 'Do we have the time?'

Though he had the inclination, he was unsure he had the energy, so he shook his head. 'We have work to do.'

Back in her room she discovered the maid had removed the towels and not yet provided fresh ones, so she collected together a few things and returned to his room. 'I was going to have a shower but my towels have been taken. May I use yours?'

'Yes, of course; we'll share them. You can go first.'

She unselfconsciously removed her clothes. As she prepared to step into the shower cubicle, she asked, 'Do you wish to come in with me?' He smiled as he dropped his pants and walked into the bathroom. Once the water temperature had settled down to bearably hot, she stepped in first and he followed immediately behind. He took her shampoo and gently washed and rinsed her silky blonde hair, then used his hands to chase the suds down to her thighs, enjoying the intimacy of his permitted thoroughness. She continued the process down to her feet by raising one leg at a time, then turned to face him, taking a moment to press her body against his. On stepping out of the cubicle, she pulled the largest towel from the rail and began to dry herself, leaving the smaller ones for him to use.

He completed his shower and stayed in the steamy bathroom, where he found the two remaining towels insufficient to dry his hirsute body. When he walked into the bedroom, he saw her looking at herself in a mirror, statuesque and revelling in her nakedness. Holding her towel away from her body, she asked, 'Do you think I am in good shape for my age?'

He greedily examined her body minutely. His eyes worked slowly upward from her delicate feet, past her tightly-muscled calves and slim thighs to her mound of Venus with its wisps of blonde hair, then over her trim abdomen, lingering on her perfectly shaped breasts, smoothly sloping above and heavily bulbous below, adorned with pink nipples that stood proud within pale brown areolae against milk-white skin. He continued up to her slender neck, her soft blonde hair, her elfin face with unblemished complexion, finally resting his gaze on her glacial blue eyes. 'You're in fantastic shape for any age.'

Looking pensive, she cupped her right hand under her left breast. 'I wonder for how much longer they will remain so firm.' She held out her used towel. 'This end is still dry.' He took it from her and dried the hair on his chest a little more.

While putting on her clothes, she watched him continue to dry himself. When he began to dress, she collected together her various accoutrements. 'I am going back to my room to get ready. Come for me when it is time to go.'

He checked his e-mails again; there was nothing requiring a response, except a note from Helen: "Did you like your surprise?" His response affirmed he had enjoyed meeting Lily, but made no mention of Anna.

When he knocked on Anna's door, she opened it immediately and prepared to leave. He saw she was dressed in shiny black pumps, artistically distressed blue jeans with parallel diagonal slashes, and a short jacket over a cotton T-shirt that imitated broad hoops of paint in alternating white and pale blue. He gave her a troubled look. 'The hotel provided me with a little sewing kit; do you want to borrow it to mend your jeans before we go?'

She giggled. Stepping into the corridor, she kissed him warmly on the lips; as she drew away, she saw his look of concern. 'I am sorry, I forgot it is a secret.'

He grimaced. 'What happens in Paris may not stay in Paris if someone spots us.' Seeing how crestfallen she appeared, he kissed her back in similar fashion.

'That's all you're getting for now.'

They exited the hotel and walked side by side, each making a conscious effort to overcome their desire to touch the other. As they approached the gallery, he reminded himself of his earlier thoughts on how to handle their visit. 'Perhaps we should agree rules of engagement for the gallery. If you're going to examine the Piscaro really closely, I think it's going to be obvious you're an expert, so there's no point in trying to hide it. Then there's the question of who I am.'

'You could simply be my lover.'

'No, Anna, I don't think that would play out very well. I can be your minder, your bodyguard; then I don't have to say much. Perhaps I should be working for a Russian oligarch, so I don't have to speak at all. How would you feel about doing all the talking?'

'Yes, that is fine. And physically you look like a bodyguard, except your face, which is too perfect, too unmarked.'

'What if they want to know more about you?'

'I can say I am an expert examining the picture on behalf of someone else, which is of course true.'

'And what if they ask if you're intending to buy it?'

'I would say I am the agent, hired to report back.'

'That's good. One final thing: I need to photograph it. My phone has a decent camera.'

'So does my iPhone. Do you wish to take the photographs or should I?'

'Maybe both of us, just to be on the safe side.'

As they entered the gallery, a woman approached them with short, rapid steps, constrained by her black pencil skirt. '*Bonjour, monsieur-dame.*'

He thought her clothes looked expensive but the

black roots to her peroxide blonde hair spoiled the overall effect. Resisting the urge to respond to her in French, he positioned himself behind Anna and rapidly glanced around as though checking for threats.

Anna replied simply, 'Hello.'

'Ah, English.'

'No, though I speak English.'

She gave a professional smile. 'Welcome to the gallery. Is there something particular you wish to see?'

'Yes, a painting by Milo Piscaro.'

Priestley felt a little uncomfortable, realising they had not agreed the details of how they should play this scene. The woman led them to the painting, where he noticed the price label: 100 thousand euros. She nodded deferentially to the painting. 'One of a set of thirteen, and the only one in France.'

Anna peered at the painting from two metres away. 'I should like to examine it closely.' She turned to Marcus. 'Go away; I may be some time.'

He responded in a gravelly voice, '*Da, Madame.*' Seeing her look of surprise, he frowned at her to discourage any laughter, before turning on his heel and marching back to the entrance.

The woman stood looking over Anna's shoulder. 'Is there anything you would like to know about it?'

Picking up on his theme, she corrected herself in time, changing 'Niets,' Dutch for 'Nothing,' to 'Nyet,' Russian for 'No.' She added, in a voice reminiscent of Marlene Dietrich, 'I wish to be alone.'

As she examined the painting at distances varying from a metre to a decimetre, the woman walked away to stand near the entrance. She smiled at Marcus, who scowled back before stepping outside the gallery and overtly checking the area for snipers.

Anna inspected every square centimetre of the painting, examining the brushwork minutely. After a quarter of an hour of scrutiny and contemplation, she took out her iPhone. Priestley saw her through the window and assumed she was about to photograph the painting, so re-entered the gallery and joined her, ready to do likewise. Anna called up photographs of the other twelve paintings, which she compared with the one in front of her. Then she checked the signature in the bottom right-hand corner against more of her photographs. Finally, she held the phone forward and prepared to take a picture. The woman immediately rushed to stop her, calling out, 'It is not permitted!'

As she made a grab for Anna's hand, Priestley wrapped his arms around the woman's waist from behind and dragged her backward, leaving her too shocked to speak. When Anna snapped in their lingua franca, 'Let her go, Dimitri,' the woman gratefully assumed the choice of language was for her benefit. He released his hold and stepped around her, physically blocking her from moving toward Anna, while holding her in position with a mesmeric stare.

When Anna had taken her photographs, she peered past Priestley and smiled at the petrified woman, before walking past them; as she reached the door, Priestley released his hypnotic gaze and moved to follow her.

Outside, Anna walked several paces along the street, with Marcus still catching up; then she began to sprint, taking him by surprise. He ran after her, feeling like a child who had almost been caught scrumping in an orchard. They were well clear of the gallery by the time she finally stopped running. While fighting to catch her breath, she began to laugh irrepressibly. Finding her laughter infectious, he joined in, rediscovering a feeling of innocence he had not known in years. Suddenly, all the laughter drained from him, as he realised he was in danger of falling in love with her.

Anna's giggles finally subsided, leaving her with a broad smile and laughter lines by her eyes. 'That was exciting, *da*?'

'Yes, it was fun.'

She became serious. 'But now you wish to know what I discovered.'

He sighed. 'It's what we came for.'

'You wish to know if it is a forgery. My answer is: I am unsure. Let us sit somewhere and I shall explain.'

'We'll go and have a bite to eat. Any preference? It's all on expenses, within reason.'

'You know what is suitable, so you should choose.'

'I'm glad you said that; there's a place not far from here I've always wanted to go to.'

'What is it?'

'A café called *Les Deux Magots*.'

'The two maggots?' She acted annoyed, raising her voice and pointing at him repeatedly. 'You think we should eat at a place that is named after maggots?'

Playing his part, he looked downcast during her performance, and only smiled when it was over. 'French for "maggot" is "*asticot*". A *magot* is a figurine from the Far East.' He added as an afterthought, 'It's also slang for a pile of cash.'

CHAPTER 51

They strolled along *rue Bonaparte* before turning onto *boulevard Saint-Germain*. He recognised the café by the words *Les Deux Magots* spelled out in large letters attached to the wall above a blue awning. 'This is it, Anna; we're following in the footsteps of Pablo Picasso and Ernest Hemingway.'

He navigated them past the outdoor tables and into the interior, then pointed up at the two seated Chinese mandarins on pedestals. 'They're what gave the place its name.' Seeing an unoccupied chair opposite a space on a bench seat, he led the way through the crowded café, noticing in passing how tourists appeared to outnumber residents by at least two to one. He reserved the chair by resting a hand on the top of the curved back, inviting her to sit on the red moleskin-upholstered side-bench at the other side of the mahogany table. When she was comfortably settled, he sat down, remarking, 'The décor hasn't changed here since it opened at the end of the nineteenth century.'

Pointing discreetly toward a waiter dressed as from that era, she responded, 'Neither have the staff.' Glancing through a menu, she remarked, 'Have you seen the prices? I think we should just have a coffee; I would not wish to get you into trouble by costing you too much.'

A concern instantly flashed across his mind: how much would she really cost him, in the end? He shook his head. 'It'll be fine.'

'No, we shall eat later.'

'Perhaps we should have absinthe; it's what they used to drink here. Absinthe makes the heart grow fonder.' Despite his English pronunciation, she appeared to have missed the pun. 'Absinthe sounds like absence. There's an English expression, "Absence makes the heart grow fonder." I should have had that sign made up to tell you it was a joke.'

She looked at him sorrowfully. 'I understood what you meant, but I am already too fond of you. Tomorrow we return to England and you return to your family; I will miss you terribly.' Her face lightened a little. 'Perhaps we could still see each other, sometimes?'

He found himself unable to respond, torn between various wrong answers and unsure whether there even was a right one. She waited with the patience, if not of a saint, then of a mistress. He chose delaying tactics. 'The idea of not seeing you leaves me feeling sick in the pit of my stomach. Give me time to think what we can do. But for now, you need to tell me all about the painting.'

She stayed with the earlier theme in the hope of receiving reassurance. 'I have no right to expect anything from you.'

'We'll work something out.'

A waiter walked over to them. '*Vous désirez?*'

Anna responded, 'A black coffee, thank you.'

Marcus added, 'Me, too.'

They were still admiring the décor when the waiter brought over a pot of coffee and poured two cups for them. After he was out of earshot, Marcus asked, 'Now, what about the painting?'

She put on what she felt was her professional face, as though readying herself to deliver a lecture. 'In the past, famous Dutch and Flemish painters employed others to perform tasks appropriate to their level of competence. At one extreme, another master may have been invited to add their specialism. In Antwerp, Peter Paul Rubens was often paid to add cherubim, and is known to have added Venus and Cupid to a painting by his neighbour, Jan Brueghel. Joos de Momper also collaborated with Brueghel. So, an excellent painting may have contributions from different experts.

'At the other end of the spectrum, apprentices within a studio may have completed some of the work; for example, simple patches of sea or sky. He, always a "he", would be encouraged to imitate the master's style so that the overall effect was consistent; for example, in terms of brushstrokes. This was not to fool the public, but simply to create the correct impression. How do I know it was not intended to deceive? Because the studio would produce price lists that clearly indicated whether the principal artist would be the master himself, or someone more junior, or even an apprentice. The prices reflected who actually did the painting.

'Over the centuries, some of the original information has been lost. Now, a painting may be described in an auction catalogue as "Workshop of..." or "Studio of..."; this indicates that the artwork was created in the studio of the famous painter, but it was not the master himself who wielded the brush. It is possible he contributed one small part, or even none at all, though he would have supervised the work to make sure it achieved a sufficient standard.

'Now to the Piscaro we have just seen. If Milo had had other artists working for him, I would say that the painting was that of an apprentice; it showed sufficient similarity of brushstrokes, but insufficient confidence of movement or application. As he had no apprentice, the choice is this: either it was created by Milo on a bad day, or it was painted by someone else who was familiar with how he worked.'

Priestley reflected on her words for several seconds. 'For criminal trials, the test is "Beyond reasonable doubt." Do you have any doubt that someone else painted it?'

'I do have a little doubt; not much, but too much to satisfy your definition.'

'What about the test used in civil cases: "Balance of Probability". Could you be confident at that level?'

'Yes, *I* could be. But the history of attribution indicates for every expert who expresses an opinion, another expert can be found who will state the opposite. Take a Renoir of uncertain provenance, for example: in Paris, I know of one expert who will always disagree with a certain other expert, on principle.' She displayed a tragic smile. 'I fear I have failed you.'

He shook his head. 'Not in the slightest. What you have done is convince me the case is worth progressing on the basis that someone watched him working and copied his style. That makes for quite a small pool of suspects. Well done, Anna; you've been brilliant.'

Though she smiled in acknowledgement, he was unsure whether she appeared subdued due to the limitation of her assessment, or if it harked back to the earlier part of their conversation about continuing their relationship in the UK. He squeezed her hand, hoping it was an appropriate response to whichever subject was uppermost in her mind. After a moment, he returned to practicalities. 'I need to let my colleagues back home know your conclusion, and I'd better let *Jean-Luc* know as well. Then I'd like a bite to eat.'

She brightened up. 'I have a suggestion for food: we could have a picnic by the Seine.'

'That's a great idea. I'll send *Jean-Luc* a text; if I talk to him, he might want to meet us, and that would get in the way of the picnic.' He typed a simple message: "Painting probably a forgery but cannot be certain. See you later." Showing it to Anna, he asked, 'Are you alright with this?'

She nodded. 'Yes; "probably" is the correct word.'

'Good. I'll send the same message to my team back home.'

When they stood to leave, Anna pointed to the various paintings that were on display around the café in a small exhibition of French art. 'I would like a moment to look at these.' Ten minutes later they emerged into the sunshine. 'There is a covered market just around the corner on *rue Lobineau*; I went there yesterday for the Champagne. It is open from eight to eight; we can buy our food there.'

They discussed what to purchase. Marcus was about to choose a small punnet of French strawberries, when Anna noticed a large punnet of Spanish ones and pointed to the price label. 'These are much cheaper.'

He shook his head. 'Surely, we have to have French ones in Paris; besides, they're only seven francs a kilo.'

She looked puzzled. 'How do you know that? All the prices are now in euros.'

He smiled. 'It's in an old song, "These Foolish Things Remind Me of You."'

'I have not heard it; sing it to me.'

'What, here? I can't!'

She giggled. 'Coward! Sing it later, then.'

They purchased the French strawberries and a bottle of Muscat, along with apples, cheese, bread and pâté. Anna looked thoughtful. 'We have no glasses for the wine. The hotel is on the way; we should call in and borrow some from the bar, like I did yesterday.'

'So that's where they came from.'

'Yes. I just asked the barman if I could borrow three champagne glasses. He handed them over straight away and asked for my room number.'

'Did you tell him?'

'Of course.'

'You didn't think he might have had an ulterior motive for wanting to know your room number?'

She blushed uncomfortably. 'Oh, I see; I did not think of that. How naïve of me.'

He smiled at her. 'Oh well, it's a good thing you were in my room before the bar closed.'

Back in the hotel, Anna retrieved the three glasses. 'Will you sing me the song about strawberries?'

'It would annoy the neighbours.'

'There is only one neighbour, and I know she is out.'

'Well, I can't remember much of it, anyway.'

She took out her iPhone. 'I can look it up.' They found several versions on YouTube and chose one by Leslie Hutchinson. Sitting side by side on the bed, they listened in silence. At the end, she tapped the screen a few times to close the music option.

He turned to ask her what she thought of it, but saw tears were trickling down her face. 'What's wrong, Anna?'

'The song is about us. I shall forever be reminded of you by foolish things; even strawberries will bring back the memory of these days with you in Paris.'

He smiled as he shook his head. 'Don't think about that now; we have the rest of the day to enjoy together. Let's go and have our picnic.'

She brushed away her tears and gave him a brave smile. A moment later she adopted the Rodin *Thinker* pose with her hand to her chin. 'I have had another idea: let us have the picnic in bed.' Pointing to the back of the door, she added, 'The sign says no food should be consumed in the room; you must be a bad influence on me, making me wish to break rules.'

He shook his head. 'Don't blame me. Anyway, I'm sure we can avoid making a mess.' After imitating her Rodin pose for a moment, he switched styles and pressed his right index finger to his temple. 'I've had an idea: let's go to bed now and have the picnic later. I can't perform with a full stomach, anyway.'

She gave him a theatrically quizzical look. 'You are going to perform? I must watch!'

His laugh was coarser than he had intended. 'I expect you to do a lot more than watch!'

'What shall we do, then?'

He began gently peeling the clothes off her, starting with her jacket and T-shirt. 'Let's just make it up as we go along.'

CHAPTER 52

After showering, Priestley checked his phone for messages. He told Anna there was one from *Jean-Luc* requesting more details from her. 'We'd better go and see him in person. At least, you should; he didn't ask for me.' He picked up the bottle of Muscat and took a corkscrew from a small side-pocket in his case. 'But let's have that picnic first.'

They drank the bottle of wine with a little food, before walking to the *gendarmerie*. As the building came into view, he held her back for a moment. 'Let's try not to look like we've just spent the afternoon in bed together; it doesn't take much to start a rumour.'

Dubois led the way into his office and invited them to sit in the visitor chairs facing his desk; he noticed they re-positioned them further apart. When they had settled, he smiled at Anna. 'Will you please tell me why you believe the painting is a forgery.' He listened patiently to her explanation, which was a reduced version of the one she had given earlier to Priestley. When she reached the end, he nodded in assent. 'I have already acted on your assessment, Anna. This afternoon, I myself, personally, went to the gallery and spoke to the lady who is employed there. I explained there was a suspicion that the painting was a forgery, and that if she sold it as the genuine article, then she could be committing a criminal act. While I waited, she telephoned someone who ordered her to take it off the wall until the position became clear.'

Priestley asked, 'Was she upset about it?'

Dubois turned to him. 'Less than I had expected. It would seem they do not own the painting and have not paid anything for it. A gallery in England sent it to them to see if they could sell it over here. In fact, the lady was more upset about having been visited by two members of the Russian mafia earlier in the day.'

Anna immediately turned to Marcus, looking to him to respond. *Jean-Luc* intercepted the signal. With a smile, he stared directly at Anna. 'Is that something you know anything about?'

Anna's gaze remained firmly fixed on Marcus, who begrudgingly gave a response to *Jean-Luc*. 'We never said we were mafia; we didn't even say we were Russian. If the woman misinterpreted our few words of conversation, that was entirely down to her.' He allowed a smile to cross his lips. '*Da*? *Nyet*?'

Jean-Luc grinned at Marcus before turning back to Anna. 'Clearly, you have hidden talents. Perhaps I could investigate them this evening with you if you are not busy? I know some excellent restaurants.'

Anna responded curtly. 'I am busy.'

Jean-Luc turned to Marcus, his frown, jutting lips and extended arm with out-turned hand all asking what it was that he had failed to understand. Marcus responded with raised eyebrows, a shrug of the shoulders, a sideways glance and a tip of the head in her direction, which collectively denied any knowledge of the reason for the rejection.

Jean-Luc asked Marcus, 'Are you also busy, Dimitri?'

Marcus laughed, then sighed. 'Unfortunately, yes, I'll be having to work on the case. Now that we think the painting is a forgery, the investigation is changing direction and I need to get involved in re-planning.'

Jean-Luc stood and shook hands with them, Marcus first. 'Then I wish you well. Do please keep me informed of how the investigation proceeds.'

Once away from the *gendarmerie*, Anna stopped and looked at Marcus with a serious expression. 'Is this what we will do in the future? Act our parts? Be deceitful? I have never known this situation before; it makes me uncomfortable.'

He looked pained. 'You're not the only one; I've never done this before, either.'

'Do you mean I am your first lover since you became married?' Seeing he was about to respond, she put her finger to his lips. 'Do not answer my question, but I shall assume it is "yes".'

They set off again. Soon after, Anna announced, 'I wish to make a love lock on *pont des Arts*. Or maybe *pont de l'Archevêché* or *pont Neuf*; they are not much further away.'

He shook his head. 'That practice has been banned; it damages the bridges.'

'Mine shall be a picture love lock. I wish to make a photograph of us together, which I shall keep private for me to look at sometimes. People used to lock in their love on the bridges; we shall lock in our secret.' She saw the concern on his face. 'You refuse?'

'What if someone hacked into your phone? Hacking is a really widespread problem. People take a private photo today and find it has eighty million viewers tomorrow. If only I could be certain no one else would ever see it, I'd be very happy to know we were locked together in some way.'

She looked pensive. 'We would be locked into our secret, but not locked into love.' Taking hold of his hand, she searched his eyes. 'And yet I know I love you.' He was stunned into silence, as she had uttered the words he had not dared to speak. She interpreted the lack of response. 'How easy it would have been for you to tell me you love me; but you cannot, because you wish to be a moral man, and so you refuse to lie to me.'

He squeezed her hand tighter. 'The problem isn't that I can't say it because it's a lie, Anna. The problem is that I can't say it because it's true.'

She felt her face glow as though in religious ecstasy, imagining herself as Simon Vouet's *Saint Cecilia* sitting at an organ. 'Whatever happens to us, I shall always remember this moment.'

They walked back to the hotel in a deep silence that was disturbed only by the occasional mundane observation. Anna floated along in the joy of knowing she was loved and in love. Marcus felt burdened down by the thought of loving two women; for him, feeling love for Anna did not undermine his love for Helen, but he knew she would not see things that way. He remembered reading that the concept of monogamy was a pernicious restriction placed on male behaviour by the Catholic Church; believing Anna would find it difficult to understand how he could feel current passion against an inconvenient ecclesiastical doctrine from a past millennium, he kept his annoyance to himself.

When they reached the hotel, she invited him into her room to discuss plans for the evening. Seeing her bed, he immediately recognised a need for dissembling. 'We can't have the hotel staff knowing your bed hasn't been slept in; we shall have to unmake it.'

She waited in vain for clarification. 'Do you mean we should have sex now in my bed, or are you imagining we could create a so-called work of art?'

He smiled at her interpretations. 'I just meant we don't want to advertise the fact that you'll be sleeping in my room tonight. You will be, won't you?'

'Yes, of course.' She pulled back the sheets. 'If we wish to make it believable, perhaps we should get in for a while. Yes?' He smiled and nodded. She quickly stripped off and jumped into bed. As he was about to join her, she pointed to her case. 'There are condoms in there.'

Finding a half-empty box of twelve, he held it up as though a courtroom exhibit. 'Twelve? Seriously?'

'I took six into your room and kept six here. I did not know what would happen, if anything.'

He took two out of the bag, just in case. After using one of them, they drifted off to sleep.

Anna was still sleeping when Marcus woke and tried to slip silently out of bed; she stirred and opened her eyes. 'What time is it?'

'Time we went for something to eat; I'm starving.'

They showered in her room. As they decamped to his room to clean their teeth, he realised her brush in his bathroom was evidence of occupation, and worried how many more clues they had left around.

She asked, 'Where should we dine? Do you know somewhere? Are you expecting Lily to join us?'

He replied succinctly, '*La Procope*, yes, and no.'

'Do explain yourself, Marcus.'

'Your three questions, answered in sequence. One: there's a place called *La Procope*; it's the world's first literary café, and that's where I'd like to eat. Two: yes,

I do know somewhere; I refer you to my earlier answer. And three: no, I'm not expecting Lily to join us. But then I wasn't expecting her yesterday, either. Now I have a question for you. Last night you brought two bottles of Champagne and three glasses. What would you have done if you'd found me in bed with Lily.'

She replied in a matter-of-fact voice. 'I would have joined you, of course.'

'Really? I mean, really, really?'

'There is only one way to be certain.' Seeing his broad grin, she added, 'That is not a suggestion!'

They walked the short distance to the café, where they enjoyed a two-course meal with a bottle of red wine. Sitting gazing at her across the linen-covered table, he suddenly realised they must look for all the world like a couple in love.

On returning to his room, he found himself hoping she would just let him sleep. She, on the other hand, had no wish to appear to be limiting her favours, and he was too polite to decline her offer.

Afterwards, as he lay awake with her sleeping soundly beside him, he found he had the beginnings of a headache.

CHAPTER 53

Anna woke in the night, thrilled that Marcus was there with her; she decided she should share the pleasure of the moment with him. In the gentle light, filtered by the pale green curtains, she observed him smiling in response to her whispers and kisses, yet he remained in a deep sleep.

Marcus woke in the night, finding Anna disturbing his sleep by whispering in his ear, kissing him on his eyelids and nibbling at his earlobes. As her hand caressed his torso he could not stop himself from smiling. He quickly made a gentle snoring sound, hoping it would encourage her to desist.

When her seven o'clock alarm began to beep quietly, she woke immediately and quickly turned it off before it could increase its volume. Her probing hand established his inclination for sex, so she decided to have one last session with him before they had to leave Paris. She pulled back the cover and knelt by his hip, facing away from him, a condom already to hand.

He opened his eyes and saw what she was about to do. 'Shall I put that on?'

She turned her head and looked at him over her shoulder. 'No, I shall do everything. All you have to do is to lie back and enjoy it.' From her kneeling position, she placed one leg over him until she was straddling him. As instructed, while she rhythmically moved up and down on him, he lay back and enjoyed it.

After showers and breakfast, she collected her

possessions and returned to her room for final packing. When he had completed his own packing, he made a last check that nothing was being left behind. Feeling grubby, he took a condom wrapper out of the bathroom bin where she had thrown it, and put it into a small disposable bag with the other empty wrappers he had collected during their stay. After initially placing the bag in a corner of his case, he transferred it to his pocket, having decided he should dispose of it as soon as possible in an anonymous rubbish bin.

The walk to the Metro and the ride to the Eurostar terminal took place with little interaction, as each attempted to process their thoughts and imagine what the future may hold. Their minimalist conversation continued on the train until it entered the tunnel under *la Manche*. Anna turned to Marcus and leaned close to him, resisting her impulse to touch him. 'I promised you I would keep our secret; everything that has happened will remain locked away. Now we have to go back to being who we were.'

He looked at his watch, as though to register the time that this transition was happening; quickly, he reset it to UK time. Looking up, he saw the melancholy in her eyes. 'What do you mean, back to who we were? Are you wishing to end it? Us, I mean.'

'No; I wish for us to go on forever. I meant only that our behaviour has to be what it was before.' She looked earnestly into his eyes. 'Do not ever say to me, "We can always remain friends." We have been so much more than friends, we cannot ever truly go back to being what we were.'

'Well, I don't want it ever to end, either; I just don't know what will happen to us in the future.'

'If you wish to see me, telephone me. I shall await your call.'

He felt ashamed that his first reaction was relief not to find himself the subject of a fatal attraction, and that his second was concern their relationship may be exposed if he contacted her in Sheffield. Yet her quiet dignity reminded him he had genuinely felt love for her in Paris. He wondered if it was possible to segregate his feelings geographically; in Paris he would be in love with Anna, and elsewhere he would be in love with Helen. For a moment, he envied sailors who had a wife or a mistress in every port.

She was certain she loved him and equally certain he loved her. How noble of him, she thought, that he would revert to being the dutiful husband and father that he had been before their sojourn, even though he would miss her terribly.

He realised he would not wish to be seen with her close to home, for fear of discovery. He asked himself if what he most wanted from her was sex. He was certain her love for him was on a much higher plane. What a low, base creature man is when compared to woman, he thought.

She remembered how much she had enjoyed having sex with him, and wondered if he would be able to see her every week at her home, so that they could continue to delight in the closeness of each other's bodies within a loving relationship.

He wondered how easy it would be to arrange to see her every week so that they could continue to enjoy having sex together.

All the way to London they ate nothing and drank only water from the two small bottles he had bought in

Paris. As they disembarked a little before midday at St Pancras, he asked, 'Shall we have lunch?'

She felt that somehow by starving herself he would understand the depth of her feelings for him. 'I cannot eat a thing.' Seeing his disappointment, she added, 'But if you wish to eat, I will perhaps manage a little something.'

At a local pub, he had a pint of Fuller's London Pride and a double round of sandwiches, except for the one she had with her bottle of Heineken lager.

When the Sheffield train set off, he prepared to send a text to Helen. Finding the number function too fiddly for quick entry, he settled for "On train ETA three."

The quiet that had descended on them when they had set out from Paris continued into the final leg of the journey, interspersed only with short bursts of banal conversation. When the triangular lodge came into view, he directed her gaze and attempted to sound brighter, but knew his voice remained flat. 'Look, Anna, over there; it's the hunting lodge I told you about.'

'Yes, I see it. What an unusual design.' She knew they sounded like colleagues rather than lovers, but accepted these were the rules of the game for a married man and his mistress.

As they were entering the outskirts of Sheffield, he pointed through the window. 'Look, that's Millhouses Park; I take my children there.' He never used the vernacular in relation to his or anyone else's children; for him, "kids" would always be young goats. He wondered if she had interpreted his use of "children" as an indication that he wished to be formal with her.

She wondered if he had mentioned his children in

order to emphasise how he was returning to his family.

When the train was drawing into Sheffield Midland Station, she felt an overwhelming desire to kiss him, as though it were somehow essential for terminating their excursion. She remained seated as other passengers prepared to save a few seconds by standing in the aisle in readiness for a rapid exit. As the carriage was disgorging the last of the other travellers, she stood and picked up her case; he did likewise, standing behind her. Approaching the exit, she put down her case and turned to him. 'May I kiss you goodbye?'

He kept his case in his hand. 'Someone might see us. Besides, this isn't goodbye, it's *au revoir*.' He smiled, 'We'll see each other again soon.'

On the platform, standing awkwardly, too far apart, fingering their case handles, looking at each other obliquely, unsure how to take their leave, he was shocked to hear a familiar voice very close to him. 'Marcus, I thought you might like me to collect you.'

He turned to find Helen standing watching him, and rushed to answer. 'Thanks, Helen, that was a good idea.' He gave a sweeping movement of his hand to indicate Anna. 'This is Ms van Honthorst. She's the art expert I told you about.'

Helen held out her hand, which Anna shook with minimal movement. 'May I drop you somewhere?'

'No, thank you. I shall walk to the gallery.'

'Then we'll be off. Goodbye.'

Marcus gave Anna a cheery, 'Bye.'

Anna remained tight-lipped, bearing a tragic smile.

CHAPTER 54

Helen led Marcus to her car in the short-stay car park near the station. 'Tell me what you've been up to, then.'

'Never,' he thought. 'Later,' he responded.

In the car, he glanced at his watch. 'I hope we aren't late for picking them up.'

Manoeuvring around a tight corner, her gaze remained steadfastly on the road. 'Amanda's collecting them and taking them to the ball-pool with hers.'

'That's good of her. Any particular reason? Not someone's birthday is it?'

'No; I just thought it would be nice for the two of us to have some time to ourselves.'

During the fifteen minute journey, she brought him up-to-date with practical minutiae and gossip: their schooling, the house, the garden, speculation on what might be happening with the couple up the road.

She parked her car on the driveway and unlocked the house. Inside, she leapt her way past the pressure pads as though playing hopscotch. When she had disabled the intruder alarm, he trudged into the kitchen with his suitcase. She re-locked the doors, then joined him and put her arms around him from behind. 'I've a treat for you.'

He turned his head to look over his shoulder at her, but she remained hidden, squeezed tight to his back. 'What is it?'

'It's me; I'm your treat. You can take me to bed straight away. Unless you're worn out.'

'Shouldn't I unpack, first?'

'What? I thought you'd jump at the offer. I thought you'd have missed me as much as I've missed you.'

Relieved she could not see his face, he began the inevitable stream of lies. 'I missed you ever so much.'

'Have you been getting enough…'

He dived in. 'I haven't been getting any!'

'I was going to say "sleep". Have you been getting enough sleep?'

He was appalled at his own stupidity; having led so many others to give themselves away in interviews, he knew he had made an obvious error that he would find difficult to expunge from the record. 'No, I haven't been sleeping too well; I missed you being next to me. Let's go to bed right now, and to Hell with my dirty clothes!' He doubted his weak humour was enough misdirection, but at least it was a start.

She repeatedly pushed him in the back as he climbed the stairs, as though she could hardly wait. 'I've bought another nightie; it's from India. Tell me what you think of it.' Before he was down to his shorts, she had thrown off all her garments and pulled on a simple white calico nightdress. She delivered her rehearsed line. 'It's just like me, plain and simple and a little bit coarse, so I think it suits me down to the ground.'

So, not at all like her, he thought. 'It looks great on you. Now take it off.'

'As you command, my lord and master.' She removed it as quickly as she had put it on, before adopting a coy pose with an arm across her chest and a hand positioned in lieu of a fig leaf. Effecting a Cornish accent only good enough to fool an outsider, she asked, 'And what must I do for ee now, sur?'

Thinking he would be less likely to give away his guilty secret if she could not see him as they made love, he pulled the sheets off the bed and lay back on it. 'Come and kneel just here.' He patted the bed next to his hip. She knelt facing him. 'No, not that way around; face away from me.' She turned as instructed. 'Now put your leg over me.'

Her West Country accent drifted toward Somerset. 'I zee what ee be wanting there, zur.' She straddled him. 'Now don't ee be a-troubling yourself there, zur; I 'ave it all in 'and.'

The intercourse was brief, as he had felt an enhanced pleasure at having sex with her for the first time in that particular way. Afterwards, as she lay down beside him, pulling the sheets up to cover his shoulders, he thought the short duration supported the premise that he had been missing both her and sex.

She looked intently at his face. 'Has someone in Paris been teaching you new tricks?'

He swallowed hard. 'No one. I just thought of it.' Even to his own ears it sounded false.

'Well, you certainly enjoyed it. When you mentioned unpacking, I thought you were just trying to put me off, as though you'd lost interest in me.'

He hoped humour might rescue him. 'I wasn't indifferent to you... unless that's two words.'

Her laughter was short-lived. 'Is there something you'd like to tell me, Marcus?'

Use of his name warned him she was once again becoming his psychiatrist. He sought to drive her back to being the loving wife. 'Yes, my darling. I just want to say I love you more than anyone in the whole wide world, and I'll love you for ever and ever.'

She imagined an 'Amen.' Then she considered an alternative ending: 'No matter what.' She had an uneasy feeling there was an unidentified problem she would need to uncover.

He turned away from her penetrating gaze. 'I'd like a bit of a snooze, now, if that's alright.'

She lay behind him. 'I'll keep your back warm.'

Hormonal release and lack of sleep contributed to his rapid descent into a deep slumber. She remained awake, thinking through various scenarios covering his time in Paris, but recognising she had insufficient facts on which to base a working hypothesis. She saw how his eyelids were flickering, an indication he was in REM sleep; knowing it was generally characterised by muscle atonia, she was alarmed when he overcame the usual paralysis and began to move violently. She decided to wake him by repeatedly shaking his arm. His eyes sprang open and she saw the look of a frightened rabbit caught in car headlights. 'Marcus. Marcus. Were you having that dream again?' She was familiar with his most frequently repeated nightmare that harked back to a lethal action when he had been in the army.

'No, it wasn't that one; it was a different one.'

'What was it, about?'

'A young woman was standing in a garden with a slice of bread in her hand.'

'Who was the woman?'

'I don't know.'

'What did she look like?'

He knew she was blonde and in her twenties, but it was not simply Anna and not simply Lin; she seemed to be more a composite of the two, but then perhaps she was neither. 'I've no idea; could have been anyone.

You know how dreams are.'

'Try and retain the image. What about the bread?'

'It was wholemeal and buttered. I mean it looked brown and somehow I knew it was wholemeal.'

'And the garden?'

He knew it was their back garden. 'It was just a common-or-garden garden.' She gave a tiny laugh. 'A butterfly landed on the bread. Then the woman folded over the slice, trapping it inside. And then she started to eat the butterfly sandwich.'

Her initial interpretation was of an Apollo connection, high ambition with a looming threat to achievement coming from a woman. She pressed for more information so she could analyse it later in greater depth. 'Was it a real butterfly?'

'Yes; it flew like one.'

'Was it a real species?' They had recently prepared for a butterfly count with the children by examining photographs of almost sixty species; as she remembered them clearly, she thought he should also.

'Maybe.' A twitch told him she had expected more.

'What colour was it?'

'Yellow.'

'Was it a brimstone?'

'I don't know; it could have been. But it was much bigger than any ordinary brimstone.'

'You could paint it; their things are still out.'

'You know I can't paint.'

'Anyone can paint a butterfly; it's easy.'

'I don't think I can remember it well enough.'

'Well, if you don't want my help analysing your dream, I can't force you. Anyway, we'd better get up; one of us needs to go and collect them.'

CHAPTER 55

Priestley arrived early at the station to check through the case documentation and bring himself up to speed ahead of the 8:30 team meeting. He found Witty already working on collating and cross-checking the team's reports, and at 8:15 called him into his office. 'You tell me what progress there's been here and I'll tell you what happened in Paris.' He felt a prickly sensation as he realised he had just lied to his sergeant.

Witty gave a brief summary that cncapsulated the limited progress and the absence of a breakthrough. 'After you let us know that picture was probably a forgery, Cargill decided to interview other people at the studio with painting on their list of talents, which is virtually all of them. He rushed through several but we didn't get any kind of a break; most of them had solid alibis. Anyway, there's more to go, so you never know.

'The three owners of the other Birds paintings have been interviewed, but they were a dead end. And they were nothing like the descriptions Campbell gave you: an accountant, a dentist and a retired teacher.'

'What about CCTV?'

'It's being processed, but it's such a slow job. Isn't there supposed to be some fancy software that can read car number plates straight off the screen?'

'You mean retrospective ANPR for grainy pictures of vehicles travelling at speed at night, taken at a sharp angle. Yes, I think we're due to get that upgrade installed sometime this century.'

Witty gave the obligatory laugh. 'What about Paris? Lily said your art expert seemed a bit of a cold fish, but maybe not so bad when you got to know her.'

Priestley was relieved Witty's feedback from Lily had focused on the negative. 'That's fair comment, though I'd say she was very professional. She examined the painting really closely and was quite confident it had been done by someone else, but she wasn't certain enough to stand up in a criminal court and state it as a fact; in the end, it was still just an opinion. Even so, I got the impression she was close to being certain, so we're proceeding on that basis.'

Plummer arrived at the office door, gave a perfunctory double-knock and walked in. 'Have I missed anything? I didn't know there'd be a pre-meeting meeting.'

Priestley observed her closely as she lifted the top chair off the stack. He reprimanded himself for watching her lithe body as she moved across the room, and wondered if Watt was right about men being sex-obsessed. When she had seated herself next to Witty, he tried to sound unaffected by her entrance. 'Hello, Lin. Neil's updated me on progress, and I was just saying to him, though the expert's opinion isn't strong enough for criminal prosecution purposes, she's almost certain the painting's a forgery.'

She nodded. 'So, how was Paris? Did you see much of it? What did you get up to?'

'I had dinner with Lily on Tuesday. It was nice seeing her again.'

'Just the two of you? Sounds cosy.'

Witty interjected. 'There were two other people there: a stunning blonde, and a gendarme who joined them for a drink after the meal.'

Plummer's eyes widened. 'Who was the stunning blonde?'

'Take no notice; he's exaggerating. The only stunning blonde was Lily; the other woman was just the art expert.'

Plummer fidgeted on her chair. 'Is this the same one who's old and wrinkled? Or is it a different one?'

'Well, maybe I did overstate that a bit.'

Witty turned to Plummer. 'Lily described her as mid-twenties, elfin-faced, and elfin-slender: that's an expression she heard an Icelandic model use.' He hesitated for a moment before plunging on. 'And she had a really good pair. But she wasn't very friendly.'

Plummer stared at Priestley. 'Did you find her very friendly?'

Priestley looked at his watch. 'I found her very professional. Now, we need to get to the incident room; it wouldn't do for us to be late.'

They walked into the MIR five minutes ahead of the scheduled meeting, resulting in anxious checking of watches by those who arrived subsequently.

Priestley noticed some of the officers welcomed him back with a little more formality than he was accustomed to. When invited to give the progress report to the team, Witty responded, 'Would it be alright for DC Plummer to give the update, sir?'

As Priestley was wondering about the significance of the "sir", he looked at Plummer to check how she felt about Witty's proposal. She responded with a firm, deep nod of the head, which he interpreted as indicating she was fully prepared and that she and Witty had planned this. He returned her nod, adding, 'Go ahead.'

Plummer gave a thorough briefing, incorporating details of the three previous 8:30 meetings from which Priestley had been absent. She ended, 'Now it's over to you, sir. What exactly did you do in Paris?'

He felt the start of a flush of embarrassment, though inwardly he applauded Lin's tactic of using the meeting as an opportunity to coerce him into revealing more details of his overseas trip. 'The art expert assessed the painting and concluded it was probably a forgery created by someone who had seen Milo working; that means we should be focusing on people at Green Lane Studios. Any comments?' Berry raised his hand. 'You're not at school, Tony; just spit it out.'

'Well, even if the painting is a forgery, does it necessarily mean the forger is the same person as the one responsible for the death?'

'Good point. There are places in China that do top notch knock-offs at very low prices; it's just possible the actual forger may not be local, but they'd probably have needed access to an original Piscaro to imitate the brushwork. So, more likely, it is someone local who did the forgery; but as you rightly ask, is it the same person who was involved in the death.

'That means there are two threads to the investigation: the forgery and the death. If there's a common motive, then we're probably looking at one perpetrator; otherwise there are two. For now, I don't propose splitting the case, but we do need to keep an open mind that there may be more than one crime and more than one criminal. And then potentially there's the question of co-conspirators.'

As there were no more questions, Priestley closed the meeting. He called over to Cargill. 'Frank, let's go and have a chat in my office.'

Priestley sat down and invited Cargill to do likewise. 'How are things going, Frank?'

Cargill looked defensive. 'I think it's a good thing for the more junior members of the team to get the experience of a formal way of behaving in meetings. They won't always be working for you, so they might get into bother if they don't call the boss "sir", or "boss", or ask permission to speak.'

'Ah, I see. I thought things were a bit more formal this morning. Yes, you could be right. But I was really meaning about the case. I'm told you've been getting through interviews quite quickly; are you sure you're not being too quick and missing something?'

'I'm doing them by the book, but there isn't much coming out of them. I've been getting similar impressions to the ones you got; so far, no one has come over as murderer material. But that's not the same as not being forgers; I thought any of them could be forging stuff, because they're all a bit unconventional.'

'I know exactly what you mean. Would you like me to divide up the remainder of the list, or do you wish to take them all on yourself?'

'Which would you prefer, sir? I mean Marcus.'

'I'd like you to do them all, Frank. That gives us commonality of assessment, and you can then rank them separately from most to least likely of killing and of forging. How does that sound?'

'I'll get right on it.' He stood up. 'Thank you for the vote of confidence in me, Marcus.'

CHAPTER 56

Priestley closed his office door. He wanted to hear her voice, but wondered if it was too early to call her. Though he had no clear idea what he wished to say, he took out his mobile phone and selected her number.

She answered immediately. 'Yes?'

'How are you?'

Her voice was breathless from fearful excitement. 'How should I be? Should I be happy that you are calling me? Or are you just calling to say goodbye.'

The pain vibrating through her last quavering words entirely removed the latter option for him; not that he had intended to finish with her. 'You should be happy; happiness suits you. I just wanted to talk to you, but I don't have anything to say. It's stupid of me, isn't it?'

'I cannot really talk now, but I am happy to hear your voice. Call me when you wish to see me.'

'It's lovely to hear your voice, too, even if only for a moment. I have to get back to the investigation. Bye.'

He wondered if it would be better for her if they finished straight away, before she had invested more time and emotion. He convinced himself the best option for her would be for the relationship to diminish slowly until she no longer felt the depth of attachment she obviously felt right now; she could then decide when to finish with him.

Eventually, he turned his attention back to the case. Having assigned all the people at the studio to Cargill, and excluded himself from speaking to Campbell, as well as putting Witty and Plummer in charge of running things in the office, he knew the key threads of the investigation were no longer in his hands. He accepted there was no alternative but to wade through his e-mails and other correspondence, to clear the backlog of work that had accumulated since Monday.

Looking in his private e-mail account, he found the photographs of the painting she had taken in Paris. There was one of the whole picture, another four showing it in quadrants, and a final close-up of the signature. As she had stated her love for him in the original missive, he attached the pictures to a new e-mail, which he sent to his work account with a message that detailed the contents.

Ploughing through the mundane correspondence, he imagined he was doing penance for having been with her; he felt better for receiving punishment, and for a moment he wished he were Catholic, believing no one does guilt like the Catholics.

On hearing a familiar knock, he hoped his boredom would soon be relieved. Feeling his muscles had been setting rigid in the seated position, he flexed his shoulders, stood up, walked across the room and opened the door.

Witty was standing outside. 'I didn't hear you call me to come in.'

'I didn't; I wanted the exercise. Have you got something?'

'Andrea Carter: do you remember her?'

'Yes. She's living with William Campbell.'

'Wrong. She was living with William Campbell. I telephoned on her landline to check something with her and got an answering machine, so I called her mobile number and mentioned I'd tried the landline. That's when I discovered she's moved out. It might mean nothing, but I thought you ought to know.'

'It might mean nothing and it might mean something. Well done for picking up on that, Neil. Why were you calling her, anyway?'

'Frank's interview with her didn't really get to the bottom of things, to my mind. She says she watched the BBC national and local news with Campbell. If it was a recording they watched later, he may have a rock-solid alibi, but if it was live, he could still be in the frame.'

'Good point. I for one never watch live news; I can often condense an hour down to five or ten minutes, depending on whether anything's happening that's worth knowing. Sometimes it's just fillers, or interviewers who like the sound of their own voice.'

'Well, if it was live and finished just before seven, she didn't see Campbell for the next two hours and twenty minutes; not 'til he came and spoke to her at twenty past nine. She assumed Campbell didn't leave the house because she didn't hear him go out, but she was always in a separate room so didn't actually see him. What should we do?'

'Let's you and me have a chat with her, shall we? See if we can't get more out of her. If I remember rightly, there's also a teenage son who hasn't been interviewed; let's have them both in.'

'I'll go and give her a call.'

'Do it from here. You can sit at my desk, but don't go getting ideas above your station.'

Witty made the call and spoke to Andrea Carter. He relayed some of the discussion to Priestley, first pressing the mute button to keep their conversation private. 'She says her son's at school so it needs to be this evening or the weekend.'

'Weekend's fine by me; what about you.'

'I'm OK.' He turned off the mute function. 'Tomorrow morning alright?' There was a lengthy pause. 'What time do you get back from the market?' A shorter pause followed. 'Yes, of course. So, 11:00 a.m.?' Priestley gave a thumbs-up. 'That's agreed then.' He reiterated. 'We'll be looking forward to meeting you and Lewis here at Midshaw Police Station at eleven o'clock tomorrow morning. Thank you, Mrs Carter. Goodbye.'

Witty put down the telephone and vacated Priestley's chair. While they remained standing, Priestley asked, 'What else do we need to do now?'

Witty frowned for a moment. 'Book a room?'

Priestley attempted to make a joke of the response. 'I'm not that fond of you!'

Witty grimaced. 'I think that expression's "Get a room." Nice try, but no cigar.'

'Well, what else do we need to do?'

He thought of several related administrative tasks, but felt certain they were not what Priestley had in mind. 'You'd better tell me.'

'We should do some research into Campbell before we talk to Mrs Carter. Find out what vehicles he owns and check the CCTV specifically for those registrations. Get someone who knows how to be discreet to talk to the neighbours and find out if they've ever seen him out cycling; it isn't that far from his house to Piscaro's, so a pushbike ride could get him there in ten minutes.'

'Lin would be good for talking to neighbours.'

'She would, but we can't use her; what if she were

seen by Campbell? Don't forget she's our ace in the hole if we need to schmooze him.'

'Ace in the hole? Schmooze? I thought you went to Paris; you sure it wasn't New York?'

'Alright. I mean she's our star performer if we need to charm him. Here's me trying to be with-it and all I get is criticism.'

'Anyone who says "with-it" is definitely without it! Maybe you're more "past it". You just need to accept you're not as young as you used to be, and grow old gracefully.'

'Says he who is just a day younger.'

'Make that four years.'

'Anyway, I've no intention of growing old gracefully; I plan to grow old disgracefully.'

Witty gave a snort in lieu of the laugh that was expected of him. As he left the office to implement the plan, he wondered why Priestley was trying so hard to be amusing. He recalled how he himself had found humour essential when his life had been a mess.

CHAPTER 57

By eight o'clock on Saturday morning the Priestley household was fully active, if not hyperactive in the case of Edwin. Marcus attempted to speak with Helen as she multitasked to accommodate the various breakfast preferences and provide Alice with paper and crayons. He drained his coffee mug, then stood to stretch over and pour milk onto the absent Edwin's cereal. 'I'll need to be off by half ten at the latest.'

'Are we doing the shopping early?'

'Not sure we'd have the time.'

'Well, do I wait 'til you're back?'

Marcus guiltily aimed to keep his options open. 'I've no idea how long I'll be; you'd better do it by yourself.'

'What's so urgent, anyway? Going in on a Saturday morning. I thought you said things were plodding along slowly.'

'A witness might hold the key, but she can't come 'til after she's done her shopping down the market.'

'And you're fitting in with her wishes because...'

'I'm such a nice person.'

'... you believe she'll be more willing to disclose information if she appreciates how accommodating the police have been.'

He realised he should have known better than to attribute a simplistic interpretation to her observation. 'Depending on what we find out today, the case may really take off. It's a pity we couldn't prove that painting was a forgery; it would at least have given us a basis for a criminal trial of some sort.'

'It is a homicide, though, isn't it?'

'I'm expecting to link forgery with homicide, but I can't guarantee there aren't two separate perps.'

'Perps.' she repeated with disdain. 'What is the world coming to.' She turned to Alice, who was holding up a sheet of paper. 'That's lovely, sweetheart. And it's a ...'

'Bird.'

'Yes, of course it is, and it's a lovely bird. Do you know what type of bird it is?'

'A garden bird.'

Marcus lifted Alice high into the air. 'I went to Paris to see a painting of a bird, but I think yours is better.'

Helen grabbed Alice off Marcus and sat her back down at the table next to her cereal. 'You can keep crayoning if you like, but you must keep eating your breakfast as well.' She turned to Marcus. 'She may as well learn to multitask from an early age; it'll be good training for when she's older.'

'So you don't think things will change for women in the future, then?'

'I can't see feminist ideals making much headway in the wider world when they struggle even to get a toehold in this house. Take shared responsibility for making breakfast, for example.'

He looked excessively hurt. 'I poured Edwin's milk.'

'So you did. Well done!' They found a few milliseconds to exchange smiles. 'Do you have a photo of that painting, by the way?'

'I've one of the whole thing and five of parts of it.'

'I'd like to take a look at them.'

Edwin appeared in the doorway and chanted to no one in particular, 'Twelve is a dozen. Thirteen is a baker's dozen.'

Marcus turned to him. 'And what's a dozen dozens?'

'A gross; that's a hundred and forty-four.'

'And what about a dozen baker's dozens? And what is a baker's dozen of baker's dozens?'

Edwin raced away.

Helen spoke delicately with studied politeness. 'Thank you for that, Marcus; he hasn't eaten his cereal yet.' She switched to her normal voice. 'Put the photos on the computer for me before you go.'

'But you've a hundred and one other things to do.'

'And that makes a hundred and two.'

'I thought multitasking results in lack of focus.'

'Oh, it does; when single-mindedness is needed, men really excel. But for the other nine hundred and ninety-nine situations it's women's willingness to do everything that puts us miles ahead.'

Edwin came to the door and shouted, 'One hundred and fifty-six and one hundred and sixty-nine.'

Helen knew he was correct, but pretended to need Marcus to check. 'Is that right?'

He grinned. 'How do you expect me to know?' Turning to Edwin, he asked, 'Did you use a calculator?'

Edwin chuckled. 'No! I worked it out with a pencil and paper, like when somebody can't do a poo!'

Helen pointed at him fiercely. 'Don't you go saying things like that when we're eating, you bad boy!'

Interpreting the achievement of a "bad boy" as an alternative form of praise, he ran away, still chuckling.

Marcus raised his eyebrows. 'Haven't *kindbezogene Epitheta* been banned?'

Helen turned on a strong Northern Irish accent. 'Do I even sound like an American psychologist?'

Alice asked, 'Why is Edwin a bad boy?'

Helen responded, 'I was only joking; he knows that.'

Marcus added, 'Boys like being bad, sometimes; it makes us what we are.'

Helen knew she lacked the time to critique his assertion, so filed it away for a less hectic moment. Seeing Edwin running into the kitchen, she bellowed, 'Stand still! I don't want you crashing into something; we've no time for taking you to the hospital again. Now sit down and eat your breakfast.'

Edwin correctly interpreted the change of tone. He sat at the table and picked up his spoon, pushing the muesli to the edge of the bowl to make a deep indentation. Marcus pointed to it. 'Is that art? It could be worth a fortune.'

His widened eyes betrayed his insincerity. 'I'd better not eat it then.'

Helen snapped through clenched teeth. 'Marcus!'

He smiled at Edwin. 'I think you need to, and soon.'

Edwin toyed with his spoon. 'What do you think it looks like?'

'A caldera. That's the name for the crater that's left when a volcano blows its top, like what your mother's about to do if you don't get it eaten.'

He pushed the cereal away from the edge of the bowl and created a high peak in the centre. 'Now it's a mountain.' He plunged the spoon deep into the centre. 'Now it's a volcano.' He flicked the contents high into the air. After it had landed all over the table and the floor, apart from the deposits that had attached themselves to the ceiling, he pointed to the bowl again.

'Now it's a proper caldera.'

Helen screamed at him. 'Edwin! You bad boy!'

Alice turned to Edwin, laughing sweetly. 'It's alright, Mummy's only joking. You're not a bad boy, really.'

Helen snapped at Alice. 'Yes, he is a bad boy.'

Alice began to cry. 'But before, you said…' Her words were lost in a series of sobs, each one beginning with a double intake of breath and ending with a burst of air and saltwater.

Helen rushed around the table to cuddle Alice. 'It isn't always what I say, sweetheart; it's how I say it that matters. And look, he's made a mess of your picture.'

Alice stopped crying and smiled at her. 'It's alright Mummy, I can do another one for you.'

Marcus pointed at Edwin. 'Eat your cereal right now and don't move from there 'til you've finished.'

Edwin plunged the spoon deep into the remaining cereal to pile it as high as he could, then stretched his mouth wide open and deposited the whole amount.

Marcus shook his head in despair. 'And don't choke on it.' He stood up and located a clean cloth. Rinsing it in hot water and squeezing out the excess until it was barely dripping, he wiped the tephra from the table and the floor, leaving the ceiling for later.

Helen took a moment to smile warmly at him. 'Well done, love; that's two helpful things you've done this morning. Before I know it, you'll be making breakfast.'

CHAPTER 58

Priestley devoted some time to helping with household chores before setting off for the station. When he arrived shortly before half past ten he found Witty already beavering away at his desk in the main office. He called over to him without slowing his pace. 'Morning, Neil. I'll talk to you in a bit about the interviews.' On entering his own office, he closed the door quietly before phoning her. 'Hello, how are you?'

She breathed her words, feeling the thrill of hearing his voice. 'Hello, Marcus. Are you coming to see me?'

'I'm busy this morning, at work. I hope to be away by noon; would you be home at, say, half twelve?'

'I shall make sure I am.'

'Marvellous. Anyway, must go, someone waiting.'

He went to see Witty. 'Are you ready for them?'

'Yes, sure. Do we need to talk tactics?'

'I was thinking "Good cop, better cop." If Andrea's split with Campbell, I don't see her doing him any favours. But then, we need to make sure she doesn't go the other way and lie to try and get him into trouble. I reckon we talk to her on her own, first. Then we talk to the boy with her present, unless it seems like he won't say anything in front of her. If we think he's holding back because she's there, we'll have to consider replacing her with an appropriate adult, which would mean reconvening. Let's hope it doesn't come to that.'

'What shall we do with the lad when we're talking to her on her own?'

Priestley rubbed his chin in contemplation. 'Let me see, he's fourteen years old. Get a young WPC to take him to the canteen; that'll keep him fully occupied.'

Feeling a little uncomfortable with the implication, Witty's mandatory laugh fell short of regulation length.

Priestley noticed. 'Something troubling you, Neil?'

'Not really, Marcus. Except, I don't think we're supposed to say things like that anymore. I'm trying to be Politically Correct all the time, nowadays, so I don't get into bother with anyone. Half the time I don't know what's acceptable and what isn't. It doesn't really matter for you; you could say anything you like and no one would complain.'

'I wouldn't say that, Neil. Just between you and me, Frank complained about me as soon as he got here. He doesn't like my informality, for a start.'

'That's for sure. While you were away he insisted the morning meetings be more formal.'

'What exactly did he say?'

'We should call him "sir", for a start. His motto was "remember rank". He said he'd take it up with you when you got back. Has he said anything?'

'Not a dicky-bird. Oh, hang on; yes, he did say something about it, but I didn't take it as a proper complaint. I might even have agreed with him a bit.'

'So, do we need to be more formal in future?'

'Neil, you're getting all uptight about nothing. You need to relax a bit; you need to chill.'

Witty looked surprised. 'You did just say "chill", then, didn't you? And you didn't mean cool myself? I've heard you complain about the "American linguistic disease"; I never expected you to catch it.'

Priestley laughed longer than was justified, in the

hope that it would encourage more of the old Witty to reveal itself in the future. He had heard murmurs from a few constables that, since making Sergeant, Witty had become "standoffish", "stuck-up" or "one of them".

Witty waited for Priestley to fall silent. 'I'd better check with reception.'

'Good idea. I hope she's on time; I've much better things to do today than be waiting around.'

Witty spoke with the two women on reception, who confirmed they were primed to contact him as soon as Andrea Carter arrived with her son. He reflected on how sympathetic the reception staff were perceived to be, not only by victims or witnesses, but even local lowlife; he wondered if, as civilians, it was perhaps easier for them to distance themselves from the underlying crimes.

Witty located a WPC and asked her to join them in interview room one. Back at his desk, the telephone rang and a receptionist informed him his visitors were waiting. He walked to Priestley's office to let him know. 'They're here.'

'They're early.'

'I'm ready for them; are you? I assume you'll be leading the interview?'

'Yes; I've got to keep my hand in. But we can make it a three-way chat with Mrs Carter if it seems like that might work better; all friends together, you know.'

Witty went to reception to collect the visitors. Priestley went directly to the interview room where he found nineteen-year-old WPC Paige Anderson waiting for him. He quickly checked over her uniform, before focusing on her face: if plainness were a virtue then Paige would be a saint. With her flat, dark hair, strong jawline and oversized nose, she could have been mistaken for a young man, were it not for a substantial pair of protuberances. 'Hello, Paige. You're looking smart this morning. Hope you don't mind working Saturdays.'

'We all have to take our turn, sir. Anyway, I'm not on the duty roster for next weekend.'

'So, you turned the page over and found your name wasn't on the list.'

She looked puzzled. 'Was that a joke, sir? You know, turning the page over.' She smiled weakly. 'It wasn't very original.' Brightening visibly, she added, 'Though it's nice to know you're interested in when I'm available.'

Before he could respond, Witty arrived with the Carters. Priestley noticed Andrea appeared a little over-dressed for shopping at the market, so assumed she had changed before leaving for the station. He led the introductions, which included shaking Lewis's hand so he might appreciate the implication of being treated as an adult, even though legally he was still a juvenile. 'Now, Mrs Carter, I'd like to have a chat with you on your own, first of all.'

When he gave her a perfunctory smile, she responded with a wholehearted one. 'Just the two of us? That would be nice.'

'Sorry, I meant with Neil as well. Paige, will you take Lewis to the canteen? Get him a drink on my tab.'

Before anyone could disagree with the proposed arrangement, Lewis had moved closer to Paige, and was standing looking at her with a face that suggested he could not believe his good fortune. Priestley waited for the two of them to leave the room.

CHAPTER 59

Priestley invited Andrea to sit opposite him across the desk, with Witty positioned off to one side. He began, 'Would you like a drink, Mrs Carter?'

She shook her head. 'No thank you. Will my Lewis be alright with that policewoman?'

He smiled. 'I'm sure she'll look after him very well.'

'He's only a boy, you know. He isn't used to being on his own with young women.'

'They'll only be in the canteen; they'll probably just chat about pop music, or something. Now, can we talk about you, Mrs Carter.'

She frowned. 'Why do you want to know about me? I'm not very interesting; I'm not anybody, really.'

He refrained from disputing the logic of her assertion. 'You're certainly of interest to us; though you may not know it, you might hold the key to solving a mystery.'

She appeared unconvinced. 'Well, if you say so.'

'First of all, let's go back to when you were sweet sixteen.' Witty knew Priestley played a wide variety of mind games, but nevertheless felt uncomfortable with his opening line; she, on the other hand, appeared thoroughly pleased with the idea. 'What I mean is, start with when you were single and then go forward in time. What was the first big thing that happened in your life?'

'I got married.'

'How old were you then?'

'Twenty-two. Ken Carter was twenty-six.'

'Is he still alive?'

'Yes, more's the pity.'

'Are you still legally married?'

'No, we got divorced. We seemed to be going along fine, and then all of a sudden he ups and says he's leaving me. Men can be such bastards you know. I don't mean you of course, Mr Priestley; I'm sure you're ever such a nice man.'

His smile set rigid on hearing the endorsement he feared he could no longer justify. 'And you have remained single ever since.'

'What do you mean by "single"?'

'Your name suggests you didn't re-marry. Unless you found another Mr Carter.'

She laughed for a moment. 'No, I didn't re-marry.'

'And what about boyfriends? Tell me how many; I'll give you time to count them all.'

She laughed dirtily. 'Just the serious ones?'

He guessed her "serious" meant "sexual". 'That would be a good starting point.'

'Let's say, five.'

'And is William Campbell among those five?'

She frowned at him as though she had seen through his charm. 'Not really. He's the one you want to know about, isn't he?'

'Yes, Mrs Carter. Could you tell me where and when you first met him.'

'It was last year when he took me on at his gallery to do the cleaning.'

'Since then, have you come to know him well?'

'I didn't really get to know him until just six weeks ago. Three weeks before that, I gave him four weeks' notice, because the tenancy on my flat was due to end and I hadn't been able to find anywhere local to live; I was having to move back in with my parents, and they're too far away. At first, he didn't seem fussed about my finishing; but then, with just a week left, everything changed. He invited me to move into his house when my tenancy expired, and start working in the gallery during the day. One time, he even let me help out at an auction of his. He always paid me by the hour, cash in hand.' She stopped abruptly.

Believing she now appeared worried due to having disclosed an illegal practice, he deliberately looked unconcerned. 'What did you do at the gallery?'

'I kept the place clean, made cups of tea, ran errands. But there wasn't anywhere near enough for me to do; it was like he was inventing jobs for me just to make me feel busy. I think he was simply being nice to me; helping me out, you know. Have you ever met him?'

Priestley was taken aback by the unexpected question; he gave a slight shake of the head. 'So you moved in. How did that work out for you?'

'Not how I'd expected. Most people think he's really confident, the way he can talk to anyone. But I thought maybe he was shy underneath it all, and he really wanted me for... Well, you know. But he didn't. He never once suggested anything like that. So I guessed he was probably queer.'

'I believe homosexuals prefer the term "Gay" nowadays. So, he didn't make any advances toward you, and you just lived there as his guest?'

'Well, I looked after the place, kept it clean, did the shopping, the cooking, the washing, the ironing. He didn't charge me anything at all for living there. I mean, for both of us living there; Lewis, as well.'

'Then what happened? Why did you leave?'

'He asked me if I'd have somewhere to go if I had to move out, and I said yes it's what I would have done before, back with my parents. So he said, he was ever so sorry, but he just liked living on his own. And that was that. He helped me to move out straight away. He also said there wasn't enough for me to do at the gallery during the day, but I could go back to being the cleaner if I liked. It wasn't worth the effort of travelling for me, so I had to turn him down and finish altogether.'

Priestley played back her earlier comment, hoping to trigger further testimony. 'You said you thought he was simply being nice to you when he invited you to stay at his house and to work at the gallery during the day.'

'I believe there was more to it than that. I think he was wanting to try to be like the rest of us, but you can't fight your nature, can you?'

'That's very true,' he responded emphatically. 'Now, can we go to the night Milo Piscaro died.'

'You mean Miles Percy; that was his proper name. I knew him when he was growing up.'

'How well did you know him?'

'Not very; he was just a local boy.'

Priestley waited but no more was offered. 'Going back to that night, you were watching television in the evening with Mr Campbell.'

'From twenty past nine.'

'And before then you watched the news together. Was that on live or was it a recording?'

'They were live programmes. National news, six to half past; local news, half six to seven.'

'Did you watch the local news to the end?'

'Yes; and then the national weather forecast.'

'And after that you left the room. What time would that have been?'

'Just before seven o'clock.'

'So you went to your own room; the downstairs one. Did you see Mr Campbell at any time between seven o'clock and twenty past nine when he came and asked if you'd like to watch TV with him?'

'No, I didn't actually see him.'

'But you think he was there.'

'Well, he must have been, mustn't he? He'd have said, if he was going out.'

'Was there any other way you'd have known he was in? Take your time; have a good long think about it.'

After several seconds of looking down with eyes almost closed, she raised her head and stared directly at Priestley without blinking. 'I couldn't say.'

He asked the reverse question. 'Was there anything that might have led you to believe he had gone out?'

'What do you mean?'

'A telephone left ringing. A car being driven away.' She shook her head. 'A lavatory being flushed?'

'I wouldn't have heard from my room.'

'Would it be fair to say you can neither confirm nor deny... Let me start again. You simply don't know if he was in or out, from seven o'clock to nine twenty. You can't say whether or not he left the house. Is that true?'

'Yes, I suppose it is.'

'Well, thank you, Mrs Carter. We need to keep this interview confidential, so I must ask you not to divulge details of it to anyone.'

'My lips are sealed, Mr Priestley.

CHAPTER 60

Priestley sent Witty to bring Lewis and his minder to the interview room. When he was alone with Andrea, he engaged her in casual conversation. 'It must be difficult, bringing up a boy on your own.'

'Two boys, Mr Priestley. My Ryan is at university.'

'He doesn't live with you, then?'

'That's down to lack of space; he didn't want to share with Lewis anymore. It's to be expected, isn't it?'

'It's normal for fledglings to wish to fly the nest; it's usually the expense that holds them back.'

'Ryan gets by without asking me for money. He works in a bar, and then there's his student loans. I don't see him very often; he works all hours, what with one thing and another, studying and all that.'

'Did Mr Campbell ever invite him to stay at his house when you were living there?'

'He said he wasn't sure he could cope with having a third guest; he likes his quiet, you see.'

'So he never stayed. Did he ever visit?'

'No, though he did phone me one time to say he'd like to. I think he wanted to check out Mr Campbell, make sure he wasn't taking advantage of his mum. He's a nice boy, is Ryan.'

Priestley heard footsteps outside followed by a knock at the door. 'Come in.' The three of them entered, Anderson moving the remaining empty chair for Lewis to sit down next to his mother, before she and Witty leaned against the wall.

Priestley looked at Lewis for a moment, attempting to assess his maturity from his appearance. Though Priestley's personal preference was for short hair, he recognised the long, dark, unkempt greasy locks were probably a teenage rebellion or fashion statement of some sort. He wondered if the spots along his forehead stemmed from the greasy hair, or if they were more down to the fizzy pop he obviously liked to drink. 'Now, Lewis, I just want to ask you about the evening that Miles Percy died.'

'Milo Piscaro,' he stated, as though a correction.

'Yes, the artist. Do you remember what you did? Start with your evening meal and work forward.'

'We had spag. bol. at half five. I went upstairs to do homework. Half ten, mum came in to say goodnight.'

Andrea interjected, 'And he wouldn't let me kiss him.'

Lewis reddened and he turned to glare at her. His voice barely concealed his irritation as he uttered through clenched teeth, 'Mum!'

Priestley offered Lewis a discreet sympathetic glance. 'What exactly did you do between six o'clock and nine twenty? Did you keep an eye on the time when you were doing your homework?'

'There was a clock next to the bed.'

'Did you often go and look at it?'

'I could see it from where I sat.'

'Would you say you're generally aware of the time when you're doing your homework?'

'I suppose so.'

'How long do you usually spend doing your homework?' Lewis twisted his mouth, unwilling to respond. Priestley guessed the problem was a truthful reply would displease his mother. 'Actually, I'm only interested in that particular evening. Tell me, as accurately as you can, what you did from six onwards.'

'I didn't have much homework to do, so first I put on my headphones and listened to some music. Then I did a bit of history and some English.'

'Did you at any time remove your headphones?'

'No; I kept them on, even between playing stuff.'

Andrea barged into the conversation. 'He wears them all the time, morning noon and night.'

Priestley briefly registered a look of concern for her benefit. 'So, that evening, you wouldn't have been aware of anything happening in the house, such as someone going out, flushing a loo, anything like that?'

'Not a thing.'

Priestley paused, then started speaking more slowly. 'Tell me, Lewis, why do wear them all the time?'

Lewis struggled to make his mouth settle on a word to begin a response. He unconsciously reached to his right to pick up his can of pop; without drinking any, he held it between him and Priestley. 'Why not? They're comfy, and I like listening to music all the time.'

Priestley recognised the significance of the symbolic barricade, interpreting the last response as a lie. He made an attempt to look deeper into the boy's psyche. 'Do you find it a bit lonely, being on your own with your mum?'

'There's my brother, Ryan.'

'But he doesn't live with you.'

'No, but I see him sometimes.'

'Though not at home; at least, not when you were at Mr Campbell's house.'

'I did see him there; he called in one time. It was a

Saturday.'

Andrea scolded him. 'You never told me that, Lewis. Why not?'

Lewis turned to her. 'Because he didn't have time to stop, and he knew you'd be sorry you'd missed him.'

She responded, 'Well, what did he want?'

'Just to have a look around the house.'

Priestley decided to allow her to take over the questioning.

'He didn't go anywhere he shouldn't have, did he?'

'I don't know.'

'He didn't nick anything or break anything?'

'No, I'm sure he didn't.'

'So he wanted to see the house, but not his mum.'

'He wanted to get an idea of what Mr Campbell was like. He asked me what I thought, and I told him.'

'And what was that?'

'I said I didn't believe he was really interested in you.'

She turned to Priestley. 'Out of the mouths of babes.'

Priestley smiled at Andrea. 'You've obviously a very smart boy, here. I think that's all, then.' He turned to Anderson. 'Just give Mrs Carter the opportunity to use our facilities, won't you?' Turning back to Andrea, he stood and thrust out a hand for her to shake, at a height that forced her also to stand. He added, 'Lewis can stay here with us for a couple of minutes 'til you're back.' Andrea had no wish to appear ungrateful for his consideration, so followed Anderson out of the room.

When the women were out of earshot, Priestley addressed the seated Lewis from his standing position. 'Now, tell me why you really wear headphones all the time. Come on, we're all men together, so out with it.'

'It's just a habit.'

'When did it start?'

'A few years ago, when my parents were fighting; I didn't want to hear them.'

'And why didn't you stop wearing them, once they'd separated?'

He looked worriedly into Priestley's face, unable quite to make eye contact. 'Because I didn't want to hear my mother shagging all the time.'

Priestley calmly acknowledged the revelation. 'Well, let me give you some advice. Listening to music can be distracting when you're meant to be studying; don't you want to go to university like your brother?'

'Yes.'

'To study hard and get a good job?'

Lewis's face suggested he was in the throes of an internal conflict; finally, the words burst out. 'I want to go, so I can meet lots of girls.'

Priestley wagged his finger at him. 'Then focus on your work and stop spending so much time listening to music. And another thing: wearing headphones can stop you from engaging with the real world. You need to get out and meet people, especially the female variety. Do you know how to chat up girls?' Lewis's face froze. 'Talk to them, ask them about themselves; it's a common mistake to spend all your time talking about yourself. And one more thing: get your hair cut, it looks a mess. You've a much better chance of picking up girls if you don't look scruffy.' He gave a hearty laugh to show his advice was meant kindly.

When Andrea returned to the room to collect her son, she found him looking happier than she had seen him for years. 'Have I missed something?'

Lewis responded. 'Mr Priestley has been giving me tips on how to chat up girls.'

Andrea thought she ought to look shocked, but decided instead to respond to Priestley's smile with one of her own. 'What he really needs is a father figure; you're not on the market, are you?'

Priestley gave no reply beyond increasing his smile and proffering a handshake. 'Goodbye, Mrs Carter, it's been so nice to meet you.' She tried to hold his gaze but he turned away to shake hands with her son. 'Goodbye, Lewis.' He adopted a more serious expression as he looked at Anderson. 'Come back here when you've taken them through to reception.'

After Anderson had left with the Carters, Witty walked toward the door as Priestley sat down. 'I'll get on with putting these notes on the system; I don't want to spend all day here.' He paused for a moment. 'You don't want me for your talk with Paige, do you?'

'Not particularly; it's just a quick chat.'

'Not a lengthy de-briefing, then?' He winked at him.

Priestley stared at Witty. 'That's not very PC, Neil. Perhaps you'd better stay, so no one starts a rumour.'

Witty ignored the insincere invitation, giving a brief wave over his shoulder as he left Priestley alone.

Anderson returned to the interview room, closing the door carefully behind her and remaining standing. 'You wished to see me, sir.'

'Yes; I just wanted a quick word with you, Paige.'

'And you got rid of DS Whittington to make it more private. I understand, sir.'

Priestley had a sinking feeling. 'Just what is it you think you understand, Paige?'

'Everyone knows how you are, sir, so I want to say straight away, just because I don't have a boyfriend at the moment, that doesn't mean I'm giving it away…'

He jumped in. 'Well, I'm glad to hear it. Other people won't have respect for you unless you have respect for yourself, including your body.'

She smiled. 'Well, it's nice to know you respect my body, sir.' She opened her eyes wider. 'What I was saying was, I'm not giving it away to just anyone, but I'd give it to you if you asked, even though you are quite old.'

Priestley put his elbows on the table, lowered his head and put his fingers to his temples. 'The only thing I wanted to ask you was how you thought the interview with Lewis went, and whether you learned anything useful from him earlier when you were babysitting.'

'That's a good cover story, sir. You're not expecting to have me right now over the table, are you?'

'No, I'm not!'

'Good, because I expect a bit of seduction first, like dinner or a nightclub or something. Well, should I expect to hear from you soon, then?'

He gave up on trying to debate rationally. 'Sorry, Paige, I have my hands full at the moment.'

'That's alright sir; just let me know when you haven't.'

Priestley thought he detected a spring in her step as she turned and walked away, carelessly leaving the door open. He sighed deeply, then went to close it before phoning the other woman. 'I'm almost finished here; I could be with you in half an hour, traffic permitting. Are you still free?'

'Yes, I am. How long will I be able to keep you?'

'I'm not sure.' After a little more conversation, he terminated the call and headed back to his office to collect his jacket.

As he passed through the main office, Witty saw him and called out, 'I'm nearly finished here. Let's have that drink we nearly had a while back.'

The words stopped Priestley dead in his tracks. 'I may have to stay a while; you just pack up and get off as soon as you're ready.'

'Come on, Marcus, it's a Saturday; surely there's nothing you can't put off 'til Monday.'

'You're probably right, but I need to check.'

'You don't sound too keen on coming out for a pint. You aren't turning over a new page, are you?'

Priestley accidentally allowed a hint of irritation to creep into his voice. 'That's, turning over a new leaf.'

'I meant Paige Anderson.' He began to laugh, then stopped quickly as Priestley failed to respond in kind. 'Sorry, Marcus, I didn't mean to put my foot in it. She's a bit young for you, though, isn't she?'

He shook his head. 'I can't believe this. No, I'm not intending to sample the delights of that young woman, not now, not ever. I can see I'll have to come to the pub; otherwise, before I know it, there'll be another stupid rumour circulating about me.'

He tried not to sulk as he headed back to his office. Guiltily, he called her again. 'I've just been summoned to a meeting. When it's over I'll give you another call and see if you're still free. I'm really sorry.'

She sighed. 'I suppose this is what I must always expect: to be fitted in between your other obligations.'

CHAPTER 61

Marcus surveyed the range of beers on offer, checking their Alcohol By Volume ratings. He intended to have a quick pint, then drive without having to wait for some of the alcohol to be metabolised. Many of the guest beers were quite strong, so he settled on Moonshine with an ABV of 4.3, a good, reliable pint, brewed locally. He knew someone of his weight might be below the current legal limit even after two pints, but he had adopted the more stringent French standard several years ago when holidaying there. He had reasoned that a fatal RTC stemming from slowed reactions when his blood-alcohol level was just within the legal limit might leave him free of criminal culpability, but would undoubtedly suffuse him with an ocean of moral guilt.

Neil questioned his choice. 'Not trying a guest beer, then? Some of them might not be back for a year.'

'Not this time. Besides, I'm supporting my local brewer; Moonshine's from Abbeydale.'

'I'll have the same then.'

Even though he was off-duty, Marcus's conditioning led him to settle in a corner where he could watch the door, as well as check for anyone who appeared to take too close an interest in their conversation. He offered the usual opening. 'Cheers!' Neil responded likewise, then waited for Marcus to begin. Marcus waited for Neil to begin, smiling encouragement.

When Neil became consciously aware they were each waiting for the other, he began to laugh. 'What's happened to us, Marcus? There was a time when we'd just sit down and start talking; now, it seems like we're both being cagey. You know how it is with me and Lily, so ask away if you want more info. But how is it with you and Helen? There are so many rumours about you, colleagues don't know what to believe anymore. I know you said it all began with a misunderstanding, but they just keep growing. Is everything alright at home?'

Marcus felt troubled that even his relationship with his wife was now being questioned. 'Everything's great between us. I wish there was some way of putting a stop to the rumours; tell me exactly what they are.'

'Are you sure you want to know?'

Marcus hit the wooden table with the side of his fist, causing the glasses to wobble slightly but without spilling a drop. 'Yes, damn it. If I don't know what they are, I can't try and kill them off.'

Neil interpreted the controlled blow as merely a dramatic gesture. 'OK, I'll tell you what I've heard, and you can tell me if there's any truth behind them. And I must remind you that you're now under oath.'

'No, I'm not.'

'Yes, you are; you said "damn it".'

He sighed. 'Very clever, Neil; now, get on with it.'

Having been slouching, Neil ostentatiously drew himself up straight, tugging at his lapels in lieu of his non-existent gown. 'I put it to you that you spend time in your office looking at porn magazines.'

'I refute that scurrilous allegation.'

'I put it to you that you have had sexual relations with one or more higher-ranking officers of the female persuasion in order to further your career.'

'I refute that allegation.'

'I put it to you that you requested the presence of a certain junior officer of the female persuasion to accompany you on your trip to Paris with a view to engaging in sexual activity with her.'

'I refute that allegation.'

'I put it to you that you are currently engaged in an affair with a certain young, blonde woman.'

Marcus was sure that was just a lucky hit. 'That's the second time you've used "certain" without making it clear who you're referring to. You need to be more specific.'

'Very well. I put it to you that you are currently engaged in an affair with a certain young, blonde woman, to wit one DC Linda Plummer.'

'I refute that allegation.' He decided to avoid the risk of any more collateral strikes. 'Is that the lot?'

'More or less; there are variations but they're all on the same theme.'

'Right then, it's my turn now.' He adopted a serious expression. 'I put it to you that the love of your life is in Paris…'

'Yes; you know she is.'

'I hadn't finished. And that as a consequence you are spending far too many hours in the office because you have nothing to do at home.'

He grimaced. 'Possibly.'

'I put it to you that you're trying so hard to be Politically Correct all the time, you're alienating some of the junior officers who don't see any harm in laughing at the odd bit of gender-related humour.'

'Am I? I never intended to.'

'I put it to you that when you see Lily you put it to her from morning 'til night to make up for lost time.'

'I'll take the fifth.'

He smiled. 'I put it to you that you are an excellent officer and a credit to the service.'

'Oh, absolutely.'

'Right, well, I think that'll do for your annual review.'

'And what about your review? As your sergeant, should I be doing more to kill off the rumours about you? I'm trusting you to have been completely honest with me, you know; I'd hate to look like an idiot when it turns out there was some truth behind them.'

'Every answer I just gave you under oath was one hundred per cent correct. Killing off the rumours isn't really your responsibility, but I have to say it would be good if people stopped spreading them.'

'I'll do my best to help.'

Marcus was trying not to appear in a hurry to finish his beer, but realised he was down to the final quarter before Neil had reached halfway. He took out his phone and began to check for messages; it startled him when it rang, as he had not anticipated the two functions occurring simultaneously. The screen indicated the call was from Helen. 'Hello, love.'

'Hello, yourself; it sounds like you're in the pub.'

'Just having a swift one with my sergeant.'

'How is Neil? It must be hard for him, Lily being away so much.'

'Just a minute, I'll ask him.' He continued to speak directly into the phone, but in a higher register and with increased modulation. 'Neil, Helen wants to know if it's hard when Lily's away.' Neil laughed dirtily, saying nothing. 'He just indicated it is.'

She refused to join in the humour. 'You'd better tell

him that's not what I meant. Anyway, if you're only having a swift one, you should be back in half an hour at the most. I'll let Edwin know you'll be taking him to the park. See you soon.'

As she terminated the call, he knew he would have to cancel his assignation. He emptied his glass. 'She wants me back; I'll have to go.'

Sitting in the car, he called the other woman. 'I'm really ever so sorry, but I can't come and see you today.'

'What about tomorrow?'

'No, I'm never free on Sundays. Maybe next week.'

He thought he heard a sharp intake of breath, or maybe a sniff, and then perhaps a sob, just before the line went dead.

CHAPTER 62

Just ahead of the Monday morning meeting, Priestley called Cargill into his office. 'You need to know what happened on Saturday, Frank. I re-interviewed Andrea Carter and established she was unable to confirm Campbell was in the house between seven o'clock and nine twenty. So, he's in the frame again.'

'And I'm at fault for not digging deep enough last time. Are we talking disciplinary, sir?'

'Of course not, Frank. We all make slip-ups from time to time; it just means you're human like the rest of us. I simply wanted you to know before the meeting, so it didn't come as a shock to you.'

Cargill stared at him for a moment. 'Why are you passing up your chance to get rid of me?'

'You're part of my team, and everyone on the team should know we always look out for each other. That doesn't go for anyone who's breaking the law, but as far as unintentional mistakes are concerned, all I ask is that everything humanly possible is done to stop them happening again in the future.'

'You're not even going to give me a bollocking? Well, I'll certainly do my best to raise my standard, Marcus.' Priestley smiled for a moment as he imagined Frank hoisting a flag; Cargill misread it. 'Supporting your team members: is that from your time in the army? I suppose back then you all had to be prepared to do anything for your mates; even to die for them.'

Unable to mask the flood of painful memories,

Priestley stood to signal the meeting was over. 'That's all in the past, Frank. I'd sincerely hope none of us ever have to lay down our lives for each other. And I certainly can't imagine one of us losing our lives over a slip such as what time someone was where, so let's not dwell on the alibi issue.'

Priestley ushered Cargill from his office and headed for the MIR; unusually, he found he was following him at a respectful distance. After taking one step inside the MIR, he turned quickly and flashed a smile. 'I'm just on time, so you must be late.'

Cargill gave a low, rumbling laugh. 'Sorry, boss.'

Priestley began the meeting a minute later, at precisely 8:30. He deliberately avoided looking in Cargill's direction as he informed the team about Campbell's lack of an alibi. Then, for the sake of anyone who had not yet read the recent updates, he explained that the painting Campbell had sent to Paris on a sale or return basis was now believed to be a forgery. Furthermore, if it was in fact a forgery, then it would probably have been painted by someone who had watched Milo working at his studio; however, though some of the painters had no alibi, none of them appeared to have a motive. After emphasising how the investigation needed a breakthrough, he ended, 'We need to brainstorm this. Any ideas?' Everyone looked at the floor or the wall. 'Any ideas at all?'

Berry began hesitantly. 'Call in the FBI.' There was a ripple of laughter around the room.

Priestley smiled at him. 'What exactly do you have in mind, Tony?'

'I think they have equipment to pick up someone's heartbeat at a distance without them knowing it. If we could find out whose heart rate increases when they're asked about the homicide, we might get an idea of who knows something and isn't telling us.'

Under their brainstorming rules, no ideas were ever rejected at this initial stage; Priestley therefore masked his belief that the suggestion was entirely impracticable. 'Fascinating! Make it a pet project of yours to find out all about it. Just at the moment, though, I doubt the budget would run to calling in the Feds.' He looked around. 'Any other ideas?'

He wondered if the dearth of suggestions was a consequence of this being early on Monday morning. Finally, Plummer spoke up. 'Why don't we have another go at Campbell? See if he reveals anything to us in our other characters.'

'You mean rock star plus trophy wife? It's possible.' He scanned the room. 'Any more ideas?'

Witty felt he should show a degree of leadership by making a suggestion. 'What about me going to Paris to liaise with the French police and have that painting examined for fingerprints?'

Priestley tried to appear positive as he highlighted a flaw. 'That could be useful, though I suppose we'd expect to find Campbell's fingerprints anyway.'

'Yes, you're right; so it wouldn't help if he's our man. On the other hand, I'd get to see Lily!'

As a few good-natured comments were being passed around, Priestley looked thoughtful. 'Aren't there forensic techniques to look for fingerprints *below* the surface of the painting? I'm thinking X-rays, infrared, UV, lasers. Then they could do ridge pattern analysis to find out who touched a lower layer of paint. If any don't belong to Milo, we may be able to find out who the forger is. We could ask the artists at the studios for their prints, and if we get a match we'd know who did it. If any refuse to give us their dabs, we could focus the investigation on them. This might just work. I'll need to take an art expert with me to Paris to consult with their forensics specialists, and I know just the person.'

Plummer spoke out immediately. 'If the budget doesn't run to you taking another officer with you, then surely it would make more sense to have the painting shipped back to the UK to do any tests here.'

Priestley tried not to appear disappointed that his plan had been scuppered. 'That raises an interesting question, Lin: where's the painting now. It was taken down by the French gallery when it was suspected of being a forgery, and they may have sent it back.' He looked pensive for a few seconds. 'Here's an idea. You give Campbell a call and ask which of his paintings from the Birds series he still has for sale. He might say just the five at the Graves, but he may include *Robin*; if he does, you could ask if we can see it again. That would give us the angle we need for having another go at him. How do you feel about that?'

'Getting dressed up again? Sure.'

'Right. We'll talk it through, later.' He looked around for one last time. 'If there are no other suggestions, we now have a plan for taking another look at Campbell, but it's a long shot. So, everyone else needs to keep plugging away at the other tasks; always tell yourself you'll be the one who turns up something that gets us the breakthrough we need.'

Later that morning, Priestley called Plummer to his office. 'Right, Lin, you're meant to be the one that likes spending money, so I think it would be best if you call

Campbell, unless you'd prefer me to make the call.'

'No, I can do it.'

'Well, in that case, don't forget you need to be in control of the conversation; I mean you mustn't sound like you're having to refer anything to someone else. Do you think you should use the landline? If he checks, he'll find it's a blocked number, though that's common enough nowadays.'

'I don't think it would be good for him to know my mobile number, so I'd still have to block that. I'll use the landline; it tends to be clearer, anyway.'

'I'd like to listen in on another handset, but that sometimes creates a funny noise, which could warn him it isn't an ordinary telephone system. I'll leave the room if you think I'd be a distraction, though I'd rather stay so that I can at least hear your half of the conversation. Do you think you could just ignore me entirely?'

'Trust me, Marcus, I know how to handle it.'

'Of course I trust you, Lin. So, what will you say about when we can visit? Any restrictions?'

'I'm free all the time but you're busy doing stuff some of the time.'

'What sort of stuff?'

'Seeing mates; something to do with a band. "He never lets me know what he's up to." Something vague.'

'And when do we wish to see him?'

'When can you get Helen's car?'

'Not 'til this afternoon, unless I go and collect it from Sheffield, which would take up to an hour there and back. But then, you'll need time to get yourself ready; how long does that take?'

'Last time, it was a couple of hours.'

'So, if it was another day, you could be ready any time; but if it's today, it would have to be much later.'

'Right. Shall I call now, then?'

'Yes. Come this side; it'll save stretching over.'

As Priestley vacated his chair for her, he recalled a rule of etiquette he had been taught as a boy by an elderly aunt: "Allow time for the heat to dissipate from a seat before inviting a female to place herself upon it." He had been instructed to afford the same consideration equally to a lady or a woman, in contrast to the correct parlance he was told he should always employ to differentiate between the two allegedly distinct echelons of females. Recalling how unchivalrous he had been to Anna on Saturday, he sought not to be ungallant to Lin, so delayed her with conversation. Gazing out of the window, he pointed to a concrete building that was replete with thick black smears. 'Have you noticed, those walls are starting to look really dirty? Do you see those stains running down them?'

Her interpretation was that he wanted to chat with her but was struggling to find something to say. She walked around his desk and stood very close to him to inspect the grime. 'Yes. No one's cleaned them since I last looked, all of three days ago! Should I call the council?'

He turned and smiled at her. Eventually, he stepped aside to allow her to sit, while he walked to the doorway. When he had checked no one was in the corridor, he closed the door. Realising that may result in some visitor knocking and perhaps entering, he opened it again and stood just inside the room.

She took her time putting herself into the correct

frame of mind, before speaking several sentences and short expressions in her coarser voice. Finally, she made the call. 'Hello, Mr Campbell? It's Lin. I came in with my husband. We looked at a painting by Milo Piscaro, but you've sold it since then. You said you had some more at the Graves Art Gallery; when will you be getting them back?' Priestley tried to imagine what she might be hearing. 'So it wasn't actually sold?' He listened to more silence. 'I could come any day, but I don't know about Marcus. Yes, Marcus is my husband.' She looked up at Priestley. 'Really? Well, I'm sure seven o'clock this evening would be fine for me.' He gave a thumbs-up. 'I can't say for definite, but I'd expect him to be back home in time to come as well. So I'll either be on my own, or with my husband. What's the address?' She picked up a pen and held it over a tear-off notepad. 'Just a minute, I need something to write it down with.' She waited several seconds. 'Right, fire away.' To ensure authenticity of timing, she wrote down the address. 'I'll see you this evening then, Mr Campbell. William? OK William.' She signed off in a singing voice. 'Laters.'

Priestley waited until the telephone was back on the cradle. 'What did he say, then?'

'He decided he liked the painting so much, he had it sent back from Paris, and it's now hanging on the wall in his dining room. We're invited to see him there at seven o'clock this evening.'

'He now knows our proper first names; it's a good thing we didn't make them up, before.'

'Sorry; I should have thought it through in advance.'

'Don't apologise, Lin; you were brilliant. Perhaps I should add, "as always". Have you done much acting?'

'Only a little bit.'

'Are you being modest?'

'No, not really.'

'Come on, tell me everything you've done.'

'In primary school, first I was a tree in Sherwood Forest, then I was one of Little Bo Peep's sheep, and then I was a wise man in a Nativity. When I went to senior school, I was a giraffe in *Noye's Fludde*.'

'Impressive!'

'Don't knock it; I even had to sing for that part. And my *pièce de résistance* was...' She used two fingers of each hand to perform a drum roll on the desk.

'I thought a *pièce de résistance* was a French virgin?'

'Well, I wasn't that.'

'A virgin?'

'French. Look, do you want to know about the pinnacle of my acting career, or not?'

'Go on then.'

'I was Juliet. That's *the* Juliet. I thought Mr Hazelwood picked me for my looks rather than my acting ability, but looking back I guess it was more to do with his fantasy; I think he imagined himself as my Romeo.'

Priestley struggled to conceal his concern. 'Did he ever interfere with you, Lin? If he did, it's never too late to do something about it.'

'It's alright, Marcus. Nothing happened, unless you count the way he used to look at me. In the end, I think he was a sort of romantic, who just kept it all in his head.' She thought he still appeared upset, so gave him an untroubled smile. 'Don't worry about it; nothing happened.'

CHAPTER 63

Having briefed Witty on the plan, Priestley set about working through various mundane tasks, though he recognised his concentration level was abysmal as his thoughts kept flitting to Anna and to Lin. He worried he was taking Helen for granted, assuming she would always be there for him regardless of his behaviour.

As midday approached, though he still felt the thrill of being in a new relationship, he was convinced it was unfair on Anna. He decided she deserved a face-to-face conversation to end it, so closed his office door and called her. 'Hi, it's me. I'd like to see you early this evening, just for a short while, if you're free. I have to come back to work later, so I won't have much time.'

'If you do not have much time, why do you not wait until you do have much time?'

Her voice retained sufficient traces of her Dutch origins to leave him uncertain how to read some of her inflexions. 'I just want to talk to you, that's all.'

'But we are talking.'

'Yes, but some things are best said face-to-face.' There was no reply. 'Anna? Are you still there?'

The calmness of her voice belied her feelings. 'You intend to finish with me. What did I do wrong?'

He saw no point in deferring the explanation. 'You haven't done anything wrong, Anna, but I'm happily married with a family. You deserve so much more than the dregs of time I can find for you. And you know I would never leave my wife.'

'I never asked you to leave your wife. I know I can only ever be your mistress, with all that that implies.'

'I wish I could make you understand how wonderful you are, and how I'm not worthy of you. Don't waste your time on me, Anna; you deserve so much more.'

'You were correct to say that some things are best said face-to-face. I need to look at you when you say these things. Come to see me this evening and we shall talk about everything and decide what we should do.'

'I've already decided; my mind's made up.'

'Perhaps I can persuade you to change your mind.'

'We need to talk, but that's all. I have to be in Shawton by seven at the latest, so I need to leave your house by six thirty. Shall I see you at six?'

'See me at five thirty. One hour is not really enough even just to talk, but I cannot arrive home before then.'

'Right, I'll see you at five thirty.' After a moment he added, 'We could still be friends.' She terminated the call on hearing the dreaded cliché.

After he had put away his mobile phone, he reflected on how he was voluntarily giving up a relationship with a fascinating and beautiful young woman. He really did think she was wonderful, but knew that to stay happily married he had to choose between sacrifices. If he continued with her, he may lose his family; if he ended it, he would lose the thrill of having an illicit affair.

Feeling too preoccupied to wish to engage with others in the main office, but needing to progress the plan, he dialled Plummer's internal number and was relieved that she took the call herself. 'Lin, come and see me, will you?'

Shortly after, he heard a knock at the door. He called out in a subdued voice, 'Come in.'

She stepped inside. 'Should I close it?'

'Yes; do.' When she was seated, he delivered his prepared question. 'I have to go somewhere else before Campbell's house this evening. If I collect you from home, we may end up a bit late. Maybe that's not such a bad thing, though; it could be more like the other "us" if we're not right on time. What do you think?'

'When I was making the appointment, I thought you may actually want us to arrive at different times, so that whoever's first might be able to go snooping around while the second one keeps him occupied at the door. That's why I hinted we might not come together, so it's no problem if we don't.'

'You've really thought this through, haven't you? I wouldn't want you to be in the house on your own, just in case he turns out to be a homicidal maniac.' She gave the obligatory laugh. 'I'll go in first at seven on the dot, and you can arrive precisely five minutes later, so I'll be able to anticipate you being at the door. Keep him occupied there for as long as you can. I don't know if I'll find anything, but it's always good to look in places people don't want us to see. Of course, even though we're invited, we still have to consider the rules on collection of evidence, so I may have to keep quiet about it if I do find something.'

'OK. It sounds like a good plan. I've got a problem, though, about what to wear. For a start, my sister's away, so I can't borrow her jewellery.'

'Do you have any of your own?'

'Only cheap stuff, and no wedding ring.'

'Would it be better not to wear any jewellery? I don't really know, I'm only a man, but I'd have thought no jewellery would be better than cheap stuff.'

'Only a man,' she echoed. You're a disgrace to male chauvinists everywhere.' He laughed a little. 'I think you're right, though. If he asks, I'll just say I didn't feel like wearing any today. But then there's the dress; the silver dress. It's the only really good one I've got. Should I dress down entirely and wear jeans, or something? I have to say, it doesn't sound right for visiting an art dealer at home if we're in the market for a fifty thousand pounds painting.'

'It'll have to be the silver one again, then.'

'Yes, I suppose it will.'

He looked at the ceiling for inspiration. 'Change of plan. Go and look for some jewellery and a dress; if I can't get them through on expenses, I'll pay for them myself.'

'And you don't think Helen would mind that?'

'I'm not usually one for keeping secrets from her, but this may have to be an exception.' His anxious laugh turned into a single cough.

'Maybe a wedding ring is the only thing that matters. I'd have to buy a platinum one like my sister's.'

'Perhaps a jeweller might lend you one. Take the afternoon off and get it sorted. And to tart yourself up like last time, of course.'

'Thank you, boss.' She tugged at her forelock. 'I'll do my hair the same. I looked good, didn't I?'

'Not 'arf! You gave me wet dreams for a week.'

She gasped theatrically. 'You're definitely not supposed to say things like that, sir, even if they are true.'

Feeling he may have overstepped the bounds of appropriate behaviour, he put forward a defence. 'You're not the only Method Actor, you know; I was just getting into character.' They laughed together, their eye contact remaining unbroken.

He escorted her to see Witty. 'Neil, just to let you know, Lin's got the afternoon off; she has things to do to prepare for the visit to Campbell's house.'

Witty nodded. 'Would you like me to act as backup this evening? I could keep an eye on the house from a distance. He's never seen me, so there's no danger of him recognising me.'

'If you're up for it, that would be great. Actually, if you wouldn't mind, do you think you could pick Lin up from home?'

'Yes, sure, no problem.'

Plummer smiled at Witty. 'Thanks, Neil.'

Priestley reminded Witty of the timings. 'Lin has to arrive at five past seven. I'll be there at seven o'clock precisely. To make sure you're not late, best get there before seven and park where Campbell can't see you.'

He turned to Plummer. 'Can you walk the last fifty yards or so in your high heels? It isn't something I've ever tried, myself.'

She addressed him dismissively, 'Stop fretting, Marcus; we'll work it out.' Seeing him lour at her, she added lightly, 'And I'm relieved to hear you don't wear high heels, by the way.'

CHAPTER 64

In the late afternoon Priestley had a ham sandwich in the canteen, so he could justify not stopping for food at home if Helen asked. He arrived a little after five o'clock and yelled to her as he rushed upstairs, 'Did you get my message about borrowing your car?'

She shouted back, 'Yes; I've taken their seats out.'

He changed into his undercover clothes and hurried down the stairs, two at a time.

To save him a few precious seconds, she ran to the inner door and opened it for him. 'Where's the fire?'

He thought she would find his haste more believable if he failed to respond to her usual joke. 'Don't know when I'll be back.' Leaving the two house doors open, he prepared to jump into her car.

She called out, 'Take care, love.'

He drove to Anna's house, ignoring the sat-nav's recommended Ecclesall Road and Bramall Lane route, instead going via Abbeydale Road to avoid the traffic streaming out of Sheffield. By 5:25 he was parked a little way from her house. Seeing her arrive on foot a few minutes later, he waited for her to enter her home before stepping out of the car. As he approached, he saw her door was wide open, so stepped inside without knocking. 'Hello, Anna. You shouldn't leave your door open like that.'

'I saw you were waiting.'

'Why didn't you give me a wave, then?'

'I thought you would not wish for me to draw

attention to you, especially as you had chosen not to park directly outside my house. You see, I am learning how to be discreet, like you.'

Fearing the bright burst of love they had shared in Paris was degenerating into a sordid affair, he put on a happy, lying face. 'What about a coffee?'

She began to perform the coffee ritual in the kitchen. 'I really do understand that you are happily married and intend to remain so. It was never my intention to try to steal you away. I only wish to borrow you, sometimes.'

His immediate thought of himself as a library book was quickly replaced by the idea of a gun for hire. 'I don't think Helen would approve of me being lent out.' He felt demeaned by using her name as a weapon.

'Then do not tell her. Or do you have absolutely no secrets from her? Does she know about us and Paris?'

'No, of course she doesn't, but I don't like to keep secrets from her.'

'That is not the same thing.'

He thought he might avoid the conversation becoming confrontational by simply agreeing with her. 'No, you're right.'

She poured him a coffee. 'Look at us.' She looked down at herself and then at him, as though the instruction were to be taken literally. 'What has happened to the happiness we felt? Where is the love? If this is goodbye, it is not the way it should be.'

'Yes, you're right.'

'So we shall have a drink, and then go to bed and be like we were in Paris, when we were so desperate for each other.'

He wondered at what point exaggeration turns into an unadulterated lie. 'I have to go on a mission with a colleague. It could be dangerous for him if I'm late.' He looked away, ashamed he had lost any claim to honesty.

'Then you must make sure that you are not late; but we still have plenty of time before you need to go.'

The conversation lightened as she reminded him of the things they had seen and done and felt in Paris.

He glanced at the kitchen clock to avoid drawing attention to the time by looking at his own wristwatch. She saw his eye movement. 'We shall go upstairs now, before it is too late.' She stood up, walked out of the kitchen and climbed the stairs without looking back. He trailed after her, unwilling to insult her by declining to follow.

In her bedroom, she was suddenly full of the overflowing laughter he had found so attractive. She helped him out of his clothes, until he stood only in his boxer shorts. She peeled off her own clothes, removing every last vestige, then pulled down his shorts for him to step out of them. Extracting a condom from a wrapper, she rolled it down onto him. As she stood facing him, she took his hand and pressed it under her. 'Make me ready,' she whispered.

A minute later, she stepped backward away from him until she was at the far side of the room. 'Stay there. You can come into my police car in a moment.' He had no idea what she meant, but followed her instruction to wait. She made a two-tone siren sound as she ran at him, then grasped him around the neck as she jumped to encircle his waist with her legs, before crossing her feet at his back to hold onto him. Once she had eased herself down on him, he turned a half circle and edged toward the wall, holding her against it as he repeatedly thrust into her.

Feeling his legs buckle, he staggered backward and collapsed onto the bed, pulling her on top of him. She moved up and down on him until certain they had both fully climaxed, before climbing off him and lying on her side. 'What did you think of my police car?'

He turned his head and adopted a serious expression, explaining dispassionately, 'The latest police cars don't have sirens like that.' After a moment he smiled into her eyes.

She smiled back. 'Now, tell me you do not wish to see me again, if you dare.'

He edged onto his side, placing her head between his hands, insisting she look directly at him. 'If it was only me I was thinking of, I would never stop seeing you, but you deserve a man all of your own.'

She frowned. 'Why do you assume I wish to have a man all of my own? I had one once, and do not wish to have another.' She smiled cheekily. 'A life spent entirely without a man would be very unfulfilling; after all, you do serve a purpose.' Her frown returned. 'But I wish to lead my own life and make my own decisions. I do not want a husband; I want a lover.'

'Well, wouldn't it be better to have a lover who's available to see you whenever you wish? Not a married man with a family.'

'And have him always asking to see me? I want a lover who thrills me when we are together, and who stays away long enough for me to miss him.'

He raised his head and rested it on his hand, his elbow pressing into the bed. 'That's a very convincing argument, Anna, but I'm not sure I entirely believe you. You see, in Paris, I was certain you were in love with me, and that you wished to be with me all the time.'

She mirrored his position. 'And I am not sure I entirely believe you, either, as I was certain you were in love with me, and that you wished to be with me all the time; at least, while ever we were in Paris. Now that we are in Sheffield, I think you would be very happy to see me some of the time, so that is what we shall do. You must call me when you wish to see me; I know you still desire me very much.'

He stood up. 'But what if I can hardly ever call you? Isn't it better you find another lover who is at least free to call you anytime? If you keep waiting for me, you could be very lonely.'

She stood and held her body against him. 'But my lover has to be someone I love and who loves me. So you are the only man who can be my lover; without you, I would be even more lonely.'

As he was wondering whether to try to debate further or simply to throw in the towel, he realised he had lost track of the time. He turned and recovered his watch from the dressing-table; it was later than he had expected. 'I need to get off.'

She opened her eyes wide. 'Again?'

'No, I'm serious. I'll have a superfast shower and then I'm out the door.'

Recognising the urgency in his voice, she rushed into the bathroom and turned on the electric shower. 'Quick, get in.' By the time he stepped out of the shower, there were two thick, warm towels waiting for him, and his clothes were stacked ready to be put on.

She called out as he hurriedly left the house, 'Until next time.'

CHAPTER 65

Priestley jogged to the car. Checking the time with the sat-nav's figure of twenty-three minutes, he calculated he had four minutes in hand. He would leave Sheffield via Ecclesall Road South and then watch out for the speed camera on Hathersage Road. Passing Fox House, he would take the A6187 and then the turn into Shawton. Nothing could be simpler, he told himself.

A section of road works wasted most of his four-minute slack, and a van driver who contrived to block a junction took more than the remainder. Long before he reached the speed camera, he pressed the accelerator just enough to regain the two minutes he was now behind schedule, then pushed it a little more to give him time in hand, in case of the unexpected.

The blue flashing light in his rear-view mirror appeared out of nowhere. He wondered if South Yorkshire police were in the habit of lying in wait off the road, just like some of his own colleagues who had turned catching speeding drivers into an art form. He braked sharply to minimise the journey interruption time. The police car stopped but no one emerged. Finally, an officer stepped out of the passenger side, the huge man strolling casually to his open window.

'What's the matter, Squadron Leader? Won't it take off?'

Priestley flashed his warrant card. 'DCI Marcus Priestley. I've got an urgent meet. It's an undercover op. that'll go tits-up if I don't get there soon.'

The officer responded slowly. 'Yes, sir, but you're speeding in South Yorkshire. You're over the border here, you know; it isn't your jurisdiction.'

'Look, what's your name.'

'Oh, so we're going to go all official are we, sir?'

'What's your first name.'

'Martyn. That's Martyn with a "Y".'

'Right. Well, Martyn, I'd like you to check with your HQ and tell them I want to co-opt you for an operation in Derbyshire. And just to hurry things along, I've some of your senior officers on speed dial if anyone would like me to escalate the request. Now, make the call, and don't forget to tell them my name.' Martyn walked back a little quicker. Priestley called after him, 'And do tell them it's urgent.'

Priestley was sweating with frustration by the time he returned. 'You must have some friends in South Yorkshire; we're yours to command. Sir.'

'Right, Martyn, you're in my car. Who's the other officer?'

'Do you want his first name?'

'Any f... First name will do fine.'

'He's Bryan. That's Bryan with a "Y". Bit of a coincidence, that, isn't it, sir?'

'You get in the front while I talk to Bryan.'

Priestley jumped down and ran to the other car. 'Bryan, I need an escort. Give me blues and twos to Shawton. Martyn's going to sit in with me and handle comms. I don't want to announce I'm arriving, so he'll tell you when to go silent, but keep the light on. Once we're on the move he'll let you know exactly where you're going. You lead the way.'

'What's happened, then?'

'Nothing. I just hate being late.'

'Well, don't tell me if you don't want to.'

Priestley ran back. 'I'll tell you where we're going and Bryan will lead us in. Let's go. And put your seat belt on; I'd hate to be stopped by the police.'

Martyn responded without the slightest hint of amusement. 'That's very funny, sir. We don't have humour in South Yorkshire; we can't afford it. It's all the budget cuts, you see.'

Bryan led the mini-convoy at high speed before decelerating rapidly to allow them to pass for the last leg of the journey. Priestley saw Witty's car parked on the left; he braked sharply and began to lower the passenger's electric window as he drew up directly alongside. Witty's window was still lowering as Priestley called out to him, 'Where's Lin?'

Witty pointed to Campbell's house. 'She's already gone in.'

'Why didn't she wait? I know I'm late, but she wasn't supposed to go in 'til after me.'

'We couldn't see your car, so we thought you must be parked around a corner and we'd simply missed you. She went in right on time at five past seven.'

'Has there been any activity at the house?'

'No. Just some door-to-door bloke; other than that, it's been quiet as the grave.'

'Right. Well, keep a lookout for anything happening at the house. I've brought two of South Yorkshire's finest with me; this is Martyn, and Bryan's parked up the road. Put Martyn in the picture.'

Priestley pulled forward to give space for the passenger door to open. 'Martyn, you sit in with Neil.'

When Martyn had climbed out and lumbered away,

Priestley drove to Campbell's house and parked directly outside. As he rang the bell, he tried to calm himself. Campbell opened the door and flashed a broad smile. 'Welcome, Marcus. I'm so glad you could make it.'

'Hello, William.'

'Do come inside.' Priestley followed Campbell into the house. 'The painting's this way. Come and have a drink.'

Priestley walked into the dining room and glanced around. 'Where's Lin?'

'I'm sorry, she hasn't arrived yet.'

Priestley stared at him, then saw his neck redden and sweat begin to pour from his brow. 'Where is she?' He noticed Campbell's involuntary flick of his eyes to one side. 'Take me to her. Now!' He grabbed Campbell's shirt collar and marched him in the direction his glance had suggested. Campbell tried to pull away as they approached a door marked "Utility Room"; Priestley pushed him until his nose was almost touching it. 'Is she in there?'

Campbell resisted. 'No, it's empty; I don't use it.'

'Open it and let me look.'

'I don't have a key for it.'

'Then I'm going to break it down.'

'I'll call the police.'

'I am the police.'

'In that case you need a warrant.'

'You invited me in, remember?'

'Well, now I'm asking you to leave.'

'And I'm asking you to open the door, otherwise I'm knocking it down with your head.'

'You wouldn't dare.'

Priestley took hold of the back of Campbell's head

and smashed his face against the door; his nose cracked and began to bleed profusely. He struck the door again, this time with Campbell's forehead, leaving him dazed and struggling to stand. After throwing him to one side, he charged the door with his shoulder, but it barely flinched. He ran out to the front of the house and waved to Witty, who came sprinting toward him. 'He's locked Lin up. I need a big red key; ask Martyn if they've got one. Or see if you can find something solid; anything to batter a door down.'

Priestley ran back inside, past Campbell who was crawling away. He sprinted toward the utility room door, a surge of adrenaline giving him the added lift to deliver his drop-kick precisely where he intended, high up at the keyhole. The jamb shattered and the door juddered open, the substantial lock still attached. He scrambled to his feet and called into the darkness, 'Lin? Linda? Lin?' Stepping inside, he saw a white switch reflecting the stray beams that were spilling from the hallway. As he turned on the light, his eyes were immediately drawn to something on the floor in the shape of a rolled-up carpet. He bent down and discovered it was Plummer's body, cocooned in soft plastic sheeting. Pulling open one end, he saw her face, still and serene, her eyes closed.

His combat experience kicked in automatically and he ran to the hallway to engage with the enemy, only to find he had bolted. Following the trail of blood drops, he turned a corner and saw him stumbling for the outer door. As the many lethal fighting techniques he had learned during his army days jostled for prominence, he screamed 'I'm going to kill you.' Campbell found a burst of energy and began to run. Priestley caught up with him just as he reached the pavement at the end of the driveway; pulling him around to face him, he prepared to deliver a fatal blow to the throat to crush his trachea, a Hungarian Krav Magra technique he had previously used in military action. As he readied his arm to make the killing blow, he found himself forced to the ground by the two uniformed officers. Martyn looked at Priestley and shook his head. 'That's not how we do things over the border, sir. And I don't think it's that different over here.'

Witty stared at Priestley. 'What the hell's happened?'

Priestley choked out, 'He's killed Lin.'

Campbell saw all eyes turned on him. 'I didn't mean to.' The inflections in his voice suggested he was asking them to believe it was just an unfortunate accident.

Witty sprinted up the steps and into the house.

Priestley struggled to release himself from Martyn and Bryan, who were using their substantial combined weight to hold him down. He looked at Martyn. 'Now will you let me kill him?' It was clear to them from his intonation that some of the fire had gone out of him, and that he was now only expressing a wish rather than an intention.

After releasing his hold on Priestley, Bryan grabbed Campbell, pulling his arms behind him and snapping on the handcuffs, then raising them high to make his head dip low to the ground. Campbell squealed in pain at the pressure on his shoulder sockets, and tried not to move. Bryan spoke evenly, almost calmly, as he repeatedly raised and lowered the cuffs for maximum effect. 'Stop resisting arrest.'

Martyn stood and positioned himself protectively between Priestley and Campbell. Priestley accepted Martyn's offer of a helping hand, scrambling to his feet and running back inside.

Ahead of Priestley, Witty had seen the damaged door jamb and had run into the utility room, where he had stooped to pull away more of the plastic sheeting enveloping Plummer; having checked her wrist for a pulse and found evidence of life, he had called for an ambulance.

Seeing Priestley's bulging eyes as he rushed into the room, Witty yelled out to him, 'She's still alive; there's an ambulance on its way.' He held out his phone as though to add weight to his statement, before stepping away to allow him more space.

Priestley knelt beside her and gently placed his fingers on her neck to check for a pulse. Feeling a tsunami of relief wash over him, he shouted to Witty who was standing just feet away, 'Find out what he's given her and tell the paramedics.' Witty ran out. Priestley eased one hand under her back, placing his other hand tenderly beneath her head to support her neck, as though she were a newborn baby.

When the paramedics arrived with Witty, they found Priestley cradling her. 'You need to let her go now, sir. We have her.' Priestley seemed oblivious to their instruction. 'She's been given ether, which is an anaesthetic. It wasn't enough to kill her, so she'll come round and be right as rain. Don't you worry about her. Now, just let us do our job.' He reluctantly released her into their care, staying close as he watched them administer oxygen.

Witty tapped Priestley on the shoulder and leaned

close to his ear; he knew this was no time for informality. 'Sir? Sir? We need to deal with Campbell.'

Priestley looked up at him with no recognition in his eyes; after a few moments his awareness returned. 'Right, Neil; I'll just make a call.' He phoned Cargill. 'Frank? Are you free right now to go to the station? Good. I want you to get there as soon as you can. I'm at William Campbell's house; he tried to kill Lin. Neil's here as well; he's going to look after things at this end. I want you to take charge at the station. Do everything by the book.' He listened for a moment. 'Me? I'm going to the hospital with Lin.'

Priestley watched intently as the two paramedics wheeled Plummer to the ambulance on a collapsible stretcher. 'I'm coming with her.'

As he climbed into the back, Martyn called out, 'What do you want doing with your car?'

He forced himself to take his eyes off Lin for a moment. 'Do you mind driving it to the hospital?'

'No problem.'

Priestley threw him the keys. 'Thank you Martyn; and you Bryan. Thank you both; you know what for.'

Bryan responded, 'Any time.' Martyn acknowledged with a nod and a hint of a smile.

CHAPTER 66

The ambulance shook the occupants as it bounced over potholes that had needed mending since last winter. One particularly severe jolt caused Plummer to open her eyes, but she was still feeling the after-effects of the ether and was unready to emerge into consciousness. Gradually, she began to regain her senses. Still suffering from cognitive dysfunction, she failed to register that it was Priestley who was looking at her. Trying to speak, she found her lips failed to operate normally, as though they were out of synch with her mind. When she finally made a sound approximating to speech, Marcus leaned in close to her. 'It's alright, love. Everything's alright.'

Finally recognising Priestley, she half-spoke, half-whispered, 'You weren't there.'

He felt her words sear his memory and knew they would haunt him for the rest of his life. 'I'm sorry, Lin; I'm so sorry.' He found his apology an entirely inadequate expression of the depth of his regret.

She was fully alert before they reached the hospital, though she remained lying down in accordance with the paramedic's instructions. When she insisted on standing and walking from the ambulance, Marcus held onto her as though she were made of glass. Inside A&E she again refused a wheelchair; he supported her as they were led away to an assessment cubicle. She asked to go to the lavatory, but the nurse insisted she wait until she had been seen by the doctor. Though she refused to lie down, she submitted to having a blood sample taken.

Dr Nagi slipped silently between the curtains; seeing Marcus standing there, she asked him to wait outside. Lin objected, 'I want him to stay.'

The doctor leaned in closer. 'I think it would be better if he left; I have to ask you some intimate questions.'

Lin responded calmly, 'We're close friends.'

Dr Nagi frowned. 'If you're absolutely sure?'

Lin nodded. 'Yes, I am.'

'I understand a man knocked you out with an anaesthetic. I should test to see if you were...' She glanced at Marcus before continuing even more quietly, 'interfered with.'

Lin's hand moved instinctively to her upper thigh. 'I'm sure I wasn't. I'd like to go to the toilet, now; the nurse said I had to wait.'

'I'll call someone to take you. You might find it a little difficult to urinate; ether can do that to you.'

When a nurse came to take her to the lavatory, she asked Marcus to hand her her handbag. He thought she seemed much more relaxed when she returned a few minutes later. As though she did not herself have the right to leave the hospital, she asked the doctor's permission to go home.

Dr Nagi was concerned at the extent to which her pupils were dilated. 'I need to perform some tests first.' She checked her blood pressure and found it was within normal parameters; her blood sugar level was also deemed acceptable. When she checked her pulse, she found evidence of paroxysmal supraventricular tachycardia; she consulted the patient's notes for any past reference to PSVT but found nothing. 'A moment ago your heart started beating quite fast, but it seems to have settled down again. Do you have any history of sudden, unexpected increases in your heart rate?'

Lin shook her head. 'No. It's probably from being in a hospital; these places make me nervous. Anyway, I'm feeling fine again, now.'

Marcus stared at her. 'Are you seriously saying that you felt alright after what you've just been through, but simply being in hospital made you anxious?'

She shrugged. 'I think it all started when I was little. I hid under a table because I didn't want a vaccination; the doctor trapped me there to give me the jab.'

Dr Nagi nodded to Marcus. 'It's called White Coat Syndrome.' She turned back to Lin. 'You really ought to stay in overnight for observation.'

Lin pleaded, 'But I'm feeling absolutely fine, now.'

'Will there be someone at home to look after you?'

'Yes,' she responded unequivocally.

As they emerged from the cubicle, Lin looked at Marcus. 'You don't have to hold onto me all the time, you know; I feel absolutely fine.'

He retained his hold. 'Is there someone at home?'

'No; but I really do feel OK.'

'Then I'll look after you.' He hoped this might assuage his guilt a little.

On stepping into the main A&E reception area, they found Martyn waiting to greet them. He looked at Lin. 'You alright then?'

Marcus answered for her. 'She's fine.'

He responded, 'I'm glad. Here are your keys; you're parked just up to the left.' He looked closely at Marcus. 'Your lot has more excitement than mine ever have. Well, goodnight then.'

Marcus pocketed the keys. 'Thanks again.'

Martyn winked at him before walking away.

When they were alone, Lin asked, 'What were you thanking him for? I missed all the action.'

He looked at the floor. 'I'll tell you later.' Wishing to change the subject, he relaxed his hold of her. 'I'll let *you* hold onto *me* if you like, but if you start to feel wobbly, just say so.' He guided her to the exit in accordance with the protocol for leading the blind.

After opening the front passenger door, he took hold of her arm again, helping her in as though she were an invalid. As he climbed into the driver's seat, she looked over at him. 'You can stop fussing, now. I just want to go home.' He drove back with added care, avoiding any rapid changes of speed or direction. As they were approaching the flats, she asked, 'Will you really be staying to look after me tonight?'

He glanced around at her for a moment. 'Yes; it's the least I can do.'

She fished into the bottom of her handbag and pulled out a small zapper, a remote control key for the car park's full height metal gates. 'Drive into the car park; it's safer than leaving it out overnight.' She pointed the device and pressed the button, the gates screeching open as they approached. Inside, she directed him to an empty reserved space near to her car. 'It belongs to my next-door neighbour; she's away, so it's OK to use it.'

When he turned off the engine, she immediately opened her door. He glanced around and saw how her short dress had ridden up. As she swung her slender legs to climb out of the car, he guiltily allowed his gaze to linger on them for a moment, expecting to catch another glimpse of her silver knickers. Disappointed at missing the shiny glint, and more disappointed in himself for trying to look, he hurried to catch up with her in case she needed his support.

As soon as they were in the flat, she closed the curtains in the living room and turned on the lights. 'Unzip me,' she commanded. 'You're going to be very disappointed in me.'

He made the obvious assumption. 'When I said I'm going to look after you, that's all I meant. I certainly wasn't expecting you to be offering me sex. Not after what you've been through.' He corrected himself. 'I meant, not anyway.'

She held her dress off her shoulders, exposing the upper regions of her breasts. 'That isn't why you'll be disappointed. Just look at me.' She allowed the dress to fall to the ground, showing her entire, naked body.

He examined her upper torso carefully, minutely. 'I don't understand. You're not at all disappointing, Lin; you're absolutely gorgeous.'

She snapped at him, 'Think!'

He looked again at her breasts, impressed with their size and shape. In his peripheral vision he saw she was indicating with her index finger that he should look lower. Glancing for a moment at her firm stomach and slender waist, his gaze settled on her mound of Venus; he saw she had just the tiniest wisp of fine blonde hair, slightly more yellowy than that on her head. He looked up and stared into her eyes. 'You look utterly fantastic, Lin. Why did you think I'd be disappointed?'

'Some detective you are.' Her words shot through clenched teeth, 'I'm not wearing any knickers.'

As she walked to her bedroom, he watched how her buttocks moved up and down, her supple limbs creating an impression of fluidity he believed only the young could achieve effortlessly. Though he accepted he had failed to notice the absence of underwear, he remained convinced any red-blooded male would have been similarly distracted on seeing her naked body.

She returned, wearing a white bathrobe. 'I took my knickers off at the hospital when I went to the loo. I rinsed them out, but I didn't want to put them back on because they were damp. Do I have to spell out why I took them off?'

'I think you'd better.'

'When he grabbed me from behind and put that cloth over my face, I peed myself.' She attempted to smile, but instead found tears streaming hot down her cheeks.

He stepped toward her, enveloping her protectively in his arms. 'It's nothing to be ashamed of.'

She fiercely jerked her head away from him so she could look at his face and he could see hers. 'Yes it is; you wouldn't have. I want to be as good as any man, but then I do something like that.'

'You're better than any man, Lin; honestly. But we're different, that's all. Don't give it another thought; I'll not tell anyone.'

'Yes, but the forensics team will find out, won't they? And then everyone will read about it in the report.'

'Maybe it doesn't have to appear in it. I'll try and have a word with someone.'

Her silent tears subsided. 'Thank you; thanks ever so much.'

'You shouldn't be thanking me for anything; not after I let you down so badly. I wasn't there on time; I put your life in danger. If there was some way I could make it up to you, I would. But I know there isn't.'

She looked into his eyes. 'Yes there is: you can come to bed with me.'

He shook his head. 'That's your emotions talking, because of what happened to you. In the morning you'll be thinking clearer, and then you'd regret it.'

'So, you're turning me down for a third time, are you?'

He frowned. 'Third time?'

'Yes. The first was when you brought me home from the gallery. I was lying in bed waiting for you, but you decided to make a phone call instead.'

'I did wonder if you'd given me the come-on.'

'I thought I'd made it fairly obvious, but clearly I hadn't. Then I asked you to take me to Paris. So this is the third time.'

'Well, there's nothing happening tonight, because I'm only here to look after you. I'll sleep on the sofa.'

'No you won't. You said you'd do anything, so you can at least sleep next to me; I mean, what if I get nightmares?' She pushed him away. 'Make yourself at home; I'm going to take a shower.'

He reminded himself he had already failed once in his earnest intention always to be faithful to his wife, and in principle he was determined not to fail a second time. But on the other hand, he reasoned, having put Lin's life in danger, he owed it to her to do whatever she wished; and if what she wished was to have sex with him, well, who was he to refuse? Only, not tonight, because of what she had been through, and because he did not deserve to have the pleasure.

While she was showering, he phoned Cargill to say he was trusting him to handle things without referral, though he could contact him on his mobile if essential. Then he phoned Witty with a similar message.

He knew he needed to let Helen know he would be absent overnight, but was concerned she would question him if he phoned her. He considered what to put in a text, then decided he should phone after all, arguing there was a perfectly valid reason for his being where he was. 'Hello, love. I'm not coming home 'til the morning.'

'Working all night?'

'I'll tell you about it later. We've made an arrest, but I nearly lost an officer. I don't want to talk about it over the phone.'

'Are you alright?'

'Yes, I'm alright. We're all alright.'

'If you're not alright, you must say so.'

'I'm alright, honestly.'

'Well, just call me anytime if you need to. You sure you're alright, love?'

'Yes, definitely. See you tomorrow, love.'

CHAPTER 67

Priestley went into the kitchen and looked around, opening cupboard doors until he found a jar of instant coffee, a canister of tea bags and a tin of hot chocolate. He went to the bathroom and knocked. She opened the door. He saw she had wrapped a small towel around her hair, and had a large bath towel covering her torso. 'What is it? I don't like talking through closed doors.'

'I was going to make a drink. Would you like one?'

'Could you do me a hot chocolate, half milk, half water.' She walked out of the bathroom and into her bedroom, carrying her bathrobe.

He used the microwave to heat enough milk to make hot chocolate for them both. When the mixing and stirring was complete, he took the mugs into the living room and placed them on coasters that were sticky with rings from repeated usage. Sitting in a chair, he waited for her to come and try her drink before he would sip his own. When she emerged from her bedroom, he saw she was wearing floral patterned leggings, with a loose-fitting T-shirt that bore a print of a cute, sleepy-looking cat. 'Sorry I don't have any pyjamas for you; I've never been one for having overnight visitors.' She smiled at him with such innocence he had to turn away, ashamed even to look at her for fear of corrupting her.

She took a sip of the hot chocolate, giving it a nod of approval. He found his to be too hot, so placed it back on the coaster. When she had settled onto the settee, he asked her to explain what had happened to her at the house. She took a moment to compose herself. 'We looked out for your car, but when we hadn't seen it by seven o'clock we assumed you'd parked around a corner. Just before seven a bus had come and blocked our view for a minute or so, which is why, when we still hadn't seen you by nearly five past, we thought you must have gone in when the bus was there. So I set off walking.' She took another sip before continuing.

'I went to the house and he let me in. I asked him to show me around, which he did, ground floor only. He ignored the utility room, so I took hold of the handle and started to open the door. He pulled it back and pushed me out of the way quite aggressively, and then stood right in front of me. I think I can remember what he said, word for word. "The room contains my dirty linen; I would not wish to offend your sensibilities." It made me suspicious, so when the doorbell went and I assumed it was you, I thought I'd take a quick look inside. I found the light switch and saw a painting on an easel; it was similar to that *Robin* painting.'

'Did it look finished, or was it a work-in-progress?'

'I wouldn't know the difference with abstract art. Having said that, the floor was covered in plastic sheeting, and there were lots of paintbrushes nearby, so I wouldn't be surprised if he was still working on it.

'Then I found myself being pulled over backward, with a cloth over my face. It smelled sweet, like a solvent; I can still smell it now, in my mind.' Her voice took on a defensive air. 'I'm sure I could have defended myself better if I hadn't been wearing high heels.'

'I'm sure you're right, Lin. Besides, you were taken off guard.'

She insisted, 'I'm sure I could have.' Accepting his

nod of agreement, she continued. 'Then there was a ringing sound in my head that grew louder and louder. The next thing I knew I was in an ambulance. You can fill in the rest for me.'

He took a moment to decide where to begin. 'I was late and Neil said you'd already gone in. When I asked where you were, Campbell said you hadn't arrived yet. I knew he was lying, so I asked him again. When he wouldn't tell me, I saw him glance to one side, so I guessed which room you were in. The door was locked, so I forced it. I thought you were dead because he'd wrapped you in plastic sheeting. I confronted him and it was clear he thought you were dead, too. But Neil checked your pulse and found you were still alive, so he called for an ambulance. And that's pretty much it.'

She had been watching him intently. 'You haven't mentioned what the South Yorkshire officers were doing there.'

'They stopped me, which made me late. So they gave me an escort to try to make up for lost time.'

'What were you thanking them for? It wasn't just for the escort, was it?'

'They stopped me from doing something I'd have regretted. I was going to hit Campbell.'

'So you didn't hit him.'

'Strictly, no.'

'And not strictly?'

He grimaced. 'I don't think I should tell you.'

'Haven't I earned the right to know?'

He reflected for a moment. 'Well, I didn't hit him when I was trying to get into that room where you were, but I did use his head to try and batter the door down.'

Her burst of laughter gave him a surge of relief.

'But that means they didn't stop you.'

'Not then. It was later when they stopped me.' For a moment she reminded him of Helen as she sat waiting patiently for him to elaborate. 'This will have to be just between us.' Still she waited. 'I shouted I was going to kill him.'

She broke her silence. 'I've often heard people say that, but it doesn't usually mean anything.'

'Oh, I meant it alright. I was within a second of smashing his windpipe. I thought he'd killed you, Lin, and I just couldn't stop myself.'

Her eyes deliquesced. 'Now I know how you really feel about me.'

He felt a powerful urge to sit with her and to put his arms around her, but foresaw the likely consequences. Looking around, he noticed the television control box and picked it up. 'Would you like to watch some TV? You never know, you might be on the local news.'

'If there are pictures of me looking helpless on a stretcher, I don't want to see. I feel really tired now, anyway; if it's alright by you, I'd like to go to bed. I'll get a toothbrush out for you. Are you staying up?'

'I'll turn in as well; the TV might keep you awake. Do you have a blanket and a pillow?'

'Your memory's failing. You said you'd do anything for me, and I said I wanted you in my bed. Or am I not to trust your word anymore?'

'I meant what I said; anything at all. But I'm not sure you really mean it; after what you've been through, you're bound to be upset and not thinking straight.'

'That sounds like the cliché we hear from men accused of rape. "She said no but I was sure she meant yes." Just stop thinking so much and do as I say.'

'Sure, Lin. Just make certain you say what you mean, otherwise how can you mean what you say?'

'Is that you being clever, again?'

'I think it was Lewis Carroll, *Alice in Wonderland*.'

Having finished her drink, she stood and walked toward the bathroom. Catching sight of herself in the hallway looking-glass, she hardly recognised the suddenly older woman staring back at her; gone were the untroubled features, replaced by a face wrought with cares and fears. She whispered softly, too quietly for him to hear, 'Perhaps you'll take me to wonderland in the morning.'

When she emerged from the bathroom, he stood to take his turn. 'Your brush is the green one.'

A few minutes later he went to her bedroom. There was a bedside light on, but she seemed oblivious to it. He knew he needed darkness to sleep, so turned it off before edging into the near side of her bed, still wearing his boxer shorts. He felt a hand touch him, followed by words delivered as a simple instruction. 'Take your pants off; there's nothing clean for you to wear in the morning.' He slipped them off and threw them toward the rectangular padded stool on which he had placed his other clothes. She turned onto her side, away from him. 'Now put your arm around me. And don't snore.'

Despite his good intentions, he had a strong physical reaction from lying close to her. He wondered if the heady perfume she had applied so liberally was intended to drown out her memory of the ether. Easing his lower torso away from her, he squeezed his feet into the corner of the bed and placed his upper arm lightly around her waist, his lower arm lying between them to provide a degree of modest separation.

CHAPTER 68

Marcus woke to find the bedroom partially illuminated. He lifted his head and turned to face the light source, the window; he saw how the pair of pink velvet curtains that reached down and rested on the windowsill had been pulled apart a little, their wrinkled folds presenting a convex gap. As he saw Lin standing naked and luminous in the shaft of light, he thought of Botticelli's *Birth of Venus*, and then of an Artemis by Titian; he realised Lin, now elevated to goddess, was looking directly at him. 'Good morning,' he offered, in a matter-of-fact voice, feeling inadequately mortal.

She leaned over and handed him a small glass bottle. 'I can't get the top off.'

His eyes were still adjusting to the half-light as he recognised the jar of Vaseline by its shape. He twisted the lid and it released with a pop that sounded unreasonably loud in the quiet room. Straining his eyes, he thought she was now manipulating something small with her fingers.

She spoke with a hint of irritation. 'I can't work it out in the dark; you'll have to put the light on.' When he did as instructed, she re-closed the curtain. He saw she was holding a condom. 'We're going to have sex now, OK?'

He breathed out audibly. 'Are you really sure you want to?'

She replied without hesitation. 'Yes, I am sure. And when I say "yes", I mean "yes". Now, prepare yourself for a big surprise.'

As she pulled back the sheets, he wondered what exotic technique she had in mind. Physically, he was fully ready, but mentally he still harboured some reservations. He thought she seemed nervous as she tried to apply the condom, so he reached down and took it from her. 'Here, let me.' When it was in position, she took a dollop of Vaseline and smeared it over the condom. As she appeared to have a plan, he decided he should leave matters in her capable hands.

She straddled him, facing him, her knees either side of his hips. As he began to enter her, he recognised the unmistakable barrier to penetration he had first encountered as a teenager. 'Stop! Good God, Lin, what are you doing?'

'There has to be a first time for everything.'

'Well, it shouldn't be me.'

'It's what I want, and you did promise.' As he had stopped pushing into her, she eased herself down on him, but found she had applied insufficient force to break her maidenhead; her second attempt, though pressing harder, still failed to achieve penetration. She raised her body higher, moving first one hand and then the other from the bed to his shoulders, carefully avoiding him slipping out of her. When she was riding him, proud and erect, she forced herself down hard, gasping at the moment her hymen split. 'That hurt!' After just a moment, she looked at him intently and asked, 'What do we do now?'

He held her firmly in position with his hands on her sides. 'I just hope you know what you've done, Lin. It's something you only part with once, so it should have been with someone special to you.'

She held his gaze with unblinking eyes. 'But you are special to me.' Quickly, she pulled herself off him.

'You shouldn't do that, either. One of us is supposed to hold onto the base of the condom so it doesn't ride up and spill its contents... not that there are any to spill.'

She climbed off the bed. 'Would you have made love to me properly if I hadn't been a virgin?'

'Yes, I'm sure I would; I did promise I'd do whatever you asked, didn't I?'

'Well, next time I won't be, so you'll have no excuse.'

'Next time?'

'Yes, next time, in about five minutes. I want to go and wash myself first; I've got some blood on my legs. And why do people use all that Vaseline?'

'They don't, Lin; you've a lot to learn.'

'Well, I expect you to teach me.'

She walked to the bathroom and cleaned herself up. When she vacated it, he went in to do likewise. A few minutes later he returned to find her in bed, having removed the duvet and straightened the top sheet. 'Now we've got that over with, I really want you to make love to me properly.' She pulled the sheet away to one side.

He felt he was free to enjoy the moment, convinced he had done everything humanly possible to remain faithful to Helen. Beginning with her toes and working upward, he lavished kisses over her entire body, and encouraged her to do likewise with him. When he was sure she was ready, and he had put on a condom, he positioned himself on top of her and slid easily into her. She looked so intently at him, he thought she was trying to learn by close observation. He rocked back and forth a few times. 'How does it feel for you?'

She answered as though it were meant to be considered factually. 'It doesn't hurt, but I'm not really enjoying it. Only, I'm starting to feel a bit different. So keep going and I'll let you know if anything happens. Just keep going a bit. Don't stop yet. Don't stop yet, please. Don't stop please. Please don't stop. Don't stop. Please. Please. Please. Please. Please, please, please, please. Now. Now. Now. Now. Now, now, now, now, now now now now now now now now.' Her words turned to screams as she gasped for air with her mouth wide open. Suddenly, she felt she had had as much as she could take, and fought him to stop, like a cat that turns on her tom after the moment of ovulation has passed.

He collapsed onto her, turning his head aside so that his heavy breathing would not be directed to her ear. When his last throb had left him drained, he eased out of her while pinching the base of the condom with a thumb and forefinger. Lying on his back, he turned to her; in a half-whisper, he asked, 'Like it?'

She tried to speak but found her mouth was too dry and her throat was hurting too much from her screaming, so she closed her lips and answered, 'Mmm.' After staring at the ceiling for a minute, she climbed off the bed and went to the bathroom. Realising she had forgotten to put the towels to dry after her shower of the previous evening, she came out again and went to the airing cupboard to fetch some more. Seeing her pass the doorway, he took the opportunity to go into the bathroom. She returned to find him there. 'Do you want to be first in the shower?'

He smiled. 'Why don't we have one together?'

They squeezed into the small cubicle and he began to wash her hair. Suddenly, he remembered washing Anna's hair in Paris, and then he recalled how he used to wash Helen's hair until she complained she could do it more efficiently herself. Even as he began to blame his extra-marital encounters on Helen for not letting him wash her hair, he knew he was lying to himself.

When they were dried and dressed, Lin made them each a mug of instant coffee. Thinking it may be the correct thing to do to appear professional, she suggested they go through the Campbell case. He shook his head. 'I want to ask you something, Lin. How did you make it through to twenty, *virgo intacta*? I thought young people nowadays were all into casual sex. Was it a religious thing?'

'It had nothing to do with religion. I know many girls do give in to pressure, but I was too strong-willed to let anyone make the decision for me. In my case, I'd say it's complicated.'

'It's alright if you don't want to tell me.'

'No, I just mean it's complicated. You see, my big sister went to university to study psychology, and she told me about some of the other girls there.'

'Others who were reading psychology?'

'That was her expression, too, "reading psychology". They may well have been, but she never let on. She gave them anonymous names, Anon-1, Anon-2, et cetera, and kept case files on them. I wonder what the other girls would have thought of her if they'd known she was analysing them?' He gave no response, taking the question as rhetorical.

'She told me about the different sexual attitudes they had. There was one girl who decided to have as many different boys in the first term as there are letters in the alphabet; she then ranked them in order of preference, A to Z. Next, she asked A to be her permanent boyfriend, though I think "permanent" means different things to different people. He turned her down, so she went to B, then C, and so on. Same thing kept happening. It seems the boys had been comparing notes, and decided, as they were all having a piece of her, she must be a tart.' He gave a short laugh. 'Many of them didn't like the idea of having a girlfriend who their mates had all had sex with. I don't know which letter of the alphabet she ended up with, if any, but I thought it was interesting.'

'So how does that relate to you?'

'Like I said, it's complicated. Perhaps the boys shouldn't have been so concerned about other boy's opinions. But there again, if she was happy to be off with so many others, what would stop her from dropping them and going off again? Maybe, if they wanted a one night stand, she could be top of their list; but if they were looking for a permanent girlfriend, she wasn't the one for them. Here's the thing, though: she wanted to try out a wide selection and then choose the best of them, as she saw it, but that very act of trying them out had made them see her as unsuitable.'

'I still don't see how this relates to you.'

'I'm getting there. My sister did a follow-up study in collaboration with a male psychology student. It was about the effects on the boys themselves. Quite a number of them had imagined she was the "love of their life", and were devastated to find they weren't the love of hers. Those particularly hard-hit were the delicate flowers who'd arrived freshly cut from their mother's apron strings. In the end, many of the boys seemed really screwed up by it all. I remember one time Sis said she'd like to do a longitudinal study and check if the effects diminish over time, or whether the boys were permanently scarred; but I suppose she was only joking.' She looked pensive for a moment. 'Actually, I'm not sure she was joking.' She refocused on his eyes. 'Are you with me so far?'

'I'm following you, but I'm still not seeing where you're leading.'

'Right. Let's jump to some of her other case studies. Imagine young male student meets and falls in love with young female student. She gives up her virginity to him, which makes him even more deeply in love with her because he sees it as something special. If it goes the distance, they live happily ever after. But let's say she dumps him because she wishes to broaden her experience, perhaps from believing all the media hype. Anyway, the bottom line is, he might remain screwed up for life. Have you got it yet?'

'Maybe.'

'Well, tell me your theory.'

'As you're so lovely and wonderful and gorgeous and stunning and ravishing and ...'

'I'm liking what I'm hearing, but you're rather wandering off the point. Start again and stay focused.'

He posed serenely with closed eyes, as though her beauty was interfering with his ability to discourse rationally. After several seconds he looked at her. 'As you're so attractive, any boyfriend you had would be bound to fall in love with you, and would be devastated if you ever split up. Your first lover would be an extreme case. So, rather than risk screwing someone up, you made sure your first time was with someone you felt sure wouldn't be screwed up.'

'That's pretty much it. I took a moral stance on who to lose my virginity to. Just one extra little bit, though; I thought it would be wrong of me to have my first experience with someone I wasn't in love with.'

He tried to replay the explanation, but found he could focus only on the corollary. 'Are you saying you're in love with me, Lin?'

'Yes, Marcus, I am in love with you. But I've let you deflower me,' she paused and smiled at the expression, 'because I know *you* won't fall in love with *me*.'

He was prepared to accept her logic, notwithstanding alternative moral arguments relating to his own marital status, but feared the final phrase was flawed. He therefore considered some alternative reasoning.

Would he fall in love with her? He had always strived to be highly principled, but knew he sometimes failed. She, on the other hand, was pure of thought, and by giving up her virginity on a moral basis had entirely eclipsed him. Conclusion: how could he not fall in love with her? *Quod erat demonstrandum.*

CHAPTER 69

Lin looked in the refrigerator and through the cupboards in the forlorn hope of finding something special for breakfast. 'There's some wholemeal bread in the freezer; it's fine for toasting, but takes a while to defrost properly. I could use the microwave, but that tends to leave it a bit snurped up.'

'I have a better idea. Let's go to the supermarket and pick up something nice.' He paused to allow her to acknowledge the merit of the idea, before adding something he knew she may baulk at. 'And then we'll go to my house so we can all have breakfast together.' To discourage any negative response, he continued without a pause. 'You've met the children before, though Alice was just a toddler; you can see how much they've grown.' He further deflected her from objecting. 'Do you remember them?'

She ignored the question. 'Do you really think that's a good idea? It isn't as though I'm going to say to Helen, "Your husband's just been having sex with me." But what if she suspects? Or even asks? It's one thing to lie to suspected criminals; it's another thing entirely to lie to your wife.'

'I'm going to have to lie to her, even if only by omission; I'll be sunk if you don't lie as well.'

She frowned. 'This isn't just a one night stand, is it? We are going to keep seeing each other, aren't we? And I don't just mean at the station.'

He looked pensive. 'Yes, of course, so long as we

can keep it under the radar.'

She smiled. 'Then I'll lie about you... and with you, and under you, and on top of you.'

He frowned. 'Don't make hidden jokes when she's there; she's very smart at interpreting what people say. And she's a highly skilled interrogator; I should know!'

At a quarter to seven they arrived at the Priestley home with bags of shopping. He turned off the alarm and invited Lin into the kitchen, where he made three mugs of coffee. 'I'll take one up to Helen and let her know you're here. I'll get changed, as well. "Always wear clean underwear in case you're knocked down by a bus," as my mother used to say when I was a boy.'

Lin sipped her coffee, watching the door for Marcus's return. It was opened by a boy who asked, with nothing but curiosity in his voice, 'Who are you?'

'I'm Lin. Do you remember me?'

'If I had, I wouldn't have asked who you are.'

'You were only little when I last saw you.'

'I'm still only little.' He conceded, 'But not as little as I used to be. Why are you here?'

'I'm going to have breakfast with you all.'

'Don't you have any food in your own house?'

'Not much.'

'Are you a poor woman? I mean, are you a socially deprived person who is female?'

'Those are big words.'

'If you're going to keep coming here for breakfast, you'll have to get used to words like that. So, are you deprived?'

'No, I'm not deprived.' She found herself blushing as she thought of an alternative meaning.

'Are you hot?'

Her flush gained strength as she considered a second interpretation. 'I am quite warm.'

'You look very, very warm.'

'I'm just nicely warm.'

'When the heating comes on in the morning it makes a noise that sometimes wakes me up. Do you have heating at your house?'

'Yes, I do.'

'You have heating but no food. Perhaps you should buy food instead of having heating.'

'I have heating and food, but I forgot to do the shopping.'

'Do you have Alzheimer's? But if you do, you wouldn't know, so I just asked a silly question.'

Marcus caught the tail end of the conversation. 'What silly question is that, Edwin?'

'I asked Lin if she has Alzheimer's because she forgot to do the shopping.'

'But we haven't forgotten to do the shopping; we brought some things in just now.'

'Is that because she forgot to do it herself? Are you her care worker? Do you have to look after her?'

'Lin doesn't need anyone to look after her.'

Edwin turned to leave, then a new question occurred to him. He looked innocently at his father. 'You didn't come home last night. Where were you?'

'I was looking after Lin.'

'You said she doesn't need anyone to look after her.'

'She doesn't usually need anyone, but she needed me last night.'

'Why was last night different?'

Marcus sighed. 'That's enough questions. Will you help us make breakfast?'

'Do you need help? Mummy often says she doesn't think you know how to make breakfast.'

He sighed again. 'Edwin, go somewhere and play.'

Helen completed her daily routine a little earlier than usual, having risen as soon as she had heard the intruder alarm being deactivated. She arrived carrying a sleepy-looking Alice. 'Hello, Lin. This is a nice surprise.'

'Good morning, Helen.' Lin's voice was hoarse from her earlier climax.

Helen immediately sent Alice to go and play with Edwin. 'Are you alright, Lin? Marcus said something had happened to an officer last night. Was that you?'

Marcus responded for her. 'Yes, it was. A man grabbed her from behind and knocked her out with ether. She could have died.'

Helen continued to ask Lin questions which Marcus answered. 'I can tell your voice has been affected. Did he try to strangle you?'

'No; he just grabbed her.'

'Was it the ether that affected your throat?'

'Possibly.'

'Did Marcus look after you alright?'

'Yes, I did.'

'Does it hurt when you try to talk?'

'Not too much; she can talk well enough.'

Helen turned to Marcus. 'Then, can you tell me why you're answering all her questions?'

Lin answered for him. 'He's been trying very hard to take care of me; he wouldn't let me do anything for myself.'

Helen asked him, 'Did you make a good job of it?'

Lin rushed to respond for him. 'A very good job indeed. If ever I need someone to take care of me again,

I know where to come.' She gave a nervous laugh. 'Thank you for lending him to me.'

Helen smiled at her. 'Anytime.'

She smiled back. 'I'd like to hold you to that.' She adopted a troubled expression. 'It was so terrifying, I think I might need someone to take care of me at night for quite a while. Did you know Marcus thought I was dead? It must have been such a shock for him. He's probably in need of taking care of, as well.'

Marcus spoke out loudly. 'I am here, you know; I can speak for myself.'

Helen responded to Lin. 'Of course he can, but answering for each other is much more interesting, don't you think?'

Marcus wondered if Helen had been reading his mind again and was just toying with him. He was relieved to hear a ting from the oven that indicated it had reached the correct temperature. After putting on a heat-resistant mitt, he opened the oven door and placed the *croissants* and the *pains au chocolat* onto a hot tray using his other hand; quickly, he closed the door before too much heat was lost.

Helen raised her eyebrows at him. 'I see you're becoming domesticated; well, not before time.'

Edwin returned with Alice close behind. 'What's cooking?'

Helen responded, 'There's *croissants* and *pains au chocolat* in the oven, but you need to have some fruit first. Daddy and Lin brought some strawberries and blueberries for us; they're our favourites. Isn't that nice of them?'

As the children ate their fruit, Marcus reinforced his domestic credentials by locating five huge, French-style cups and making hot chocolate for them all. He explained to the children, 'In France, people dip their crusty bread into their hot chocolate or coffee. We can do the same with our *pains au chocolat* and *croissants*.'

Repeated tings informed Marcus the French pastries had had their allotted time in the oven; he transferred them all to a large plate. Helen gave one each to the children in accordance with their stated choices, before taking a *croissant* for herself. Alice watched her mother pull pieces off her *croissant* and dip them into her drink; she imitated her with care and precision. Edwin plunged a *pain au chocolat* into his mug, then lifted it high to his mouth and tried to suck the liquid out of it, brown streaks racing down his arm.

When the children had finished eating and had been despatched to wash themselves again, Helen looked at Lin. 'Tell me all about your love-life, then.'

Lin made a conscious effort not to show her concern. 'What exactly do you mean, Helen?'

Marcus added, defensively, 'What makes you think she has a love-life?'

Helen pointed to Lin's finger. 'You're wearing a wedding ring, but there's no one at home to look after you. What's the story?'

Lin hoped she had not betrayed her feeling of relief. 'The first time we went undercover, I borrowed my sister's jewellery, including her rings. She wasn't around this time to lend them to me, so I just bought a wedding ring that looks like hers, and wore that. It's platinum. I think I might keep wearing it, to discourage men from trying it on with me.'

'Are you not interested in getting married, then?'

'I'm married to the job, Helen. At least for now.'

CHAPTER 70

Witty had contacted everyone on the team, Priestley and Plummer excepted, to instruct them to assemble in the MIR ten minutes ahead of the 8:30 meeting. At 8:20, as the chatter showed no signs of abating, Witty called out loudly, 'Quiet, everyone.' The room fell silent. 'There's been a major breakthrough in the case, which we'll be covering from eight thirty. Before then, I'd like to address a growing problem.

'Now, I'm as ready as the next man, or woman, to have a bit of a laugh about what colleagues have or have not been up to, but it seems to me the spreading of unfounded rumours is getting out of hand. I'm not going to dignify any of them by repeating them here, but no doubt you've all heard some of the latest ones regarding DCI Priestley. On Saturday I asked him about them, and he denied them all. Now, I for one respect him, and accept his word as the gospel truth.

'A fortnight ago DCI Priestley went on a joint undercover operation with DC Plummer, and I annoyed her later when I implied there was something going on between them. It was intended as a joke, so it shows how any of us can get it wrong if we're not careful. I apologised, of course, when I realised how embarrassed and upset she was at having to deny it. But how much better not to say the wrong thing in the first place. So, absolutely no rumours on that front, if you don't mind; otherwise I'll take a very dim view of it. Comments, anyone?' He saw Berry muttering something to the person next to him. 'If you've something to say, Tony, I'm sure we'd all like to hear it.'

Berry looked around, as though trying to avoid Witty's eyes. Finally, he met his gaze. 'Strictly, assuming we trust our colleagues to have been truthful, the evidence you've presented indicates there was nothing going on between them as at Saturday. It's now Tuesday.'

Before Witty could respond, several people shouted out various comments.

'Don't be so anal, Tony.'

'That's just stupid.'

'You certainly put the "P" into pedantic.'

As Plummer opened the door, she heard someone call out, 'You're splitting hairs.'

She froze when there was a general roar of laughter at someone's response of, 'And not Lin's.'

Witty saw the shock on Plummer's face. When the raising of both hands and arms failed to restore quiet, he bellowed, 'Shut up!' The room immediately fell silent as they followed his gaze to the doorway and saw Plummer standing there. 'Lin, I've just been telling everyone there is absolutely no truth in the rumour that you're in a relationship with DCI Priestley.' He turned his head to scan the room. 'And let me add, if I hear any of you suggesting otherwise, I'll be treating it as a disciplinary matter.' Everyone found a sudden reason to inspect their footwear.

Witty continued, 'When the boss is here, we'll have a run-through of yesterday's events. But let me say, right away, how brave Lin is to have come into work this morning after what happened; so I expect you all to afford her the ultimate in courtesy and consideration.'

He lowered his voice substantially, though only to a level that could still be heard by everyone in the subdued room. 'Lin, are you sure you should be here?'

She spoke just audibly. 'I'll be fine, so long as people don't keep fussing over me.' Hearing her cracked, hoarse voice, looks of concern passed quickly amongst her colleagues.

Witty checked his watch against the wall-clock. 'DCI Priestley should be arriving any moment now. I don't wish to steal his thunder, but, for anyone who doesn't yet know, he and Lin went undercover again yesterday and cracked the case. We now have a suspect in custody.'

The door opened and Priestley strode in. The combination of unspoken apologies for past rumours, sympathy for Plummer, and knowledge that the case had been broken, resulted in an eruption of cheers and applause. He looked around, uncertain of the reason behind the appreciation. Witty called out for everyone to hear, 'Well done, sir. You and Lin were fantastic.' Priestley turned to Lin, who shook her head to deny knowledge of the reason for the ovation. Witty called out above the continuing applause, 'Well done for cracking the case, sir.' Priestley looked relieved.

After the room had quietened, Witty accepted Priestley's invitation to give his report of the events at Campbell's house; he did so without mentioning the injury to Campbell. Cargill was next, giving a detailed explanation of the key actions since Campbell had been taken into custody, but excluding mention of the medical treatment given to him. Other reports were delivered, including the identification of Campbell's car on CCTV a mile from Milo's house, travelling first toward and then away from Nethershaw. When someone called out, 'Better late than never,' Priestley admonished him and thanked the original officer for her diligence. After all reports had been heard, Cargill added one extra piece of information. 'Campbell's raised a formal complaint against an officer; I think we'd better discuss it offline.'

In his office, Priestley met with Cargill, Witty and Plummer. Cargill explained to Priestley that the complaint was against him for using unnecessary violence. He responded, 'While ever I'm the subject of a complaint, I think it would be best if I stayed behind the scenes and let you continue to run with it. Are you alright with that?'

Cargill nodded repeatedly. 'More than alright. I'll make sure there are no slip-ups. Thank you, Marcus.'

'I'm not sure you should be thanking me, Frank; you'll have a lot to do, and you don't get overtime.'

Cargill looked him full in the eyes, not something he generally did with colleagues. 'Thank you for putting your trust in me, Marcus; yesterday and today.' The three of them left Priestley in his office, Plummer forcing herself not to look back.

While Cargill carried on his way, Witty took Plummer aside in the corridor. 'Are you really alright, Lin? You can tell me if you're not.'

'Trust me, Neil, I've got the mental strength to get over it, so don't go treating me like an invalid.'

'Sure, Lin. Perhaps I should be more worried about Marcus; I saw how upset he was about you. But I can't just ask him; men don't do that sort of thing.'

'What do you mean, how upset he was?'

'Well, when you were unconscious, I saw how

broken he looked. He was kneeling down and holding you up so carefully, with his hand under your head, and looking at you like you were an injured child.' He tried to laugh but it failed after the first sound. 'The paramedics had to prise you away from him.'

She found herself empathising with Marcus, forgetting for a moment the more substantial trauma she herself had suffered. Realising Neil was watching her intently, she gave him a smile. 'Don't worry about him, Neil; leave it with me. I'll give him some TLC.'

CHAPTER 71

Cargill arranged for Campbell to be brought from his cell and put into an interview room. Campbell appeared agitated, and demanded to know why his solicitor was absent. Cargill responded calmly, 'This is just a friendly chat. I'm not asking you any questions, and you don't have to say anything if you don't want to. I just wanted you to know something. Now, would you like a cup of coffee?'

'I suppose so.'

Cargill turned to the uniformed constable. 'Would you mind fetching a coffee for Mr Campbell? Make it one of those nice ones, the sort with the infuser and the plunger and everything. We'll be alright here 'til you get back.'

The officer gave Cargill a concerned stare; when he responded with a smile and a shake of the head to suggest nothing untoward was about to happen, he went away to make the coffee.

Cargill began as soon as the door was closed. 'Now, Mr Campbell, I know you've pleaded not guilty, but that's never going to work; there's too much evidence stacked against you. So, you're going to be doing time.

'You've raised a complaint against DCI Priestley; I'm making no comment on whether or not it's justified, though I think you know as well as I do he was simply reacting to a very unpleasant situation. But here's the thing. Mr Priestley is a friend of mine, and I wouldn't want him to have a blot on his record. So, if you withdraw your complaint against him, I'll not do what I will do if you don't withdraw your complaint.'

Campbell had intended to remain silent, but decided he needed Cargill to explain his threat. 'What would you do if I don't withdraw my complaint?'

'I'd make sure that for the whole of the time you're inside, you're banged up with the shittiest blokes I can find, and there'll be plenty to choose from. There's the sort who won't leave you alone at night, for a start. I don't need to spell it out to you, do I, Mr Campbell? I can tell you're the sensible type. So, think about it, but don't take too long. An hour should be plenty of time for you to come to a decision.' The two sat in silence.

When the drink arrived, Cargill chatted to the PC. He allowed Campbell to finish his coffee, before having him taken back to his cell.

After Campbell had withdrawn the complaint, Priestley arranged to see him in an interview room. The same uniformed officer was in attendance. Priestley began, 'I'm sorry about your injury, Mr Campbell.'

He responded, 'I've withdrawn my complaint, so you don't need to threaten me.'

Priestley recalled what he had screamed at him yesterday. 'I'm not here to threaten you, Mr Campbell. Quite the opposite, in fact. There's something I want to say to you, that's all; and you don't have to respond unless you wish to.'

The officer thought he had understood the code, so spoke up. 'Should I go and make Mr Campbell a nice cup of coffee, sir?'

Priestley looked surprised. Campbell responded, 'Yes, a cup of coffee. Let's get it over with.'

The officer closed the door behind him. 'I appreciate

you withdrawing your complaint against me, Mr Campbell, and in return I'm going to say something that might just help you when it comes to sentencing. The young woman you knocked out with the ether was very upset when you grabbed her, as you might expect. You thought you'd killed her, didn't you? Why was that?'

Campbell eventually decided to speak. 'I'm not answering questions without a solicitor.' As Priestley continued to hold his gaze, he decided to imply the reason without admitting to anything. 'When I was a boy, my father took me out shooting rabbits. One time, I picked up a rabbit that he'd just shot, and I held it up to look at it. Only it pissed in my face. My father laughed at me; I hated him for that. But he explained to me that when the rabbit dies, it loses control over its muscles, making it release the contents of its bladder.'

When Campbell again fell silent, Priestley decided to respond in kind. 'Here's the thing. What if the rabbit wasn't dead, and afterwards didn't want anyone to know that she'd peed herself, because she was embarrassed, being a very proper sort of rabbit. It could do the boy more harm than good if he told people about the rabbit having peed herself; a judge might be especially annoyed, having sympathy for the rabbit.'

Campbell nodded but remained silent.

When the officer returned, Campbell asked to be taken back to his cell at once, without first drinking the coffee.

Later, Campbell was again brought to an interview room. His solicitor, a gaunt-looking man in his forties, dressed in a dark blue suit that had seen better days, sat to his left. Witty sat at Cargill's right, as the four faced each other across a table for the First Account interview. Cargill began, 'This is an opportunity for you to give your version of events. What you say won't be challenged at this stage, so feel free to explain things as you think fit. Let's start with yesterday evening, when you knocked out DC Plummer with ether.'

Campbell launched into his story. 'I didn't know she was a policewoman, so it's misleading to say I knocked out a detective constable. As far as I'm concerned, an unknown woman tricked me into inviting her into my home by pretending she was interested in buying a painting. When I went to answer the door to a double-glazing salesman, she went into a room that I had specifically told her was out of bounds. The woman looked very fit and athletic, so I thought she might be able to overpower me. I therefore looked for something to subdue her, and noticed a bottle of ether lying around. So I applied some to a cloth and put it over her nose and mouth. She quickly became unconscious, so I wrapped her up in some plastic insulating material to keep her warm, and locked her in the room in case she recovered from the anaesthetic and became violent toward me. When a man she had previously stated was her husband came looking for her, I thought it was best not to tell him where she was, as he looked the violent sort. I had no way of knowing he was in fact another police officer, so I ran out of the house seeking help. There were other officers outside who afforded me protection from the man. All I did was what any law-abiding citizen might have done under the circumstances.'

During the story, Cargill and Witty had struggled to maintain the straight faces protocol demanded. Cargill now asked, 'Do you wish to say anything about the unfinished painting found in your house?'

Campbell responded glibly. 'It was something I was attempting as an *hommage* to my dear departed friend, Milo Piscaro.'

The officers remained poker-faced. Cargill asked, 'What did you do on the evening Milo Piscaro died?'

'I was at the gallery 'til five o'clock; then I went home and dined with Mrs Andrea Carter and her son Lewis. I watched TV with her from six 'til seven, then read 'til nine twenty, and then watched more TV with her 'til half ten when we went to bed.'

'Just to clarify, did you go to the same bed?'

'We had separate sleeping arrangements; I went to my bed and she to hers.'

Cargill looked at Witty. 'Anything from you?'

Witty responded to Cargill. 'That painting that sold at auction for forty thousand pounds; there's a suspicion it was a forgery.'

Cargill bounced it as a question to Campbell. 'Is there anything you would like to tell us about that?'

Campbell puffed himself up in his chair. 'I have seen many paintings by Milo Piscaro and there is nothing about that particular one which would suggest to me it is anything other than the genuine article.'

'What about the price it fetched at auction?'

'That was the most welcome and unexpected good fortune for me, though it saddens me to think Milo's talent was only recognised after his demise.'

'That good fortune you mentioned, did you know Mr Piscaro was leaving his entire estate to you in his will?'

'Anyone who knew him might have expected him to show appreciation for his closest friend in that way.'

Cargill echoed, 'His closest friend?'

'Yes, me; I was his closest friend.'

'Right, well, thank you Mr Campbell. Is there anything you'd like to add to your testimony?'

'No; nothing.'

The solicitor spoke up. 'I trust everything has now been clarified to your satisfaction and you will be releasing my client.'

Cargill gave him an acid smile. 'Our twenty-four hours isn't up yet; we'll be retaining the pleasure of Mr Campbell's company a while longer.'

As Campbell was being taken back to his cell, Cargill and Witty went to Priestley's office. After Cargill had reprised the interview, Priestley asked, 'His story about Lin: is it good enough to fool a jury?'

Cargill looked downcast. 'That depends entirely on the jury; I've seen some really stupid decisions come out of jury rooms. I think some must come down to one person getting it wrong, accidentally or deliberately, and persuading everyone else to change their minds.'

Priestley responded, 'I can recall some really obvious miscarriages of justice. Whenever a new one comes along, my wife always reminds me there's no point in fretting about something I'm powerless to alter. But it doesn't make it any easier to swallow.' He turned to Witty. 'If you were on a jury, Neil, would you buy Campbell's story?'

Witty grinned and shook his head. 'Maybe when it comes out in paperback.'

CHAPTER 72

Priestley telephoned the Lead CSI about the crime scene report relating to Campbell's house. 'You can see how embarrassing it would be for her, can't you?'

'I'm not missing anything out of our findings.'

'I wouldn't expect you to, Steve. All I'm asking is that you make it less prominent, so it's there if someone goes looking for it, but it doesn't leap out at anyone who's just skimming through.'

'What about this? "Evidence was found indicating relaxation of a pubococcygeus muscle." Will that do?'

'If that means the same as you had before, let's go with it. Cheers, mate.'

He telephoned Plummer and she came to his office. 'Do you know what a pubococcygeus muscle is?'

'Not really, though "pubo" is probably a hint. Why?'

'Relaxation of aforesaid muscle results in the release of urine. The CSI report is going to use that term, so it shouldn't be too obvious what happened. And I've also suggested to Campbell it might be in his interests not to mention it, either. It's the best I could do, Lin.'

'Thanks, Marcus; I do appreciate it.'

'So, how are you feeling, anyway?'

'Guilty, to be honest.'

'Does that mean you're regretting what we did? I think I'm the one who should be feeling guilty.'

Lin laughed lightly. 'It isn't us I'm feeling guilty about; I don't regret that at all.' She shook her head. 'No; it's what's just happened with the Chief Super.

She knew all about the incident at Campbell's house, and when someone told her I could barely speak this morning, she put two and two together and made five. She had me in her office to tell me how brave I was, a credit to the service and an example to women everywhere. Some example, eh? I suppose I'd better try and keep my mouth shut next time.'

He stifled his laughter and spoke quietly. 'We'd both better keep our mouths shut; the door's open. We'll have to get into a work mindset whenever we're on the premises, and block out the other.'

'Yes, of course. So, if we're in work mode, what's happening with the case?'

'Frank and Neil talked me through Campbell's interview, and then I read the transcript. He says you're a powerful woman and he feared for his safety.' He waited for her to reciprocate his smile. 'You'd better read it as well, and then get them in here for a confab.'

When Cargill, Witty and Plummer arrived at Priestley's office, he explained his latest thoughts on the case. 'If we could prove that the *Robin* painting is a forgery, and that Campbell painted it himself, then we'd have a really solid case.' He locked his fingers together as though in prayer. 'Neil, when is that forensic accountant going to investigate the auction?'

'He's already on it. I told him what had happened to Lin, and it went straight to the top of his pile.'

'And what about the will?'

'Different bloke, same reaction; it's being looked at today. We should try this method more often.'

When Priestley adopted a worried frown, Plummer sought to lighten his mood. 'Are you really suggesting I should be attacked more often so as to get the work done quicker, Neil? You'd better not be!'

Only two of the men laughed; Cargill pursed his lips, then addressed Priestley. 'What about getting more experts to say they think the painting's a forgery?'

'Our expert is probably the best there is.'

'Couldn't you put some pressure on her to "up" her opinion? You must have got to know her a bit in Paris; is she the pliable sort?'

Priestley stifled a smile. 'If you mean pliant as in lying, I'd say she's far too principled ever to bend to anyone's wishes. I'll have a word with her, though.'

Priestley closed the meeting and telephoned Anna. 'Hello, it's Marcus; this is a work call.'

'Go ahead then.'

'Is there any basis on which you could be more certain about your assessment of the Piscaro? Could you see yourself standing up in court and declaring it definitely a forgery?'

'Not without more evidence. If you wish, I could track down some of his earlier work and see if there is something that might increase my certainty.'

'That would be very helpful, Anna.'

'And when will I receive a call from you that does not relate to work?'

'I've got my hands full at the moment... with this case. Call me if you find something; otherwise, I'll call you later to check on progress.'

Even though the conversation had been work-related, he nevertheless experienced a twinge of guilt, so telephoned Helen in the hope that that would assuage the feeling. 'Hello, love. How's your day going?'

She responded in a business-like voice. 'By which you mean you wish to tell me how your day's going, so fire away.'

'It's the Piscaro case; it seems to hinge on whether we can prove beyond all reasonable doubt that the painting's a forgery. Are there any art experts at the university who might have a different angle on it?'

'Are you asking if there's anyone who's susceptible to bribery?'

'No, of course not. I only want people with integrity, though I expect the defence team will be buying a few so-called experts to argue it's genuine.'

'Leave it with me. Keep your pecker up, love.'

Priestley wondered why she had said "pecker", when she usually said "chin". Telling himself he must stop trying to reinterpret every little thing she said, he put it down to his feelings of guilt about Anna and Lin, and the concern that Helen would find out.

He was still musing, when his telephone rang. 'Hello, it's Jim Pickard, about that painting that was auctioned. Just tracing through a single transaction is a piece of cake; I've got all the evidence you need to prove the money went a circular route and ended up back where it started. Campbell bought it off himself.'

'Thanks, Jim; that's brilliant. We needed something to go in our favour; the guy's denying everything at the moment. Now we've something we can definitely charge him with, it'll give us breathing space to put the rest of the case together. You're worth every penny.'

He responded gruffly. 'I charge a lot more than pennies. Anyway, you can charge him with shilling.'

'Is that what passes for accountants' humour?'

'Glad you don't think that's an oxymoron.'

Priestley laughed down the telephone. 'When will I get your report?'

'It's on its way. Next thing for me is a trip to Bermuda to check on some drug-laundering money, if only I can get it past my boss.'

'Best of luck with that, and don't forget the shorts.'

'Cheerio.'

Priestley called together Cargill, Witty and Plummer in the MIR. 'Good news. The accountant has proved Campbell bought his own painting at the auction, so we should be able to charge him with shill bidding.'

Cargill added, 'And that's not all; we can do him for forging the will as well, or at least for getting it forged. They've just phoned me with the results; I was coming to tell you straight away.'

'Right. If there's any more good news, let me know.'

Witty asked, 'And what about any bad news?'

'Just bury it; today's a very special day, so good news only.' When Priestley laughed, the other two men joined in, while Lin gave him her sweetest smile.

Priestley returned to his office, where he received a call from Steve, the CSI. 'Hello, Marcus.'

'Hello, Steve. You haven't changed your mind about our little conversation, have you?'

'No, it's fine. I'm just ringing to give you a bit of good news.'

'That's the type I like. What is it?'

'The ether bottle at Campbell's house: it came from the same batch as the one found at Piscaro's house. They hadn't sold any more from that batch; all the rest of their customers have been buying the litre bottles because they work out a lot cheaper. That means the two bottles they sold must be these two we've got here in the lab.'

'This day is just getting better and better.'

'One slight problem, though. The supplier forces buyers to register, and the name on the order was Andrea Carter. Could she be an accomplice?'

'I think it's more likely he used her name to place the order without her knowing, just like he used her to try and get himself an alibi.'

'Right. I'll get the report written up.'

'Cheers, mate.'

Priestley went to the MIR to inform the other three key members of the investigation team. Rubbing his hands together, he declared, 'The noose is tightening around his neck.'

Witty responded, 'That's not allowed anymore; didn't you know hanging's been repealed?'

Back in his office, Marcus received a call from Helen. 'Hello, love. If you're calling to check on me, I can tell you I'm much happier now. I've had some good news on the case; it's all coming together nicely.'

'Well, people sometimes get what they deserve.'

'So, what are you wanting?'

'A meeting with you and Anna van Honthorst.'

He felt a momentary, unpleasant shrivelling feeling in his scrotum; he swallowed hard and managed a strangulated, 'Really?'

'Yes, really. I have something important to say to you both.'

'What is it?'

'It's better if the three of us meet up at the gallery.'

'Are you sure?' He hoped she was not intending to make a big scene in public.

'It's important. Can you come straight away?'

'Yes; I'll be right over.'

'Don't you need to check she's available, first?'

'Yes, you're right; I'll phone her.'

He terminated one call and made the next. 'Hello, Anna. Have you spoken to my wife at all?'

'No. Why do you ask?'

'She wants to meet us together; she said she has something important to say to us. I just can't imagine how she found out. She wants me to come over right away.'

'I would not want anything unpleasant to happen at the gallery; as I work there, it would be very bad for me. Perhaps we should meet somewhere else.'

'I agree. Where do you suggest?'

'My house, I suppose. I cannot think of anywhere else that is not public.'

'I'll ring her and call you back.'

He telephoned Helen again. 'I spoke to her. She asked if you would like us to meet at her house.'

'Well, that's very generous of her, but it needs to be at the gallery.'

'But...'

'There's no "but" about it, Marcus. I'm having to squeeze this in between meetings. I'll be there in thirty minutes. Don't be late.' The line went dead.

He telephoned Anna again. 'She'll be at the gallery in thirty minutes. She wouldn't talk on the phone. I'm setting off right now. Don't worry; I'm sure she won't want to make a scene. I'll see you soon.'

Feeling that all the joy of the day had been wiped out at a single stroke, he dragged himself to Witty's desk to let him know he was going to the gallery in Sheffield. Witty asked, 'Is everything alright? I thought this was a day for good news; you look like something's up.'

He put on a brave smile. 'No, no, everything's fine.'

CHAPTER 73

Anna took Marcus into the curators' private library, where art books and catalogues spanning many decades filled the shelves to overflowing. Her darting eyes reflected her deep concern. 'Does she know all about us, or is she only guessing?'

'I just don't know; she's totally inscrutable when she wants to be. If she says it's you or her, I really have to stay with my children. I hope you understand that.'

'I never meant to come between you and your wife. Are you sure she knows? I was hoping simply to have you as my lover. I still think about you all the time. Last night I dreamed you were having me in the gallery, up against the wall between *The Hours* by Edward Coley Burne-Jones and *The Execution of Marshal Ney* by Jean Leon Gérôme. But we triggered the alarms; perhaps it was an omen.'

They sat staring into space.

Anna jumped when there was a knock at the door, both quickly standing up as her colleague announced, 'I've got a visitor for you.'

They received Helen in silence, unsure who should speak first or what they ought to say. Helen looked at Anna. 'Hello again.' She offered her hand; Anna held it rigidly for a moment.

Helen tapped Marcus on the back. 'Well, come on, then; I haven't much time.' She led them out of the library, through the curators' office and into the corridor, then stopped and turned to Anna. 'You'd better lead the way.'

'To where?'

'To the Piscaroes, of course.'

Anna turned and looked at him, stretching her eyes wide and pushing her lips forward in a look of puzzlement. He averted his gaze, as Helen had half-turned and was now looking past her and at him. Anna spun away and rushed ahead of Helen. Marcus brought up the rear as they filed along in silence.

When they reached the Piscaroes, Helen pointed to seven symbols on the first painting. 'The name of the bird is in code. It uses the initial letters of the colours of certain symbols. These spell *Bluetit*: Brown, Lilac, Ultramarine, Emerald, Turquoise, Indigo, Turquoise.' She repeated the explanation while pointing to symbols on the next five paintings. '*Curlew*, Copper Ultramarine, Red, Lilac, Emerald, White. *Grouse*, Gold, Red, Orange, Ultramarine, Silver, Emerald. *Merlin*, Magenta, Emerald, Red, Lilac, Indigo, Nickel. *Osprey*, Orange, Silver, Purple, Red, Emerald, Yellow. *Plover*, Purple, Lilac, Orange, Violet, Emerald, Red.'

She paused for breath. 'When I checked the *Robin* painting, I knew it was a forgery; the coloured symbols don't spell out the name of the bird, you see.'

She looked at Marcus for a moment. 'Are you paying attention? I know you had a hard night, but you look like you're not with us.' He blinked and nodded to show he was still functioning. 'Now, Marcus, I was thinking, if everyone knows the code, it's going to be more difficult in the future to detect a forgery, so it seems to me the best thing would be to keep it secret. That way, if someone says they have another painting in the series, Anna,' Helen turned and smiled at her before switching her gaze back to Marcus, 'could check the painting for the things she knows to look for as an expert, and could also check the code embedded in the painting. If it satisfies both checks, it's probably the real thing; if it fails on either, it's definitely a forgery.' She looked at Marcus with an air of self-satisfaction that had crossed the border into smug.

He remained silent for several seconds. 'That's brilliant,' he finally managed to say, though with little emphasis as he was feeling dazed and dazzled.

Anna edged forward and gazed directly at Helen. 'I now know why Marcus thinks you are so wonderful.'

Helen found the words quite touching and slightly embarrassing. 'Yes, well, I have to get off straight away, or I'll be late.' She turned and hurried away through the double-doors.

Marcus followed Anna back to the art library, closing the door behind him. They remained standing as she broke the silence. 'I like your wife and I would not wish her to be unhappy. Would you be terribly upset if...', he assumed she was about to end their affair, '...I said we should only see each other in Paris?'

'I agree with you totally.'

'And other distant places, such as capital cities?'

'It's possible.'

'Good. I shall be visiting Amsterdam on the first weekend of next month. Will you come with me?'

'I'll let you know. I have to go now.'

She smiled cheekily. 'I can show you all the sights.'

He returned to his car and drove back to the station, intending to deliver the good news in person.

Witty intercepted him as he was passing through the main office. 'You've a call from Anna van Honthorst.'

'Switch it through to me.'

The telephone began to ring as he approached his desk. In case Anna's call had been queued behind another, he answered neutrally, 'Hello?'

Anna spoke rapidly. 'I have been looking at pictures of other paintings by Piscaro; ones from before the Birds series. Knowing what to look for, I can see he has always colour-coded his work. Thanks to your wife, I am now the world's leading expert.'

'Would you be prepared to testify the *Robin* painting is a forgery, without revealing the code?'

'Yes, though it may be necessary to disclose it if another expert disputes my findings.'

'We'll keep that option up our sleeves. Anyway, we can now put together a strong prosecution case.'

'We should go somewhere to celebrate together.'

'Where were you thinking of?'

'My bed.'

'I thought you said only places that are far away?'

'I have reconsidered.'

'I'll call you soon, Anna. Bye.'

He found Witty talking with Plummer. 'Neil, could you get hold of Frank and we'll all have a chat in my office.'

When they arrived, he stood up and walked around his desk to greet them. 'More good news. Our art expert will testify that the painting is a forgery.'

Cargill asked, 'Did you apply a bit of pressure, then?'

He shook his head. 'No, Frank. She's added a dimension to her analysis that makes her more certain. If we could just prove the painting was done by Campbell, I'd say the investigation is complete. Neil, call a full team meeting, will you. I think everyone should be given the good news.'

In the MIR, the news triggered spontaneous cheering, before Priestley reminded them the case against Campbell would benefit from tying the painting directly to him at a date before Piscaro's death. Nevertheless, the general mood remained celebratory.

He walked back to his office, not noticing WPC Paige Anderson trailing him. As soon as he sat down, he heard a quiet knock at the open door, and looked up. Knowing she would not normally have any reason to contact him directly, he assumed she was there to repeat her earlier offer. 'What is it, Paige? Tell Neil if you have something to report.'

'I think you'll want to hear this for yourself, sir.'

He believed that confirmed his expectation. 'I'm busy right now.'

She remained at the doorway. 'You really want to see what I've got for you, sir.'

'How can you be so sure of that?'

'Believe me, I'm sure.'

'Well, come in then, and out with it.'

'You know about social media, don't you, sir? It's what young people use.'

'I'm not that old, Paige.'

'Well, let me show you something.' She walked around to his side of the desk and typed away at the computer keyboard. 'You see this picture?'

'No, I can't see anything from this angle; the light's reflecting on it.'

She turned the screen to face him, then stepped behind his chair and stretched over him to point at the relevant image. He quickly pulled the hydraulic lever to drop his seat, so she could see more easily; she responded by cradling the back of his head with her breasts. 'That's it there, sir. Ryan Carter took a selfie; that means a picture of himself. It's when he was in Campbell's house on the Saturday before Milo died. It shows Ryan next to the *Robin* painting, except it wasn't quite finished, so it shouldn't have been there. So that ties up the case, doesn't it, sir?'

'Marvellous, Paige; I owe you one.'

'I'll let you know when I want to collect.' She began to rub her breasts up and down over his head and neck.

Lin shouted from the doorway. 'What's going on?'

He looked up. 'There's something here for you to see, Lin.'

'I've seen enough, thank you.'

'No, don't go. You really need to see this.'

She asked sulkily, 'What?'

'Just come and look. Move over Paige, let Lin see.'

Lin decided not to be outdone; she stood behind his chair, with her breasts pressed up against his head. 'What am I looking at?'

'It's a picture of the unfinished forgery taken in Campbell's house not long before Milo died. Campbell must have at least completed it, which indicates he will have painted the whole thing. I don't see any way he can worm his way out of this one.'

Chief Superintendent Barbara Watt bellowed from the doorway. 'What's going on, here?'

He jerked his head back for a moment to force Lin to move away. 'It's this photograph, ma'am. It's the final piece of the jigsaw.' As she walked toward his desk, he began to clamber out of his low chair.

Watt ordered him, 'Stay where you are.' Standing

behind him, craning forward to see, she squeezed her matronly bosom over his hunched head.

He gulped as he pointed. 'It's that image there, ma'am. It's a photograph of a painting we now know is a forgery. It wasn't finished and yet it was already in Campbell's house instead of still being at Milo's studio. The metadata will prove it pre-dates Milo's demise by just two days; that indicates Campbell must have completed it, which logically argues he forged the whole thing.'

'So we've got him, then.'

'Yes, ma'am.'

'Very good.' She stepped away from the chair and headed for the door, turning back to face him at the last moment. 'And in future, don't force women to squeeze up against you like that to see your screen. It's an amber light situation; it might even be a red.'

His eyes widened as he flushed in embarrassment at the public reprimand. 'I didn't really mean to, ma'am; it just happened.'

She smiled to herself as she walked away.

CHAPTER 74

Cargill and Witty reconvened with Campbell and his solicitor for the Disclosure interview where the accusations would be presented; Priestley and Plummer watched remotely on a monitor. As the allegations were delivered in chronological order, Campbell responded "No comment," after each.

The first accusation put to him was that he incited Miles Percy to commit fraud, though the team knew there was no realistic prospect of the CPS wasting resources on taking this to a formal charge unless he admitted the offence.

The second allegation was that he conspired with another to procure ether in preparation for a criminal act. The team had no intention of progressing this, as they were confident Mrs Carter had had no involvement; the purpose was merely to give him the opportunity to admit he had purchased the ether himself.

The third allegation was that he had forged a painting in imitation of the work of the late Miles Percy, an artist known as Milo Piscaro.

The next allegation was that he administered ether and other substances to Miles Percy, resulting in his death.

The allegation that he had forged the will was put to him with an alternative that he had arranged for the forgery to be made.

Cargill made the bid rigging allegation in two parts:

first, his own involvement; and second, conspiring with person or persons unknown to place the telephone and internet bids. They hoped Campbell would confess and give the name or names; otherwise, they would have to consider expending resources on investigating further.

Attempting to sell the forgery, both in England and France, brought a further raft of allegations that the CPS would in due course specify as charges.

Finally, there was the assault on DC Linda Plummer. The whole team wished to push this really hard, for Lin's sake, but they knew the CPS would have some issues with the way she had gained admittance to the property and failed to disclose her true identity.

After the final "No comment," Cargill terminated the interview and went with Witty to see Priestley, who invited them and Plummer to his office.

When they were seated, Priestley began, 'I'd like to be there myself for the Challenge interview, but after that little fracas I had with Campbell it's best I keep out of the way. Lin, you're obviously excluded as well. So, Frank, it's with you and Neil to see this through. Do you have any thoughts on how you wish to play it?'

Cargill responded without hesitation. 'I'd like to let the fish run before reeling him in; give him the chance to lay down his lies before facing him with facts.'

Priestley nodded. 'It's a method I've used myself plenty of times, though I'm not sure it's quite right for this particular fish. What if he refuses to comment until there's hard evidence in front of him?'

'Yes, I've known that happen often enough, but I still think it's worth a try.'

Priestley turned to Witty. 'What are your thoughts on the whole interview strategy, Neil?'

'It's always good to put the suspect under pressure, so they're more likely to slip up. Maybe we should build up slowly, drip-feeding the evidence like Chinese torture, taking one offence at a time.'

'Yes, that could work. And what do you think, Lin?'

'Me?' She had been taken by surprise, believing herself too junior to be asked for an opinion.

'Yes, you, unless there's someone else here called Lin.' He smiled at her. 'Just say what you think.'

'Well, I don't believe it's possible to know exactly what to do 'til we see how he reacts, so I'd have thought we can't do any more than work out various tactics for different situations. But that isn't really a proper strategic plan, so I don't suppose it helps.'

'Thank you Lin, and it does help. Right, gentlemen and lady, I believe all three of you are correct. Let me tell you how I see it. Start off by inviting him to speak, and if he does, let him take as much line as he likes, but if he clams up, feed him some evidential bait and see if that sets him going. If he still won't run with the hook in his mouth, feed him some more. Be ready with tactics for each step, depending on whether he does or doesn't start to speak. In the end, all the evidence has to be put to him, so the skill is knowing when to hit him with each different piece.'

Cargill responded, 'Do you want to tell us if we're missing a trick? You could be on the phone to us.'

'One thing I've learned over the years is that, when it comes down to split-second choices on how to react, it's always necessary to let the officer on the ground make the decisions. It works best with a top quality officer who has reliable judgement; an officer such as you, Frank, so I'm trusting you to deliver the goods.

'Another thing: I know you'll be keeping your wits about you, but don't overlook the fact that you'll have one of the smartest guys around with you.' He turned to Witty. 'Aren't you, Neil? A natural when it comes to reading people and knowing how to react.'

Plummer frowned at him. 'If you're dishing out the praise, sir, don't I get any?'

Priestley smiled at her. 'You've already had your fair share today, Lin: the Chief Super told me she'd told you you're the best thing since sliced bread. I agreed, of course.' Plummer blushed and looked away.

He turned to Cargill. 'Alright, Frank, you and Neil have a chat with each other to make sure you're both singing from the same hymn sheet, and let me know when you're good to go. I'll be watching on the monitor with Lin, but don't let that put you off your stride. You've been doing a great job since you joined the team, so I've very high expectations of how well you'll land this slippery customer.'

Plummer remained seated as Cargill and Witty walked away. 'I just wanted a quick word.' She played for time as they left the office. 'It's just something that occurred to me that I thought I'd run by you, but I didn't want to waste the others' time by asking you when they're here because they've obviously better things to do with their time than listen to me prattling on about nothing.' She judged they were now out of earshot. 'Why all the praise for Frank? You know he made a big mistake, don't you?'

'He needs confidence to do a good interview. I think he's like a beaten dog; if people stop hitting him, he'll respond positively and do better.'

'So, how do you think the interview will go?'

'I can't say; it depends on both pairs of combatants.'

'Won't you even venture a guess?'

'Well, Campbell clammed up last time, and for him things haven't changed, so I expect he'll start out as he left off. Then, when the evidence in front of him reaches a critical mass, he'll either start talking non-stop, or he'll go into a huddle with his solicitor and concoct a story. He's fundamentally a talker, so in the end I'm sure he'll eventually find a lot to say for himself. Maybe it'll be the truth, but my money is on him spinning us a yarn.'

CHAPTER 75

The allegation that Campbell had attempted to incite Miles Percy to commit fraud was treated with disdain by the solicitor, who objected to hearsay evidence.

The allegation of conspiracy with Andrea Carter to purchase ether was dismissed with a "No comment."

When the *Robin* painting was described as a forgery, the solicitor demanded more evidence than a mere opinion. Cargill looked Campbell in the eye. 'Our expert has been described as the leading authority on Piscaroes; I'm confident you won't find any credible witness to contradict their opinion.' Cargill smiled inwardly when Campbell was the first to blink.

The solicitor dismissed the allegation that Campbell had administered ether to Miles Percy as based merely on circumstantial evidence. He also fielded the allegation that Campbell was directly or indirectly responsible for forging the will. 'My client was merely the unwitting beneficiary.'

Cargill presented the evidence of the circular route taken by the money when the *Robin* painting was auctioned; this triggered a whispering session between solicitor and client. Campbell then responded, 'I'm putting my hand up to that one. But no one lost money on it apart from me, what with the buyer's commission. So no real harm done, eh?'

The allegation of attempting to sell a forgery was dismissed by the solicitor, on the basis that even the existence of a forgery had not been accepted.

On cue, Witty raised the subject of the attack on DC Plummer. He struck the side of his fist hard onto the table. With apparent emotion shaking his raised voice, he demanded, 'Don't deny you knocked out my friend Lin with that ether.' Witty glared at Campbell, his clenched fists held forward as though he was struggling to restrain himself from punching him.

Campbell recoiled, holding his head as far away from Witty as his neck would allow. 'No, of course I'm not going to deny that, but it was only because I didn't know who she was.'

Watching on the monitor, Plummer turned to Priestley. 'Neil's losing it; do you need to intervene?'

Priestley smiled at her. 'It looks like you're not the only one who can act; keep watching the show.'

Witty raised his voice a notch. 'And you're not denying it was your ether that you used?'

'No, of course it was mine; it was in my house.'

Cargill interjected in a calm voice. 'That ether was bought along with the bottle used to kill Miles Percy. If you owned one, you owned them both. We have CCTV evidence that shows you travelled toward Miles Percy's house before he was killed, and away from it afterwards. The timing fits precisely with the autopsy evidence relating to the drugs and the ether.

'We have a photograph of that *Robin* painting when it was unfinished, taken in your house not long before Miles died. Yesterday we found another unfinished painting there that's in the same style. My betting is our expert will confirm the two paintings are by the same hand; that is to say, your hand.

'You needed Miles dead before the rigged auction took place, because you knew he'd stand up and tell everyone the painting was a forgery; you knew he wouldn't just go along with it, because you'd already tried and failed to persuade him to join you in a price-fixing scam last year. And you'd only benefit from the sale of *Robin* if you owned it; that's why you had to have the will forged. So the only thing that isn't buttoned down is whether Andrea Carter conspired with you to buy the ether. But seeing as she wouldn't give you a false alibi, and you threw her out as soon as she didn't serve a purpose anymore, I can't imagine for one moment she was really involved. So, would you like to respond, now, Mr Campbell?'

As the evidence was stacking up against Campbell, the solicitor had noticed the colour drain from his face, leaving him ashen; he demanded a comfort break for himself, citing the quantity of tea he had drunk.

Plummer was the first to speak when Cargill and Witty met up with her and Priestley. 'Neil, you seemed so angry, I thought you really were upset about me.'

He responded quietly. 'With this acting lark, you have to recall past emotions to make your performance more believable; so I simply remembered just how I felt when I was told he'd killed you.'

She quivered. 'Well, I think you deserve an Oscar.'

Priestley concurred, before turning to Cargill. 'You did brilliantly, Frank, hitting him with all the evidence as soon as he'd admitted to owning that second bottle of ether. Are you ready for the next round?'

Cargill shook his head. 'I'd like to drop out, if I may, Marcus. By rights, you deserve the honour.'

Priestley nodded. 'I would like to pick it up from here, so long as you don't mind. Thank you, Frank.'

CHAPTER 76

When Campbell and his solicitor had had their discussion and were ready to reconvene, Priestley and Witty joined them in the interview room, while Cargill and Plummer watched proceedings via the monitor.

Once the recording equipment had been started, Campbell began his defence. 'I blame the council.'

Priestley looked bemused. 'You'll have to explain that, Mr Campbell.'

'Business rates; they're killing people. Financially, I mean. It's the death of the High Street as we know it. Local government is squeezing the lifeblood out of people like me; they keep upping the rates. Paintings are only worth what you can sell them for, and I can't sell mine for enough to cover my costs.'

'Well, I don't think rates are anything you'll need to worry about for quite some time.' He recognised his words were cruel, but knew he harboured massive ill-will toward the man who had almost killed Lin.

Campbell appeared not to notice the barb. 'I needed to make more money, so last year I asked Milo if he would help me increase the market value of his paintings by rigging an auction, but he flatly refused; he said he had his reputation to protect.

'Then I came up with another idea. If I imitated his work, I could sell my own pictures at inflated prices without him dirtying his hands. So I made a start at home and invited him to look at what I'd done so far, but he just laughed and said it was an obvious forgery.

'I eventually finished the painting, and I still thought it was OK, but your expert spotted it was a wrong 'un.'

Priestley nodded. 'Yes, the expert had absolutely no doubt about it being a forgery. Now, before you continue, could I check for my own benefit exactly what order things happened. Did Mrs Carter move into your house before or after Milo had looked at your attempt to imitate his work?'

Campbell sensed a trap, thinking they probably already knew the answer. 'I didn't even ask her about moving in, until the day after Milo had visited me. I knew the tenancy was due to run out on her flat in a week's time, and she wasn't happy about having to move back in with her parents, so I invited her and her son to come and stay at my house.'

Priestley forced a smile. 'That was generous of you.'

Campbell nodded in appreciation, then paused as he tried to remember what he had intended to say next. 'What you really need to know about, though, is what happened earlier this year. I was talking to Milo at his studio, and he was pretty miserable. "The love of my life", he kept going on about. "She chewed me up and spat me out." He told me he'd decided to give up painting and become a decorator. I told him there's not much money in that, but he was adamant there was more in it than what he was currently doing. I remember saying I'm short of funds as well, and we sympathised with each other.

'I've forgotten something; I'm doing this in the wrong order. I should have mentioned last Christmas when he broke up with his girlfriend, Lisa Wye.'

Priestley shook his head slightly. 'You just carry on; we'll piece it all together afterwards.'

'I want to tell you about why they broke up. There was a Christmas party. He told me all about it; he said it was too good a do. Everyone but him, he reckoned, had chipped in double the amount they normally paid, so he felt like he was sponging off them. It stopped him from enjoying it, and Lisa didn't appreciate why; she said he should just enjoy it and pay more next year if he wanted to. That's what led him to think about giving up art and simply trying to earn a normal wage. Of course, really, the problem started before then, when Lisa adopted him as her latest pet. Have you met Lisa?'

Priestley nodded. 'Yes. I can understand how he could fall for her; she's a very attractive woman.'

'If you're into that sort of thing.'

'I take it you aren't.'

'Don't misunderstand me; I'm not into men. No, not at all. I'm not like that. I've always liked women, but not enough to want to stay with one for very long.'

'I did wonder what happened with you and Andrea Carter. Just not your type?'

'I was only helping her out, really, but it crossed my mind to give it a try, only my heart wasn't in it.'

'It was useful to have her around, though, wasn't it?'

'Useful?'

'Getting her to order the ether.'

'I'm not a bad man, Mr Priestley; I've just been unlucky. That's why I'm telling you it was me who ordered the ether, using her name. She didn't know anything about it. Do I get something for owning up?'

'I'm grateful you're coming clean about things, but I'm afraid your other offences are rather more substantial. Why did you order two bottles, by the way? Were you unsure what quantity you would need?'

'I'll come to that later, Mr Priestley.'

'As you wish. There's another thing relating to Mrs Carter that I've been wondering about: did you consider asking her to give you an alibi, rather than leaving the house quietly and returning without her knowing?'

Campbell appeared flustered. 'This is all coming out in the wrong order; let me tell it my way.' Priestley nodded. 'I didn't expect to need an alibi when I set off that evening. After I came back, I knew not to ask her, because of something-or-other she'd said recently; she was obviously far too law-abiding to lie for me.'

'And once Milo was dead, you asked her to leave.'

'Not straight away; it wasn't until after... it was after a while, when I realised we were never going to have a relationship.'

'Just after DI Cargill had interviewed her, in fact, and she had given you an alibi. So, putting things in sequence, let me check if I've understood correctly what you've told me so far. Last year you invited Milo to take part in a scam to inflate the going rate for his paintings, but he refused. Then he had a love affair that ended at Christmas. Sometime around then he decided to make a living away from art, but for the time being he continued to paint. This year he told you how unhappy he was about losing Lisa. You then tried to imitate his work, to make money, while at the same time protecting him from the accusation of being your accomplice; but you couldn't work to his standard. The day after he'd seen your attempt, you invited Mrs Carter to stay at your house, and she moved in a week later. Is all that precisely correct?'

'Yes, it is.'

'You ordered some ether under her name, without

her knowledge. Was that before or after she moved in?'

He thought the police could easily check this, so answered honestly. 'It was after she moved in; I needed to get hold of her ID.'

'Alright, so what about the actual death? Would you like to describe what happened?'

'Well, I was losing money at the gallery, so I was pretty miserable. And Milo was still grieving over his lost love, so he was miserable as well. And that's when we decided on a suicide pact. I bought two bottles of ether, and he asked me to do away with him first because he didn't think he'd be strong enough to go through with it without me. So I gave him Valium in whisky and waited for it to take effect. When he was unconscious, I put ether on a cloth and placed it in a bag that I then put over his head. After I'd eased him gently out of this world, I was supposed to do the same for myself, but I couldn't go through with it.'

Priestley and Witty stared at each other in amazement. Priestley responded to Campbell. 'I think we can terminate the interview there, thank you Mr Campbell. I expect the CPS will be instructing us to charge you with murder.'

'But I was told it would be manslaughter if it was pursuant to a suicide pact.'

'What you were told is correct, but I don't accept the circumstances warrant that classification.'

Campbell was bobbing up and down in his seat in agitation. 'Why not?'

'Because what you've just said is the biggest load of bollocks I've heard all year. Your latest money-making racket could only work if Milo was dead, otherwise he'd denounce your imitations as forgeries. You invited

Mrs Carter to live in your house only after you'd shown Milo your unfinished painting, so that was clearly an attempt to procure someone to provide you with an alibi. When you realised she wasn't the type to lie to the police, you sneaked out and murdered Milo, and sneaked back in again. Then you spoke to her as soon as you were back, to see if she'd noticed you'd left the house. She hadn't, so you kept up your pretence that you'd been there all along. If you'd really intended to commit suicide, you'd have had no reason to sneak out, and no reason to cover up the purchase of the ether by using Mrs Carter's details.'

Priestley looked at Witty, who shook his head to indicate he had nothing to add. He turned back to Campbell. 'With the clear evidence of premeditation, I haven't the slightest doubt you'll be found guilty of murder. And I expect the CPS will also instruct us to charge you with the attempted murder of DC Linda Plummer. You have a solicitor to advise you, but if you'll take my advice, plead guilty to both; at least that way your sentence might be reduced.'

Priestley terminated the interview and addressed the solicitor. 'There's an officer stationed outside, for when you've finished with your client. Have a nice day; I know I'm having one.'

CHAPTER 77

Priestley set off with Witty to meet up with Cargill and Plummer. He asked, 'Have you seen any episodes of the murder mystery they were watching that evening?'

Witty nodded. 'Yes, I've seen all of them so far. I know Mrs Carter said it was easy to pick up what was happening in the first episode, even though she'd missed the first twenty minutes, but frankly I'd have thought it would have made no sense, not knowing who'd been murdered, or how.'

'I think she'd been pleased when he invited her to watch it with him; that's why she wouldn't admit to herself she'd missed too much to know what was going on. I had a look at the latest episode, just to satisfy my curiosity. I found it quite disappointing; the way they portrayed police officers and procedures was completely unrealistic, and they made it too obvious the nanny's boyfriend did it.'

Witty groaned theatrically. 'You bastard, Marcus! There are still two episodes to go.'

Priestley laughed. 'Sorry, Neil; anyway, I could be wrong. Maybe it's the doctor's receptionist; she clearly has something to hide, as well as her secret relationship with the golf pro. And the odd-job man has a past that he doesn't want revealing, so perhaps...'

'Stop it! Stop it!'

Both were still laughing when they reached Cargill and Plummer. She asked, 'What have we missed?'

Witty responded, 'You know that murder mystery on

ITV that Campbell and Mrs Carter were watching the night Milo was murdered?'

'Yes; I've been watching it. Why?'

'If you'll take my advice, don't talk to Marcus about it. He's just given away the ending.'

Priestley grinned. 'I was only guessing how it ends. All I said was…'

Plummer stuck her index fingers in her ears and hummed loudly for a few seconds. 'I'm not listening.'

The other three laughed softly in her direction, relieved she had come through her ordeal with her sense of humour intact.

Priestley led the way to his office for a de-briefing. He asked Witty, 'Do you think the CPS will confirm the murder charge?'

Witty gave a deep nod. 'Definitely. He admitted buying the ether in advance, so we can prove premeditation…'

'And premedication; he's admitted to giving him Valium before the ether.' He turned in the direction of a strange sound and discovered it was Cargill laughing enough to loosen the phlegm from his lungs.

Witty added, 'All he was left with was coming up with some sort of partial defence. Suicide pact! My money was on loss of control.'

Cargill commented, 'I'd an each-way on diminished responsibility.'

Priestley asked, 'What about you, Lin?'

She looked pensive for a moment. 'I thought we might have been treated to a story about Milo believing he had some sort of incurable degenerative disease, and so turned to his best friend to help him terminate his life painlessly; claiming, in essence, he had killed him out of kindness. What did you think he might go for?'

'I thought "suicide pact" was possible, but only on the basis of homosexual love in a world that still doesn't understand or fully accept; he could have cited lack of relationships with women to support that line. But no, it was just that the two of them were hard up.'

Witty asked, 'Do you think they were hard up... with each other? Am I allowed to make jokes like that?'

Priestley grinned. 'I don't know; you'd better consult the manual.' The three men laughed loudly, pleased to share the risqué humour. Plummer restricted herself to an uncomfortable smile.

Priestley was the first to stop. 'Campbell was very insistent there was no homosexual angle to his relationship with Milo. Maybe he doth protest too much, methinks. Being short of money isn't generally a strong enough motive to kill someone, though by starting down the fraud route he was increasing what was at stake. But should it have been enough to push him into murder? The two of them may have been friends until Lisa came along. After that, Milo talked of dropping his involvement with the art world, which of course is what connected him with Campbell. Maybe it was about unspoken love, but that isn't his defence, so we won't mention it to the CPS. Who'd like to volunteer to see the Duty Prosecutor?'

Cargill responded, 'Me and Neil can do it together.'

Witty added, 'I'd like to do the MG3; I've never done a Charging Decision report on a murder case.'

Priestley nodded. 'You'll also need to do an Evidential Report and suggested charges. Make sure you include attempted murder; they can use the "system" argument.' He checked his watch. 'You'll have to get your skates on. We need their decisions not much after seven, when the twenty-four hours is up.'

Cargill cleared his throat. 'Actually, Marcus, we've got until nine. The detention clock was paused while he was at the hospital.' Priestley nodded his agreement.

Witty turned to Cargill with a smile. 'I feel like celebrating, Frank. How'd you like to share a Twix?' Cargill stood up and smiled back.

Priestley listened to Cargill's ruttling laughter as the two headed off, side by side, until it was out of hearing.

Lin spoke quietly to Marcus. 'I'd *really* like some more looking after, tonight.' She widened her eyes.

'Not tonight, Lin; Helen might become suspicious.'

'I'd have thought it would be easier to justify staying with me while I'm still recovering from severe trauma.'

He looked intently at her. 'I think you've survived unscathed; but if it's all an act, tell me now. Honestly.'

She glanced down. 'I can't lie to you; I'm fine.'

'Well, if you ever have night terrors, or even just flashbacks, let me know and I'll come over. But otherwise, I should spend my nights with my family.'

'What about evenings, then? Would that be easier? You could join a choral society or a folk-dancing club; that way you'd have an excuse for going out regularly.'

'I never thought of you as the devious type.'

'We're both going to have to be devious, aren't we? What if I phone you late tonight and say I'm getting anxious about things? Would that work, just this once?'

'I'd rather you didn't; I should stay home. We'll see each other soon. Try not to miss me too much.'

She gulped. 'I understand. That's what mistresses have to do, isn't it?'

CHAPTER 78

Marcus felt an intense need to be with his children all evening. He invited Helen to catch up on her reading in the living-room, while he took Alice and Edwin into the kitchen to do some crayoning. They began filling in pictures in colouring books; then he encouraged them to start again with some of their own drawings, and finally he suggested they create images that grow without the constraints of hard outer lines.

Edwin quickly discarded any sense of formality, his pictures becoming more diffuse and less recognisable. Alice put aside the crayons and picked up a pencil, drawing outlines on a blank sheet of paper. She then filled them in with crayon before attempting to rub out the original pencil lines, though she found this impossible where the wax had crossed over them. Marcus found neither of their end results especially remarkable, though he was nevertheless impressed with the different ways they had responded to the artistic challenges he had set them.

While he tidied up, they sat and read books silently. He wondered to what extent their willingness to read was down to the home environment and their upbringing, and how much came from their character. He thought Alice had the temperament to be quiet for long periods of time, whereas Edwin was sometimes too full of energy and excitement to sit still even for a moment. He was sure Helen understood them clinically, which left him free simply to enjoy them as children.

As Alice's bedtime approached, he watched to make sure he only stopped her from reading when she had reached the end of a chapter. 'Time for bed, my little love.' She raised her arms, ready for him to pick her up, clutching the book in her hand. He lifted her and she put her arms around his neck, a corner of the book digging in slightly. Looking at his son, he gave the usual instruction. 'Say goodnight to your sister, Edwin.'

The usual echo came back. 'Goodnight to your sister Edwin.'

When he heard Alice giggle a little, he wondered if she would ever grow tired of the joke, or whether she had already developed the capacity to humour her brother. He took her into the living room and offered her to Helen, who stood and kissed her on the forehead. 'Goodnight, sweetheart. Sweet dreams.'

He took her upstairs and into the family bathroom. She brushed her teeth diligently, had a final wash and changed into her pyjamas, putting her used clothes into the linen basket. As she walked into her bedroom and climbed into bed, he saw the book was again in her hand.

She smiled to ask for permission. 'I'll just read one chapter.'

'Read it aloud, then.' He listened to a story about animals who lived in a forest. Her words began to slow as she started to fall asleep. When she stopped, he gently eased the book from her hand and turned off the light. He liked to kiss her on the forehead before leaving, but sometimes this woke her, so tonight he just kissed the air above her head.

He went downstairs to Edwin and commenced their usual protracted negotiations. 'Alice is asleep, so don't be noisy when you go upstairs.'

'I'll remember, when I go.'

'I meant it's time to go so don't be noisy.'

'It's too early for me to go.'

'You're both children, so you both need lots of sleep.'

'But I'm older, so I should stay up later.'

'You have stayed up later. Now, it's time to go.'

'If you work out what time I should go to bed based on my age and her age, I think I should stay up 'til midnight.'

'If you go up right now, I'll read to you.'

'You always read to me when you're at home.'

'Well, if you don't go up now, I won't read to you.'

'That's not fair. Besides, Mummy says you should always read to me because it improves my vocabulary and pro-nun-ci-a-tion.' He smiled with satisfaction, having played his trump card.

'You win, you scamp. I'll take you to bed right now and read to you.' Edwin realised he had been outmanoeuvred; he raised his arms, not in surrender, but simply inviting his Daddy to lift him up. After a detour to Helen for a kiss, Marcus carried him upstairs.

Marcus read an Asterix book in what he hoped was a Brittany accent. When Edwin finally gave up the fight to stay awake, he gave him an air kiss before slipping quietly out of the room and tiptoeing downstairs.

Helen was still reading her textbook. 'Is he asleep, then? Or did you have to bribe him?'

'He's sleeping like an angel.'

'In contrast to his waking hours.'

'He isn't a bad boy; you know that. It's just that sometimes he has a lot of energy. Perhaps we could plug him into the mains and cut our electricity bill.'

Helen pretended to be shocked. As she put down her book, he noticed seven paper bookmarks of differing colours were protruding from it.

When he sat next to her, she turned and looked at him with concern in her eyes. 'How are you and Lin?'

'What do you mean?' He knew he had sounded defensive.

'She nearly died, and you were there. What do you think I mean?'

'I've obviously done a good job of putting it to the back of my mind.'

'So, how is she? I was wondering if the problem with her voice might be psychosomatic. Has she started speaking more normally, yet?'

'She's getting there.'

'Maybe you should give her a call? Ask her how she's feeling?'

'Good idea. I'll phone from the study.'

'No, call from here; I want to hear what you say.'

He telephoned her. 'Hello, Lin. Helen suggested I call you to see how you are; she's here with me.'

'Is she just listening to you, or is she listening in?'

He quickly concocted a response to answer Lin and mislead Helen. 'Yes and no, you know how it is.'

'So, can you come over tonight?'

'If you find you're panicking in the night, you can give me a call anytime. But try and be brave; I like my beauty sleep.'

'Message understood. Thank Helen for me, will you; she's such a considerate woman. Do you think she'd be nice enough to let me have a part-share in you?'

He tried to remain poker-faced. 'If you're feeling

desperately anxious, don't suffer in silence. I can come over if you really need someone to be with you.'

'But not tonight, I think.'

'Alright then, Lin. Goodnight, sleep tight.'

She completed the rhyme before terminating the call. 'Don't let the bedbugs bite.'

He turned to Helen. 'She asked me to thank you for suggesting I call her.'

She nodded in acknowledgement. 'If there's a chance you'll be called out in the night, we'd better go to bed soon.'

Though much earlier than usual, they followed the standard night-time procedure. As she climbed into bed wearing her red silk pyjamas, she asked, 'Would you like to make love? It might help you sleep.'

He shook his head. 'No thank you, sweetheart. I was up a lot last night, so I'm tired enough to drop off straight away.'

She looked at him with genuine surprise. 'Well, that's a first. Turn the light off, then.'

He fell asleep before her, which she recognised as another first.

In the early morning, she woke to find him tussling with the sheets. She turned on her bedside light, then tugged gently at his arm until he opened his eyes. 'You were having a nightmare. What was it about?'

He ran his tongue around his mouth before swallowing to clear the spittle. 'I was in the back garden. There was a white swan that picked up a pink cinder in its beak, then crushed it; lots of tiny bits came shooting out like little fireworks.'

'Have you ever had that dream before?'

'No, I haven't. Next thing, I was in a dream I have

had before, quite a few times. It's the one where I'm walking along a footpath at the top of a cliff and then part of it gives way right in front of me.'

'Did you remember what to do?'

'Yes. I transported myself to a beach where there wasn't any high ground anywhere near; then I walked along the sand.'

'But not too near the sea.'

'No, I wasn't too close to the water.'

She pondered for a while on these two dreams, and also on his recent one involving a yellow butterfly. For want of a better starting point, she began with a standard opening that might have applied had it not been her husband being asked the question. 'Have you had sex with someone recently?'

Suddenly he felt wide awake, but knew it was better to continue to appear almost asleep, so that his answers may seem less premeditated. 'Yes, you.'

'Have you been with Anna or Lin.'

He responded immediately, as he was certain any hesitation would lead to further questions. 'No.' He retrospectively justified his answer inwardly on the basis of the Boolean algebra he had studied in sixth form electronics, the "Exclusive OR" requiring not both but one and only one to be true.

She watched him thinking. 'Should I have said Anna *and* Lin?'

He put aside the pretence of drowsiness. 'Three in a bed; that sounds a great idea.'

'I can see you're not going to answer properly. What would you say if you were talking to me as your psychiatrist? Would it be a different answer if you were talking to me as your wife?'

'That sounds like the one about: "Does the guard who tells the truth protect the doorway to freedom?" Who am I talking to now, by the way?'

'Both; so I could respond as either.'

'What would you say as my psychiatrist if I said I'd been having it off with both of them?'

'I'd say you need to consider whether your behaviour reflects your wish to leave someone or your desire to go to someone else.'

'Well, we both know I'll never want to leave you. So, what would your response be as my wife?'

'My first reaction would be an emotional one, probably along the lines of you being a no-good two-timing...'

'Three-timing,' he interjected.

'I'd probably shout and scream,' she continued calmly.

'And your second reaction?'

'I'd realise it was my fault for not keeping you fully engaged with me. I'd make sure you had so much sex with me you didn't have the energy to go looking elsewhere.'

'So, let's be clear about this. If I were to say to you I've been having hot sex with two other women, and maybe throw in for good measure I'd had a few more offers that I've turned down, for now!, your reaction would be to give me masses of sex? I can't see a downside.'

'Well, have you?'

'Oh, absolutely. So, let's have sex now, shall we?'

'No, because you've been three-timing me.'

'But you said it would be sex all the way if I said I'd been with other women.'

'I never said how long it would be between my initial reaction and my later one. It could be years.'

'Then I withdraw my confession. And the next time you question me, I demand to have a solicitor present.'

'What, in the bed? Who did you have in mind?'

'Well, there's Tony Beresford's fiancée, Susan; she's quite cute.'

Helen acted shocked, opening her eyes and mouth as wide as they could go. 'Marcus! That's appalling! Just how low can you get!'

He smiled wickedly. 'I don't know; I'm still working on it.'

She began to laugh contentedly, confident their entire conversation had been in jest. After all, the alternative was unthinkable.

ACKNOWLEDGEMENTS

I would like to thank the following people who have generously given their time to help with research.

Eileen Basford for assistance with foreign languages and for conducting wide-ranging investigations.

Dr John Basford for sharing his knowledge of auctions, artists and the art market.

Hannah Brignell for providing an insight into the functioning of Sheffield's Graves Art Gallery and the work of the curators.

Kristan Baggaley, Paul Dearden, Paul Evans and Tim Rose, four talented artists who shared their thoughts on art and life. Also thanks to Kristan for permitting the photographing of his painting, *Distant Shower Stanage Edge*, used as the front cover.

Jennie Gill and Annette Petch, two of Sheffield's leading Jewellery makers, who explained various techniques and their use of chemicals and equipment.

Rabbi Jonathan Golomb for his broad guidance on Jewish attitudes and on the regional variations of Yiddish.

Irenie Zelickman for information on Jewish residential areas of Birmingham following post-war reconstruction.

Max Fajman who spared time on a visit from Sweden to translate my English dialogue into idiomatic Polish Yiddish.

SEND OFF SIR

The seminal Detective Marcus Priestley novel

A games master is red-carded at the annual school v. staff football match. His body is discovered shortly afterwards in the changing room, blood seeping from a wound to the back of the head.

The police set out to establish the underlying cause. A senior investigating officer has an ulterior motive when he assigns a particular policewoman to lead the investigation, which flounders due to her inexperience.

When a second teacher is found dead, the series' principal detective returns from secondment and takes over the two cases. In resolving the investigation he is forced to choose between a successful prosecution and a morally satisfactory outcome.

Send Off Sir was originally published in 2014 under the pen-name *Marc de Caen*. Future reprints will be under the author name Mark Basford.